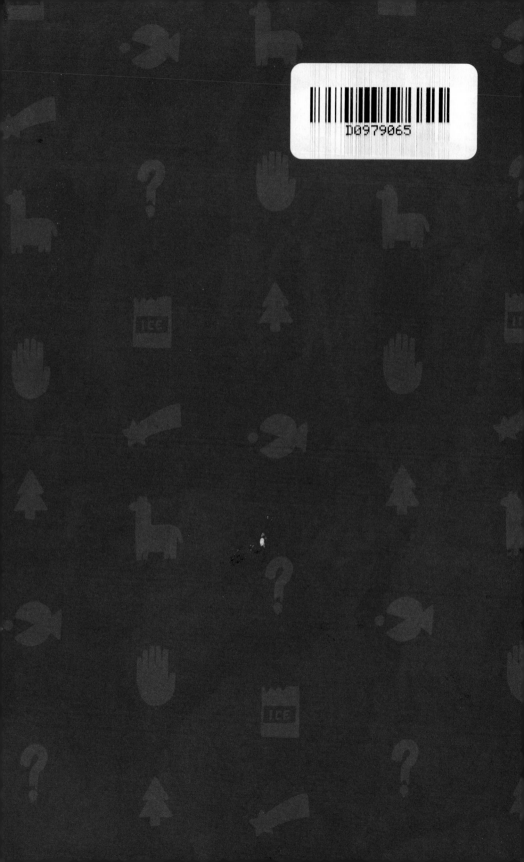

Disney

Gravity Falls

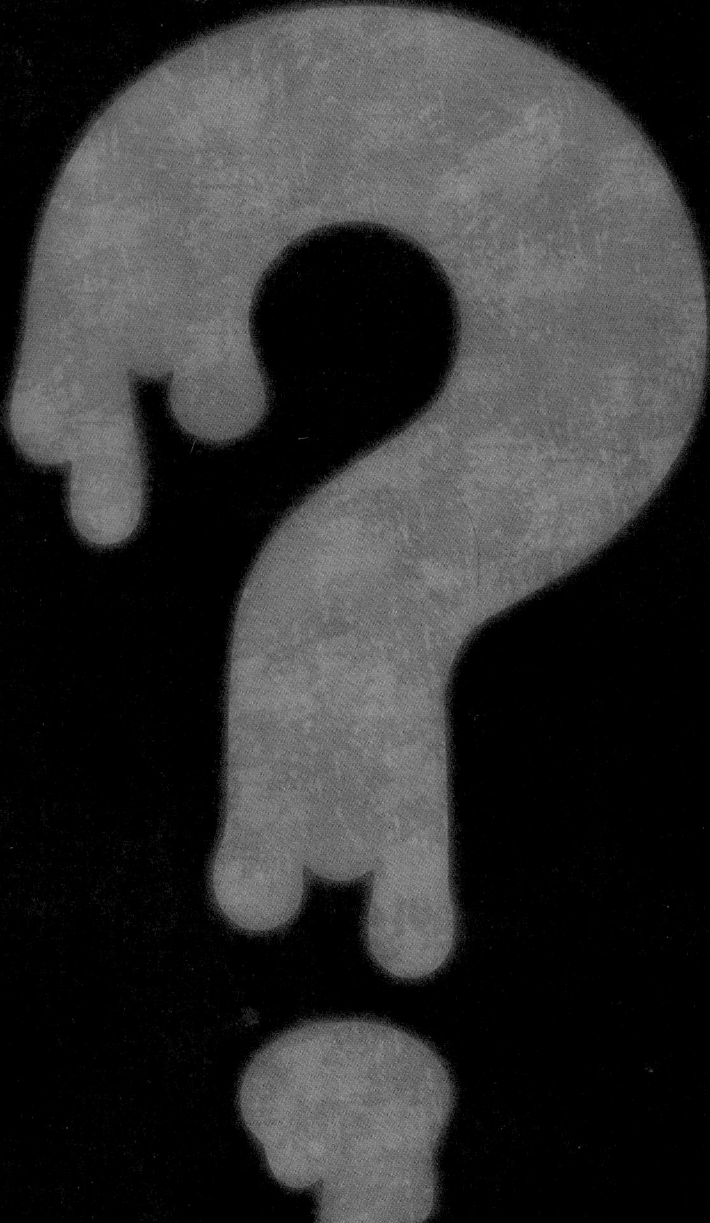

Lost Legends

by Alex Hirsch

WRITER
ALEX HIRSCH

ARTISTS

JOE PITT

IAN WORREL

ASAF HANUKA

DANA TERRACE

JACOB CHABOT

JIM CAMPBELL

KYLE SMEALLIE

MEREDITH GRAN

MIKE HOLMES

PRISCILLA TANG

SERINA HERNANDEZ

STEPHANIE RAMIREZ

VALERIE HALLA

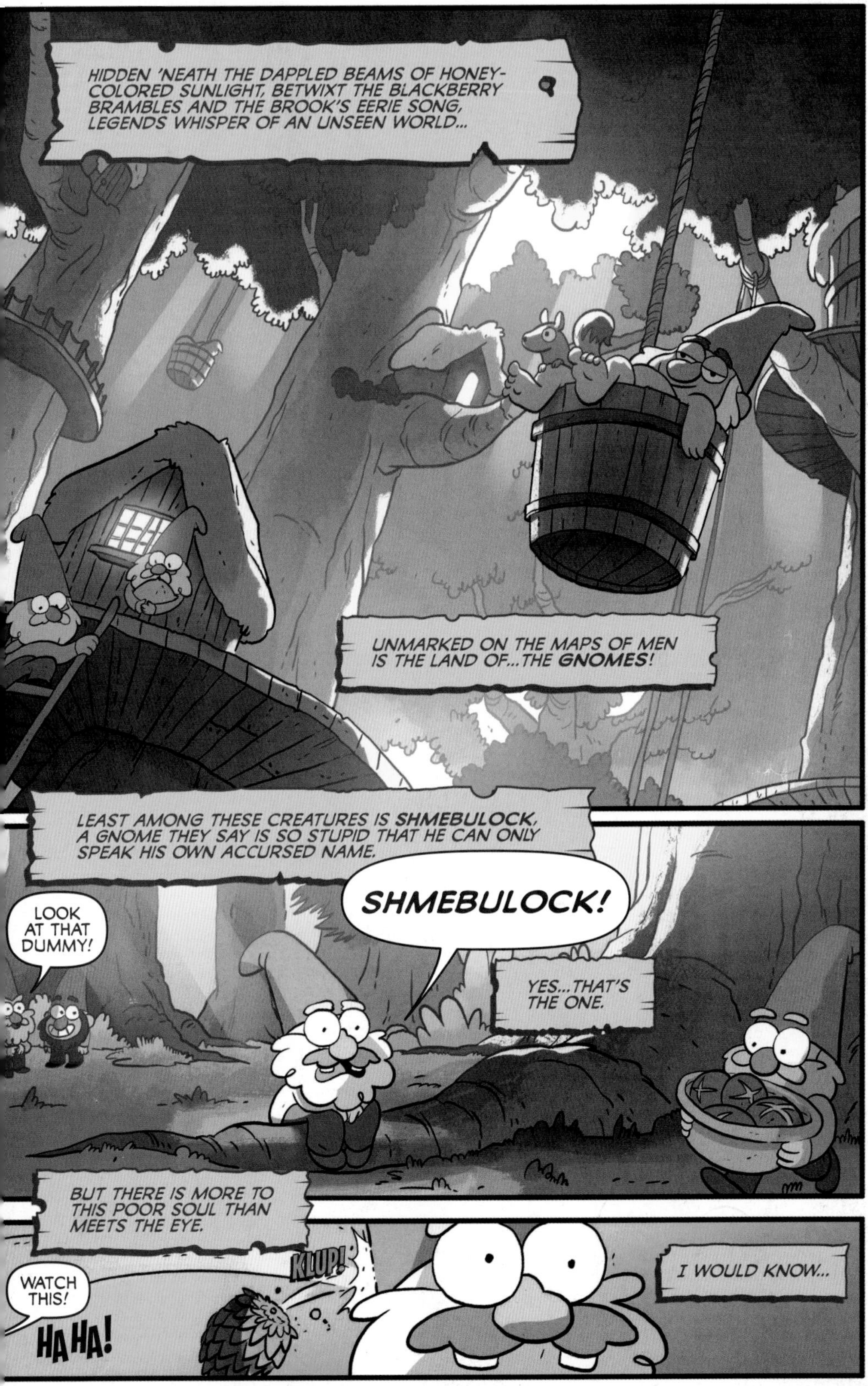
HIDDEN 'NEATH THE DAPPLED BEAMS OF HONEY-COLORED SUNLIGHT, BETWIXT THE BLACKBERRY BRAMBLES AND THE BROOK'S EERIE SONG, LEGENDS WHISPER OF AN UNSEEN WORLD...
UNMARKED ON THE MAPS OF MEN IS THE LAND OF...THE GNOMES!
LEAST AMONG THESE CREATURES IS SHMEBULOCK, A GNOME THEY SAY IS SO STUPID THAT HE CAN ONLY SPEAK HIS OWN ACCURSED NAME.
LOOK AT THAT DUMMY!
SHMEBULOCK!
YES...THAT'S THE ONE.
BUT THERE IS MORE TO THIS POOR SOUL THAN MEETS THE EYE.
WATCH THIS!
HA HA!
KLUP!
I WOULD KNOW...

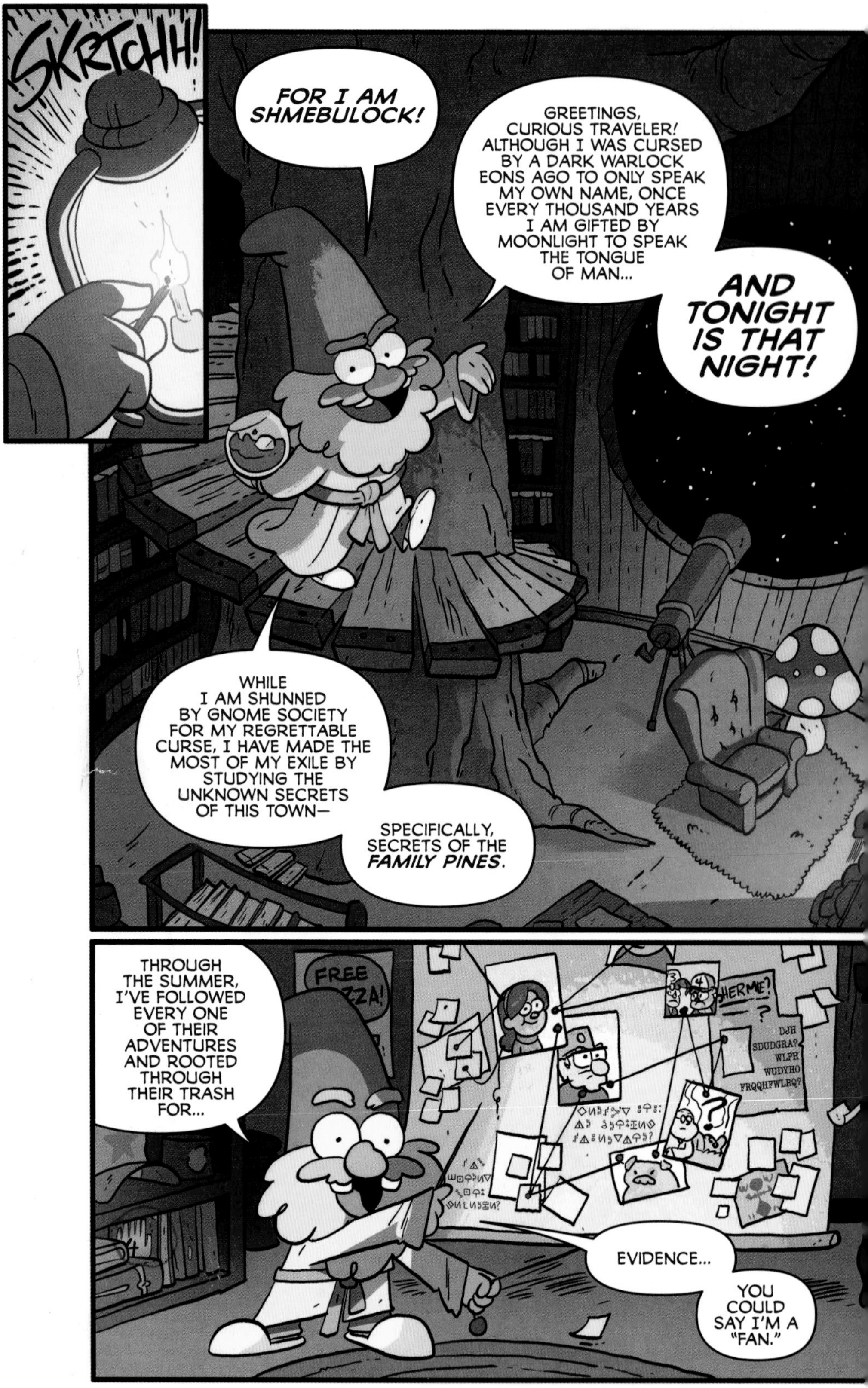

SKRTCHH!
FOR I AM SHMEBULOCK!
GREETINGS, CURIOUS TRAVELER! ALTHOUGH I WAS CURSED BY A DARK WARLOCK EONS AGO TO ONLY SPEAK MY OWN NAME, ONCE EVERY THOUSAND YEARS I AM GIFTED BY MOONLIGHT TO SPEAK THE TONGUE OF MAN...
AND TONIGHT IS THAT NIGHT!
WHILE I AM SHUNNED BY GNOME SOCIETY FOR MY REGRETTABLE CURSE, I HAVE MADE THE MOST OF MY EXILE BY STUDYING THE UNKNOWN SECRETS OF THIS TOWN—
SPECIFICALLY, SECRETS OF THE *FAMILY PINES*.
THROUGH THE SUMMER, I'VE FOLLOWED EVERY ONE OF THEIR ADVENTURES AND ROOTED THROUGH THEIR TRASH FOR...
FREE
SHERMIE?
DJH
SDUDGRA?
WLFH
WUDYHO
FRQQHFWLRQ?
EVIDENCE...
YOU COULD SAY I'M A "FAN."

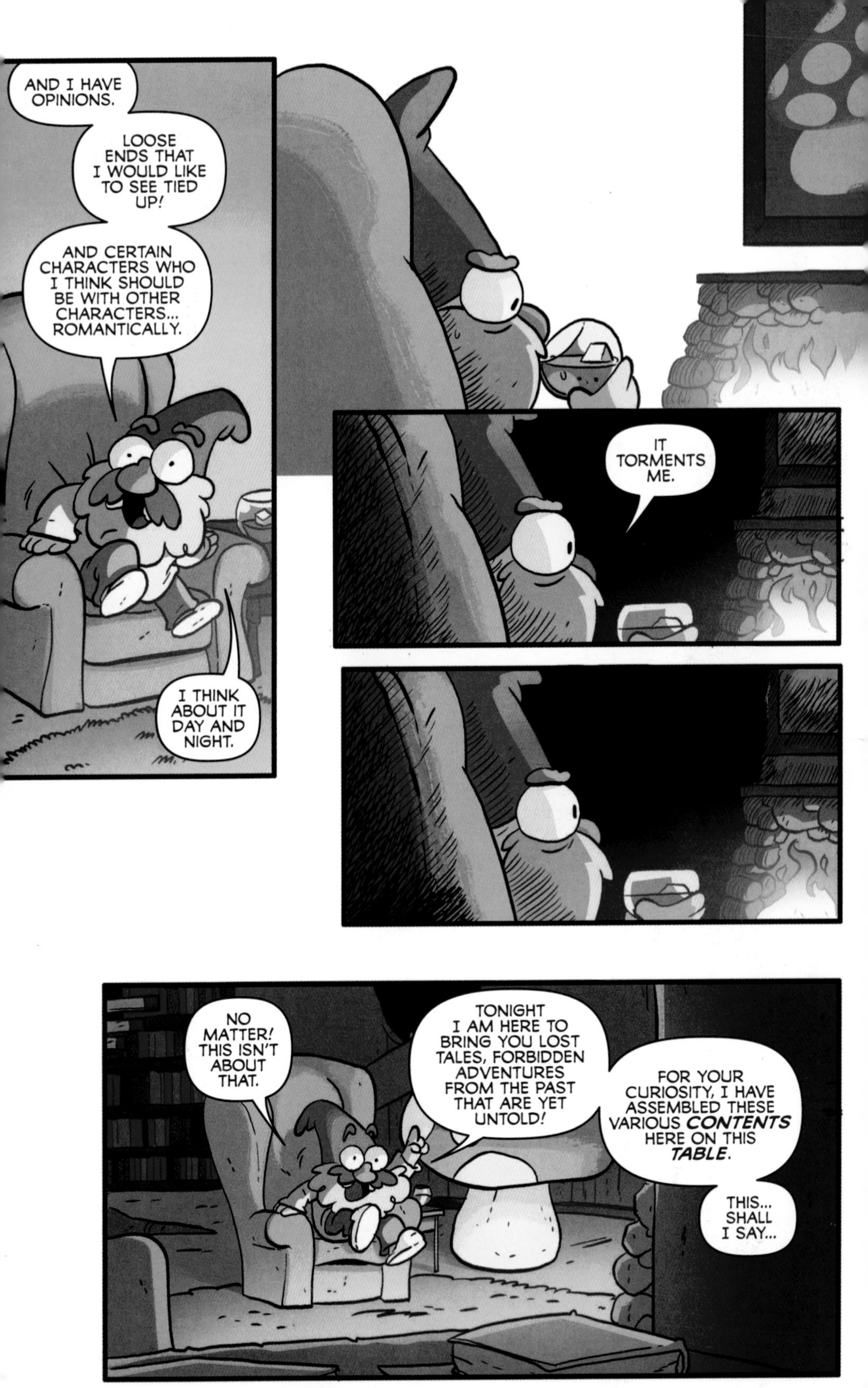
AND I HAVE OPINIONS.
LOOSE ENDS THAT I WOULD LIKE TO SEE TIED UP!
AND CERTAIN CHARACTERS WHO I THINK SHOULD BE WITH OTHER CHARACTERS... ROMANTICALLY.
I THINK ABOUT IT DAY AND NIGHT.
IT TORMENTS ME.
NO MATTER! THIS ISN'T ABOUT THAT.
TONIGHT I AM HERE TO BRING YOU LOST TALES, FORBIDDEN ADVENTURES FROM THE PAST THAT ARE YET UNTOLD!
FOR YOUR CURIOSITY, I HAVE ASSEMBLED THESE VARIOUS ***CONTENTS*** HERE ON THIS ***TABLE***.
THIS... SHALL I SAY...

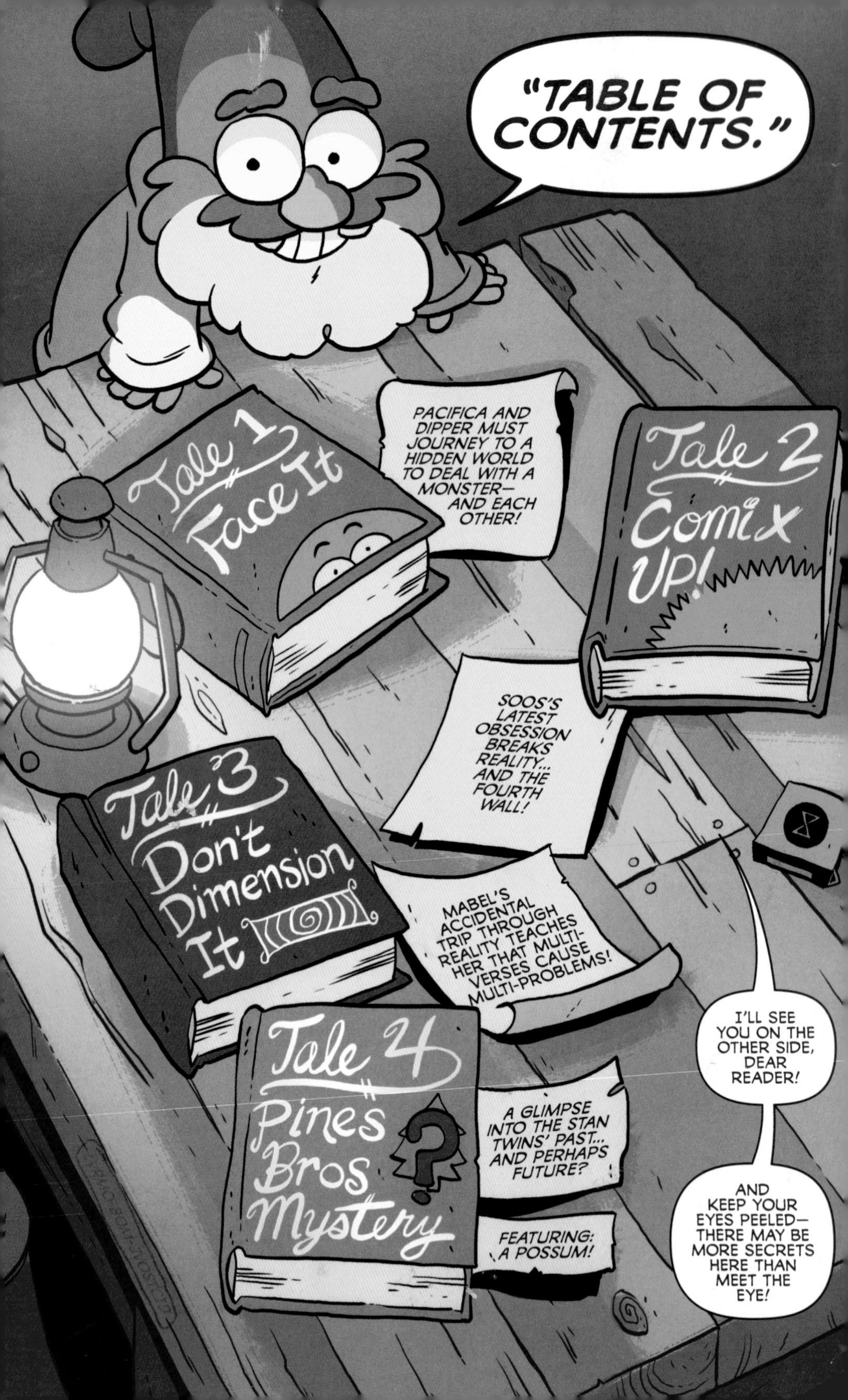
"TABLE OF CONTENTS."
Tale 1 Face It
PACIFICA AND DIPPER MUST JOURNEY TO A HIDDEN WORLD TO DEAL WITH A MONSTER— AND EACH OTHER!
Tale 2 Comix Up!
SOOS'S LATEST OBSESSION BREAKS REALITY... AND THE FOURTH WALL!
Tale 3 Don't Dimension It
MABEL'S ACCIDENTAL TRIP THROUGH REALITY TEACHES HER THAT MULTI-VERSES CAUSE MULTI-PROBLEMS!
Tale 4 Pines Bros Mystery
A GLIMPSE INTO THE STAN TWINS' PAST... AND PERHAPS FUTURE?
FEATURING: A POSSUM!
I'LL SEE YOU ON THE OTHER SIDE, DEAR READER!
AND KEEP YOUR EYES PEELED— THERE MAY BE MORE SECRETS HERE THAN MEET THE EYE!

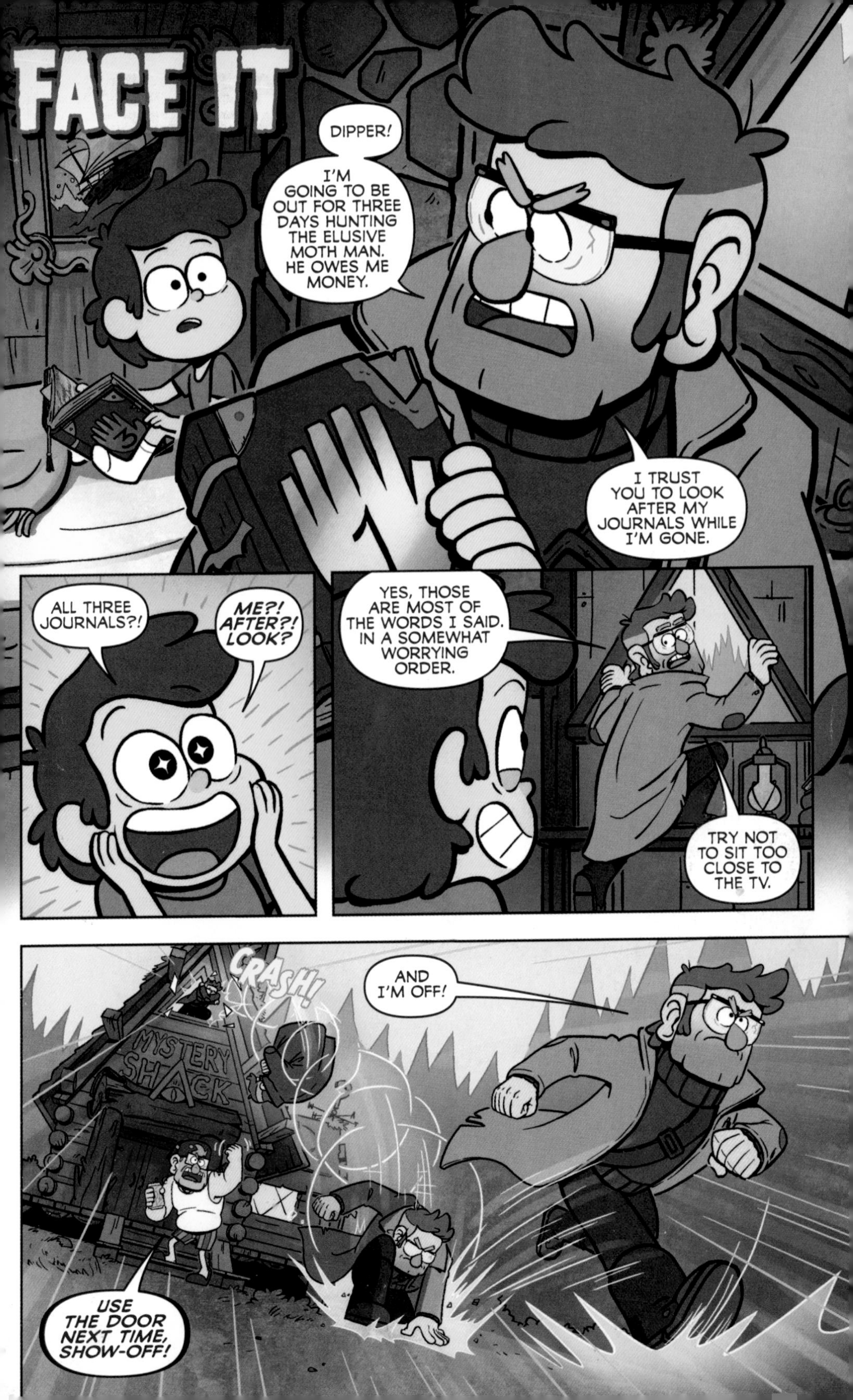
FACE IT
DIPPER!
I'M GOING TO BE OUT FOR THREE DAYS HUNTING THE ELUSIVE MOTH MAN. HE OWES ME MONEY.
I TRUST YOU TO LOOK AFTER MY JOURNALS WHILE I'M GONE.
ALL THREE JOURNALS?!
ME?! AFTER?! LOOK?
YES, THOSE ARE MOST OF THE WORDS I SAID. IN A SOMEWHAT WORRYING ORDER.
TRY NOT TO SIT TOO CLOSE TO THE TV.
CRASH!
AND I'M OFF!
MYSTERY SHACK
USE THE DOOR NEXT TIME, SHOW-OFF!

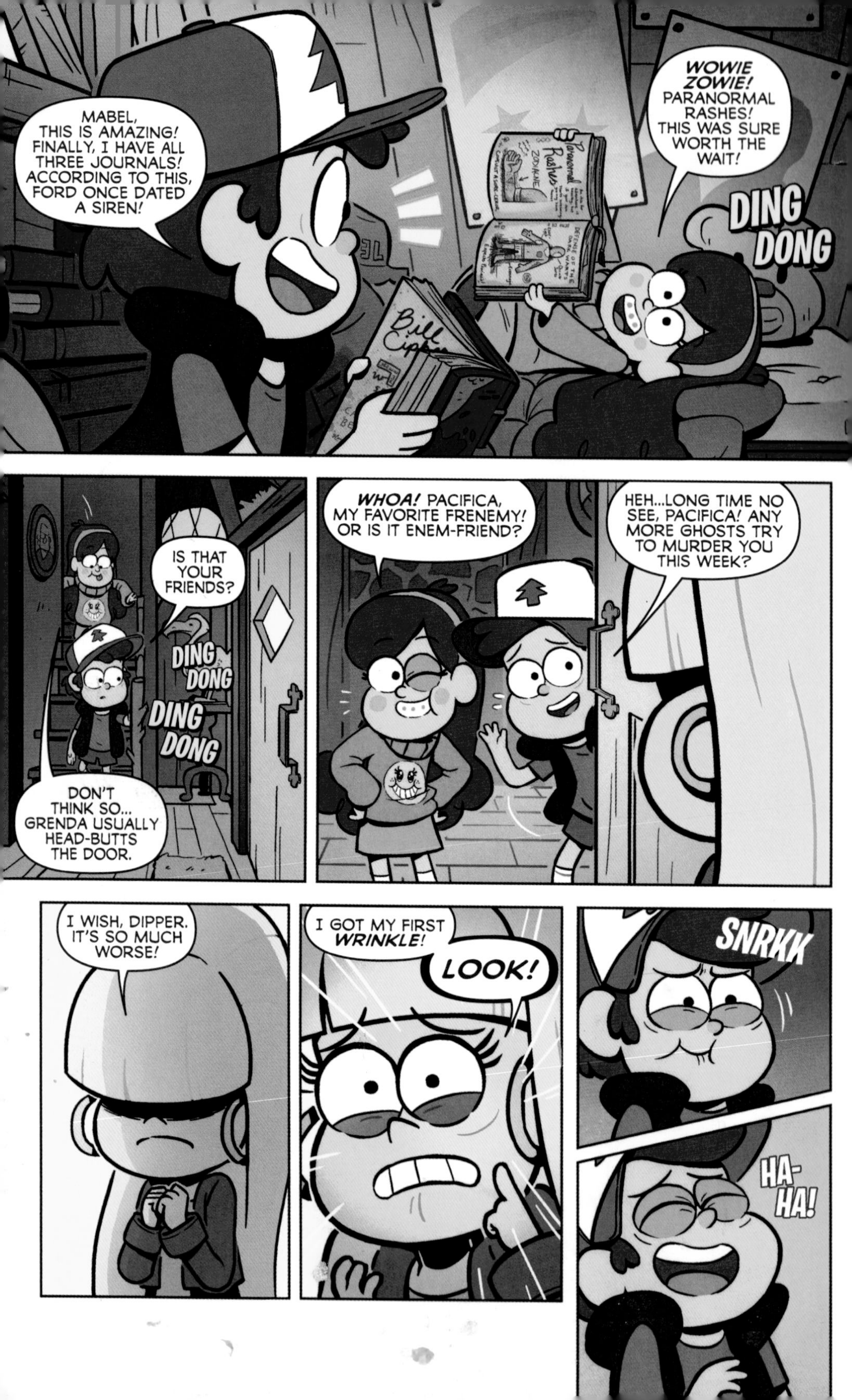

MABEL, THIS IS AMAZING! FINALLY, I HAVE ALL THREE JOURNALS! ACCORDING TO THIS, FORD ONCE DATED A SIREN!
WOWIE ZOWIE! PARANORMAL RASHES! THIS WAS SURE WORTH THE WAIT!
DING DONG
IS THAT YOUR FRIENDS?
DING DONG
DING DONG
DON'T THINK SO... GRENDA USUALLY HEAD-BUTTS THE DOOR.
WHOA! PACIFICA, MY FAVORITE FRENEMY! OR IS IT ENEM-FRIEND?
HEH...LONG TIME NO SEE, PACIFICA! ANY MORE GHOSTS TRY TO MURDER YOU THIS WEEK?
I WISH, DIPPER. IT'S SO MUCH WORSE!
I GOT MY FIRST WRINKLE!
LOOK!
SNRKK
HA-HA!

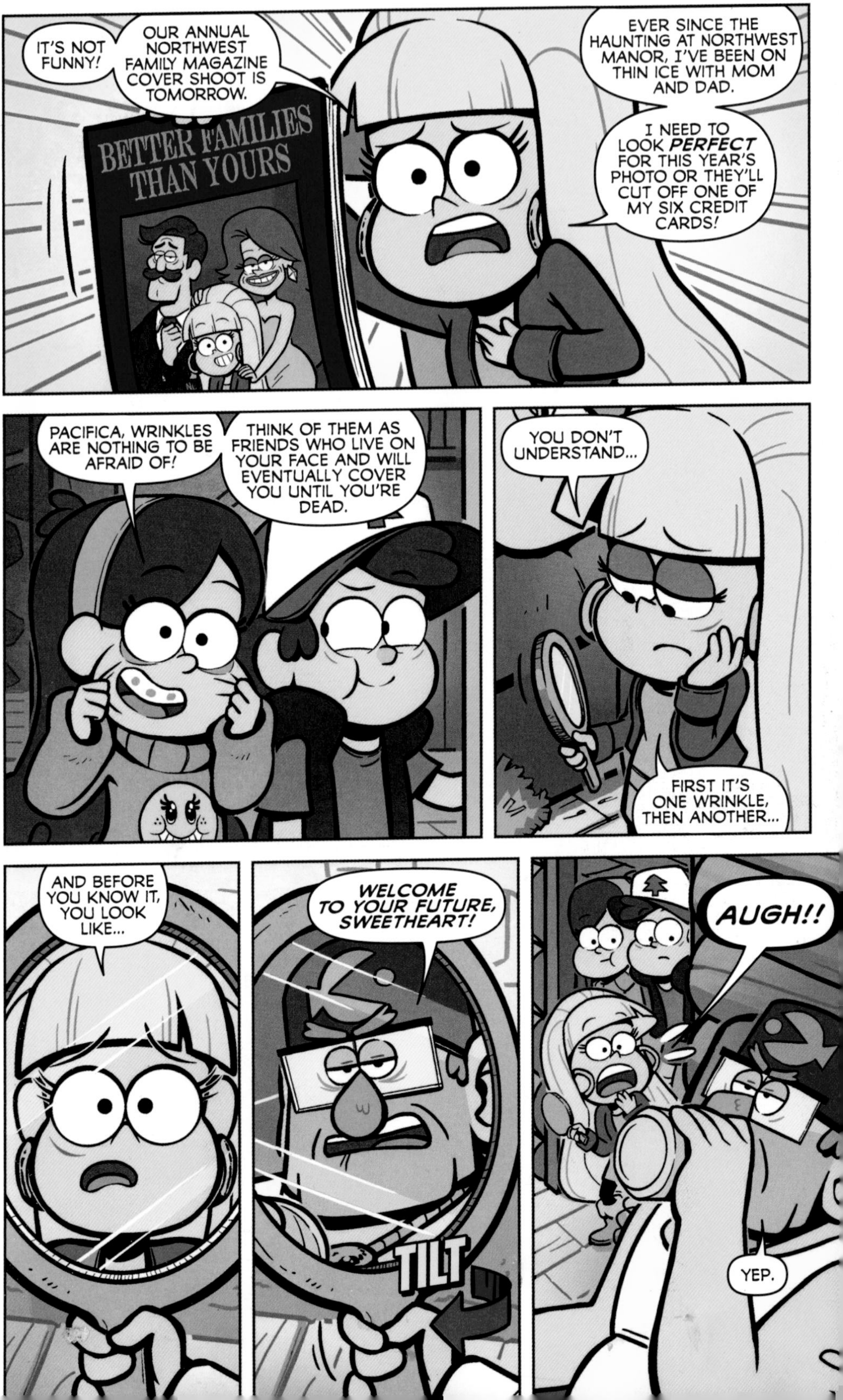
IT'S NOT FUNNY!
OUR ANNUAL NORTHWEST FAMILY MAGAZINE COVER SHOOT IS TOMORROW.
BETTER FAMILIES THAN YOURS
EVER SINCE THE HAUNTING AT NORTHWEST MANOR, I'VE BEEN ON THIN ICE WITH MOM AND DAD.
I NEED TO LOOK PERFECT FOR THIS YEAR'S PHOTO OR THEY'LL CUT OFF ONE OF MY SIX CREDIT CARDS!
PACIFICA, WRINKLES ARE NOTHING TO BE AFRAID OF!
THINK OF THEM AS FRIENDS WHO LIVE ON YOUR FACE AND WILL EVENTUALLY COVER YOU UNTIL YOU'RE DEAD.
YOU DON'T UNDERSTAND...
FIRST IT'S ONE WRINKLE, THEN ANOTHER...
AND BEFORE YOU KNOW IT, YOU LOOK LIKE...
WELCOME TO YOUR FUTURE, SWEETHEART!
TILT
AUGH!!
YEP.

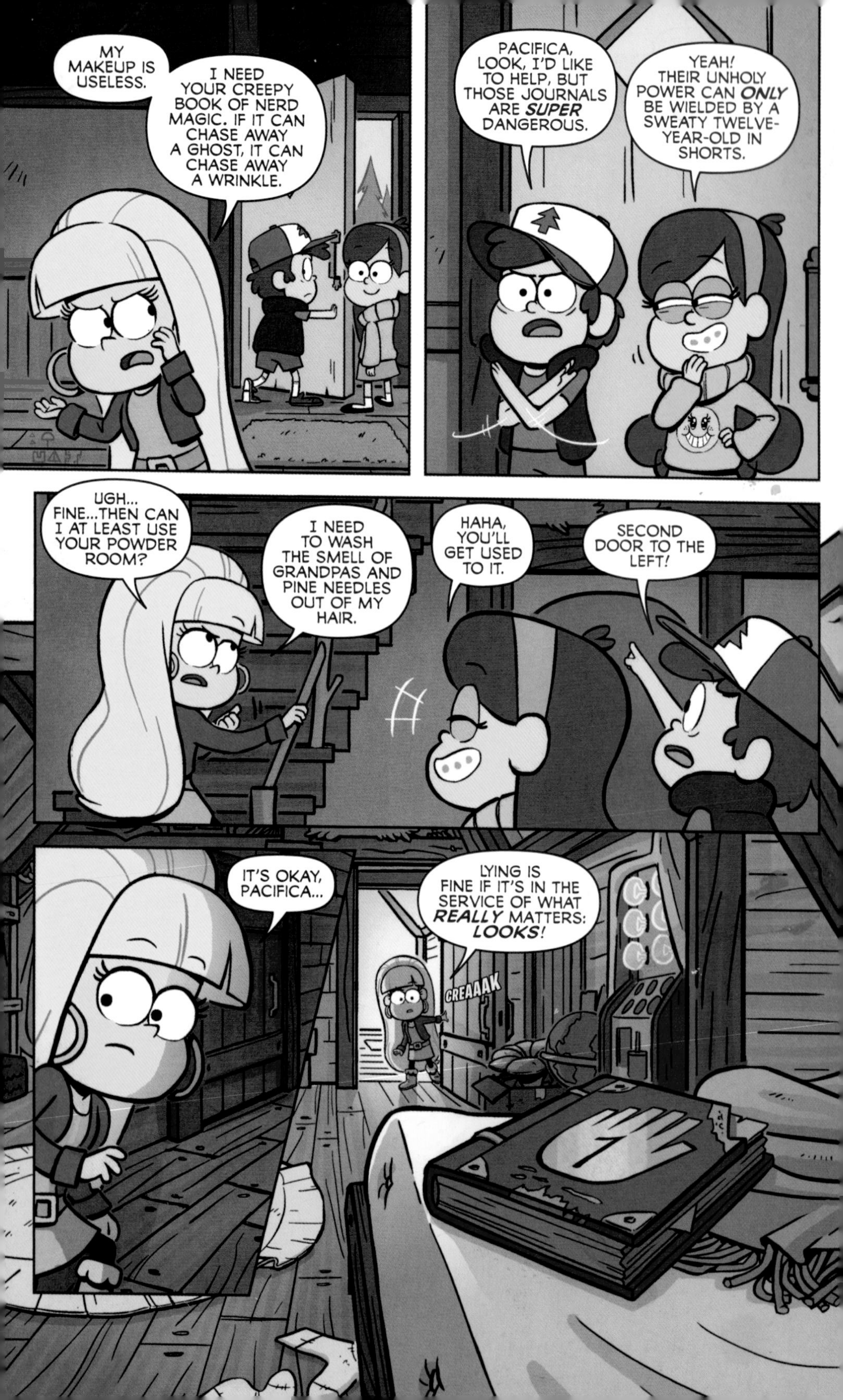
MY MAKEUP IS USELESS.
I NEED YOUR CREEPY BOOK OF NERD MAGIC. IF IT CAN CHASE AWAY A GHOST, IT CAN CHASE AWAY A WRINKLE.
PACIFICA, LOOK, I'D LIKE TO HELP, BUT THOSE JOURNALS ARE *SUPER* DANGEROUS.
YEAH! THEIR UNHOLY POWER CAN *ONLY* BE WIELDED BY A SWEATY TWELVE-YEAR-OLD IN SHORTS.
UGH... FINE...THEN CAN I AT LEAST USE YOUR POWDER ROOM?
I NEED TO WASH THE SMELL OF GRANDPAS AND PINE NEEDLES OUT OF MY HAIR.
HAHA, YOU'LL GET USED TO IT.
SECOND DOOR TO THE LEFT!
IT'S OKAY, PACIFICA...
LYING IS FINE IF IT'S IN THE SERVICE OF WHAT ***REALLY*** MATTERS: ***LOOKS***!
CREAAAK

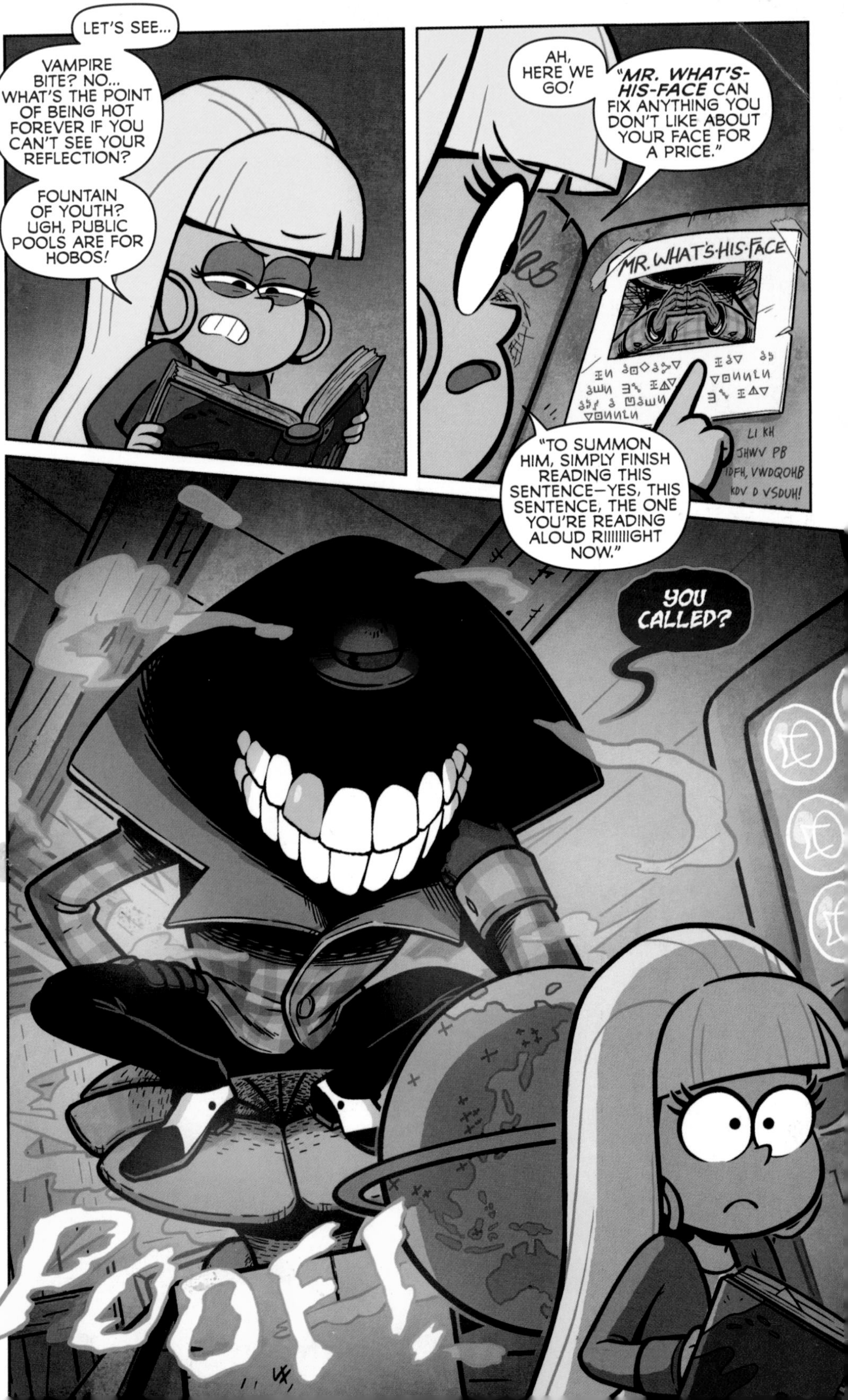
LET'S SEE...
VAMPIRE BITE? NO... WHAT'S THE POINT OF BEING HOT FOREVER IF YOU CAN'T SEE YOUR REFLECTION?
FOUNTAIN OF YOUTH? UGH, PUBLIC POOLS ARE FOR HOBOS!
AH, HERE WE GO!
"MR. WHAT'S-HIS-FACE CAN FIX ANYTHING YOU DON'T LIKE ABOUT YOUR FACE FOR A PRICE."
MR. WHAT'S-HIS-FACE
"TO SUMMON HIM, SIMPLY FINISH READING THIS SENTENCE—YES, THIS SENTENCE, THE ONE YOU'RE READING ALOUD RIIIIIIIGHT NOW."
LI KH
JHWV PB
IDFH, VWDQOHB
KDV D VSDUH!
YOU CALLED?
POOF!

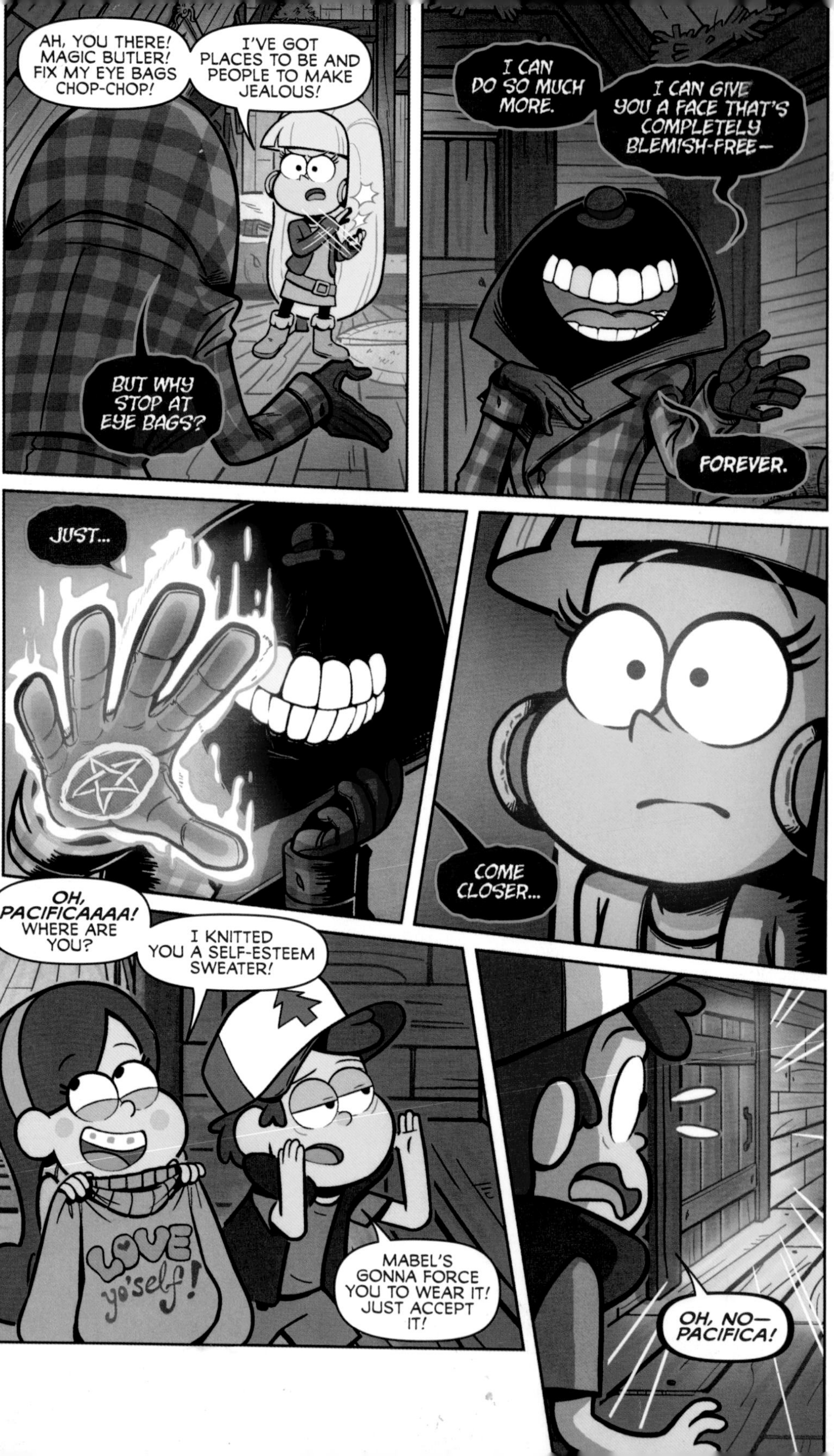
AH, YOU THERE! MAGIC BUTLER! FIX MY EYE BAGS CHOP-CHOP!
I'VE GOT PLACES TO BE AND PEOPLE TO MAKE JEALOUS!
BUT WHY STOP AT EYE BAGS?
I CAN DO SO MUCH MORE.
I CAN GIVE YOU A FACE THAT'S COMPLETELY BLEMISH-FREE—
FOREVER.
JUST...
COME CLOSER...
OH, PACIFICAAAA! WHERE ARE YOU?
I KNITTED YOU A SELF-ESTEEM SWEATER!
LOVE yo'self!
MABEL'S GONNA FORCE YOU TO WEAR IT! JUST ACCEPT IT!
OH, NO— PACIFICA!

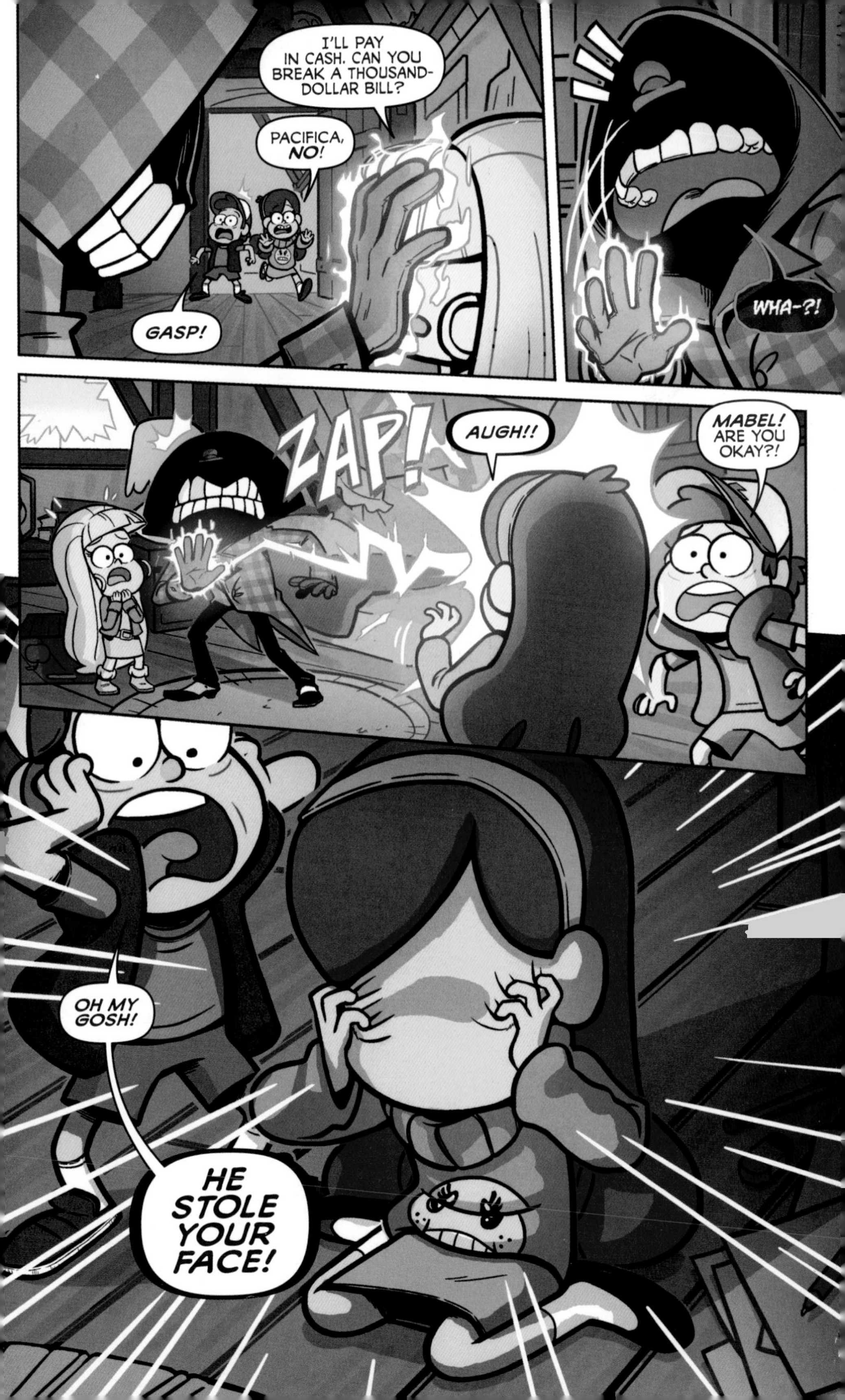
I'LL PAY IN CASH. CAN YOU BREAK A THOUSAND-DOLLAR BILL?
PACIFICA, NO!
GASP!
WHA-?!
ZAP!
AUGH!!
MABEL! ARE YOU OKAY?!
OH MY GOSH!
HE STOLE YOUR FACE!

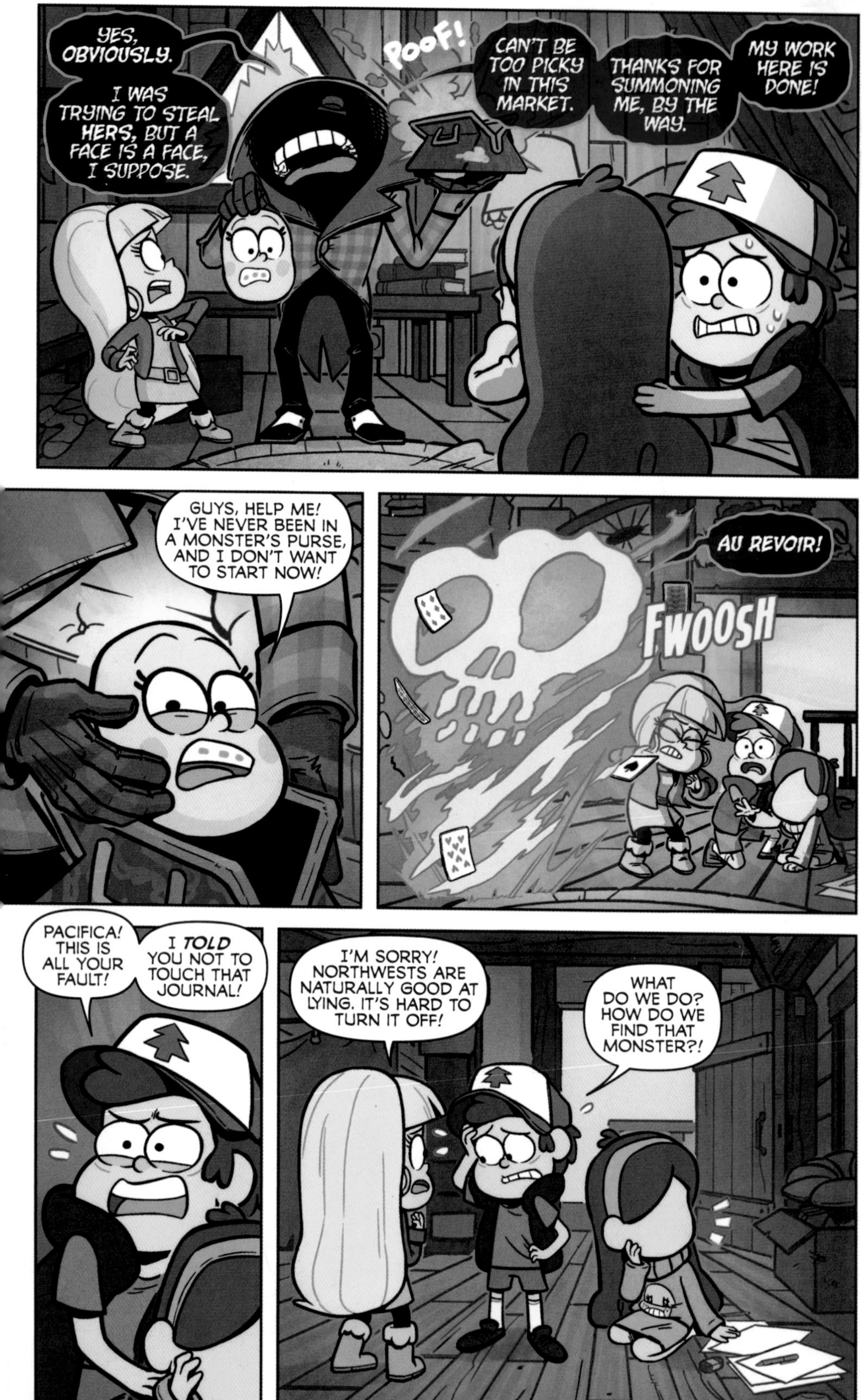

YES, OBVIOUSLY.
I WAS TRYING TO STEAL HERS, BUT A FACE IS A FACE, I SUPPOSE.
POOF!
CAN'T BE TOO PICKY IN THIS MARKET.
THANKS FOR SUMMONING ME, BY THE WAY.
MY WORK HERE IS DONE!
GUYS, HELP ME! I'VE NEVER BEEN IN A MONSTER'S PURSE, AND I DON'T WANT TO START NOW!
AU REVOIR!
FWOOSH
PACIFICA! THIS IS ALL YOUR FAULT!
I TOLD YOU NOT TO TOUCH THAT JOURNAL!
I'M SORRY! NORTHWESTS ARE NATURALLY GOOD AT LYING. IT'S HARD TO TURN IT OFF!
WHAT DO WE DO? HOW DO WE FIND THAT MONSTER?!

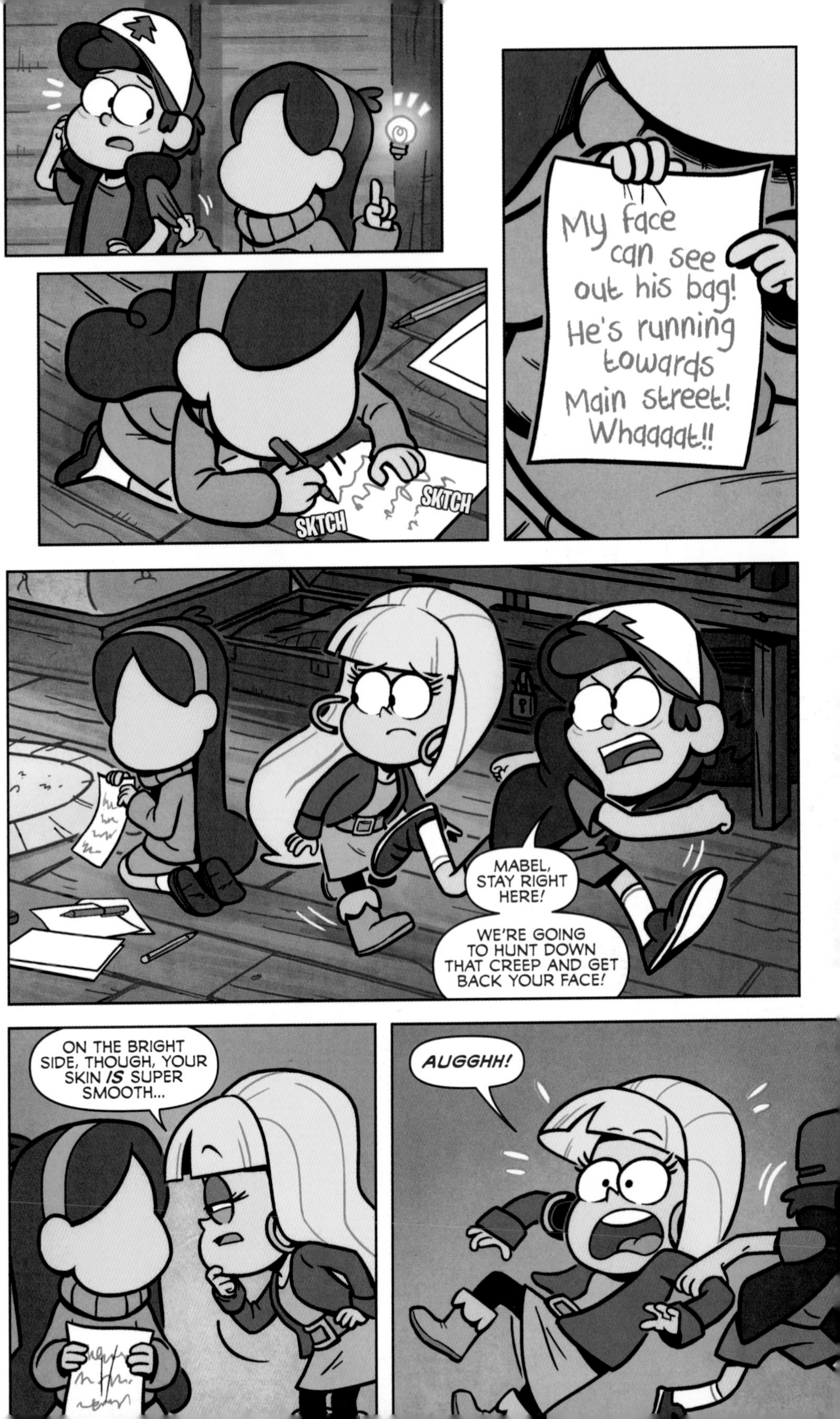
SKTCH
SKTCH
My face can see out his bag! He's running towards Main street! Whaaaat!!
MABEL, STAY RIGHT HERE!
WE'RE GOING TO HUNT DOWN THAT CREEP AND GET BACK YOUR FACE!
ON THE BRIGHT SIDE, THOUGH, YOUR SKIN *IS* SUPER SMOOTH...
AUGGHH!

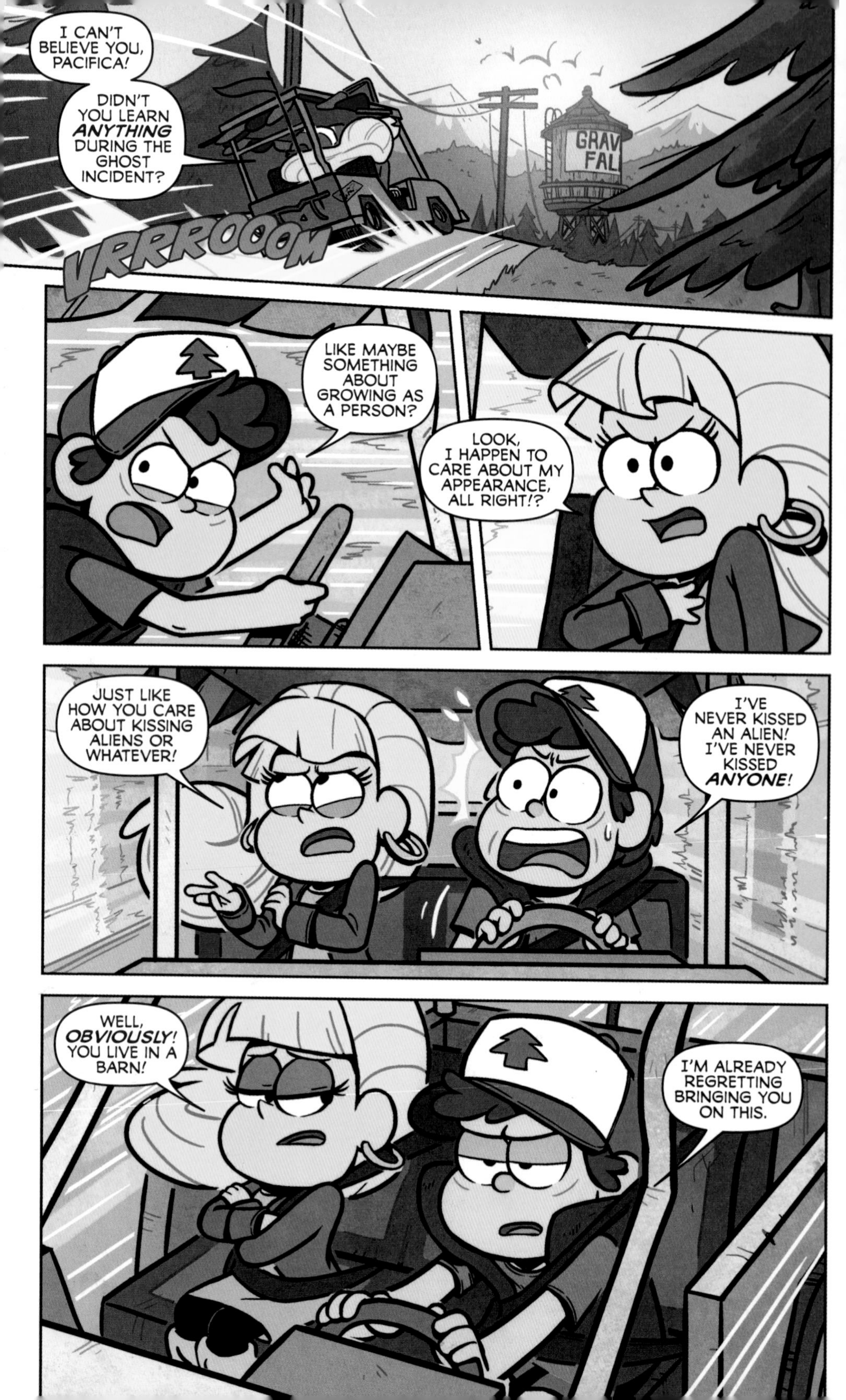
I CAN'T BELIEVE YOU, PACIFICA!
DIDN'T YOU LEARN ***ANYTHING*** DURING THE GHOST INCIDENT?
GRAV FAL
VRRROOOM
LIKE MAYBE SOMETHING ABOUT GROWING AS A PERSON?
LOOK, I HAPPEN TO CARE ABOUT MY APPEARANCE, ALL RIGHT!?
JUST LIKE HOW YOU CARE ABOUT KISSING ALIENS OR WHATEVER!
I'VE NEVER KISSED AN ALIEN! I'VE NEVER KISSED ***ANYONE!***
WELL, ***OBVIOUSLY!*** YOU LIVE IN A BARN!
I'M ALREADY REGRETTING BRINGING YOU ON THIS.

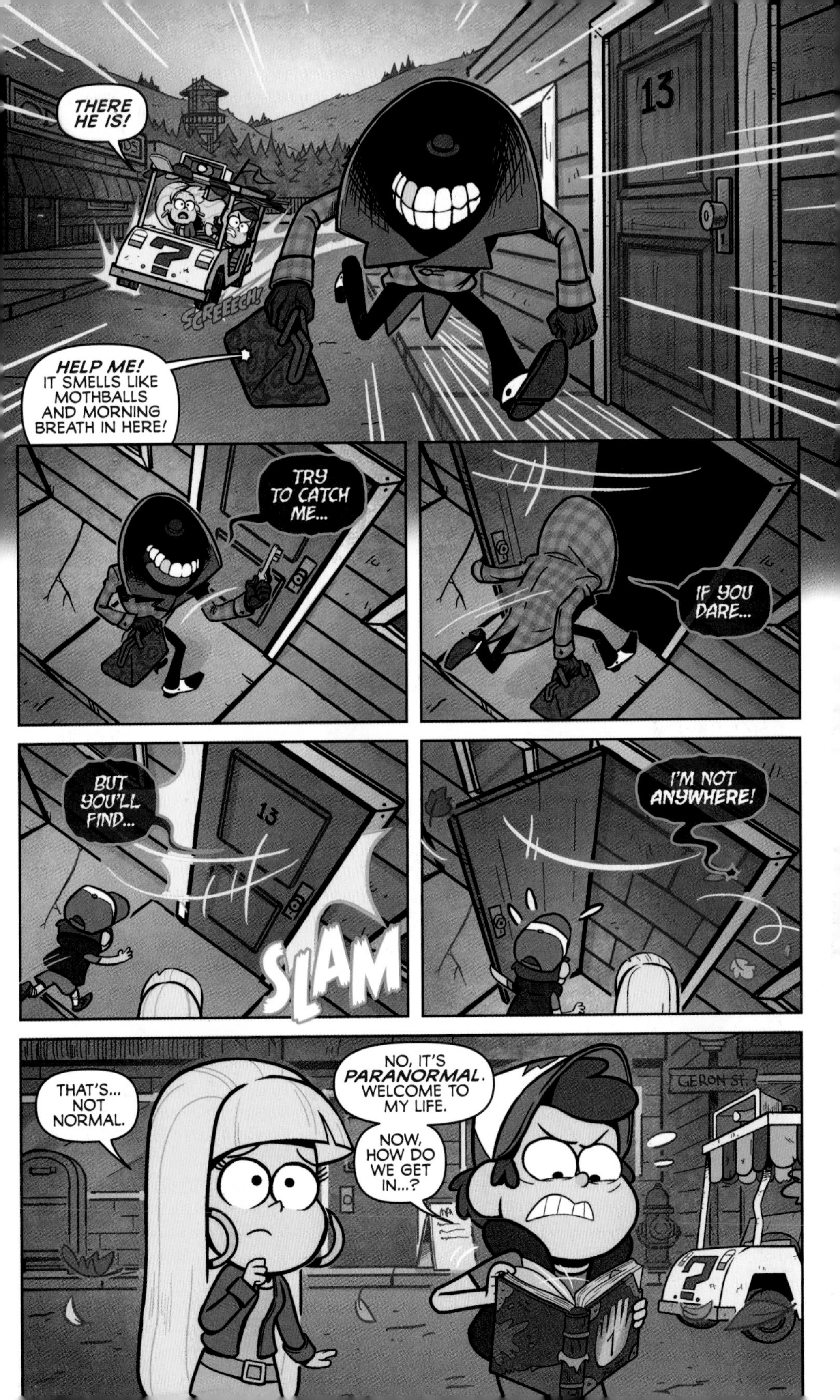
THERE HE IS!
SCREEECH!
HELP ME! IT SMELLS LIKE MOTHBALLS AND MORNING BREATH IN HERE!
13
TRY TO CATCH ME...
IF YOU DARE...
BUT YOU'LL FIND...
13
SLAM
I'M NOT ANYWHERE!
THAT'S... NOT NORMAL.
NO, IT'S PARANORMAL. WELCOME TO MY LIFE.
NOW, HOW DO WE GET IN...?
GERON ST.

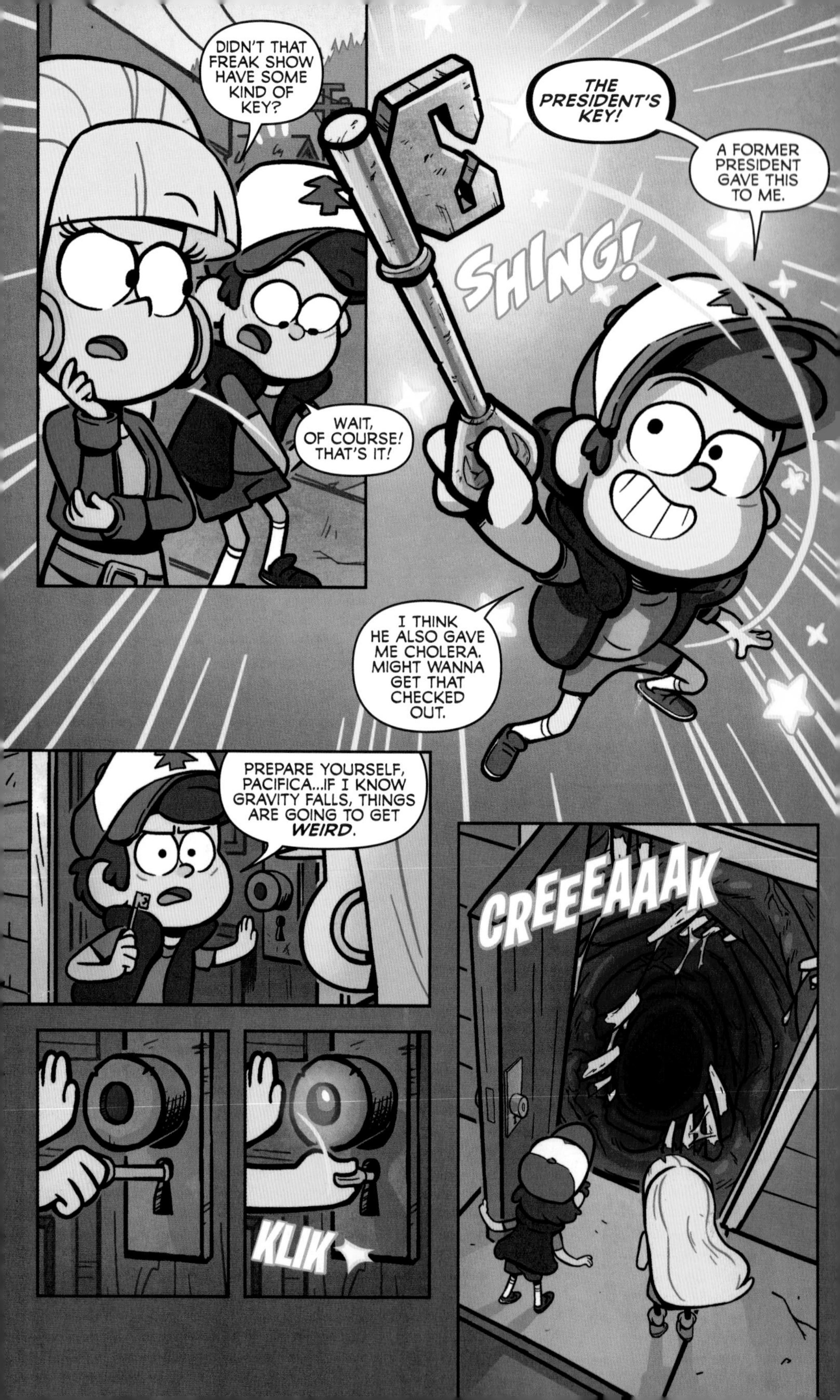

DIDN'T THAT FREAK SHOW HAVE SOME KIND OF KEY?
WAIT, OF COURSE! THAT'S IT!
THE PRESIDENT'S KEY!
A FORMER PRESIDENT GAVE THIS TO ME.
SHING!
I THINK HE ALSO GAVE ME CHOLERA. MIGHT WANNA GET THAT CHECKED OUT.
PREPARE YOURSELF, PACIFICA...IF I KNOW GRAVITY FALLS, THINGS ARE GOING TO GET WEIRD.
KLIK
CREEEAAAK

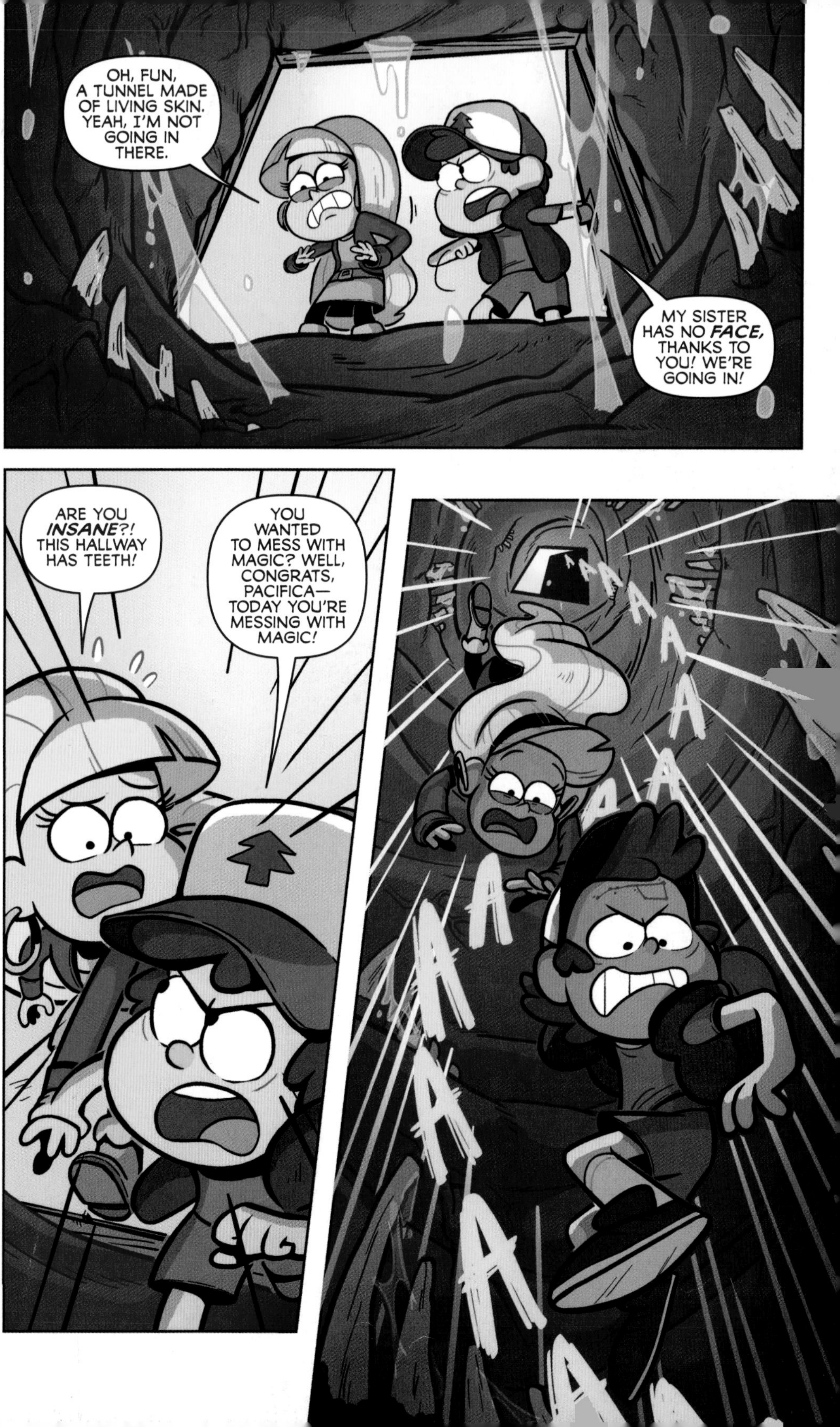
OH, FUN, A TUNNEL MADE OF LIVING SKIN. YEAH, I'M NOT GOING IN THERE.
MY SISTER HAS NO *FACE,* THANKS TO YOU! WE'RE GOING IN!
ARE YOU *INSANE*?! THIS HALLWAY HAS TEETH!
YOU WANTED TO MESS WITH MAGIC? WELL, CONGRATS, PACIFICA— TODAY YOU'RE MESSING WITH MAGIC!
AAAAAAAA
AAAAAAAA

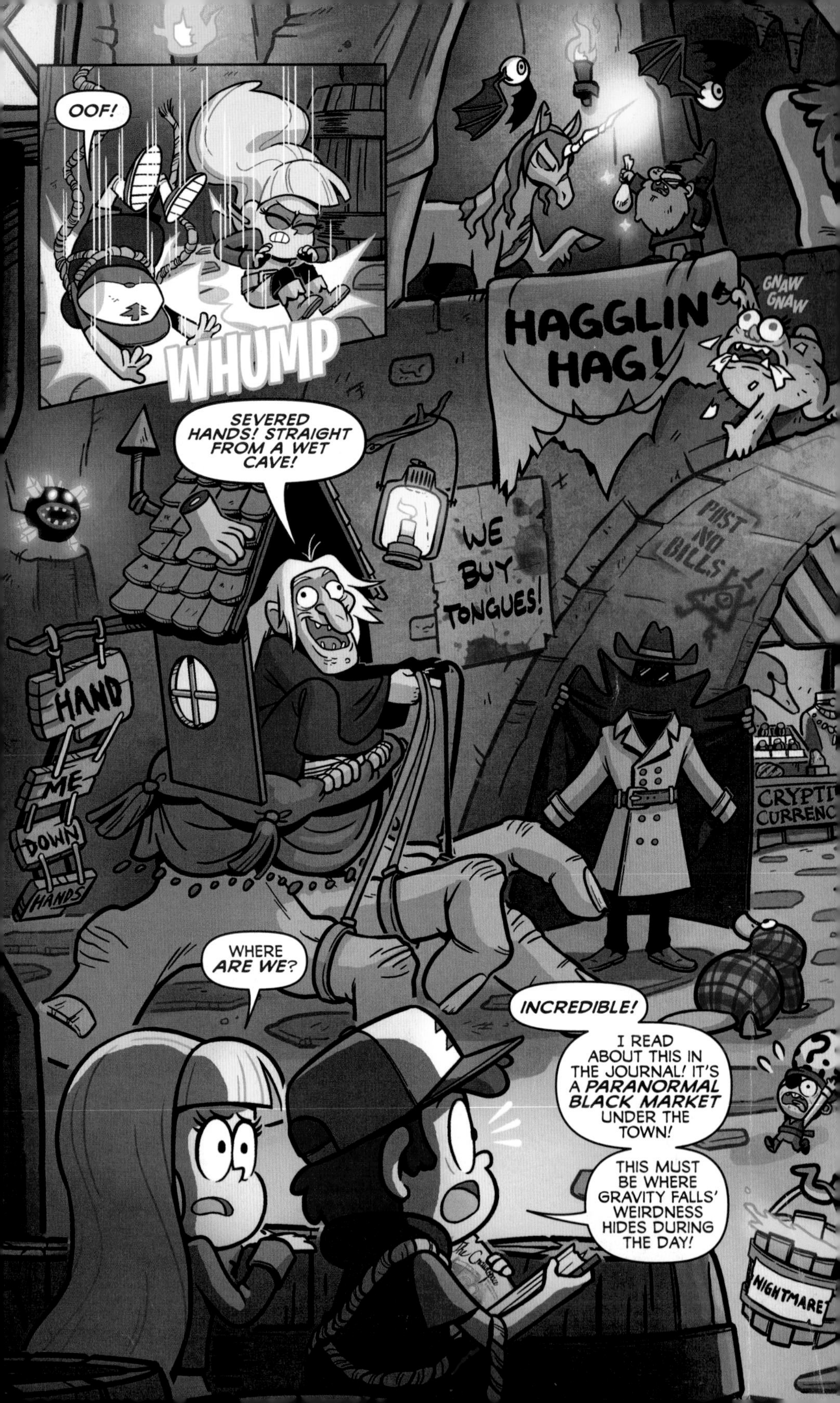
OOF!
WHUMP
HAGGLIN HAG!
GNAW GNAW
SEVERED HANDS! STRAIGHT FROM A WET CAVE!
WE BUY TONGUES!
POST NO BILLS
HAND ME DOWN HANDS
CRYPTI CURRENC
WHERE ARE WE?
INCREDIBLE!
I READ ABOUT THIS IN THE JOURNAL! IT'S A PARANORMAL BLACK MARKET UNDER THE TOWN!
THIS MUST BE WHERE GRAVITY FALLS' WEIRDNESS HIDES DURING THE DAY!
NIGHTMARE

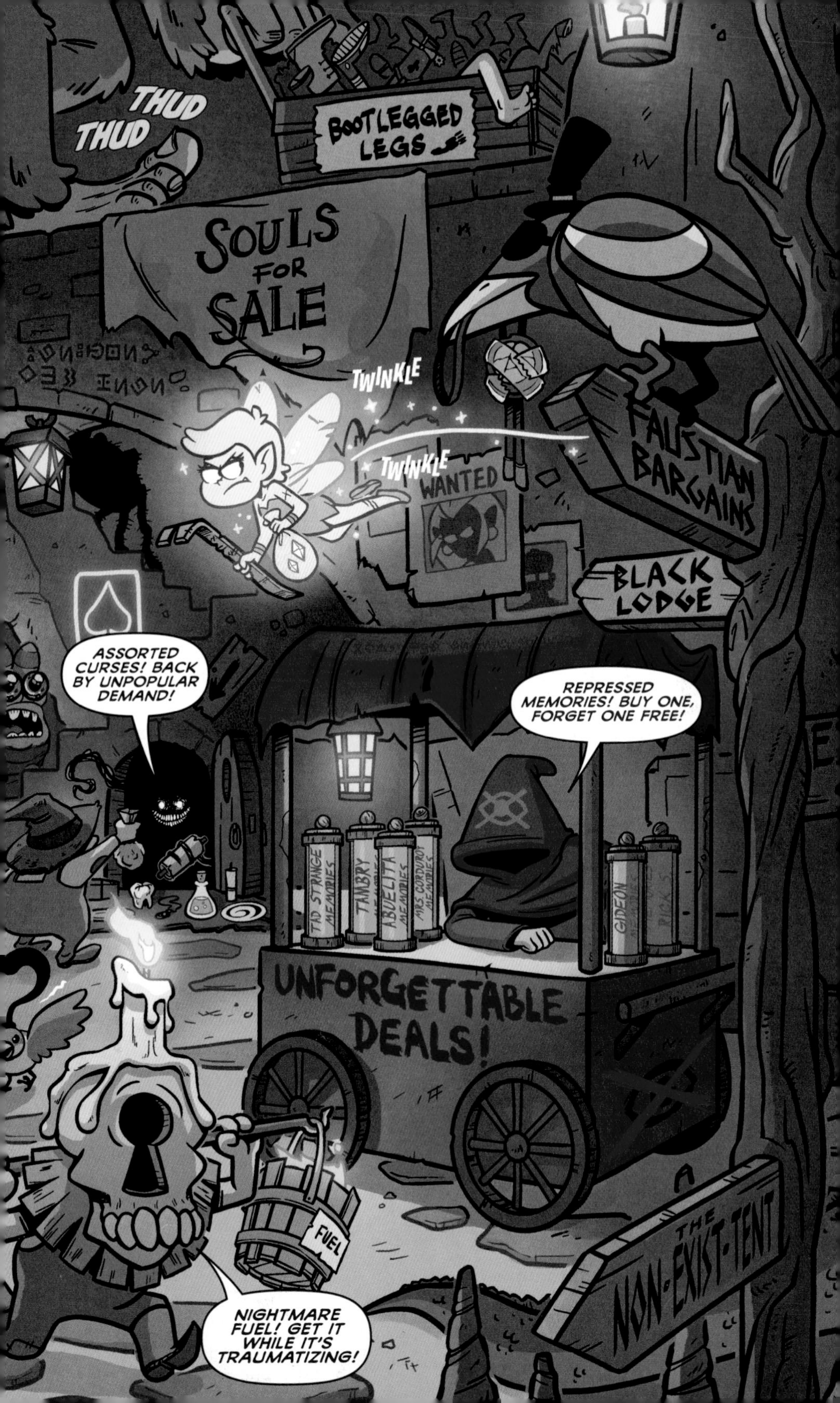
THUD
THUD
BOOTLEGGED LEGS
SOULS FOR SALE
TWINKLE
TWINKLE
WANTED
FAUSTIAN BARGAINS
BLACK LODGE
ASSORTED CURSES! BACK BY UNPOPULAR DEMAND!
REPRESSED MEMORIES! BUY ONE, FORGET ONE FREE!
TAD STRANGE MEMORIES
TAMBRY
ABUELITA MEMORIES
MRS. CORDUROY MEMORIES
GIDEON
UNFORGETTABLE DEALS!
FUEL
THE NON-EXIST-TENT
NIGHTMARE FUEL! GET IT WHILE IT'S TRAUMATIZING!

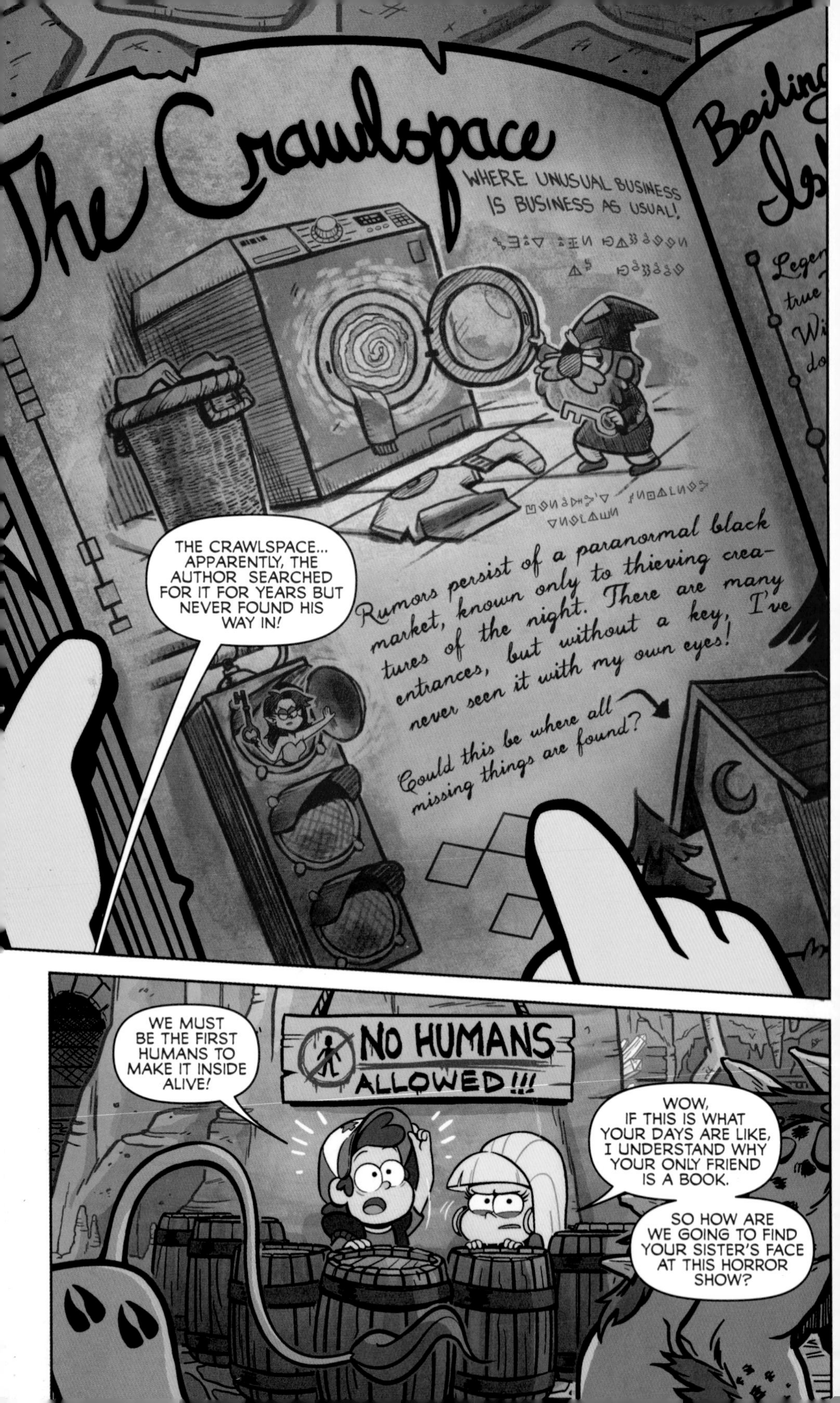

The Crawlspace
WHERE UNUSUAL BUSINESS IS BUSINESS AS USUAL!
THE CRAWLSPACE... APPARENTLY, THE AUTHOR SEARCHED FOR IT FOR YEARS BUT NEVER FOUND HIS WAY IN!
Rumors persist of a paranormal black market, known only to thieving creatures of the night. There are many entrances, but without a key, I've never seen it with my own eyes!
Could this be where all missing things are found?
WE MUST BE THE FIRST HUMANS TO MAKE IT INSIDE ALIVE!
NO HUMANS ALLOWED!!!
WOW, IF THIS IS WHAT YOUR DAYS ARE LIKE, I UNDERSTAND WHY YOUR ONLY FRIEND IS A BOOK.
SO HOW ARE WE GOING TO FIND YOUR SISTER'S FACE AT THIS HORROR SHOW?

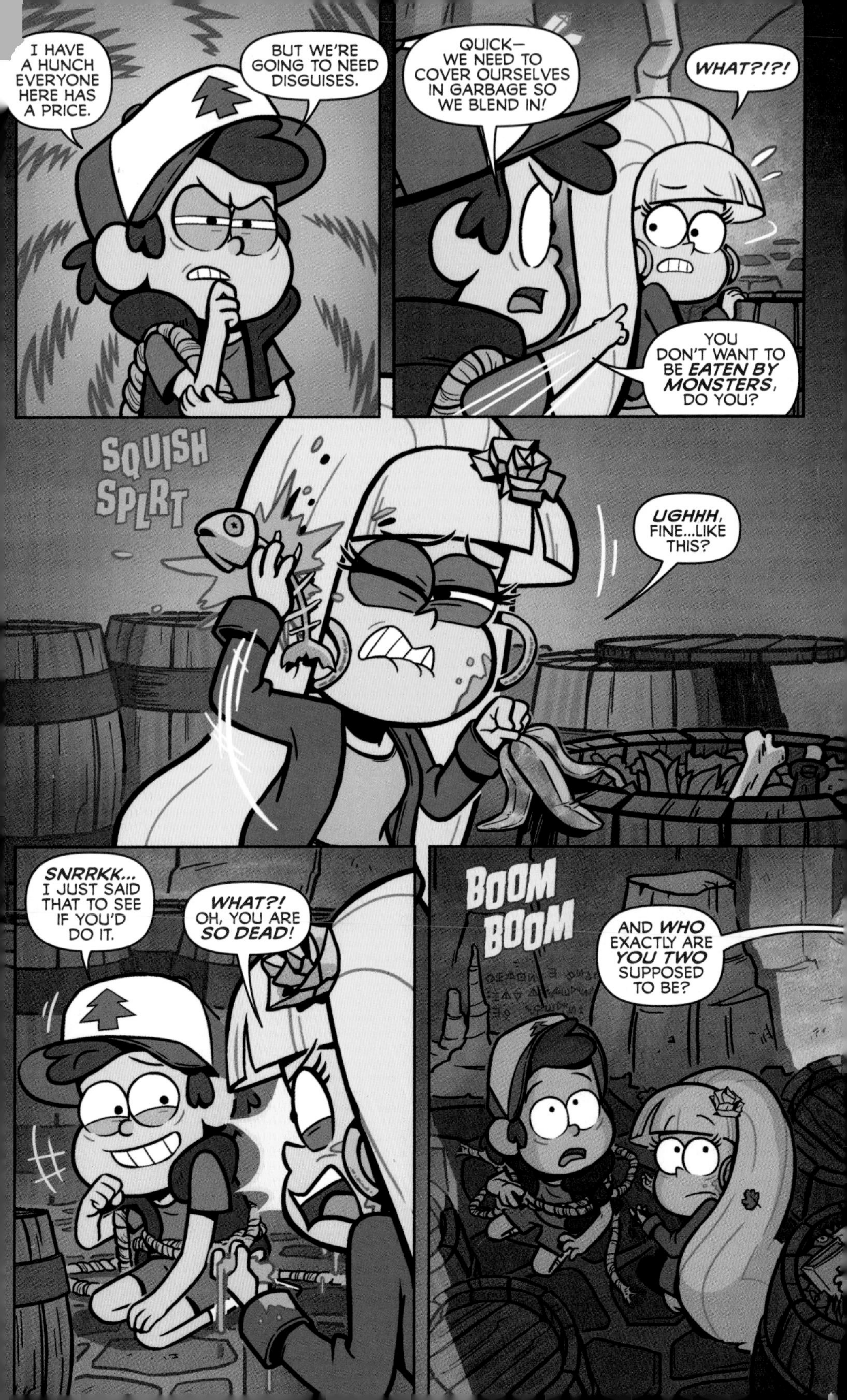

I HAVE A HUNCH EVERYONE HERE HAS A PRICE.
BUT WE'RE GOING TO NEED DISGUISES.
QUICK— WE NEED TO COVER OURSELVES IN GARBAGE SO WE BLEND IN!
WHAT?!?!
YOU DON'T WANT TO BE EATEN BY MONSTERS, DO YOU?
SQUISH
SPLRT
UGHHH, FINE...LIKE THIS?
SNRRKK... I JUST SAID THAT TO SEE IF YOU'D DO IT.
WHAT?! OH, YOU ARE SO DEAD!
BOOM
BOOM
AND WHO EXACTLY ARE YOU TWO SUPPOSED TO BE?

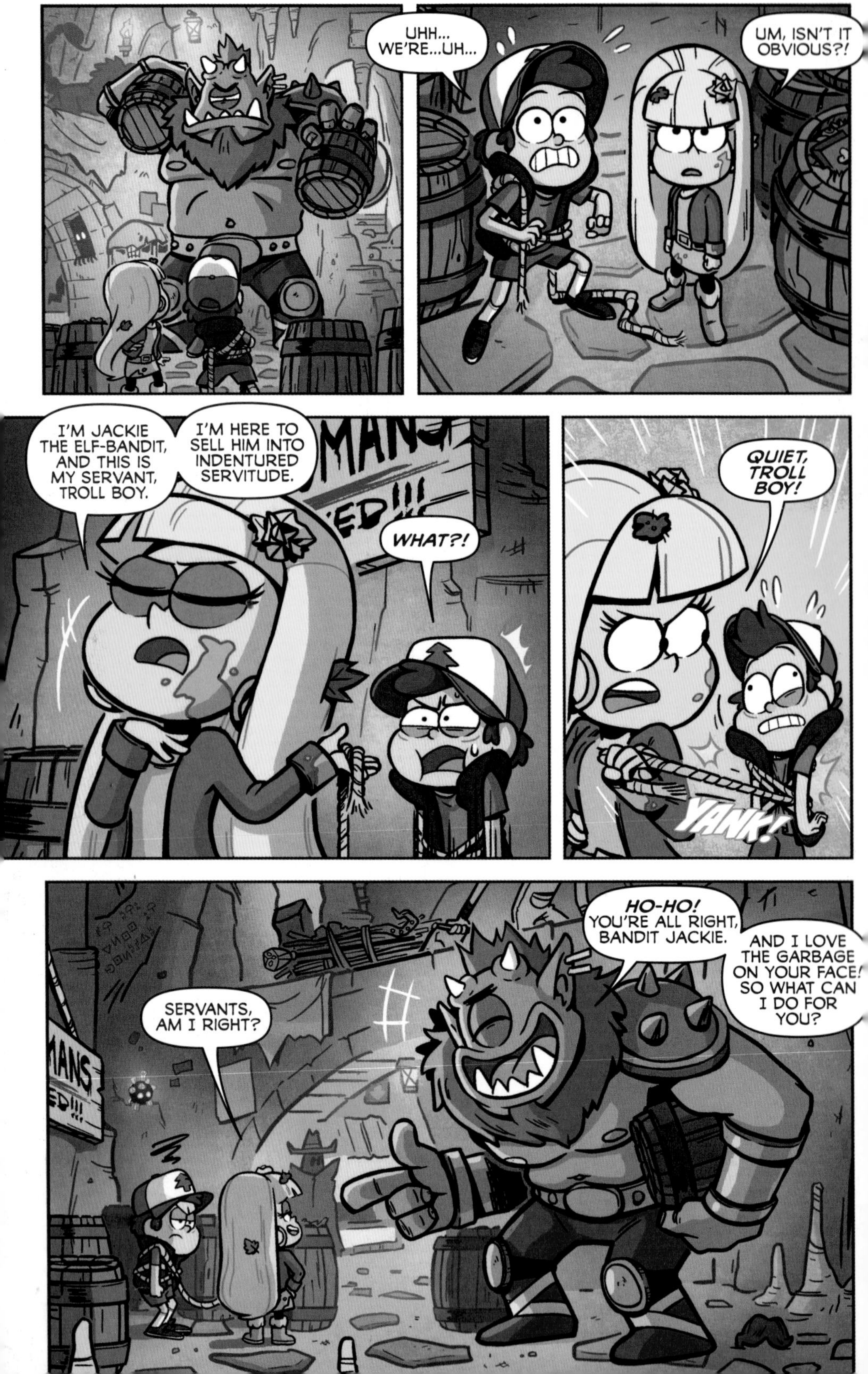
UHH... WE'RE...UH...
UM, ISN'T IT OBVIOUS?!
I'M JACKIE THE ELF-BANDIT, AND THIS IS MY SERVANT, TROLL BOY.
I'M HERE TO SELL HIM INTO INDENTURED SERVITUDE.
WHAT?!
QUIET, TROLL BOY!
YANK!
SERVANTS, AM I RIGHT?
HO-HO! YOU'RE ALL RIGHT, BANDIT JACKIE.
AND I LOVE THE GARBAGE ON YOUR FACE! SO WHAT CAN I DO FOR YOU?

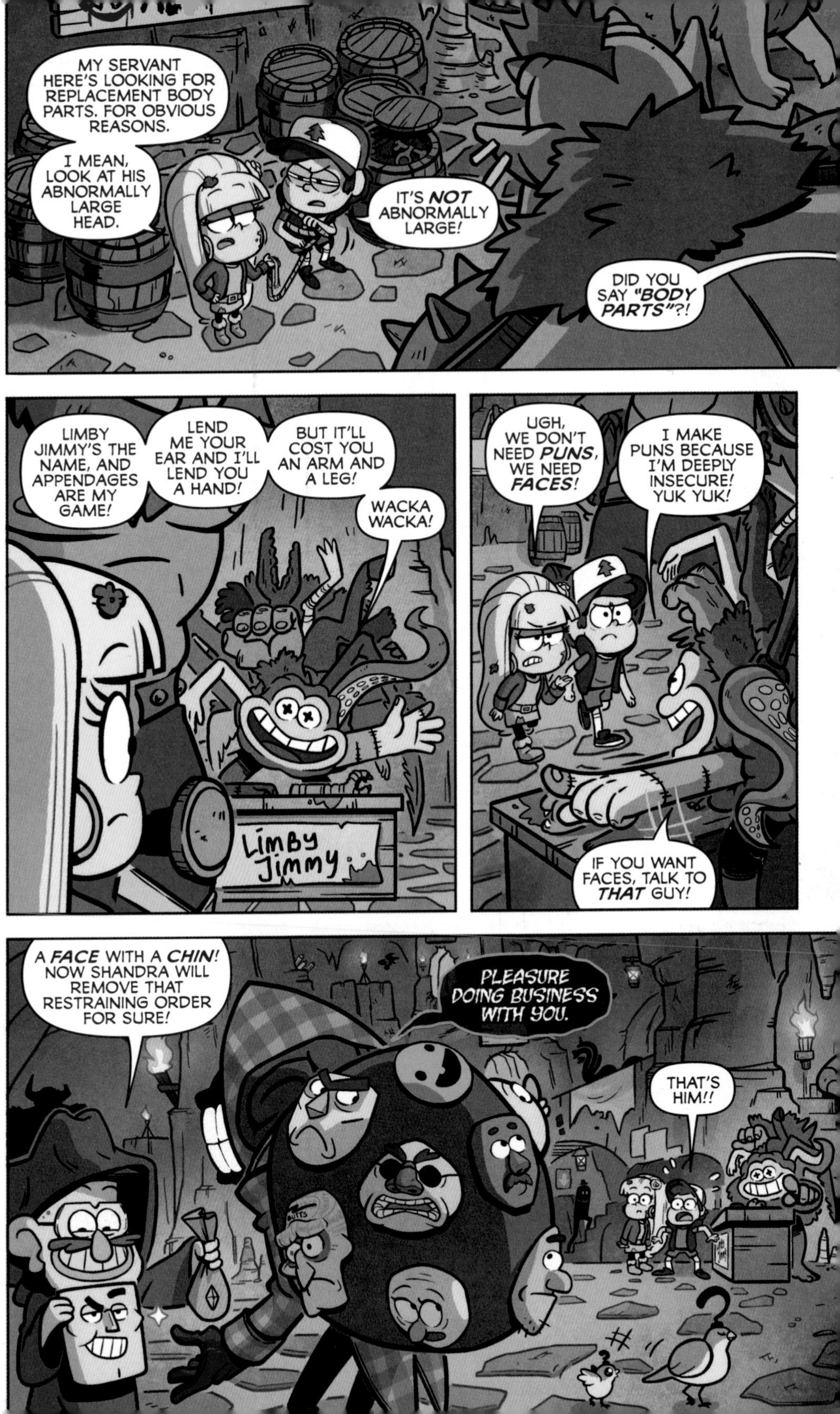

MY SERVANT HERE'S LOOKING FOR REPLACEMENT BODY PARTS. FOR OBVIOUS REASONS.
I MEAN, LOOK AT HIS ABNORMALLY LARGE HEAD.
IT'S NOT ABNORMALLY LARGE!
DID YOU SAY "BODY PARTS"?!
LIMBY JIMMY'S THE NAME, AND APPENDAGES ARE MY GAME!
LEND ME YOUR EAR AND I'LL LEND YOU A HAND!
BUT IT'LL COST YOU AN ARM AND A LEG!
WACKA WACKA!
Limby Jimmy
UGH, WE DON'T NEED PUNS, WE NEED FACES!
I MAKE PUNS BECAUSE I'M DEEPLY INSECURE! YUK YUK!
IF YOU WANT FACES, TALK TO THAT GUY!
A FACE WITH A CHIN! NOW SHANDRA WILL REMOVE THAT RESTRAINING ORDER FOR SURE!
PLEASURE DOING BUSINESS WITH YOU.
THAT'S HIM!!

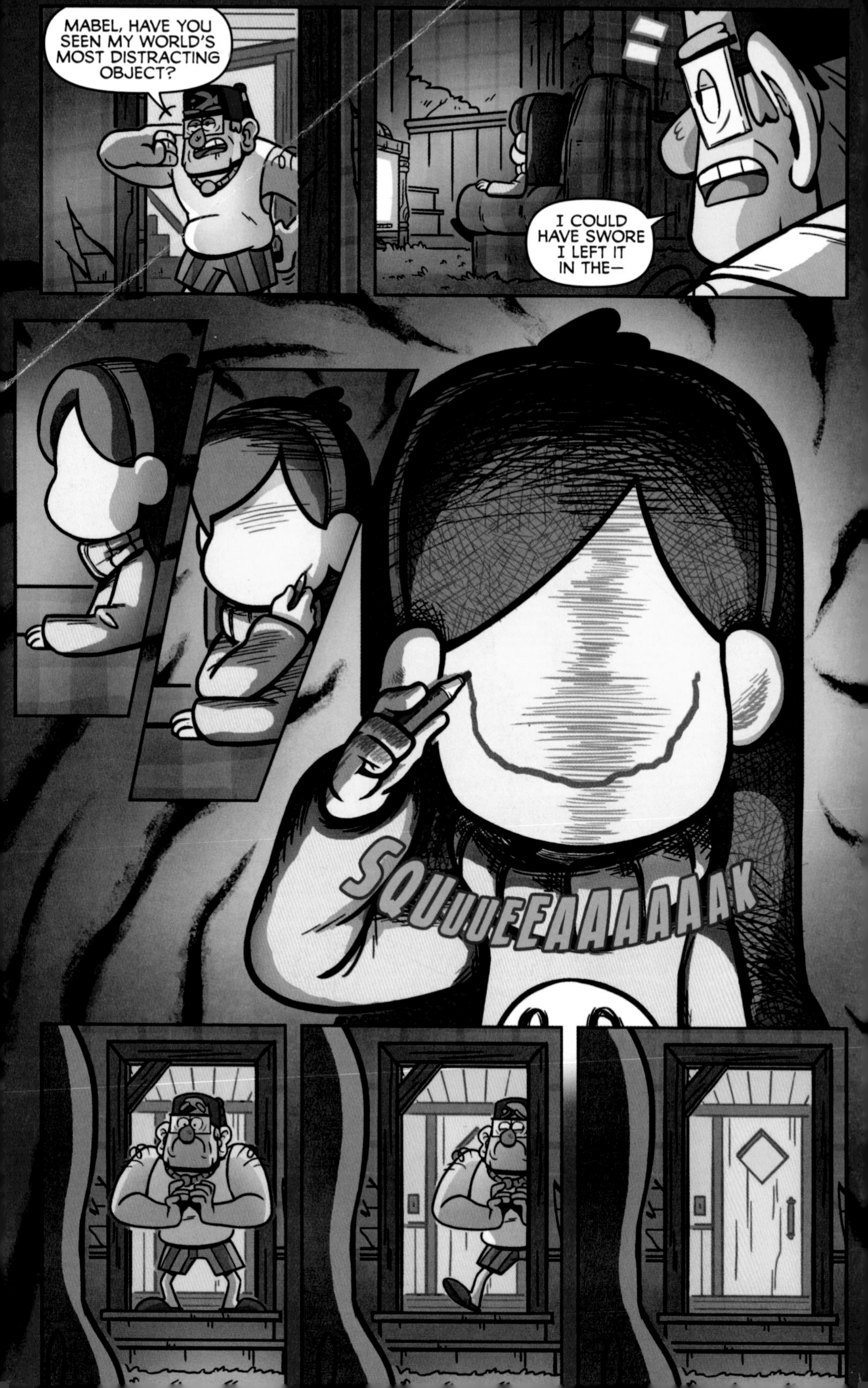
MABEL, HAVE YOU SEEN MY WORLD'S MOST DISTRACTING OBJECT?
I COULD HAVE SWORE I LEFT IT IN THE—
SQUUUEEAAAAAAK

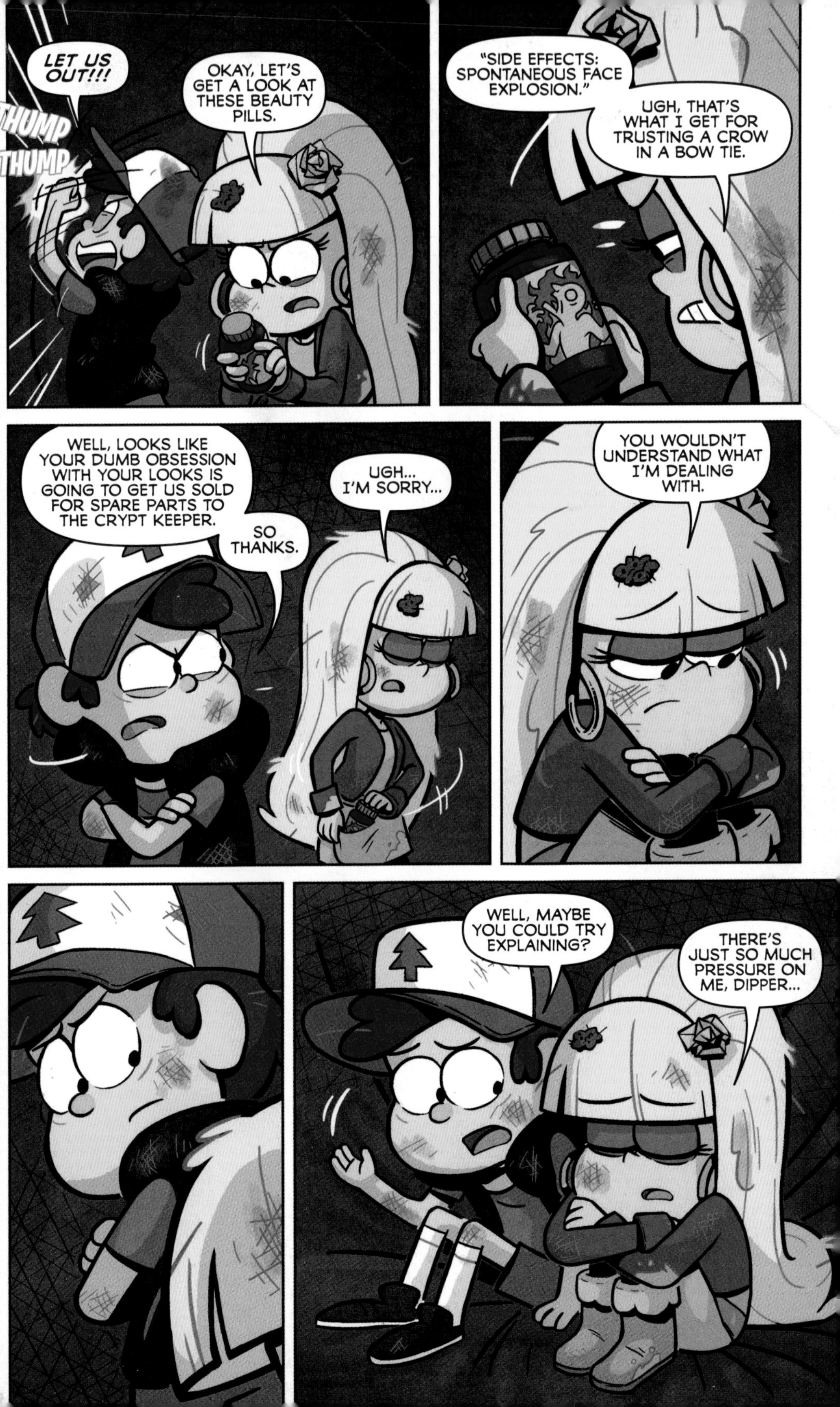
LET US OUT!!!
THUMP
THUMP
OKAY, LET'S GET A LOOK AT THESE BEAUTY PILLS.
"SIDE EFFECTS: SPONTANEOUS FACE EXPLOSION."
UGH, THAT'S WHAT I GET FOR TRUSTING A CROW IN A BOW TIE.
WELL, LOOKS LIKE YOUR DUMB OBSESSION WITH YOUR LOOKS IS GOING TO GET US SOLD FOR SPARE PARTS TO THE CRYPT KEEPER.
SO THANKS.
UGH... I'M SORRY...
YOU WOULDN'T UNDERSTAND WHAT I'M DEALING WITH.
WELL, MAYBE YOU COULD TRY EXPLAINING?
THERE'S JUST SO MUCH PRESSURE ON ME, DIPPER...

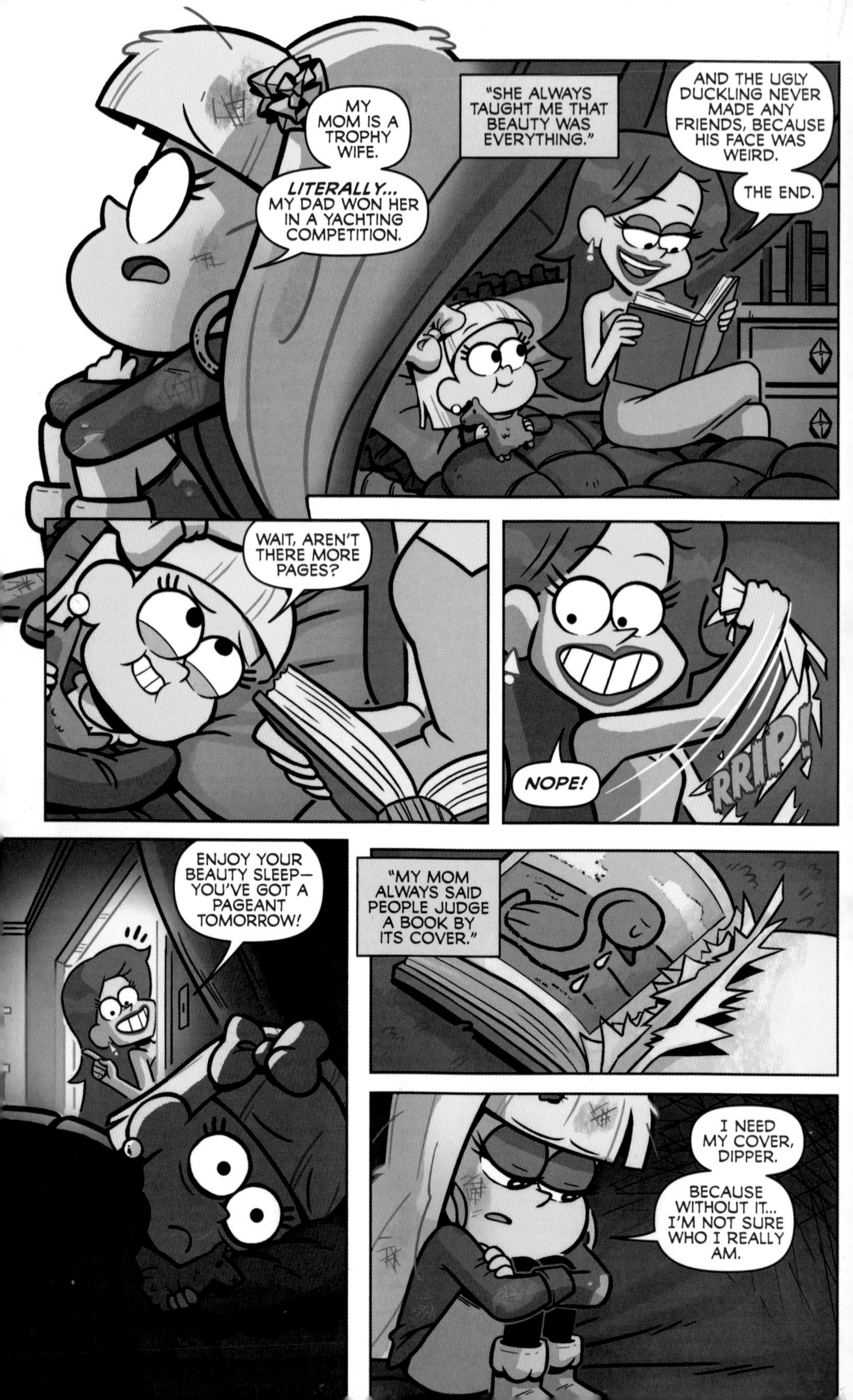
MY MOM IS A TROPHY WIFE.
LITERALLY... MY DAD WON HER IN A YACHTING COMPETITION.
"SHE ALWAYS TAUGHT ME THAT BEAUTY WAS EVERYTHING."
AND THE UGLY DUCKLING NEVER MADE ANY FRIENDS, BECAUSE HIS FACE WAS WEIRD.
THE END.
WAIT, AREN'T THERE MORE PAGES?
NOPE!
RRIP!
ENJOY YOUR BEAUTY SLEEP— YOU'VE GOT A PAGEANT TOMORROW!
"MY MOM ALWAYS SAID PEOPLE JUDGE A BOOK BY ITS COVER."
I NEED MY COVER, DIPPER.
BECAUSE WITHOUT IT... I'M NOT SURE WHO I REALLY AM.

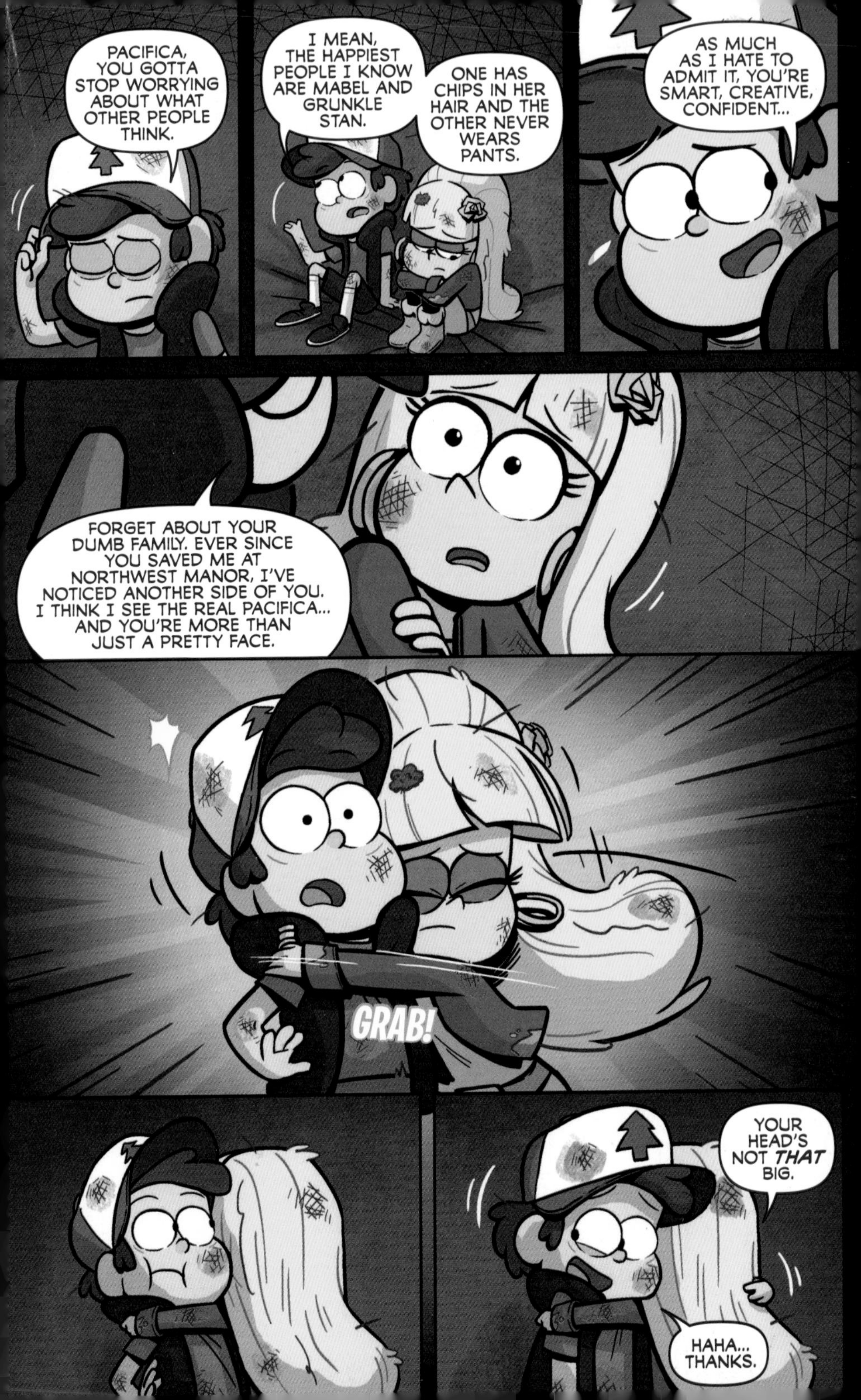
PACIFICA, YOU GOTTA STOP WORRYING ABOUT WHAT OTHER PEOPLE THINK.
I MEAN, THE HAPPIEST PEOPLE I KNOW ARE MABEL AND GRUNKLE STAN.
ONE HAS CHIPS IN HER HAIR AND THE OTHER NEVER WEARS PANTS.
AS MUCH AS I HATE TO ADMIT IT, YOU'RE SMART, CREATIVE, CONFIDENT...
FORGET ABOUT YOUR DUMB FAMILY. EVER SINCE YOU SAVED ME AT NORTHWEST MANOR, I'VE NOTICED ANOTHER SIDE OF YOU. I THINK I SEE THE REAL PACIFICA... AND YOU'RE MORE THAN JUST A PRETTY FACE.
GRAB!
YOUR HEAD'S NOT *THAT* BIG.
HAHA... THANKS.

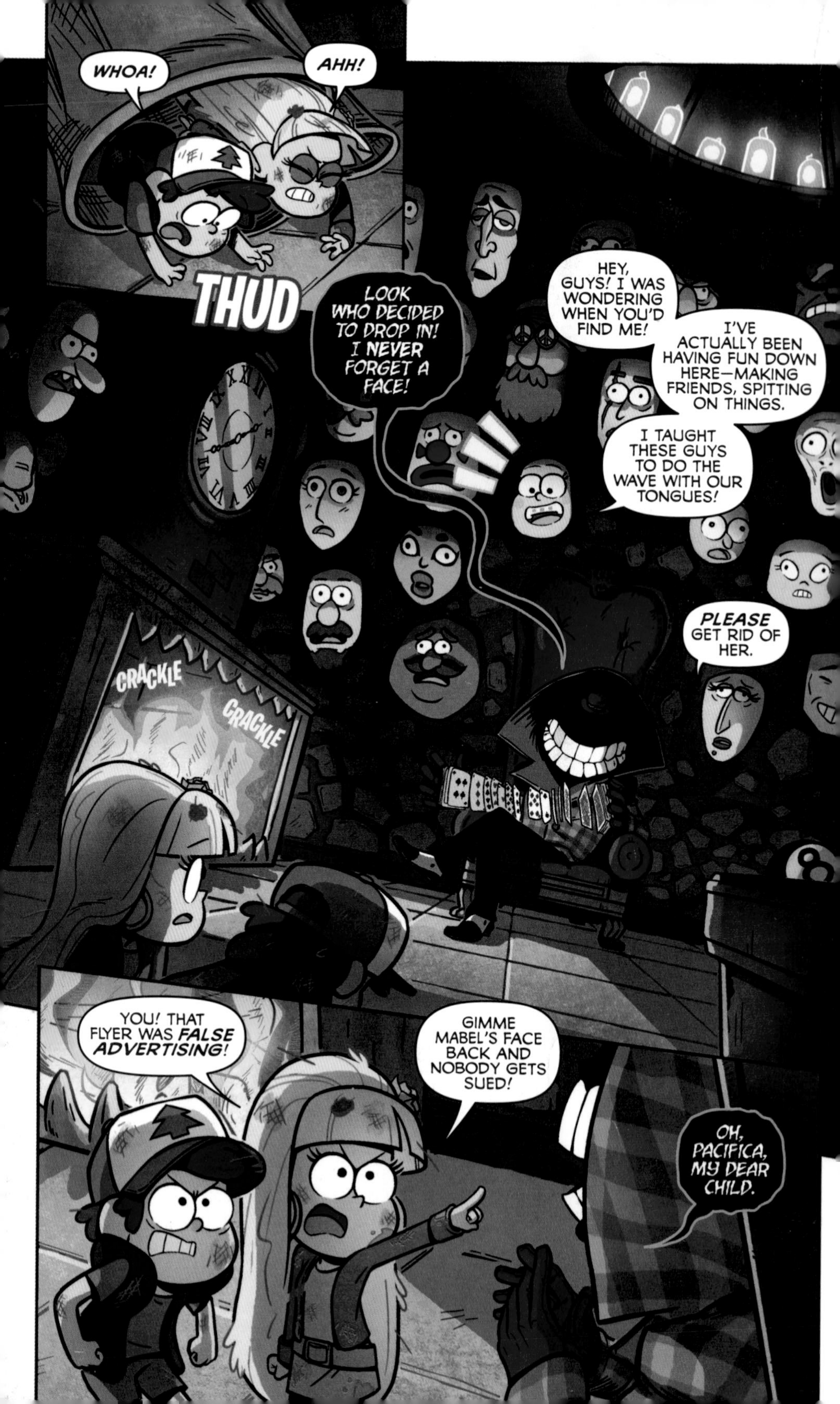
WHOA!
AHH!
THUD
LOOK WHO DECIDED TO DROP IN! I NEVER FORGET A FACE!
HEY, GUYS! I WAS WONDERING WHEN YOU'D FIND ME!
I'VE ACTUALLY BEEN HAVING FUN DOWN HERE—MAKING FRIENDS, SPITTING ON THINGS.
I TAUGHT THESE GUYS TO DO THE WAVE WITH OUR TONGUES!
PLEASE GET RID OF HER.
CRACKLE
CRACKLE
YOU! THAT FLYER WAS FALSE ADVERTISING!
GIMME MABEL'S FACE BACK AND NOBODY GETS SUED!
OH, PACIFICA, MY DEAR CHILD.

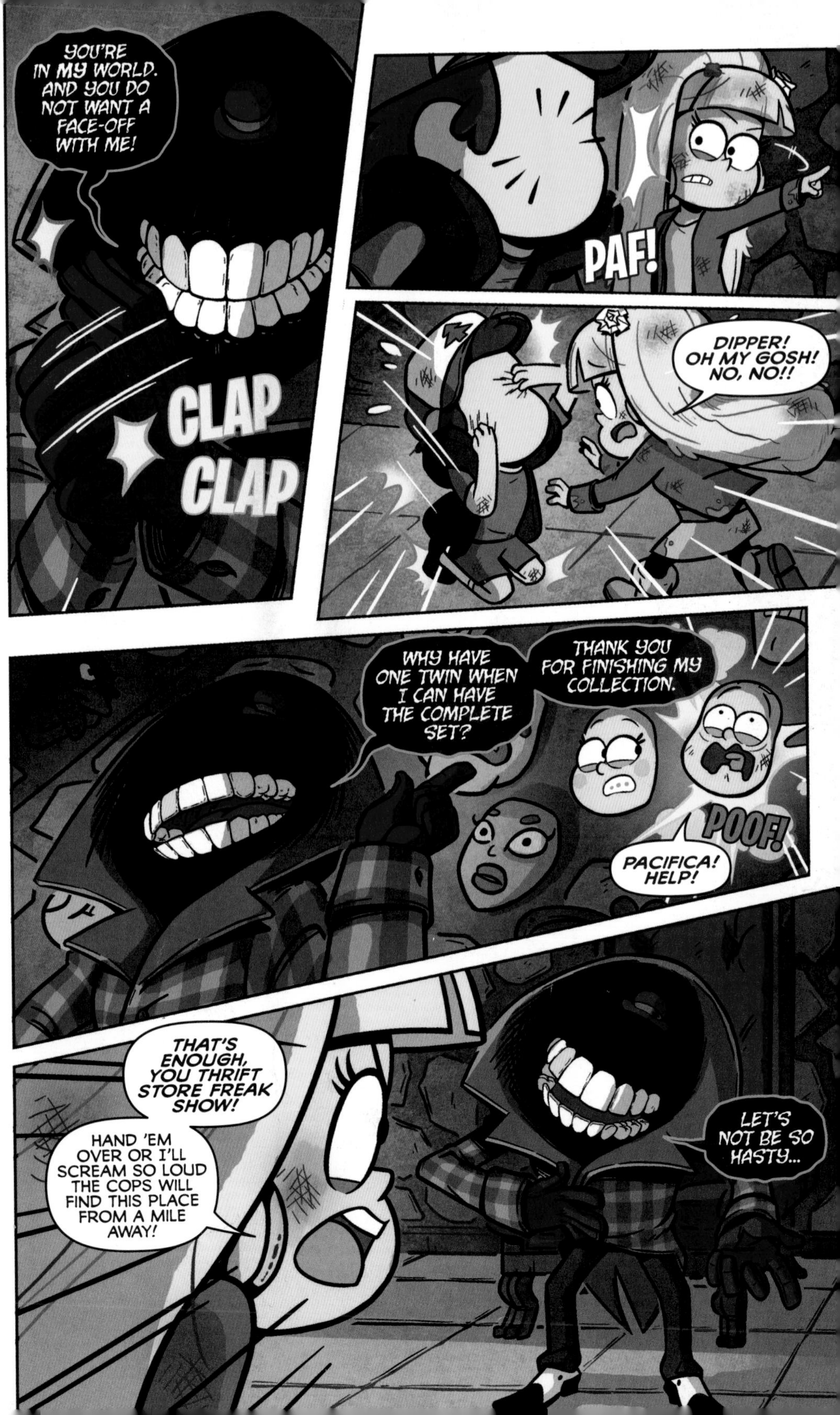
YOU'RE IN MY WORLD. AND YOU DO NOT WANT A FACE-OFF WITH ME!
CLAP
CLAP
PAF!
DIPPER! OH MY GOSH! NO, NO!!
WHY HAVE ONE TWIN WHEN I CAN HAVE THE COMPLETE SET?
THANK YOU FOR FINISHING MY COLLECTION.
POOF!
PACIFICA! HELP!
THAT'S ENOUGH, YOU THRIFT STORE FREAK SHOW!
HAND 'EM OVER OR I'LL SCREAM SO LOUD THE COPS WILL FIND THIS PLACE FROM A MILE AWAY!
LET'S NOT BE SO HASTY...

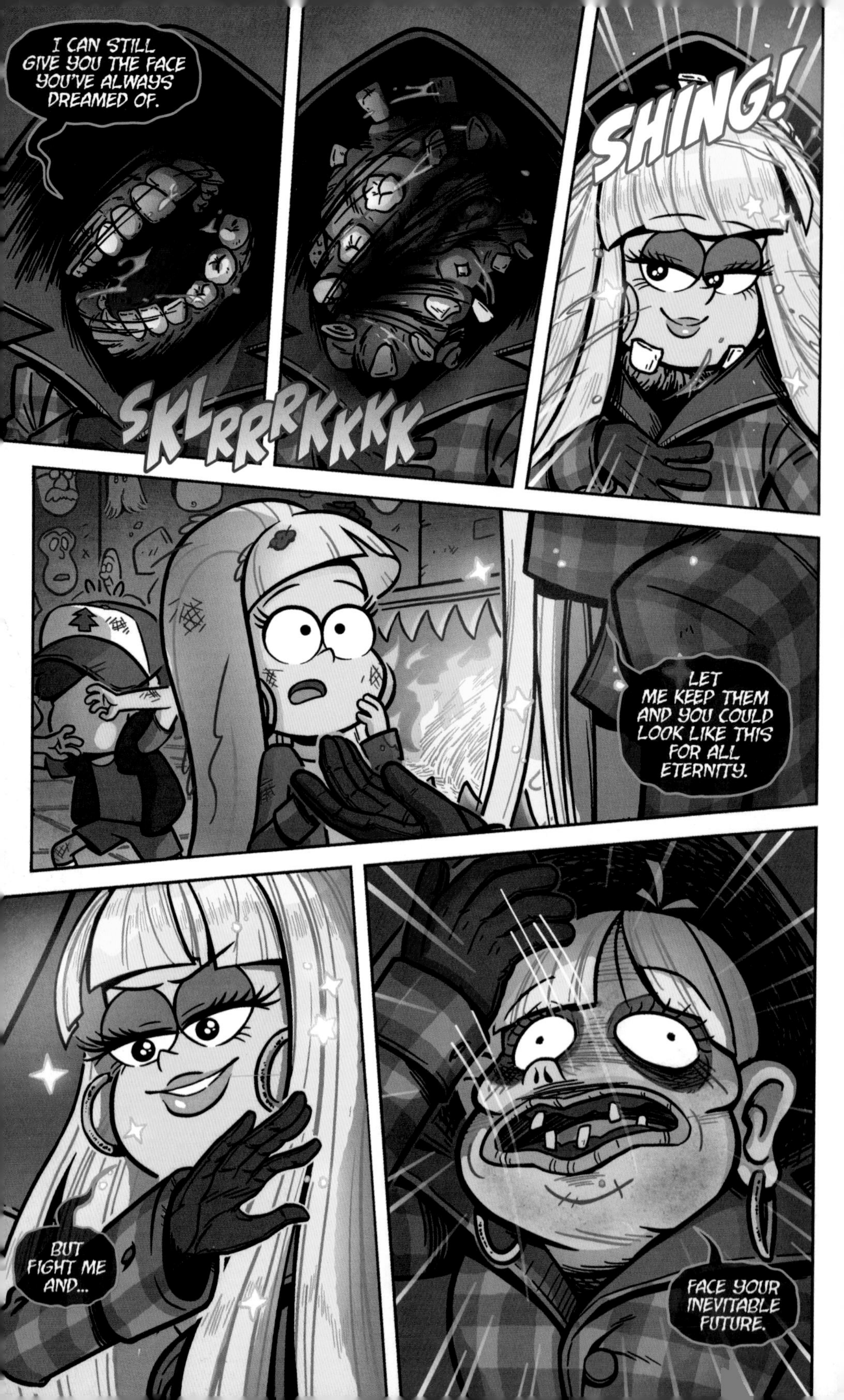
I CAN STILL GIVE YOU THE FACE YOU'VE ALWAYS DREAMED OF.
SKLRRRKKKK
SHING!
LET ME KEEP THEM AND YOU COULD LOOK LIKE THIS FOR ALL ETERNITY.
BUT FIGHT ME AND...
FACE YOUR INEVITABLE FUTURE.

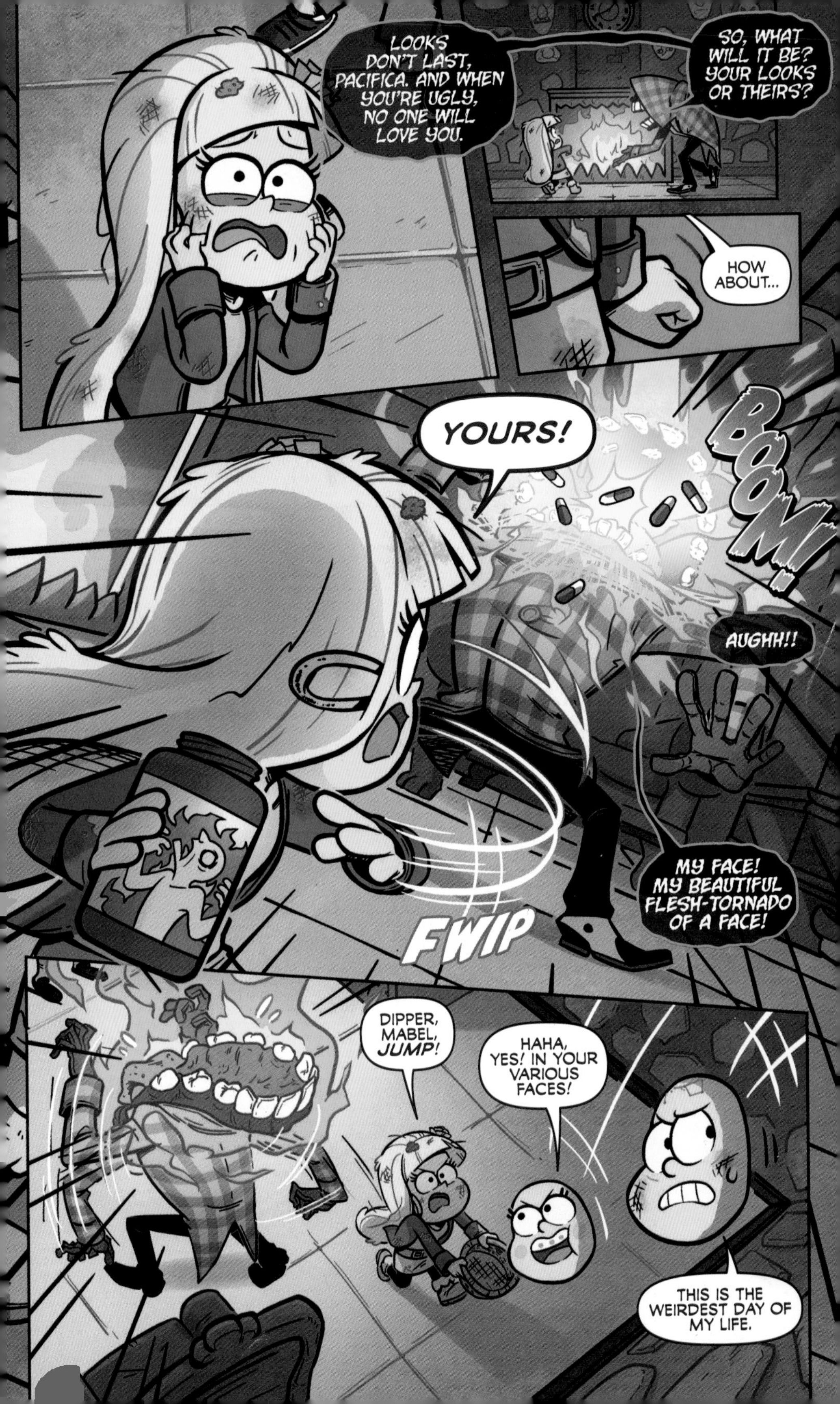
LOOKS DON'T LAST, PACIFICA. AND WHEN YOU'RE UGLY, NO ONE WILL LOVE YOU.
SO, WHAT WILL IT BE? YOUR LOOKS OR THEIRS?
HOW ABOUT...
YOURS!
BOOM!
AUGHH!!
MY FACE! MY BEAUTIFUL FLESH-TORNADO OF A FACE!
FWIP
DIPPER, MABEL, JUMP!
HAHA, YES! IN YOUR VARIOUS FACES!
THIS IS THE WEIRDEST DAY OF MY LIFE.

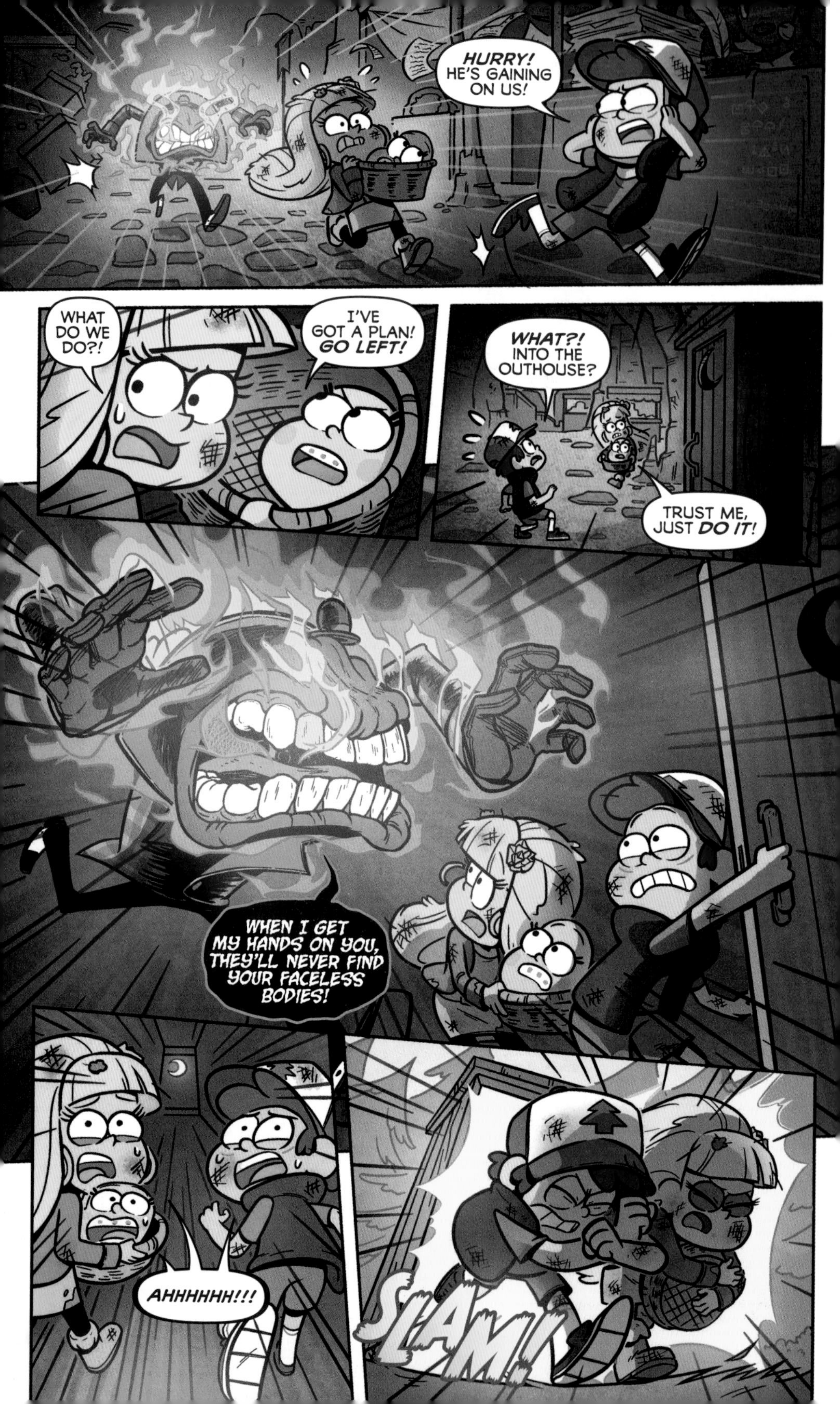
HURRY! HE'S GAINING ON US!
WHAT DO WE DO?!
I'VE GOT A PLAN! GO LEFT!
WHAT?! INTO THE OUTHOUSE?
TRUST ME, JUST DO IT!
WHEN I GET MY HANDS ON YOU, THEY'LL NEVER FIND YOUR FACELESS BODIES!
AHHHHHH!!!
SLAM!

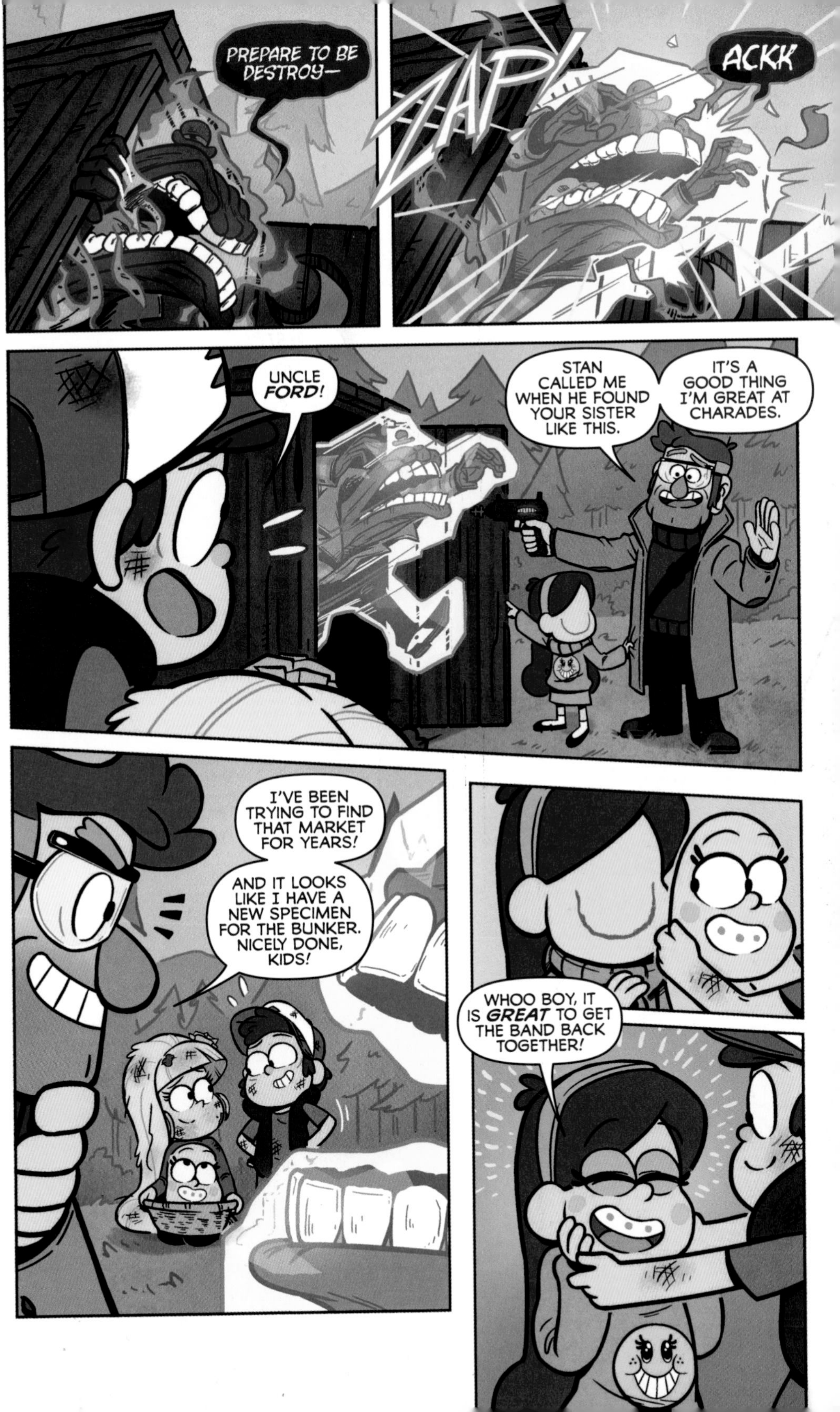
PREPARE TO BE DESTROY—
ZAP!
ACKK
UNCLE *FORD*!
STAN CALLED ME WHEN HE FOUND YOUR SISTER LIKE THIS.
IT'S A GOOD THING I'M GREAT AT CHARADES.
I'VE BEEN TRYING TO FIND THAT MARKET FOR YEARS!
AND IT LOOKS LIKE I HAVE A NEW SPECIMEN FOR THE BUNKER. NICELY DONE, KIDS!
WHOO BOY, IT IS *GREAT* TO GET THE BAND BACK TOGETHER!

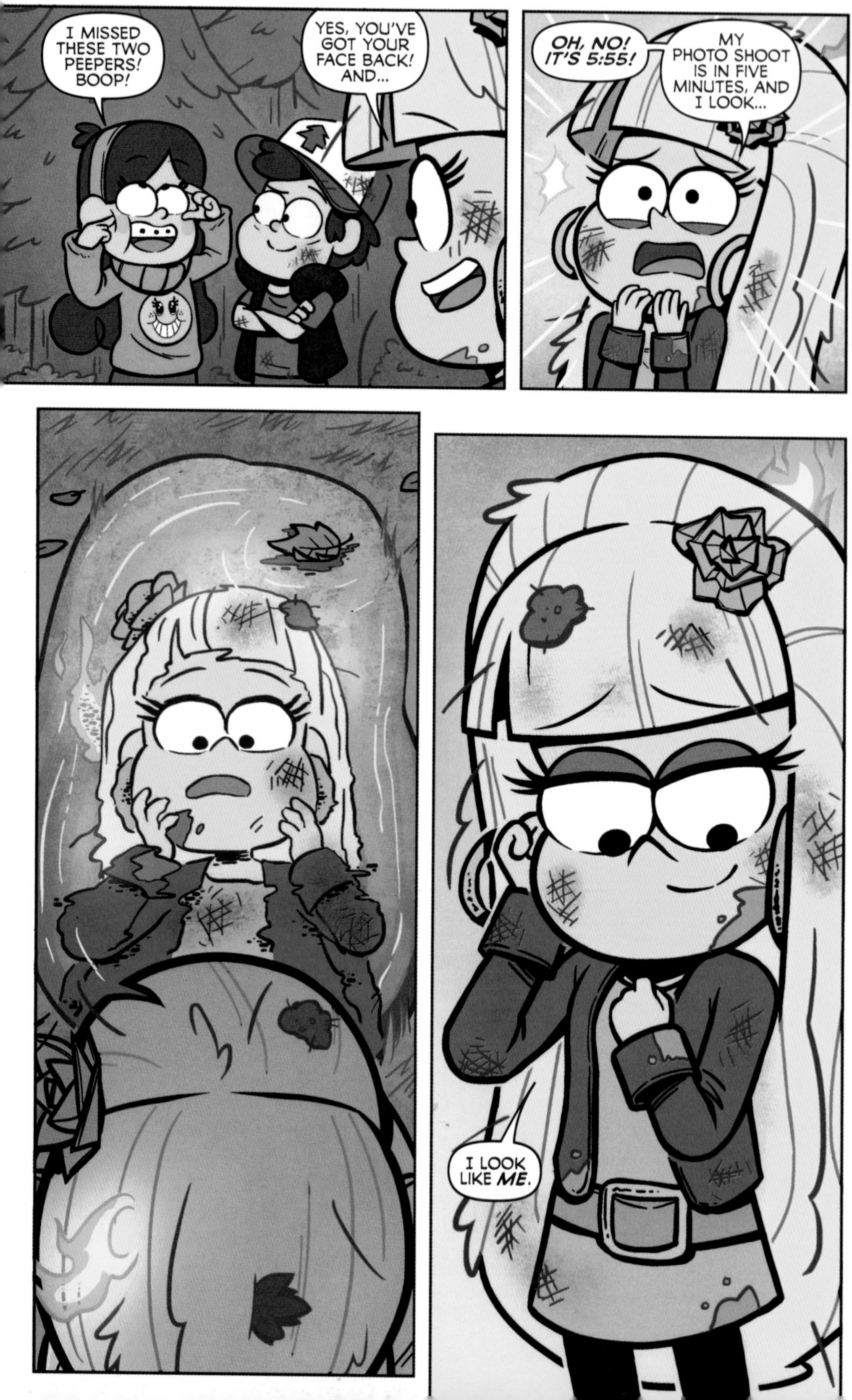
I MISSED THESE TWO PEEPERS! BOOP!
YES, YOU'VE GOT YOUR FACE BACK! AND...
OH, NO! IT'S 5:55!
MY PHOTO SHOOT IS IN FIVE MINUTES, AND I LOOK...
I LOOK LIKE *ME*.

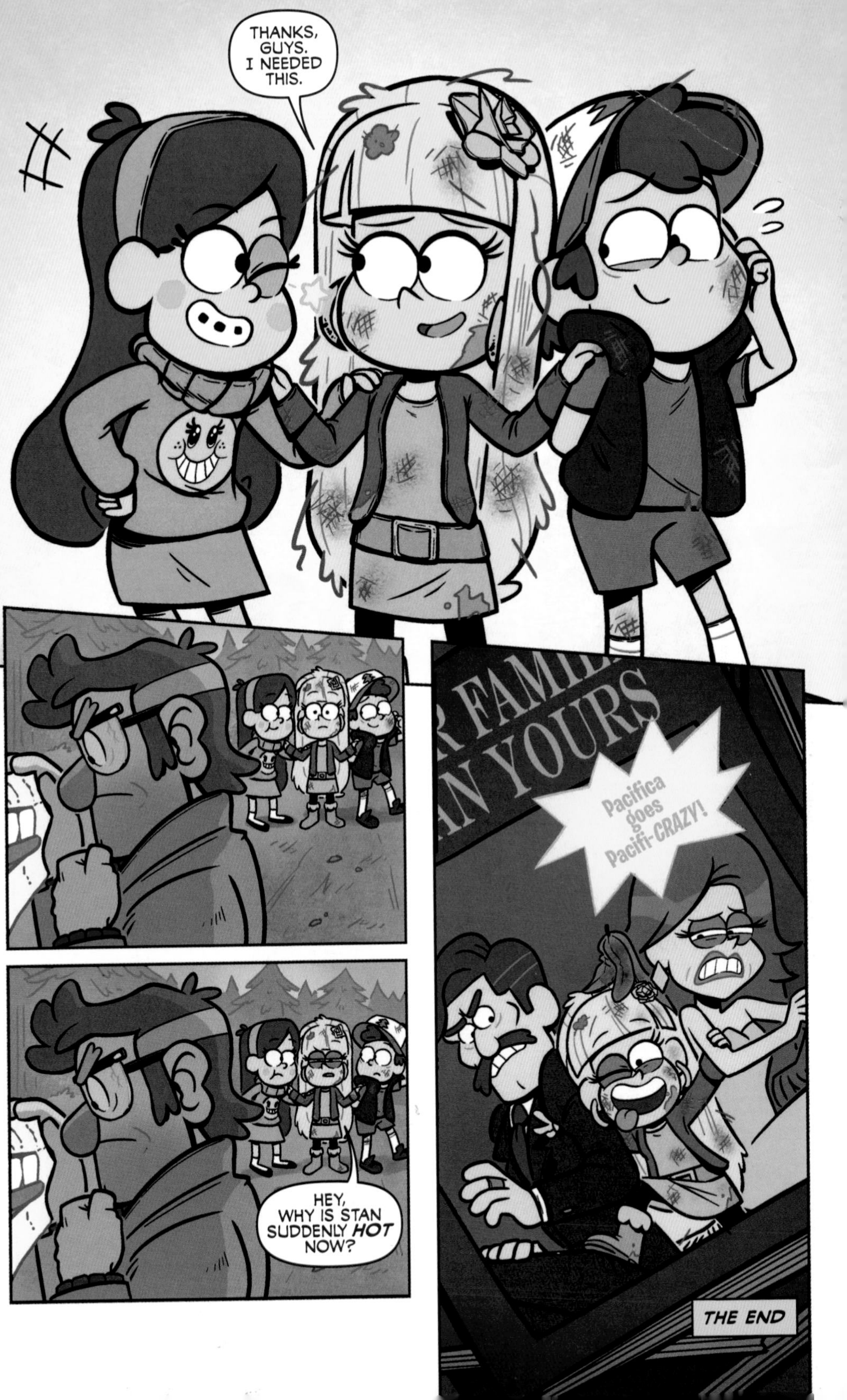

THANKS, GUYS. I NEEDED THIS.
R FAMIL
AN YOURS
Pacifica goes Pacifi-CRAZY!
HEY, WHY IS STAN SUDDENLY *HOT* NOW?
THE END

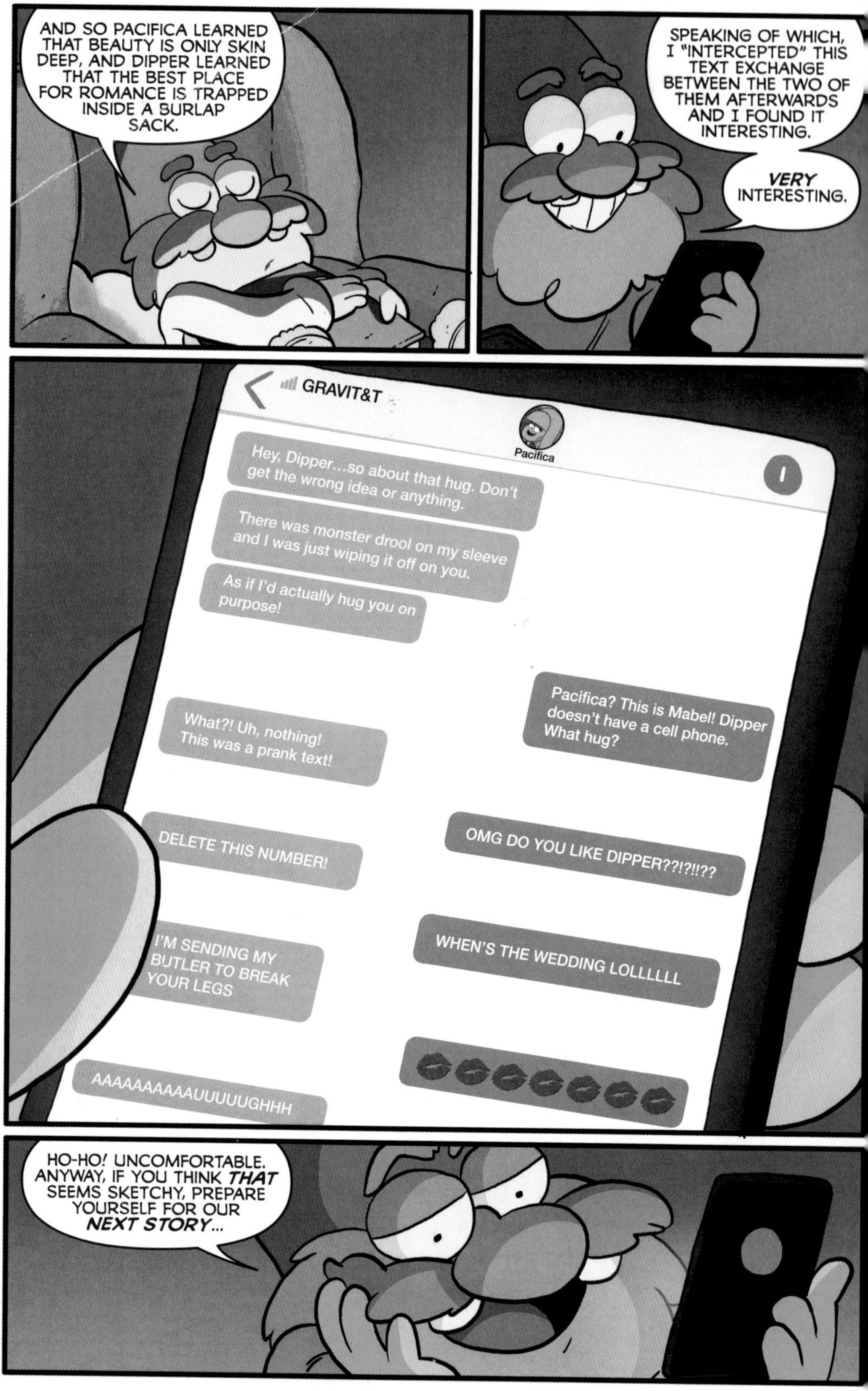
AND SO PACIFICA LEARNED THAT BEAUTY IS ONLY SKIN DEEP, AND DIPPER LEARNED THAT THE BEST PLACE FOR ROMANCE IS TRAPPED INSIDE A BURLAP SACK.
SPEAKING OF WHICH, I "INTERCEPTED" THIS TEXT EXCHANGE BETWEEN THE TWO OF THEM AFTERWARDS AND I FOUND IT INTERESTING.
VERY INTERESTING.
GRAVIT&T
Pacifica
Hey, Dipper...so about that hug. Don't get the wrong idea or anything.
There was monster drool on my sleeve and I was just wiping it off on you.
As if I'd actually hug you on purpose!
Pacifica? This is Mabel! Dipper doesn't have a cell phone. What hug?
What?! Uh, nothing! This was a prank text!
OMG DO YOU LIKE DIPPER??!?!!??
DELETE THIS NUMBER!
WHEN'S THE WEDDING LOLLLLLL
I'M SENDING MY BUTLER TO BREAK YOUR LEGS
AAAAAAAAAAUUUUUGHHH
HO-HO! UNCOMFORTABLE. ANYWAY, IF YOU THINK THAT SEEMS SKETCHY, PREPARE YOURSELF FOR OUR NEXT STORY...

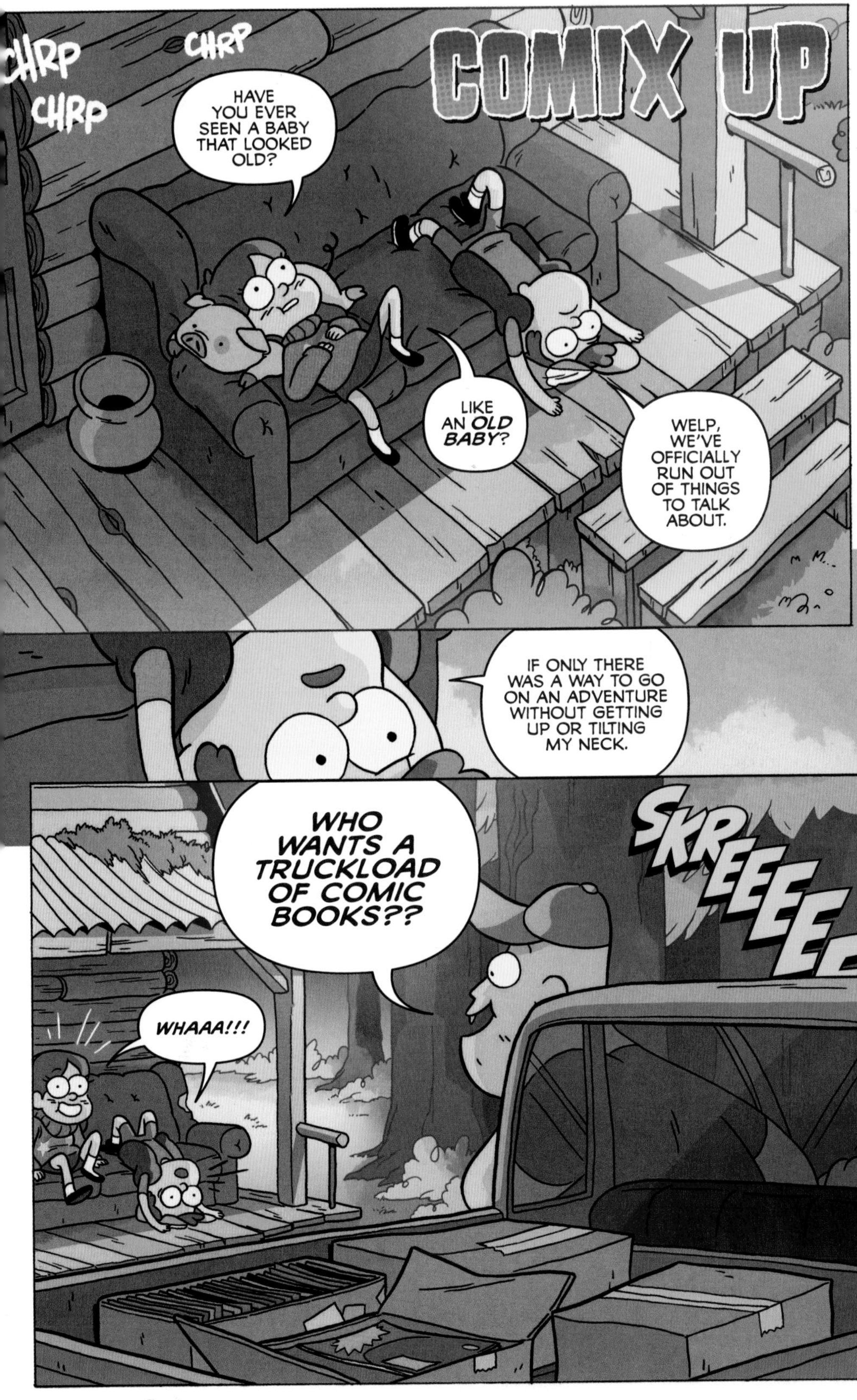

CHRP
CHRP
CHRP
COMIX UP
HAVE YOU EVER SEEN A BABY THAT LOOKED OLD?
LIKE AN OLD BABY?
WELP, WE'VE OFFICIALLY RUN OUT OF THINGS TO TALK ABOUT.
M M...
IF ONLY THERE WAS A WAY TO GO ON AN ADVENTURE WITHOUT GETTING UP OR TILTING MY NECK.
SKREEEEE
WHO WANTS A TRUCKLOAD OF COMIC BOOKS??
WHAAA!!!

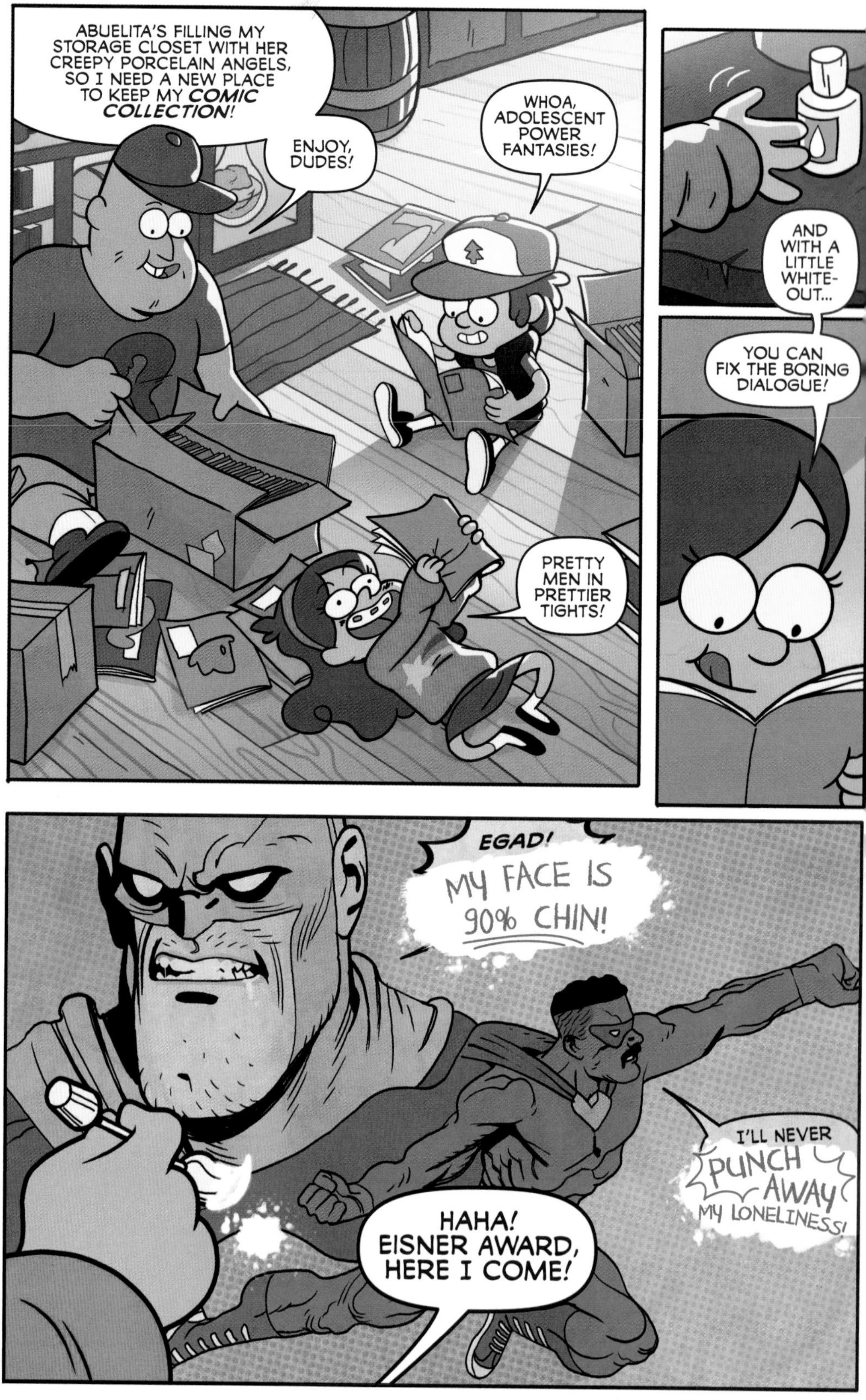
ABUELITA'S FILLING MY STORAGE CLOSET WITH HER CREEPY PORCELAIN ANGELS, SO I NEED A NEW PLACE TO KEEP MY COMIC COLLECTION!
ENJOY, DUDES!
WHOA, ADOLESCENT POWER FANTASIES!
PRETTY MEN IN PRETTIER TIGHTS!
AND WITH A LITTLE WHITE-OUT...
YOU CAN FIX THE BORING DIALOGUE!
EGAD!
MY FACE IS 90% CHIN!
I'LL NEVER PUNCH AWAY MY LONELINESS!
HAHA! EISNER AWARD, HERE I COME!

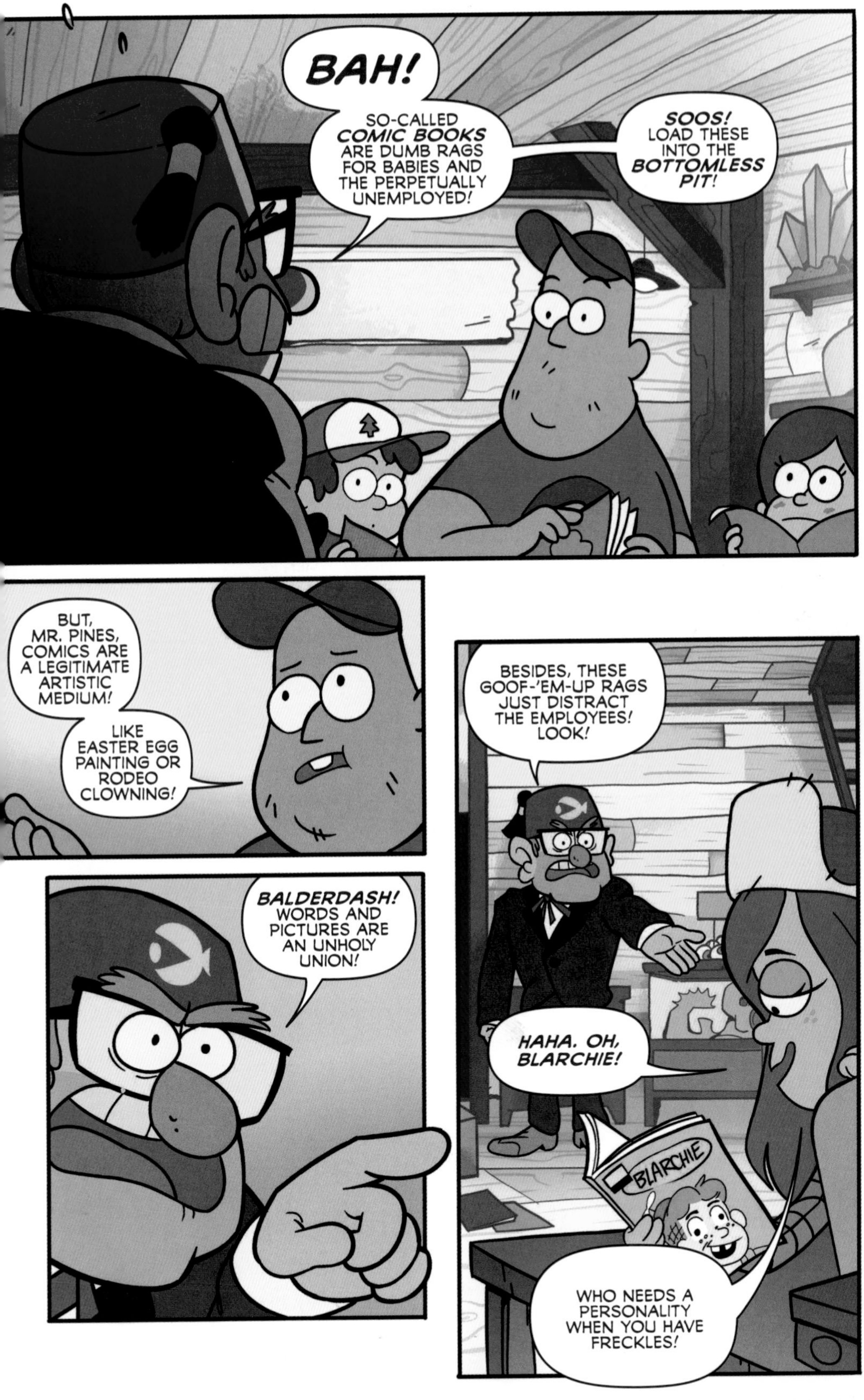
BAH!
SO-CALLED COMIC BOOKS ARE DUMB RAGS FOR BABIES AND THE PERPETUALLY UNEMPLOYED!
SOOS! LOAD THESE INTO THE BOTTOMLESS PIT!
BUT, MR. PINES, COMICS ARE A LEGITIMATE ARTISTIC MEDIUM!
LIKE EASTER EGG PAINTING OR RODEO CLOWNING!
BALDERDASH! WORDS AND PICTURES ARE AN UNHOLY UNION!
BESIDES, THESE GOOF-'EM-UP RAGS JUST DISTRACT THE EMPLOYEES! LOOK!
HAHA. OH, BLARCHIE!
BLARCHIE
WHO NEEDS A PERSONALITY WHEN YOU HAVE FRECKLES!

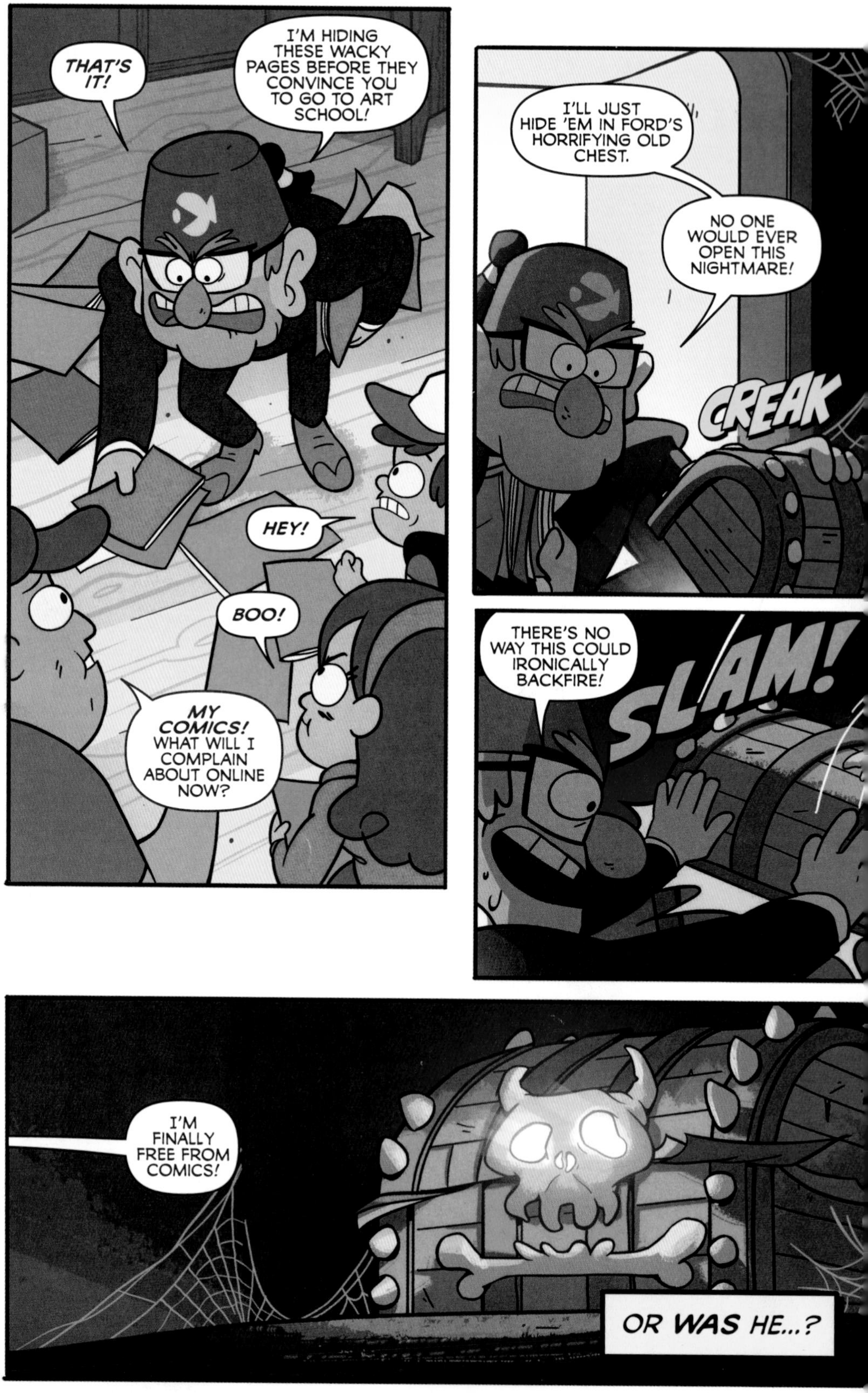
THAT'S IT!
I'M HIDING THESE WACKY PAGES BEFORE THEY CONVINCE YOU TO GO TO ART SCHOOL!
HEY!
BOO!
MY COMICS! WHAT WILL I COMPLAIN ABOUT ONLINE NOW?
I'LL JUST HIDE 'EM IN FORD'S HORRIFYING OLD CHEST.
NO ONE WOULD EVER OPEN THIS NIGHTMARE!
CREAK
THERE'S NO WAY THIS COULD IRONICALLY BACKFIRE!
SLAM!
I'M FINALLY FREE FROM COMICS!
OR WAS HE...?

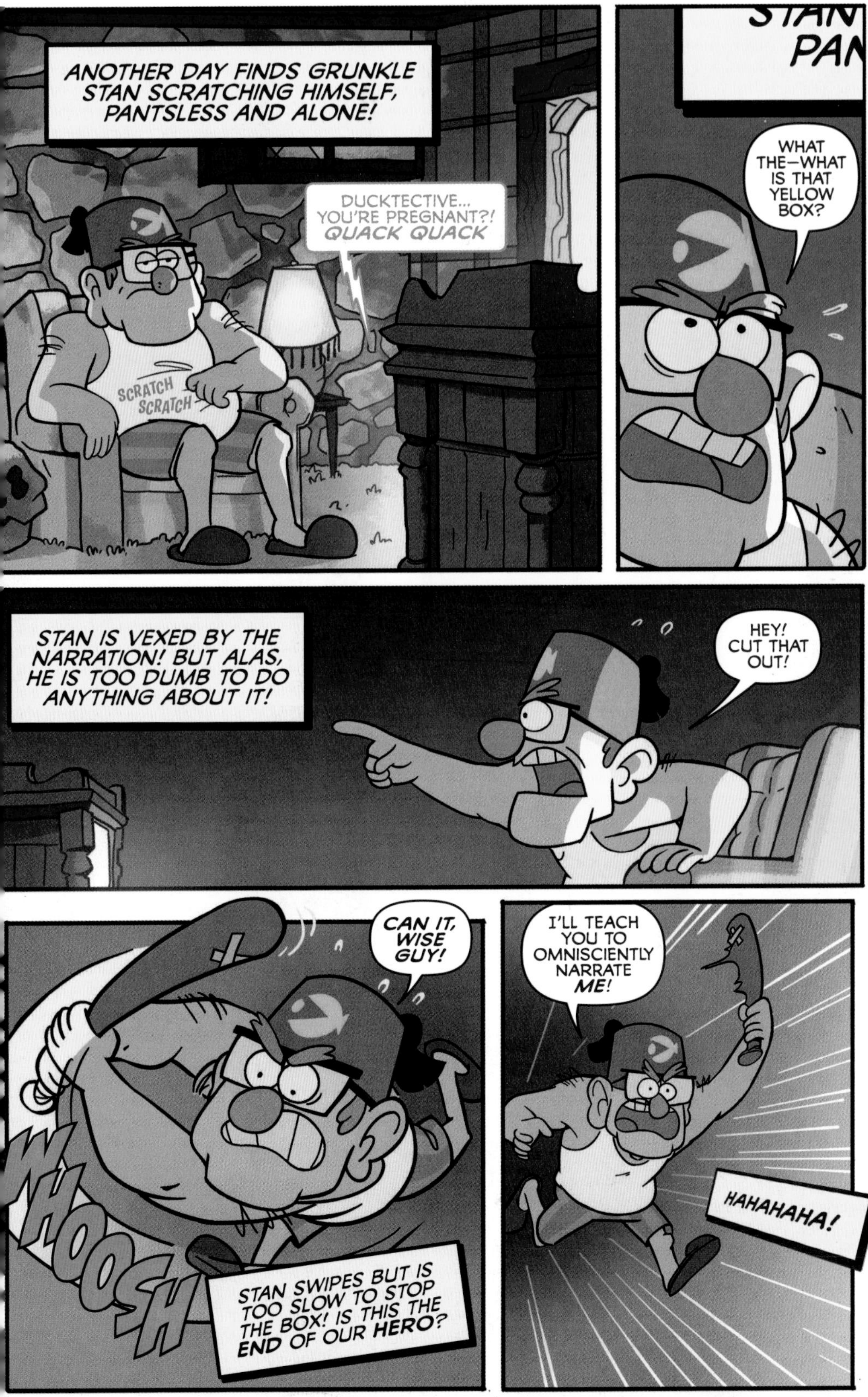

ANOTHER DAY FINDS GRUNKLE STAN SCRATCHING HIMSELF, PANTSLESS AND ALONE!
DUCKTECTIVE... YOU'RE PREGNANT?! QUACK QUACK
SCRATCH SCRATCH
STAN PAN
WHAT THE—WHAT IS THAT YELLOW BOX?
STAN IS VEXED BY THE NARRATION! BUT ALAS, HE IS TOO DUMB TO DO ANYTHING ABOUT IT!
HEY! CUT THAT OUT!
CAN IT, WISE GUY!
WHOOSH
STAN SWIPES BUT IS TOO SLOW TO STOP THE BOX! IS THIS THE END OF OUR HERO?
I'LL TEACH YOU TO OMNISCIENTLY NARRATE ME!
HAHAHAHA!

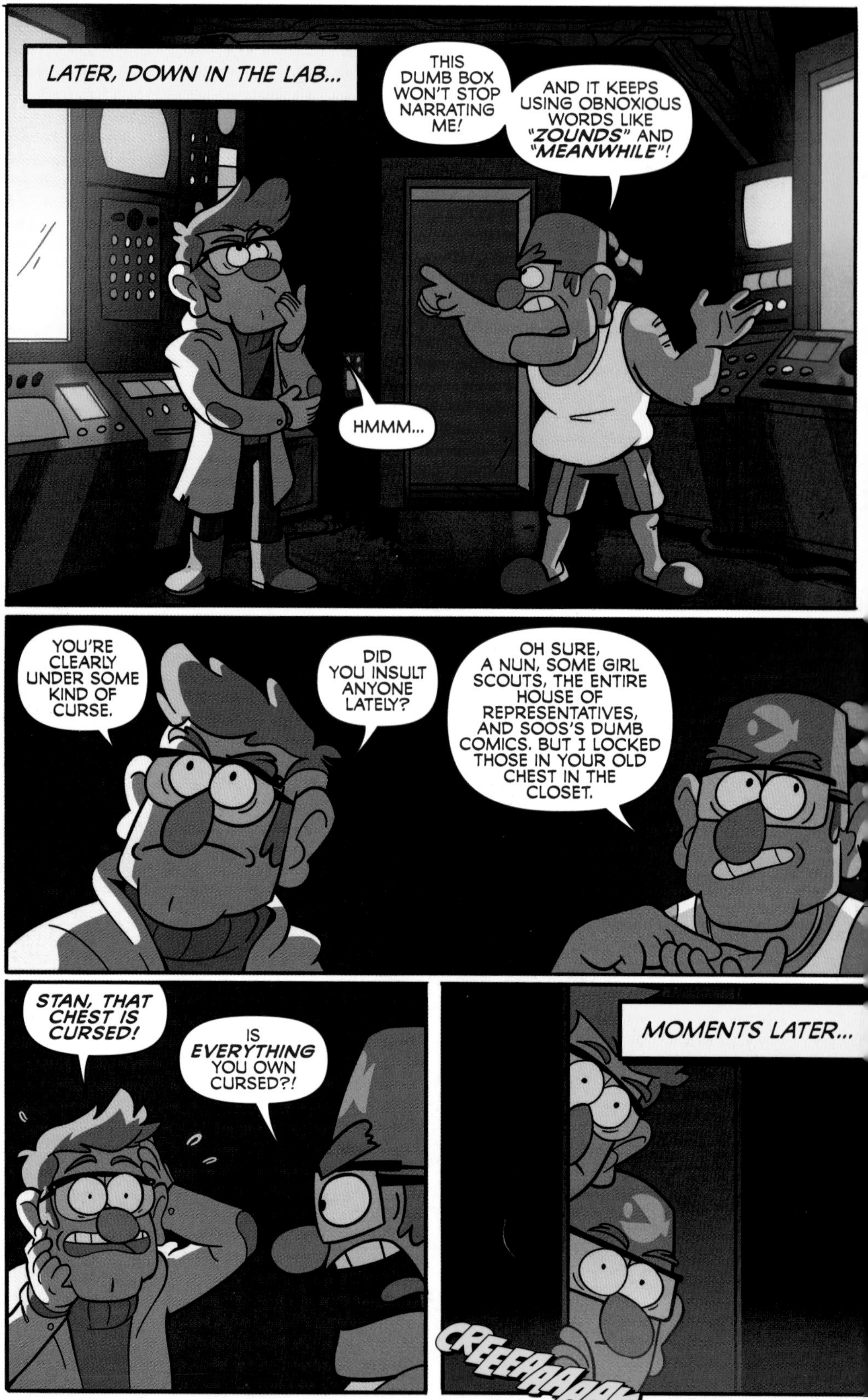
LATER, DOWN IN THE LAB...
THIS DUMB BOX WON'T STOP NARRATING ME!
AND IT KEEPS USING OBNOXIOUS WORDS LIKE "ZOUNDS" AND "MEANWHILE"!
HMMM...
YOU'RE CLEARLY UNDER SOME KIND OF CURSE.
DID YOU INSULT ANYONE LATELY?
OH SURE, A NUN, SOME GIRL SCOUTS, THE ENTIRE HOUSE OF REPRESENTATIVES, AND SOOS'S DUMB COMICS. BUT I LOCKED THOSE IN YOUR OLD CHEST IN THE CLOSET.
STAN, THAT CHEST IS CURSED!
IS EVERYTHING YOU OWN CURSED?!
MOMENTS LATER...
CREEEAAAAAK

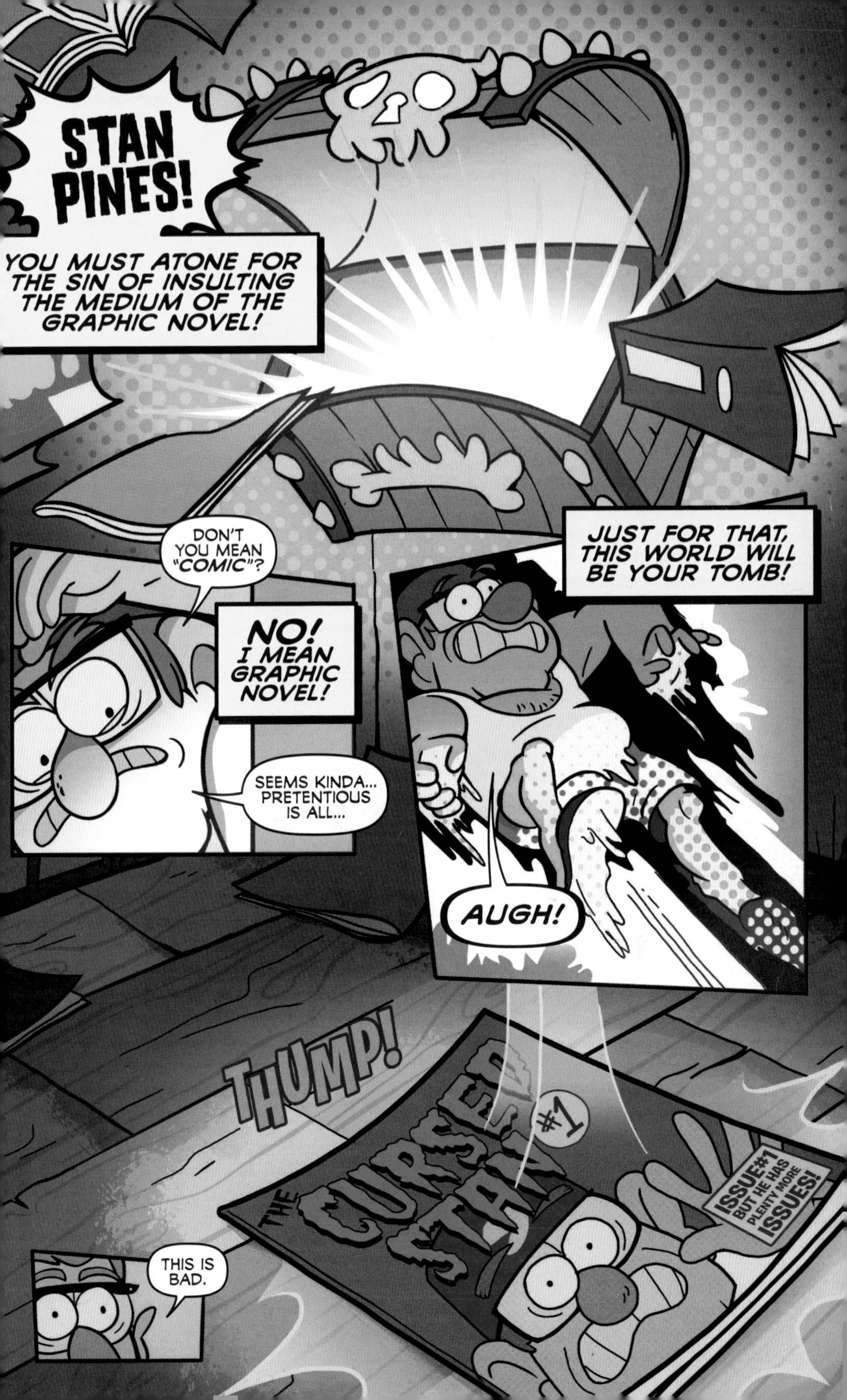
STAN PINES!
YOU MUST ATONE FOR THE SIN OF INSULTING THE MEDIUM OF THE GRAPHIC NOVEL!
DON'T YOU MEAN "COMIC"?
NO! I MEAN GRAPHIC NOVEL!
SEEMS KINDA... PRETENTIOUS IS ALL...
JUST FOR THAT, THIS WORLD WILL BE YOUR TOMB!
AUGH!
THUMP!
THE CURSED STAN #1
ISSUE#1 BUT HE HAS PLENTY MORE ISSUES!
THIS IS BAD.

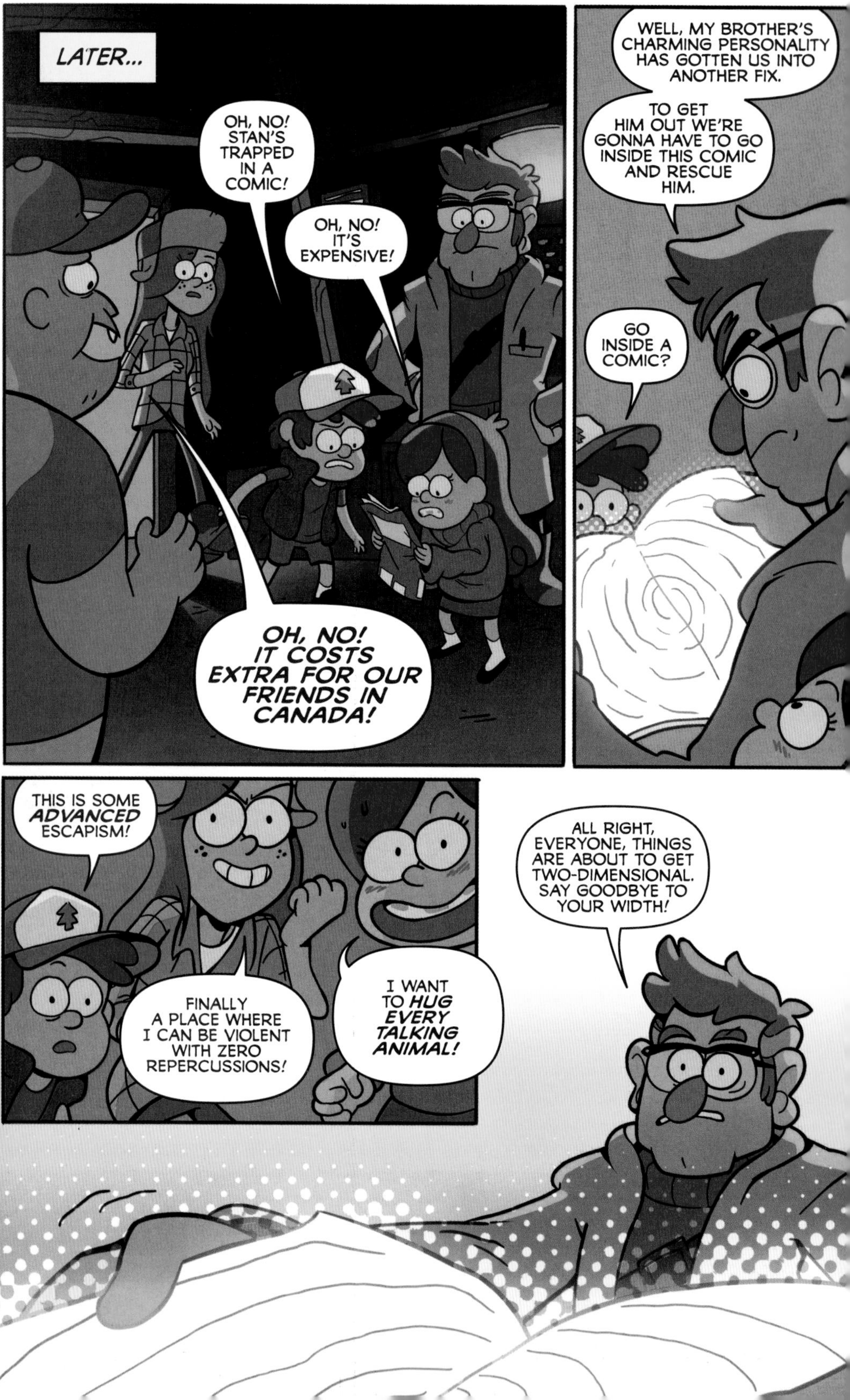
LATER...
OH, NO! STAN'S TRAPPED IN A COMIC!
OH, NO! IT'S EXPENSIVE!
OH, NO! IT COSTS EXTRA FOR OUR FRIENDS IN CANADA!
WELL, MY BROTHER'S CHARMING PERSONALITY HAS GOTTEN US INTO ANOTHER FIX.
TO GET HIM OUT WE'RE GONNA HAVE TO GO INSIDE THIS COMIC AND RESCUE HIM.
GO INSIDE A COMIC?
THIS IS SOME *ADVANCED* ESCAPISM!
FINALLY A PLACE WHERE I CAN BE VIOLENT WITH ZERO REPERCUSSIONS!
I WANT TO *HUG EVERY TALKING ANIMAL!*
ALL RIGHT, EVERYONE, THINGS ARE ABOUT TO GET TWO-DIMENSIONAL. SAY GOODBYE TO YOUR WIDTH!

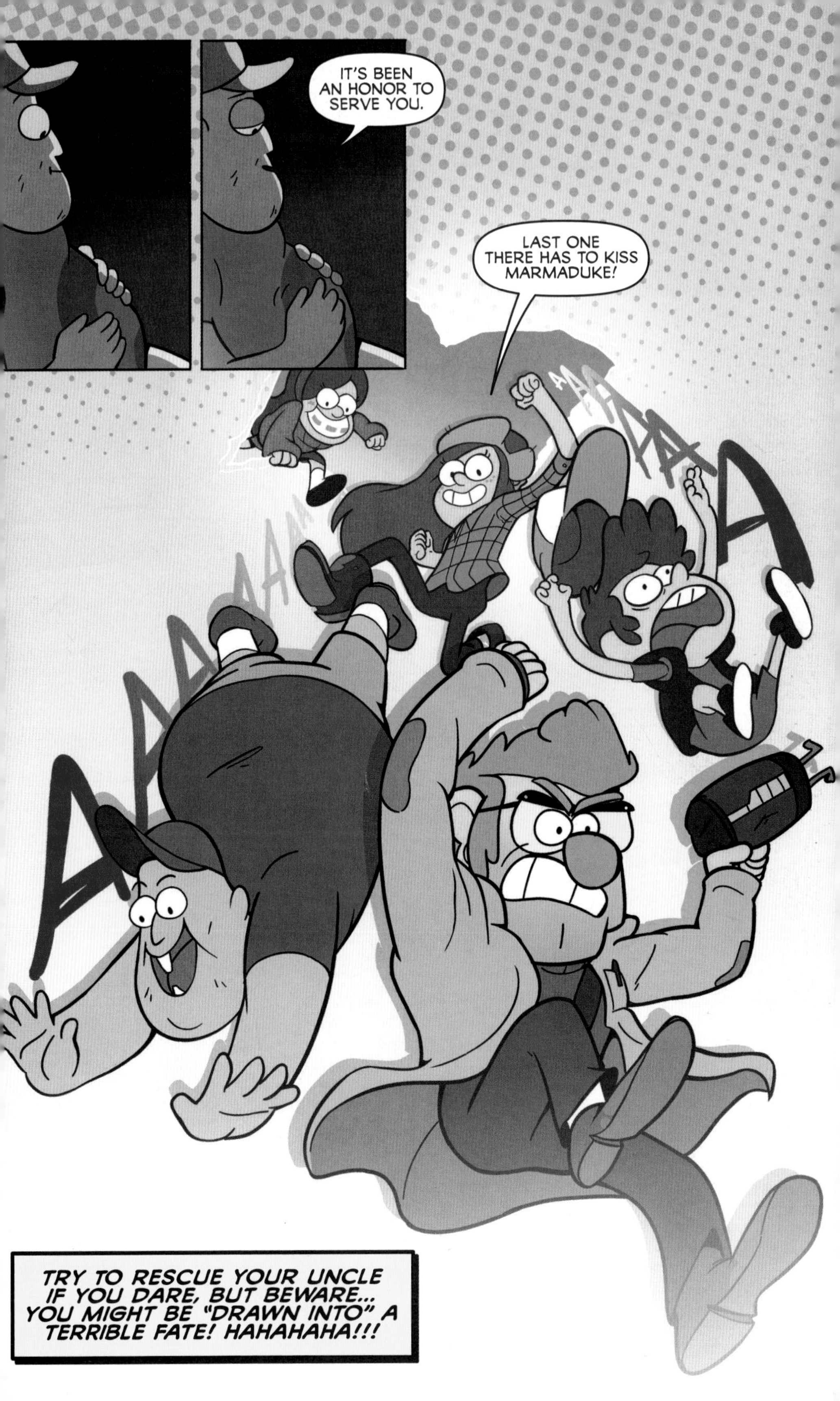
IT'S BEEN AN HONOR TO SERVE YOU.
LAST ONE THERE HAS TO KISS MARMADUKE!
AAAAAAAAAA
TRY TO RESCUE YOUR UNCLE IF YOU DARE, BUT BEWARE... YOU MIGHT BE "DRAWN INTO" A TERRIBLE FATE! HAHAHAHA!!!

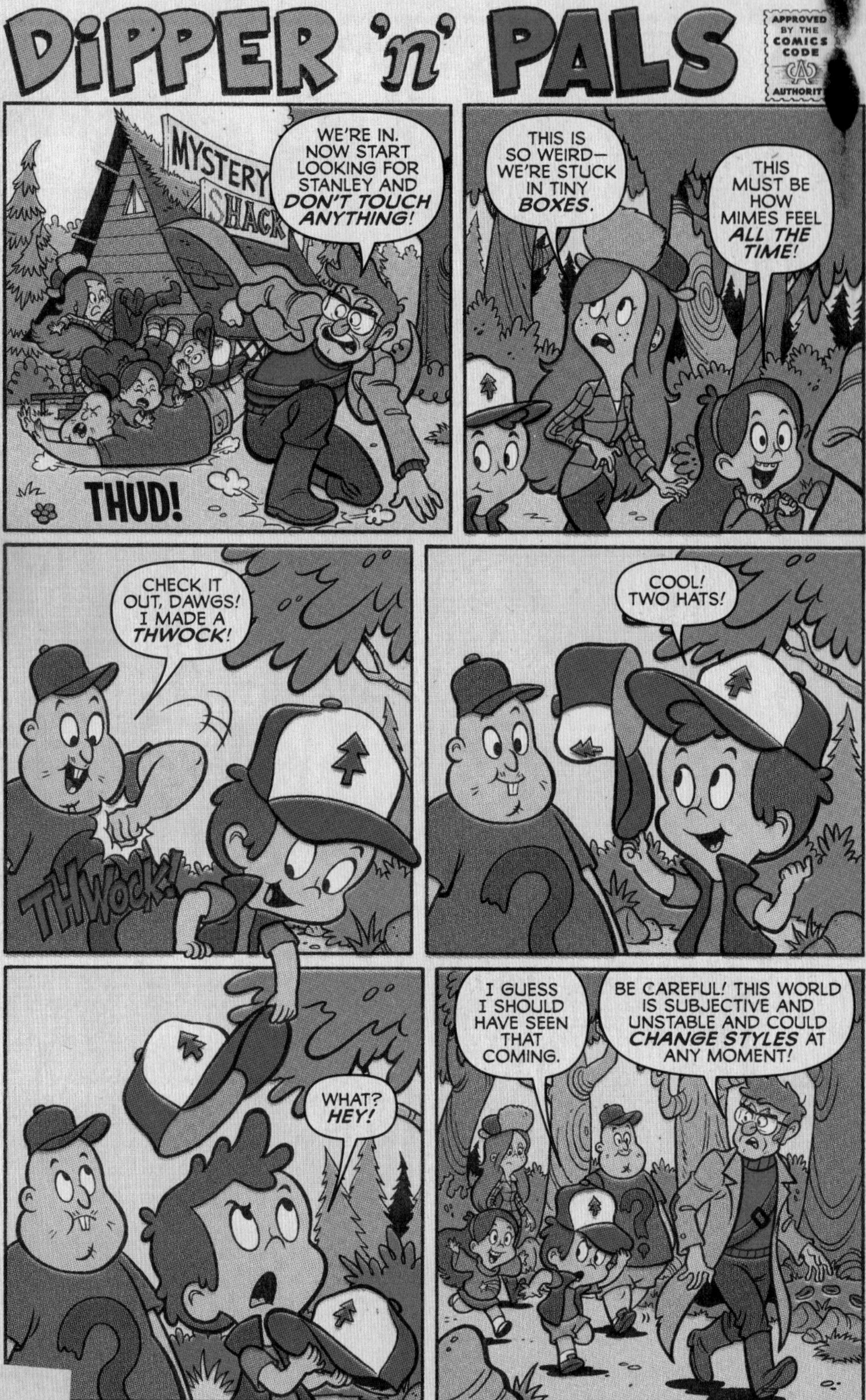
DiPPER 'n' PALS
APPROVED BY THE COMICS CODE AUTHORITY
WE'RE IN. NOW START LOOKING FOR STANLEY AND DON'T TOUCH ANYTHING!
MYSTERY SHACK
THUD!
THIS IS SO WEIRD— WE'RE STUCK IN TINY BOXES.
THIS MUST BE HOW MIMES FEEL ALL THE TIME!
CHECK IT OUT, DAWGS! I MADE A THWOCK!
THWOCK!
COOL! TWO HATS!
WHAT? HEY!
I GUESS I SHOULD HAVE SEEN THAT COMING.
BE CAREFUL! THIS WORLD IS SUBJECTIVE AND UNSTABLE AND COULD CHANGE STYLES AT ANY MOMENT!

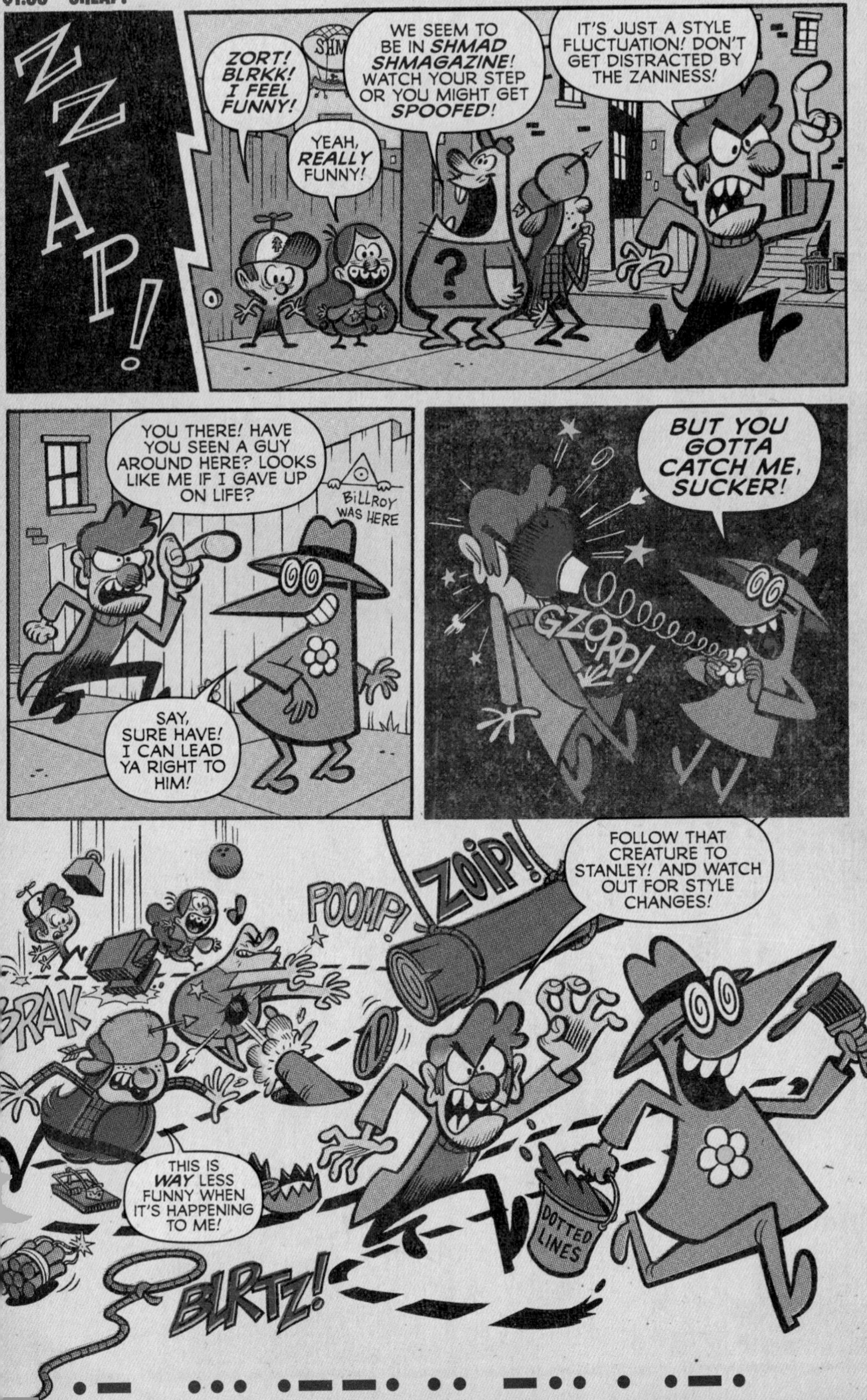
ZZAP!
ZORT! BLRKK! I FEEL FUNNY!
YEAH, REALLY FUNNY!
WE SEEM TO BE IN SHMAD SHMAGAZINE! WATCH YOUR STEP OR YOU MIGHT GET SPOOFED!
IT'S JUST A STYLE FLUCTUATION! DON'T GET DISTRACTED BY THE ZANINESS!
YOU THERE! HAVE YOU SEEN A GUY AROUND HERE? LOOKS LIKE ME IF I GAVE UP ON LIFE?
BILLROY WAS HERE
SAY, SURE HAVE! I CAN LEAD YA RIGHT TO HIM!
BUT YOU GOTTA CATCH ME, SUCKER!
GZORP!
FOLLOW THAT CREATURE TO STANLEY! AND WATCH OUT FOR STYLE CHANGES!
ZOIP!
POOMP!
BRAK
THIS IS WAY LESS FUNNY WHEN IT'S HAPPENING TO ME!
DOTTED LINES
BLRTZ!

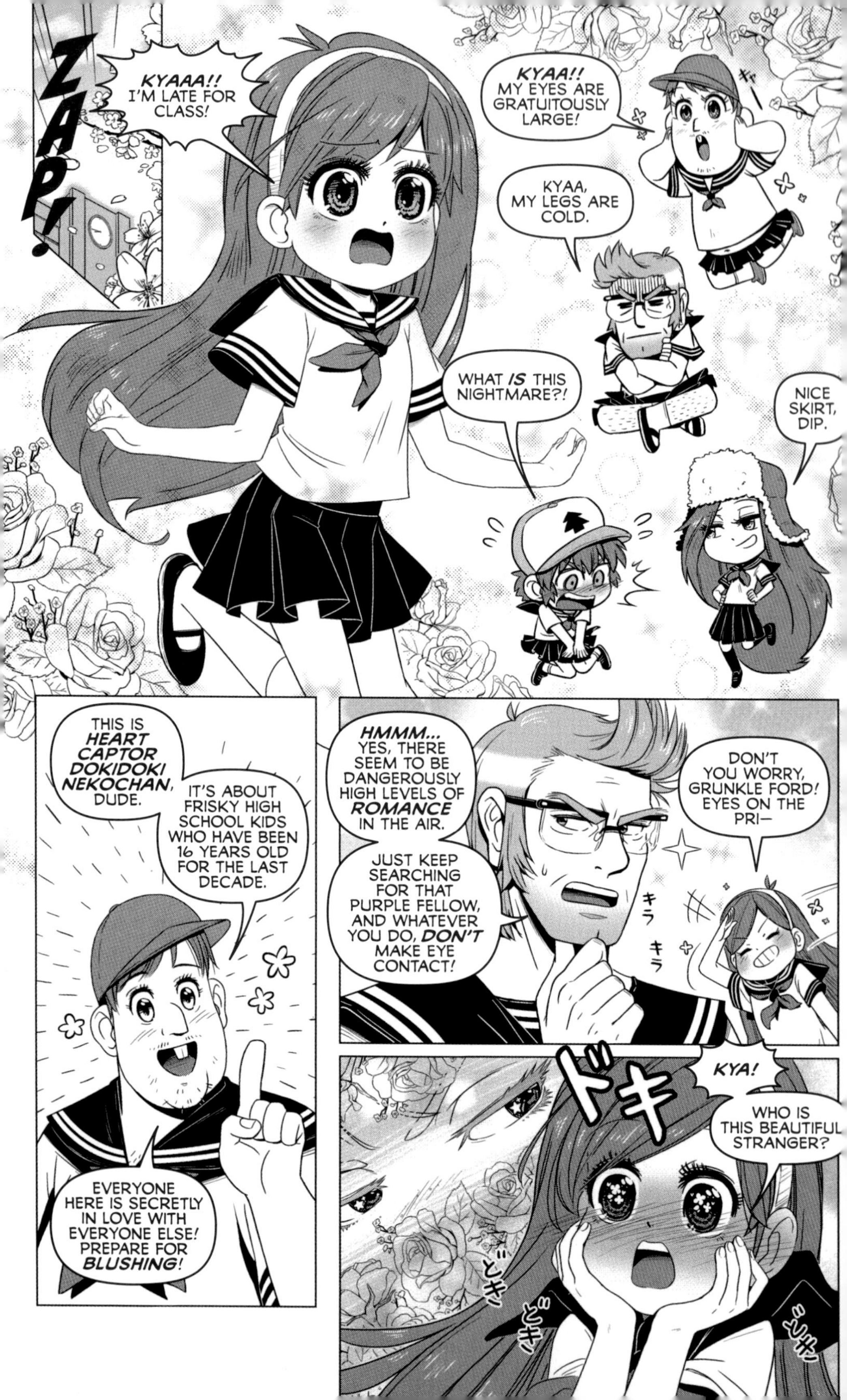

ZAP!
KYAAA!! I'M LATE FOR CLASS!
KYAA!! MY EYES ARE GRATUITOUSLY LARGE!
KYAA, MY LEGS ARE COLD.
WHAT IS THIS NIGHTMARE?!
NICE SKIRT, DIP.
THIS IS HEART CAPTOR DOKIDOKI NEKOCHAN, DUDE.
IT'S ABOUT FRISKY HIGH SCHOOL KIDS WHO HAVE BEEN 16 YEARS OLD FOR THE LAST DECADE.
EVERYONE HERE IS SECRETLY IN LOVE WITH EVERYONE ELSE! PREPARE FOR BLUSHING!
HMMM... YES, THERE SEEM TO BE DANGEROUSLY HIGH LEVELS OF ROMANCE IN THE AIR.
JUST KEEP SEARCHING FOR THAT PURPLE FELLOW, AND WHATEVER YOU DO, DON'T MAKE EYE CONTACT!
DON'T YOU WORRY, GRUNKLE FORD! EYES ON THE PRI—
キラ
キラ
ドキ
KYA!
WHO IS THIS BEAUTIFUL STRANGER?
どきどき
どきどき

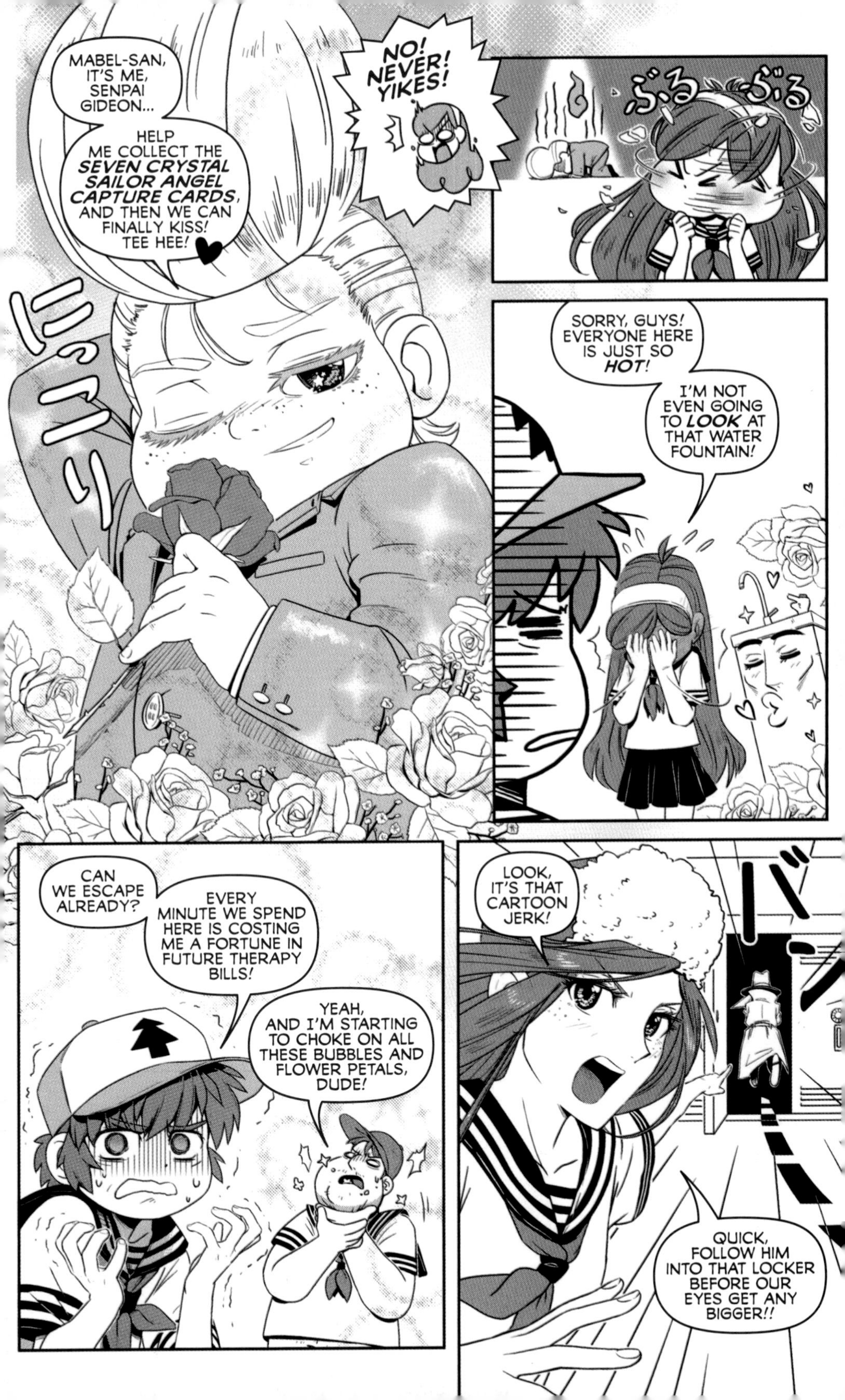
MABEL-SAN, IT'S ME, SENPAI GIDEON...
HELP ME COLLECT THE ***SEVEN CRYSTAL SAILOR ANGEL CAPTURE CARDS***, AND THEN WE CAN FINALLY KISS! TEE HEE!
ニッコリ
NO! NEVER! YIKES!
ぶるぶる
SORRY, GUYS! EVERYONE HERE IS JUST SO ***HOT***!
I'M NOT EVEN GOING TO ***LOOK*** AT THAT WATER FOUNTAIN!
CAN WE ESCAPE ALREADY?
EVERY MINUTE WE SPEND HERE IS COSTING ME A FORTUNE IN FUTURE THERAPY BILLS!
YEAH, AND I'M STARTING TO CHOKE ON ALL THESE BUBBLES AND FLOWER PETALS, DUDE!
LOOK, IT'S THAT CARTOON JERK!
QUICK, FOLLOW HIM INTO THAT LOCKER BEFORE OUR EYES GET ANY BIGGER!!

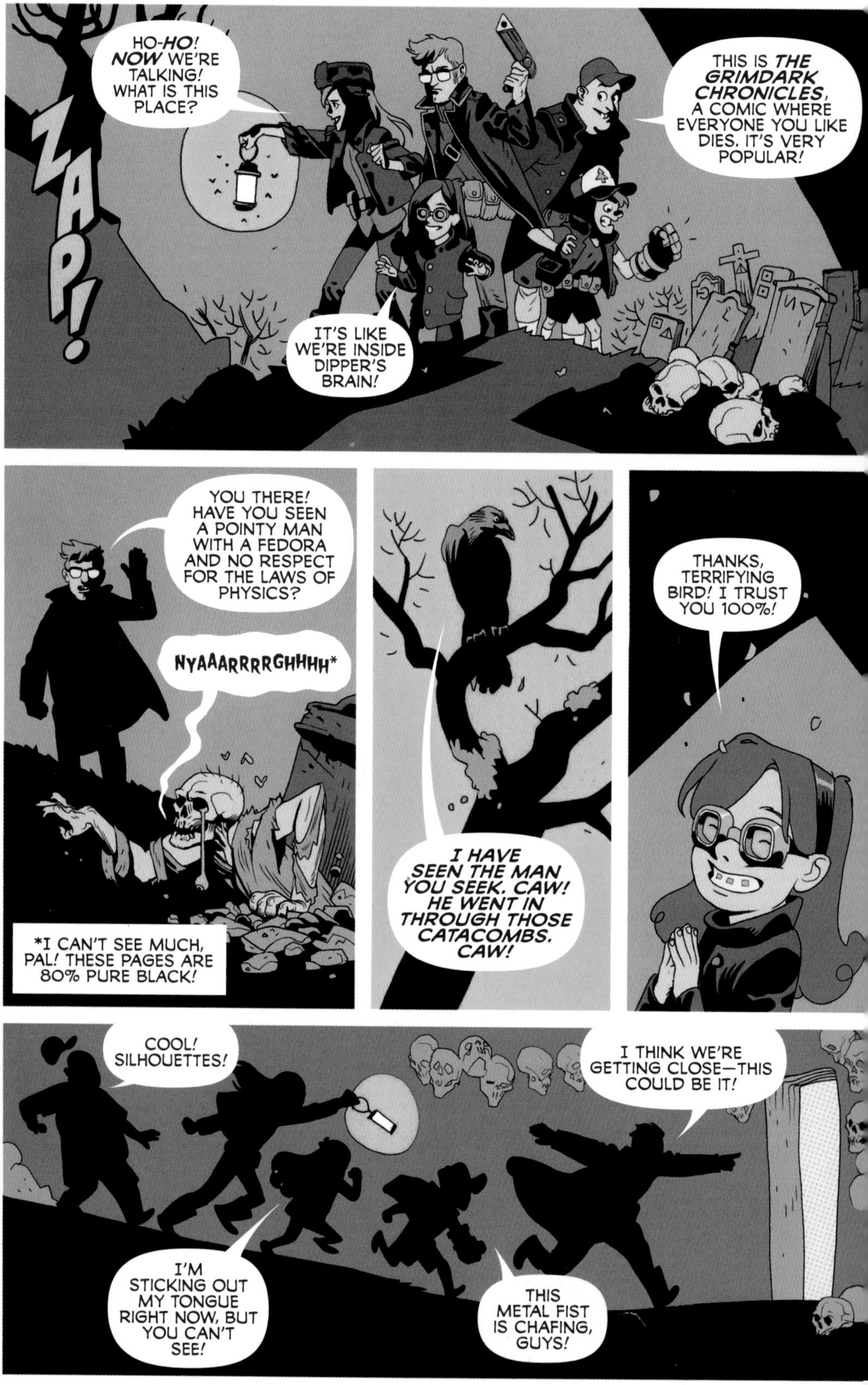
HO-*HO*! *NOW* WE'RE TALKING! WHAT IS THIS PLACE?
ZAP!
THIS IS *THE GRIMDARK CHRONICLES*, A COMIC WHERE EVERYONE YOU LIKE DIES. IT'S VERY POPULAR!
IT'S LIKE WE'RE INSIDE DIPPER'S BRAIN!
YOU THERE! HAVE YOU SEEN A POINTY MAN WITH A FEDORA AND NO RESPECT FOR THE LAWS OF PHYSICS?
NYAAARRRRGHHHH*
*I CAN'T SEE MUCH, PAL! THESE PAGES ARE 80% PURE BLACK!
I HAVE SEEN THE MAN YOU SEEK. CAW! HE WENT IN THROUGH THOSE CATACOMBS. CAW!
THANKS, TERRIFYING BIRD! I TRUST YOU 100%!
COOL! SILHOUETTES!
I THINK WE'RE GETTING CLOSE—THIS COULD BE IT!
I'M STICKING OUT MY TONGUE RIGHT NOW, BUT YOU CAN'T SEE!
THIS METAL FIST IS CHAFING, GUYS!

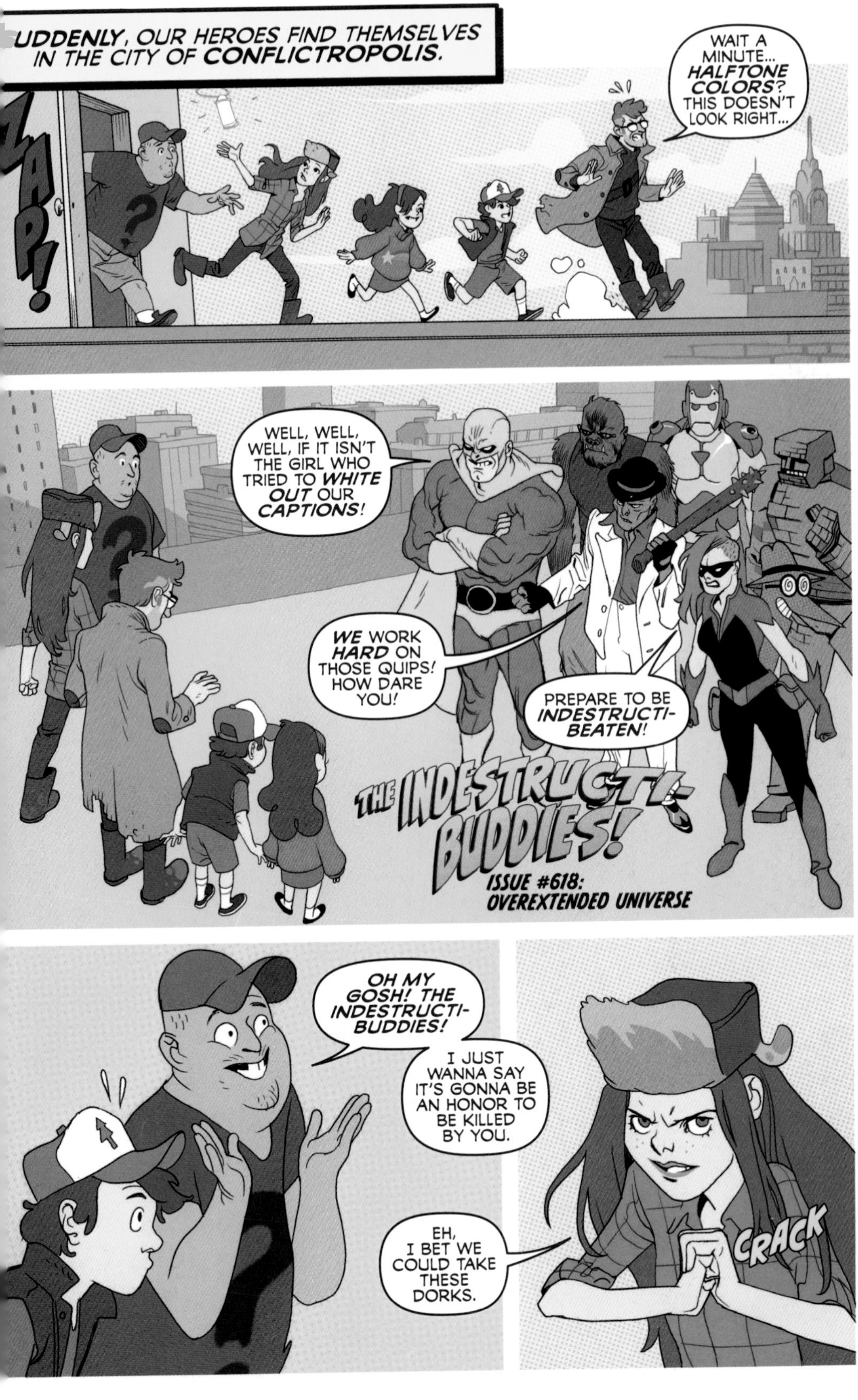

UDDENLY, OUR HEROES FIND THEMSELVES IN THE CITY OF CONFLICTROPOLIS.
ZAP!
WAIT A MINUTE... HALFTONE COLORS? THIS DOESN'T LOOK RIGHT...
WELL, WELL, WELL, IF IT ISN'T THE GIRL WHO TRIED TO WHITE OUT OUR CAPTIONS!
WE WORK HARD ON THOSE QUIPS! HOW DARE YOU!
PREPARE TO BE INDESTRUCTI-BEATEN!
THE INDESTRUCTI-BUDDIES!
ISSUE #618: OVEREXTENDED UNIVERSE
OH MY GOSH! THE INDESTRUCTI-BUDDIES!
I JUST WANNA SAY IT'S GONNA BE AN HONOR TO BE KILLED BY YOU.
EH, I BET WE COULD TAKE THESE DORKS.
CRACK

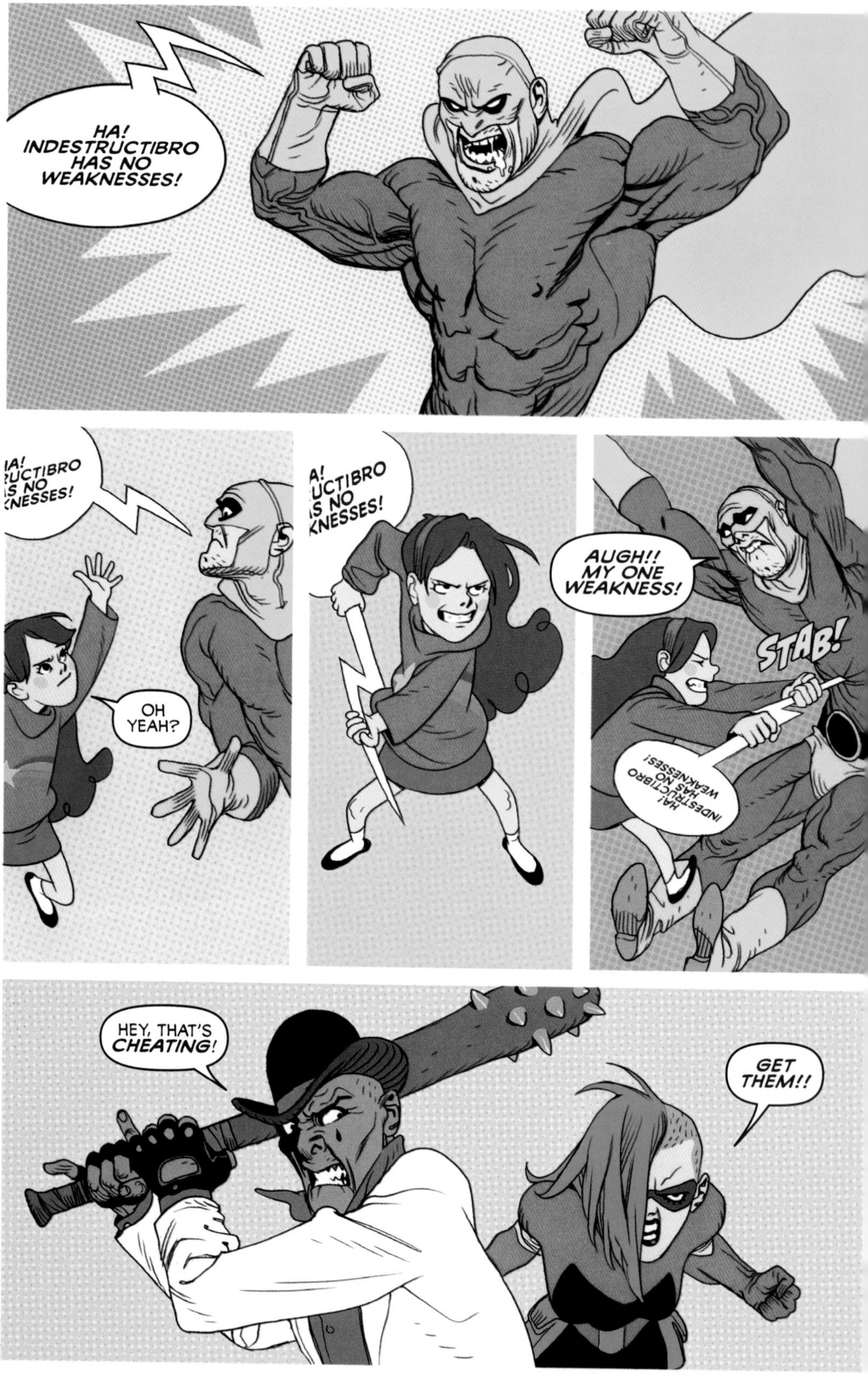
HA! INDESTRUCTIBRO HAS NO WEAKNESSES!
A! RUCTIBRO AS NO KNESSES!
OH YEAH?
A! UCTIBRO S NO KNESSES!
AUGH!! MY ONE WEAKNESS!
STAB!
HA! INDESTRUCTIBRO HAS NO WEAKNESSES!
HEY, THAT'S CHEATING!
GET THEM!!

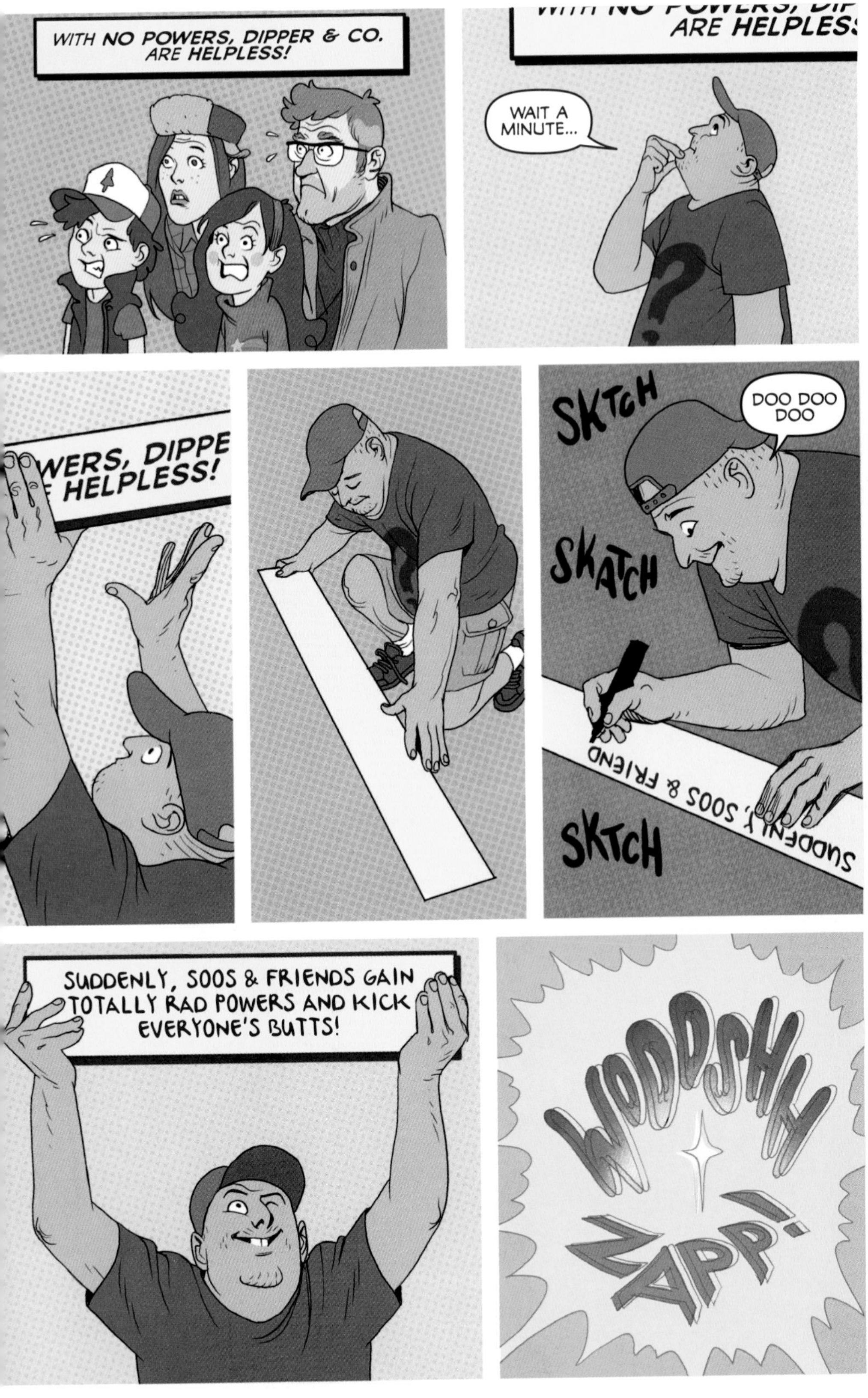
WITH NO POWERS, DIPPER & CO. ARE HELPLESS!
ARE HELPLESS
WAIT A MINUTE...
WERS, DIPPE
HELPLESS!
SKTCH
DOO DOO DOO
SKATCH
SUDDENLY, SOOS & FRIEND
SKTCH
SUDDENLY, SOOS & FRIENDS GAIN TOTALLY RAD POWERS AND KICK EVERYONE'S BUTTS!
WOOOSHH
ZAPP!

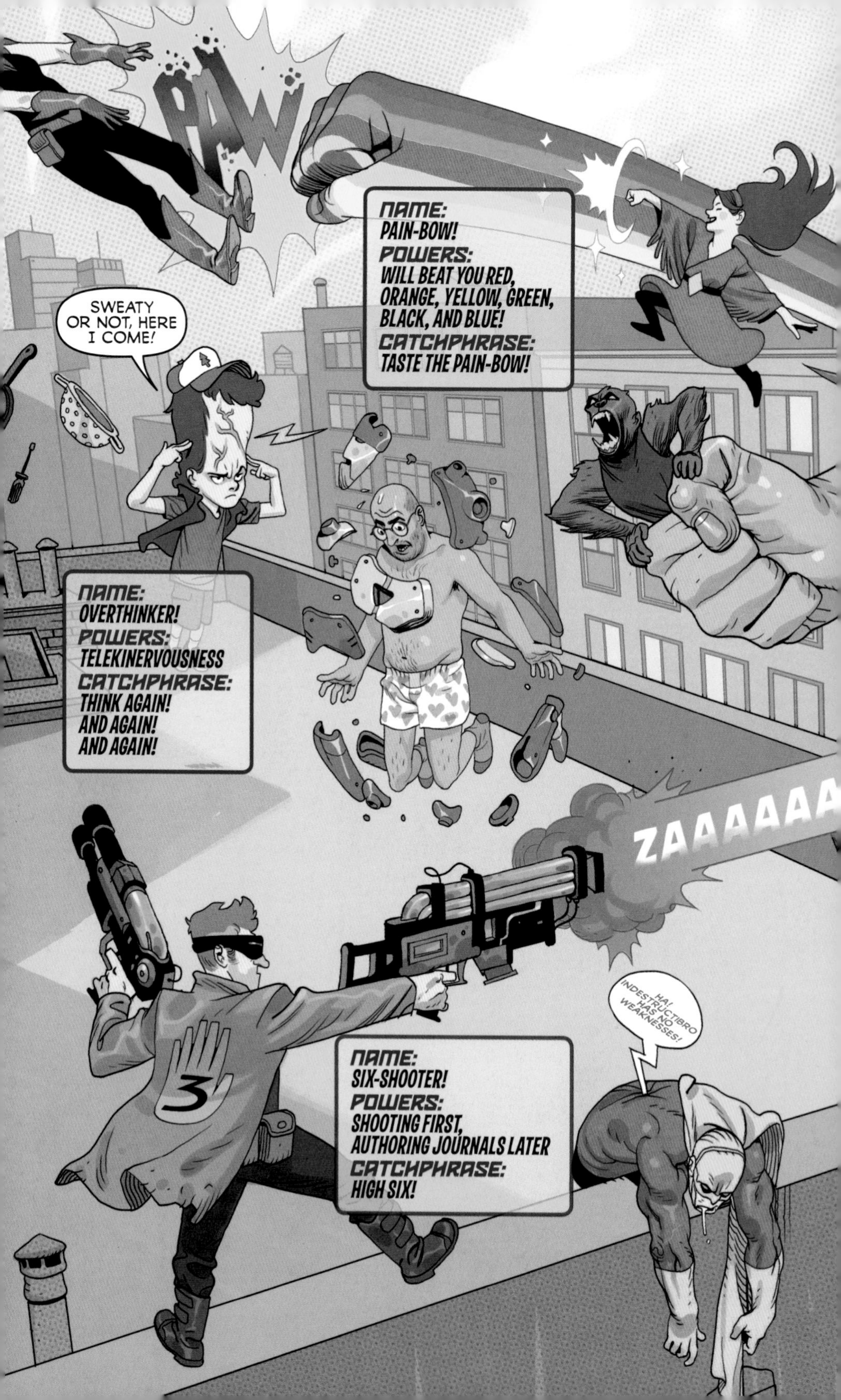
PAW
NAME:
PAIN-BOW!
POWERS:
WILL BEAT YOU RED, ORANGE, YELLOW, GREEN, BLACK, AND BLUE!
CATCHPHRASE:
TASTE THE PAIN-BOW!
SWEATY OR NOT, HERE I COME!
NAME:
OVERTHINKER!
POWERS:
TELEKINERVOUSNESS
CATCHPHRASE:
THINK AGAIN! AND AGAIN! AND AGAIN!
ZAAAAAA
HA! INDESTRUCTIBRO HAS NO WEAKNESSES!
NAME:
SIX-SHOOTER!
POWERS:
SHOOTING FIRST, AUTHORING JOURNALS LATER
CATCHPHRASE:
HIGH SIX!

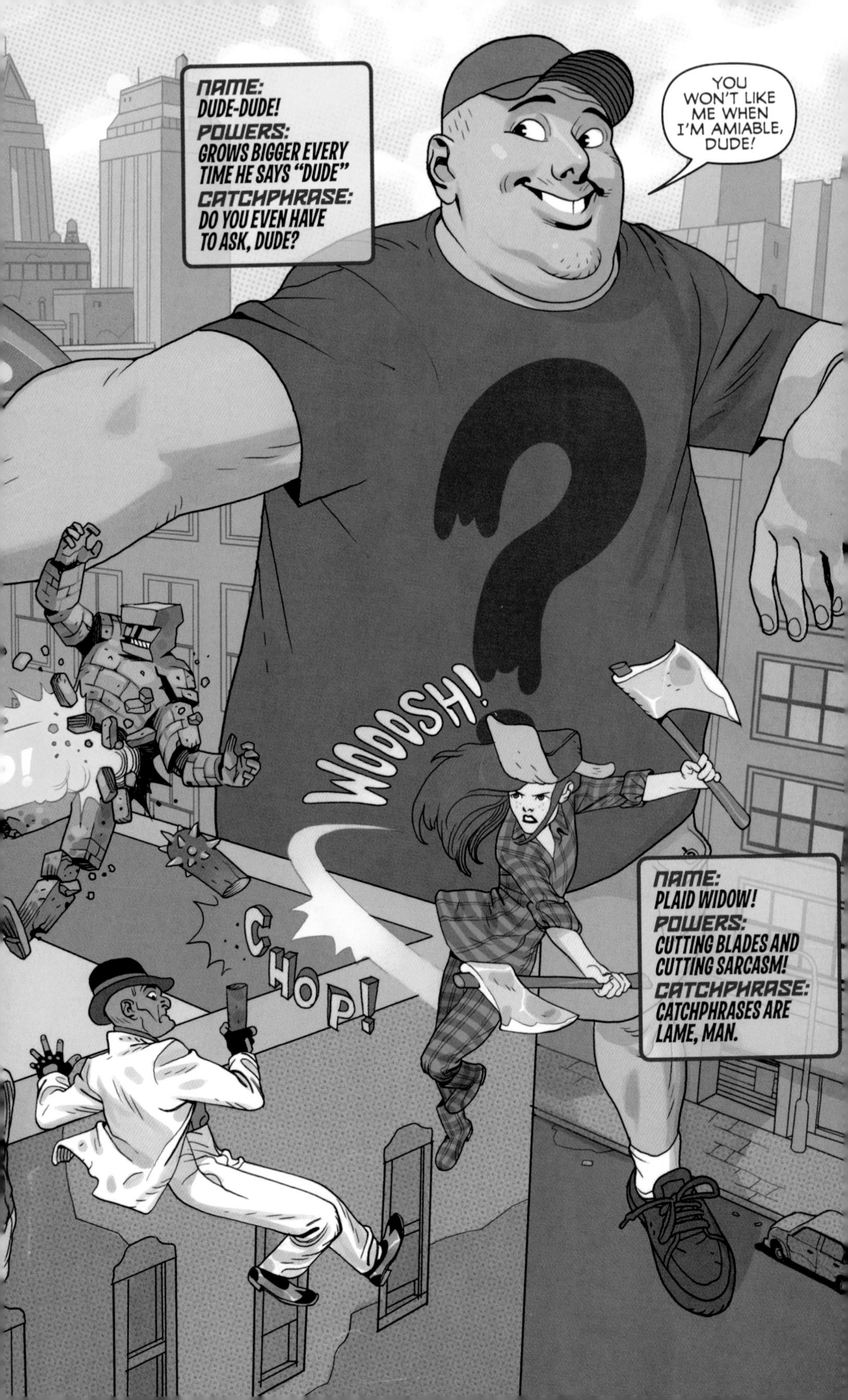
NAME:
DUDE-DUDE!
POWERS:
GROWS BIGGER EVERY TIME HE SAYS "DUDE"
CATCHPHRASE:
DO YOU EVEN HAVE TO ASK, DUDE?
YOU WON'T LIKE ME WHEN I'M AMIABLE, DUDE!
WOOOSH!
CHOP!
NAME:
PLAID WIDOW!
POWERS:
CUTTING BLADES AND CUTTING SARCASM!
CATCHPHRASE:
CATCHPHRASES ARE LAME, MAN.

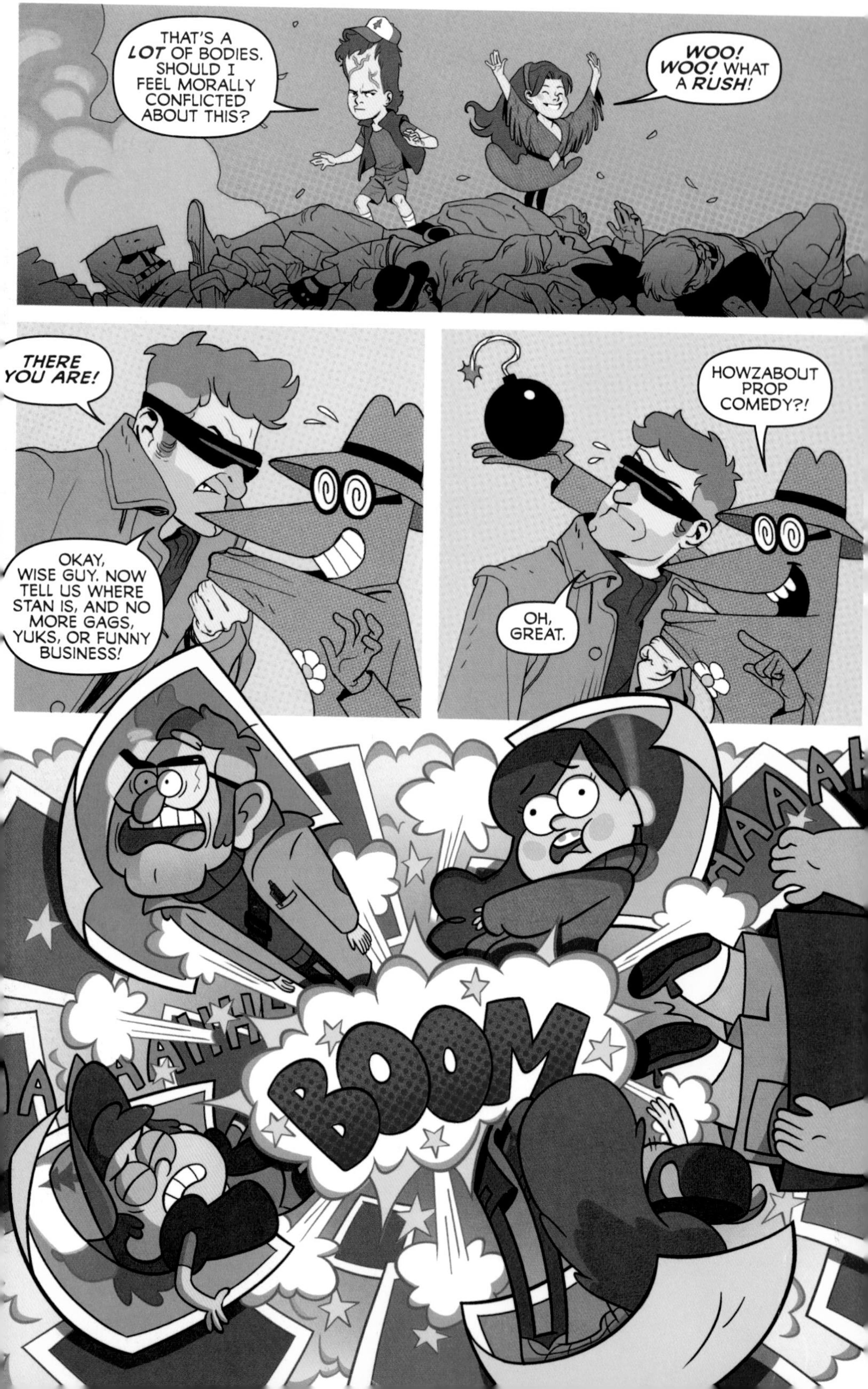
THAT'S A *LOT* OF BODIES. SHOULD I FEEL MORALLY CONFLICTED ABOUT THIS?
WOO! WOO! WHAT A *RUSH!*
THERE YOU ARE!
OKAY, WISE GUY. NOW TELL US WHERE STAN IS, AND NO MORE GAGS, YUKS, OR FUNNY BUSINESS!
HOWZABOUT PROP COMEDY?!
OH, GREAT.
BOOM

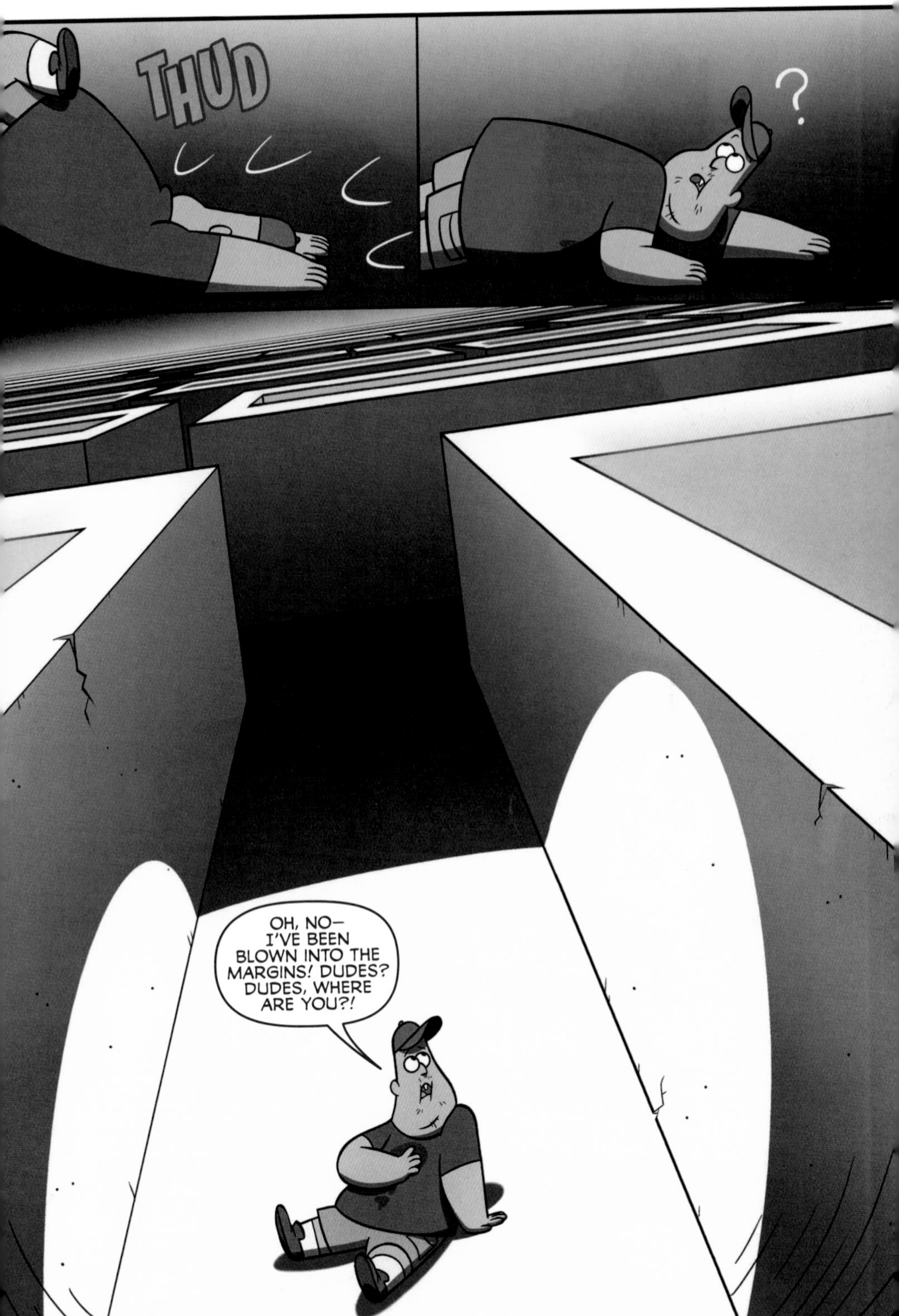
THUD
?
OH, NO— I'VE BEEN BLOWN INTO THE MARGINS! DUDES? DUDES, WHERE ARE YOU?!

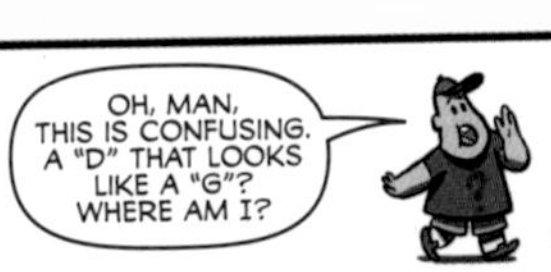
OH, MAN, THIS IS CONFUSING. A "D" THAT LOOKS LIKE A "G"? WHERE AM I?

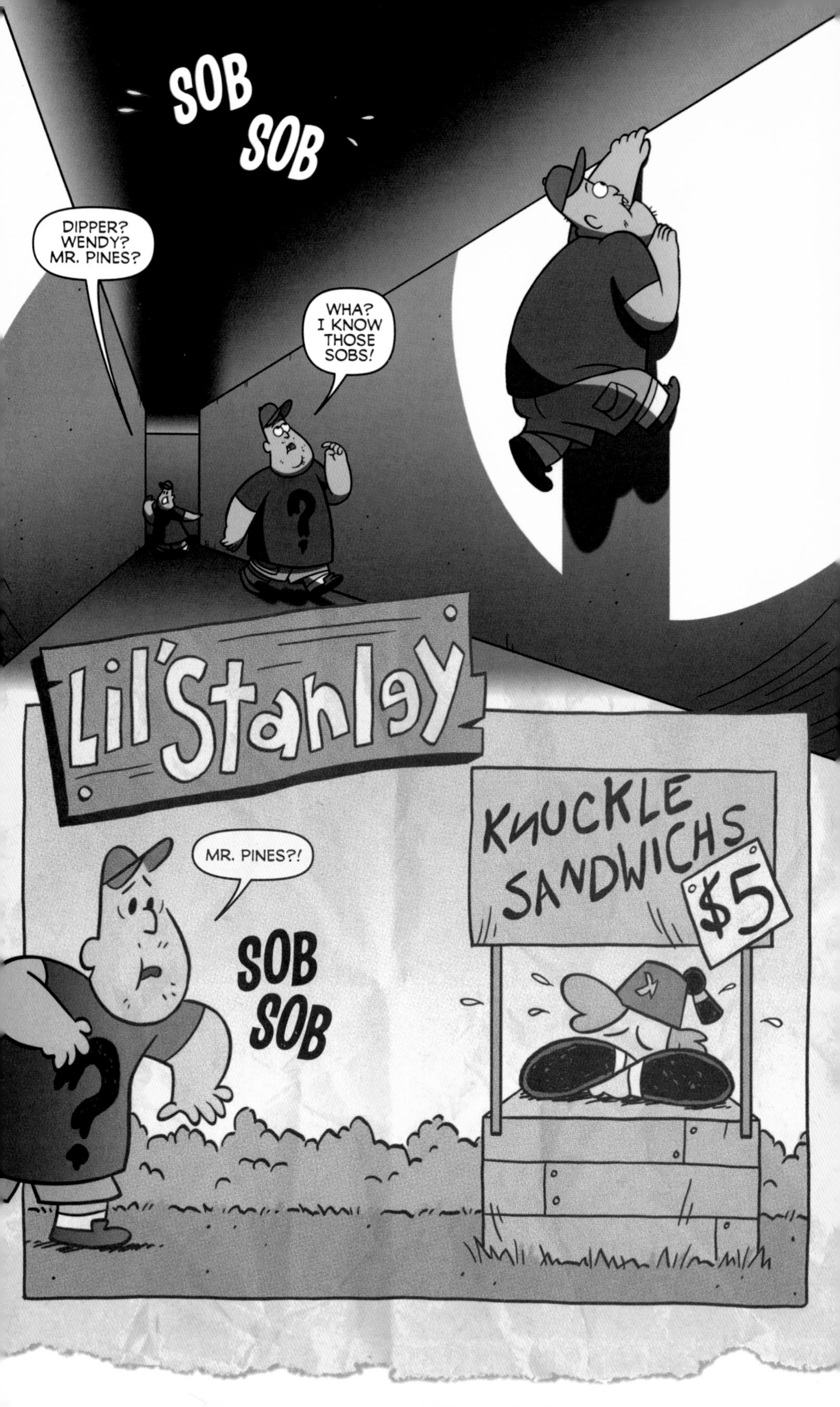
SOB
SOB
DIPPER? WENDY? MR. PINES?
WHA? I KNOW THOSE SOBS!
Lil' Stanley
KNUCKLE SANDWICHS
$5
MR. PINES?!
SOB
SOB

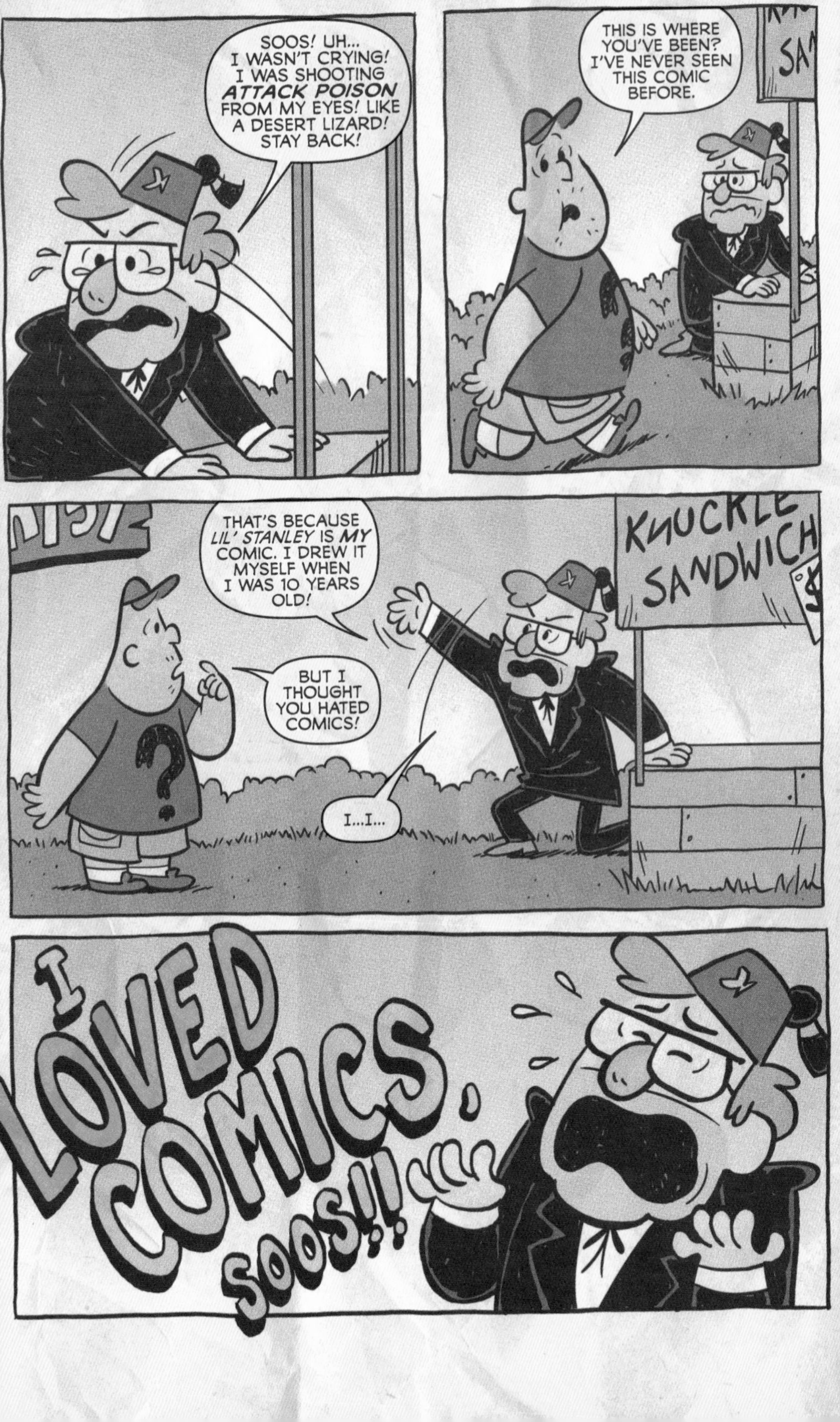

SOOS! UH... I WASN'T CRYING! I WAS SHOOTING ATTACK POISON FROM MY EYES! LIKE A DESERT LIZARD! STAY BACK!
THIS IS WHERE YOU'VE BEEN? I'VE NEVER SEEN THIS COMIC BEFORE.
THAT'S BECAUSE LIL' STANLEY IS MY COMIC. I DREW IT MYSELF WHEN I WAS 10 YEARS OLD!
KNUCKLE SANDWICH
BUT I THOUGHT YOU HATED COMICS!
I...I...
I LOVED COMICS, SOOS!!!

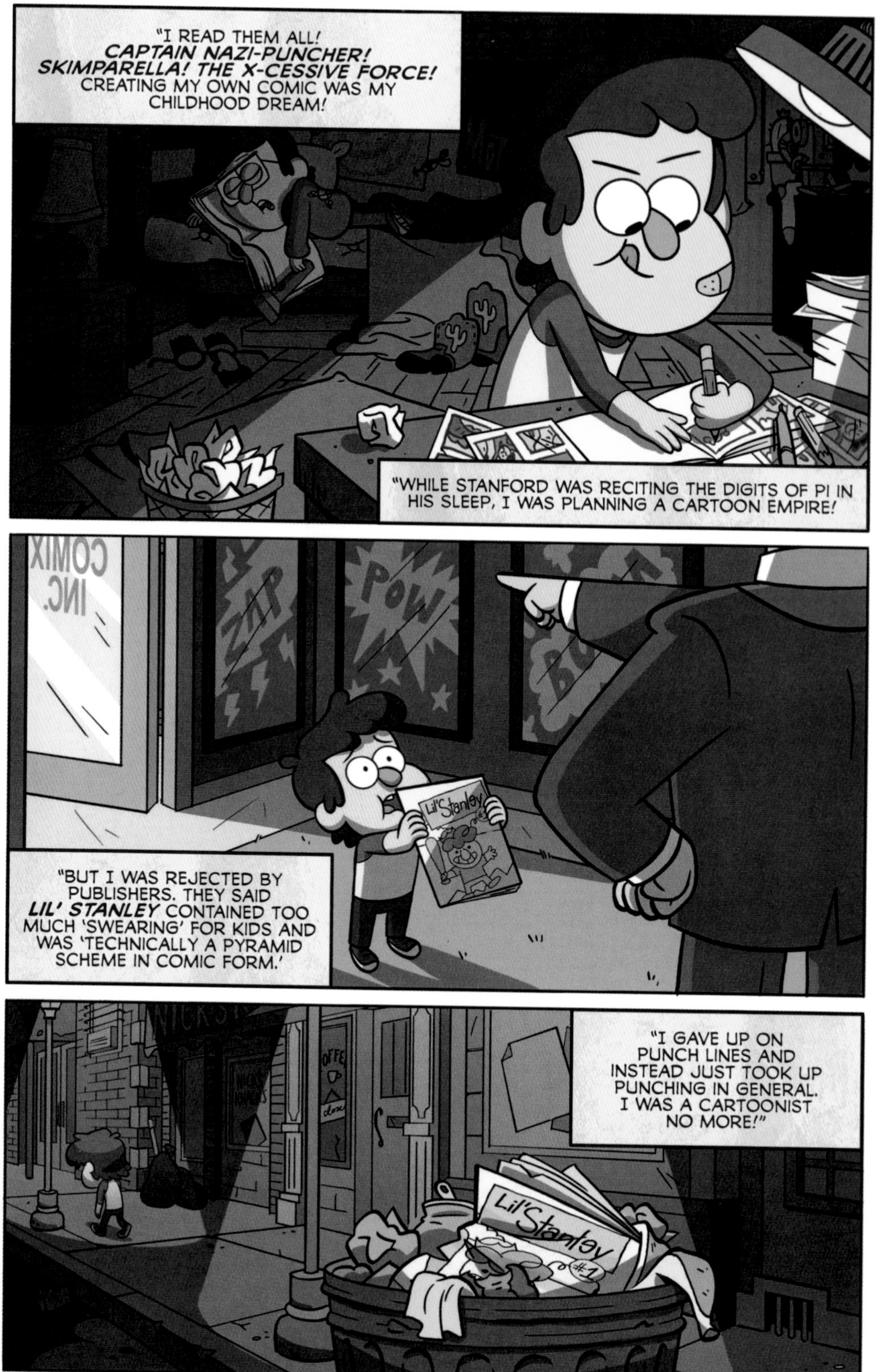

"I READ THEM ALL! *CAPTAIN NAZI-PUNCHER! SKIMPARELLA! THE X-CESSIVE FORCE!* CREATING MY OWN COMIC WAS MY CHILDHOOD DREAM!
"WHILE STANFORD WAS RECITING THE DIGITS OF PI IN HIS SLEEP, I WAS PLANNING A CARTOON EMPIRE!
ZAP
POW
Lil'Stanley
"BUT I WAS REJECTED BY PUBLISHERS. THEY SAID *LIL' STANLEY* CONTAINED TOO MUCH 'SWEARING' FOR KIDS AND WAS 'TECHNICALLY A PYRAMID SCHEME IN COMIC FORM.'
"I GAVE UP ON PUNCH LINES AND INSTEAD JUST TOOK UP PUNCHING IN GENERAL. I WAS A CARTOONIST NO MORE!"
Lil'Stanley
#1

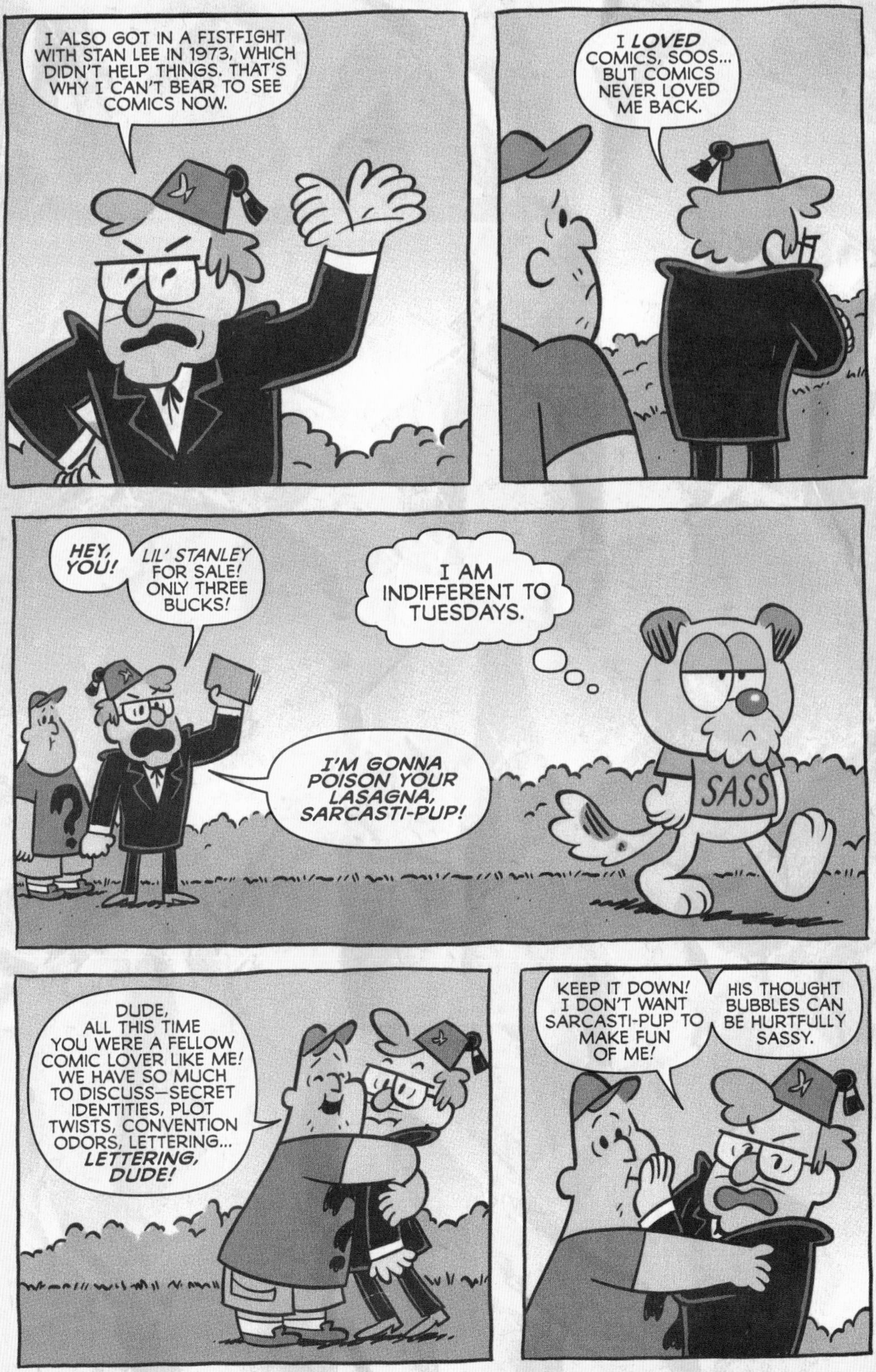
I ALSO GOT IN A FISTFIGHT WITH STAN LEE IN 1973, WHICH DIDN'T HELP THINGS. THAT'S WHY I CAN'T BEAR TO SEE COMICS NOW.
I LOVED COMICS, SOOS... BUT COMICS NEVER LOVED ME BACK.
HEY, YOU!
LIL' STANLEY FOR SALE! ONLY THREE BUCKS!
I AM INDIFFERENT TO TUESDAYS.
I'M GONNA POISON YOUR LASAGNA, SARCASTI-PUP!
SASS
DUDE, ALL THIS TIME YOU WERE A FELLOW COMIC LOVER LIKE ME! WE HAVE SO MUCH TO DISCUSS—SECRET IDENTITIES, PLOT TWISTS, CONVENTION ODORS, LETTERING... LETTERING, DUDE!
KEEP IT DOWN! I DON'T WANT SARCASTI-PUP TO MAKE FUN OF ME!
HIS THOUGHT BUBBLES CAN BE HURTFULLY SASSY.

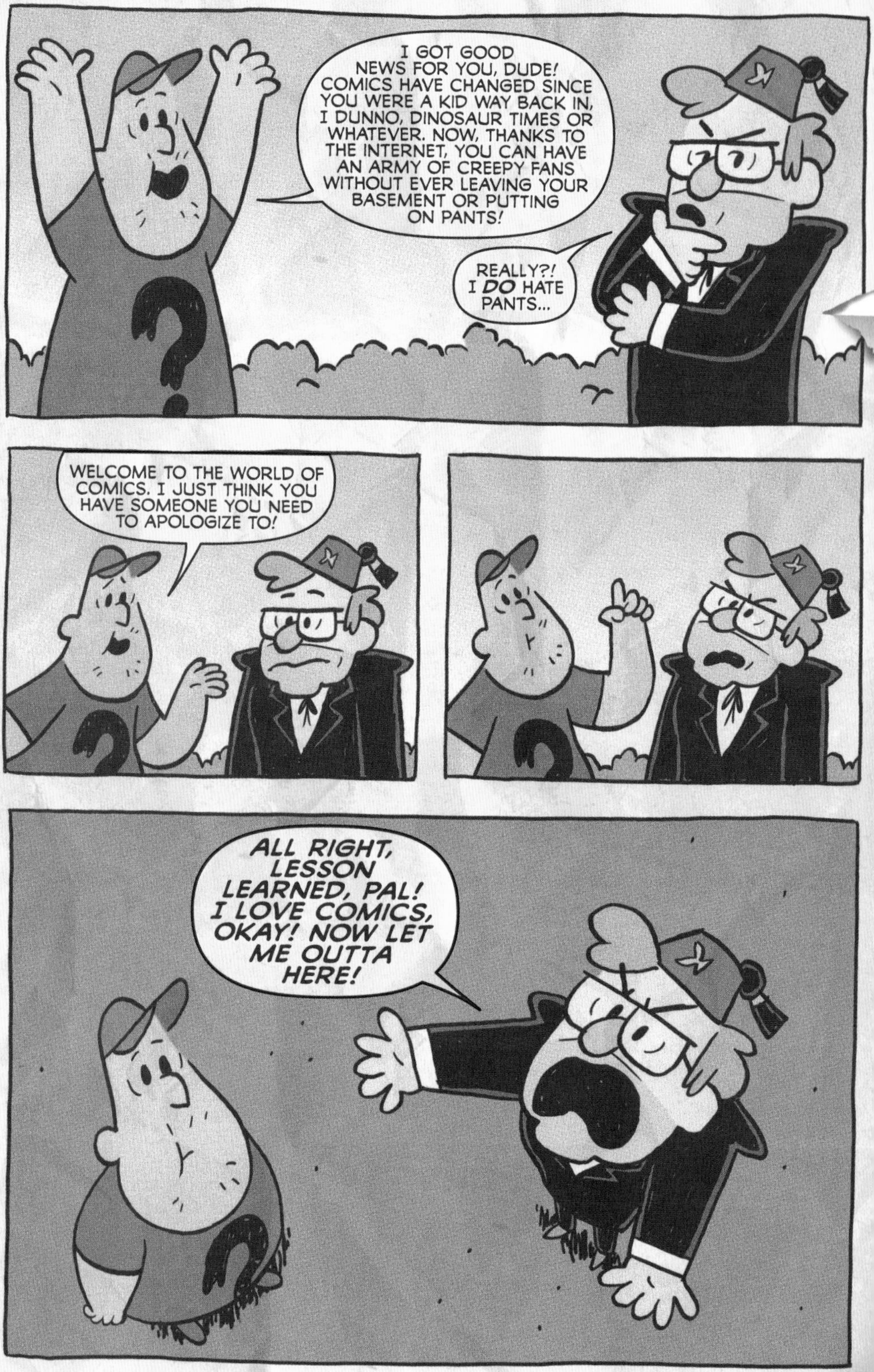
I GOT GOOD NEWS FOR YOU, DUDE! COMICS HAVE CHANGED SINCE YOU WERE A KID WAY BACK IN, I DUNNO, DINOSAUR TIMES OR WHATEVER. NOW, THANKS TO THE INTERNET, YOU CAN HAVE AN ARMY OF CREEPY FANS WITHOUT EVER LEAVING YOUR BASEMENT OR PUTTING ON PANTS!
REALLY?! I *DO* HATE PANTS...
WELCOME TO THE WORLD OF COMICS. I JUST THINK YOU HAVE SOMEONE YOU NEED TO APOLOGIZE TO!
ALL RIGHT, LESSON LEARNED, PAL! I LOVE COMICS, OKAY! NOW LET ME OUTTA HERE!

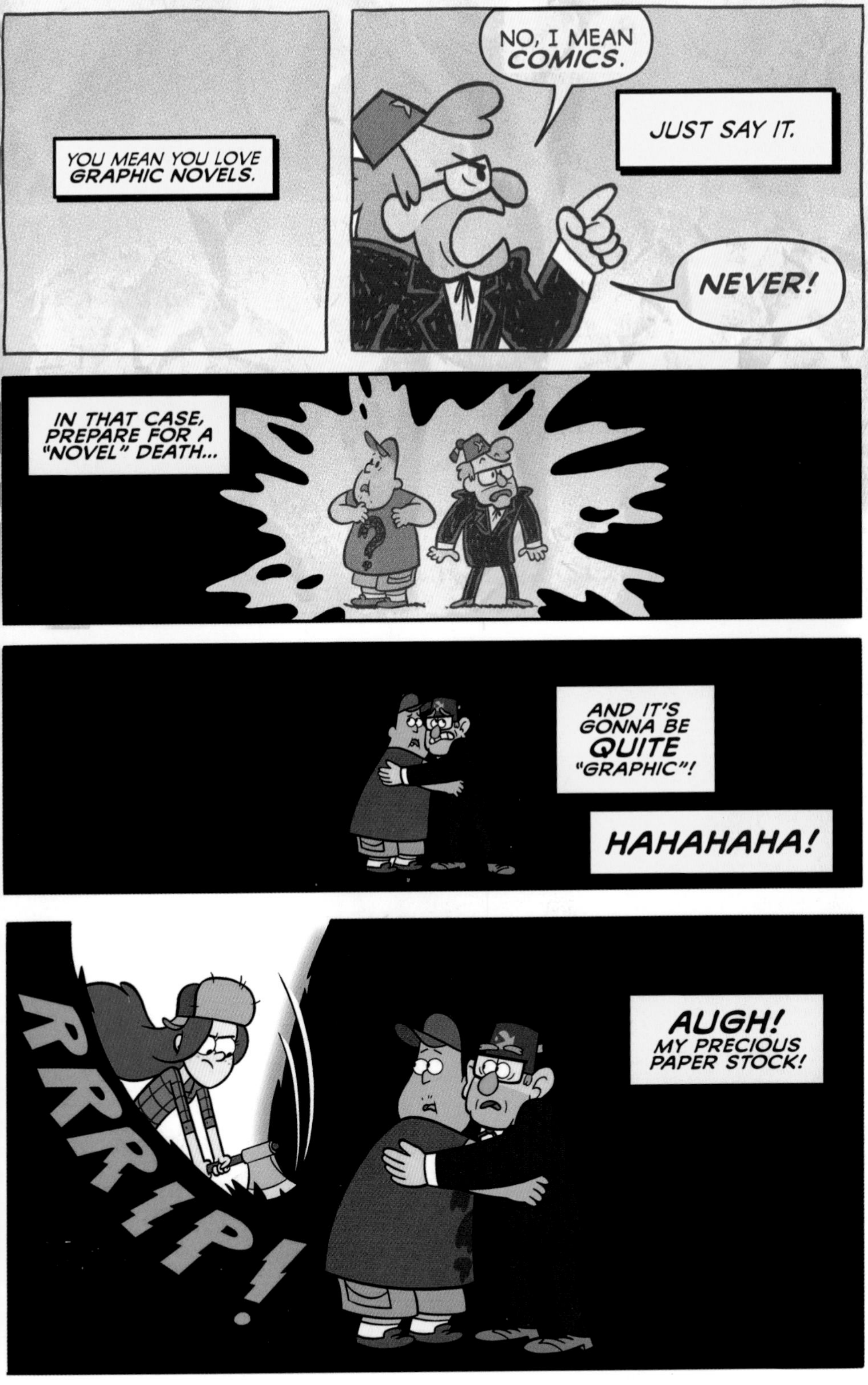

YOU MEAN YOU LOVE GRAPHIC NOVELS.
NO, I MEAN COMICS.
JUST SAY IT.
NEVER!
IN THAT CASE, PREPARE FOR A "NOVEL" DEATH...
AND IT'S GONNA BE QUITE "GRAPHIC"!
HAHAHAHA!
RRRIP!
AUGH! MY PRECIOUS PAPER STOCK!

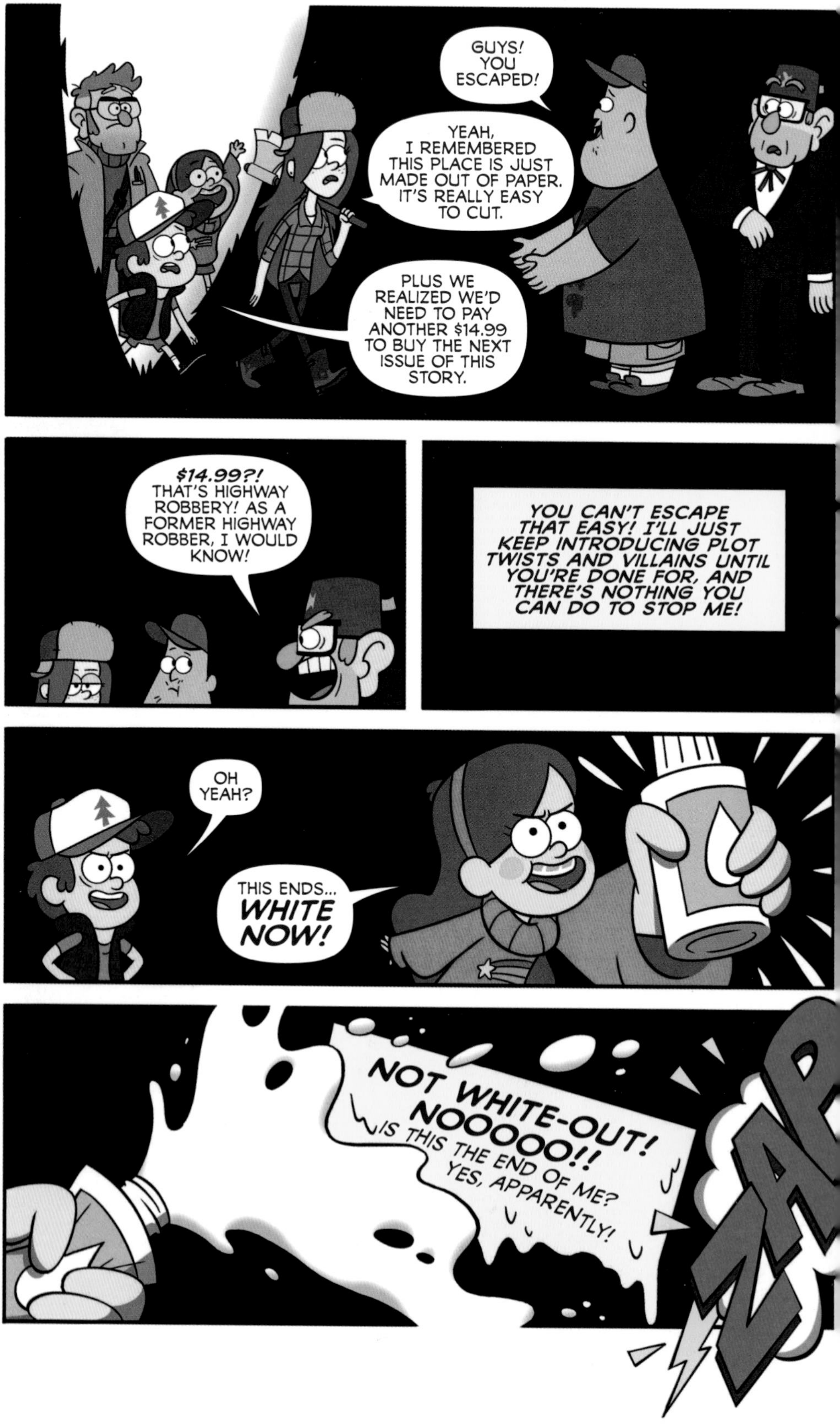

GUYS! YOU ESCAPED!
YEAH, I REMEMBERED THIS PLACE IS JUST MADE OUT OF PAPER. IT'S REALLY EASY TO CUT.
PLUS WE REALIZED WE'D NEED TO PAY ANOTHER $14.99 TO BUY THE NEXT ISSUE OF THIS STORY.
$14.99?! THAT'S HIGHWAY ROBBERY! AS A FORMER HIGHWAY ROBBER, I WOULD KNOW!
YOU CAN'T ESCAPE THAT EASY! I'LL JUST KEEP INTRODUCING PLOT TWISTS AND VILLAINS UNTIL YOU'RE DONE FOR, AND THERE'S NOTHING YOU CAN DO TO STOP ME!
OH YEAH?
THIS ENDS... WHITE NOW!
NOT WHITE-OUT! NOOOOO!! IS THIS THE END OF ME? YES, APPARENTLY!
ZAP

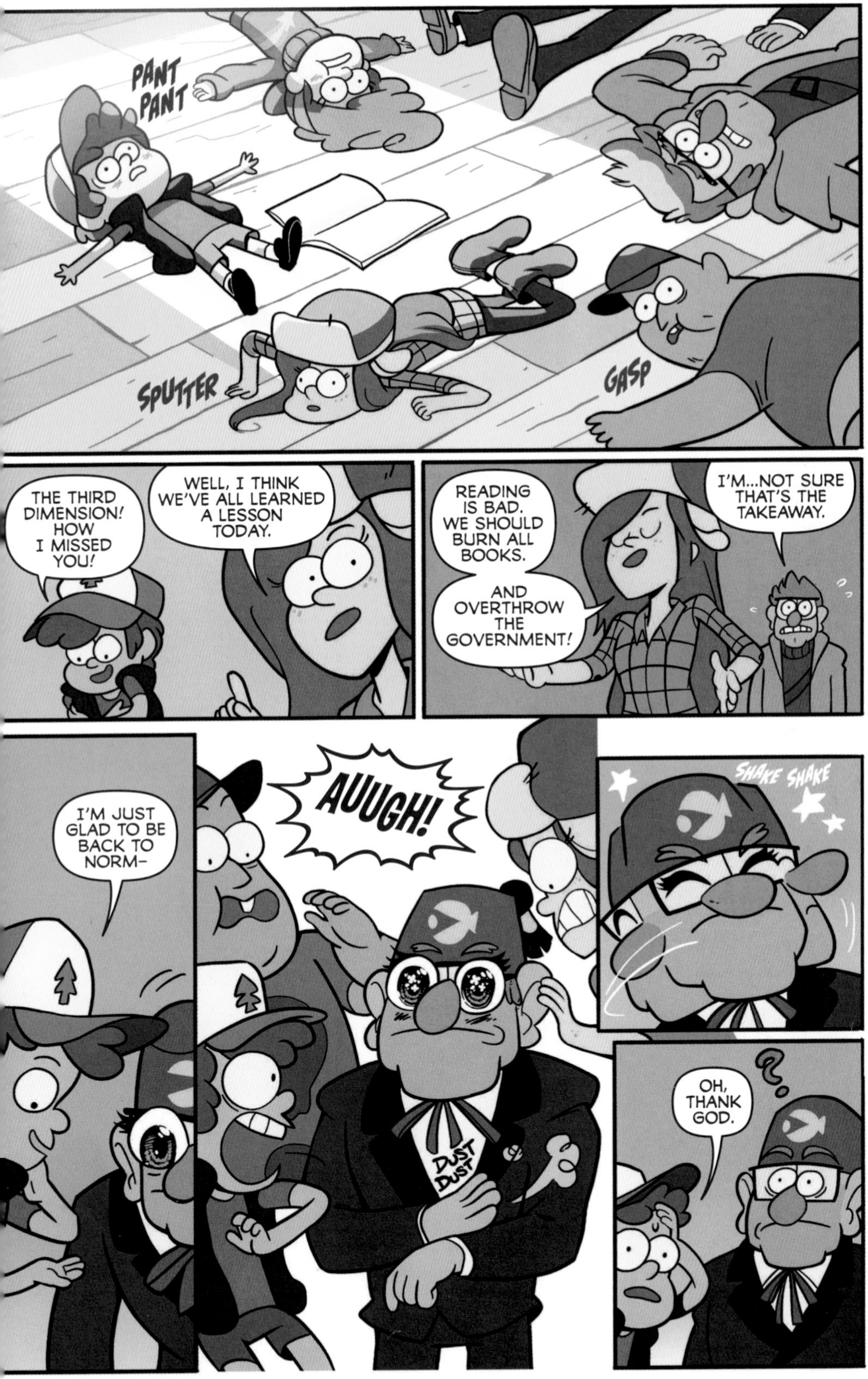
PANT PANT
SPUTTER
GASP
THE THIRD DIMENSION! HOW I MISSED YOU!
WELL, I THINK WE'VE ALL LEARNED A LESSON TODAY.
READING IS BAD. WE SHOULD BURN ALL BOOKS.
AND OVERTHROW THE GOVERNMENT!
I'M...NOT SURE THAT'S THE TAKEAWAY.
I'M JUST GLAD TO BE BACK TO NORM-
AUUGH!
DUST DUST
SHAKE SHAKE
?
OH, THANK GOD.

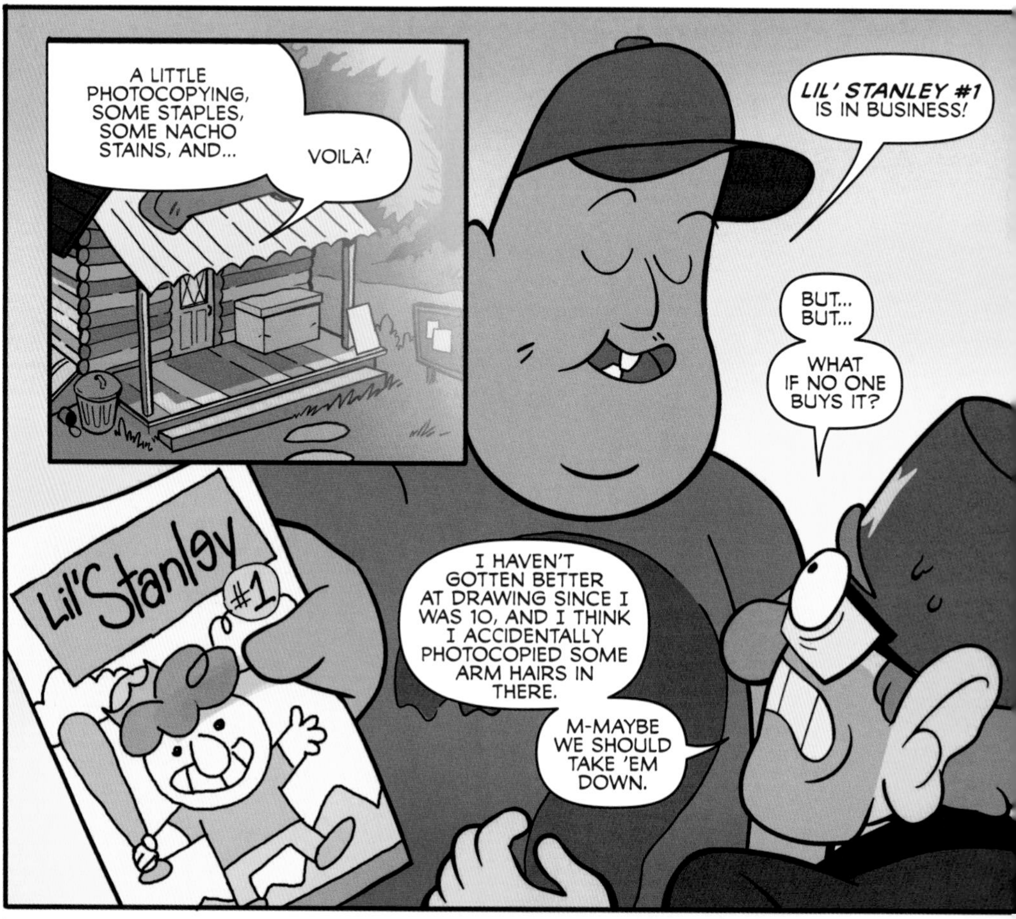
A LITTLE PHOTOCOPYING, SOME STAPLES, SOME NACHO STAINS, AND...
VOILÀ!
LIL' STANLEY #1 IS IN BUSINESS!
BUT... BUT...
WHAT IF NO ONE BUYS IT?
Lil'Stanley #1
I HAVEN'T GOTTEN BETTER AT DRAWING SINCE I WAS 10, AND I THINK I ACCIDENTALLY PHOTOCOPIED SOME ARM HAIRS IN THERE.
M-MAYBE WE SHOULD TAKE 'EM DOWN.

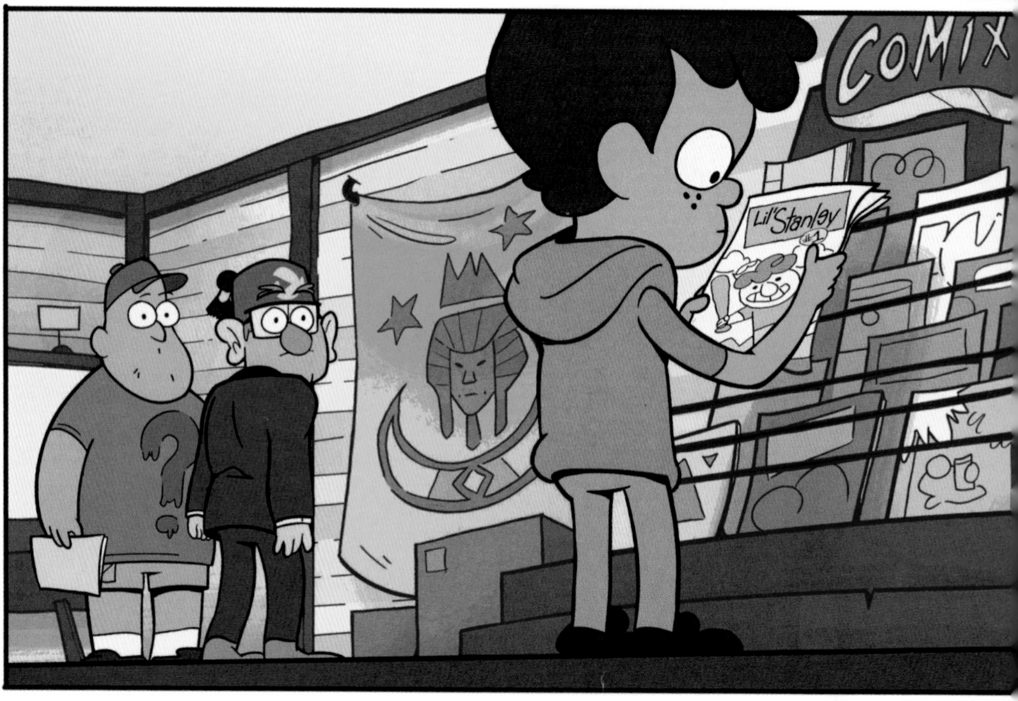
COMIX
Lil'Stanley #1

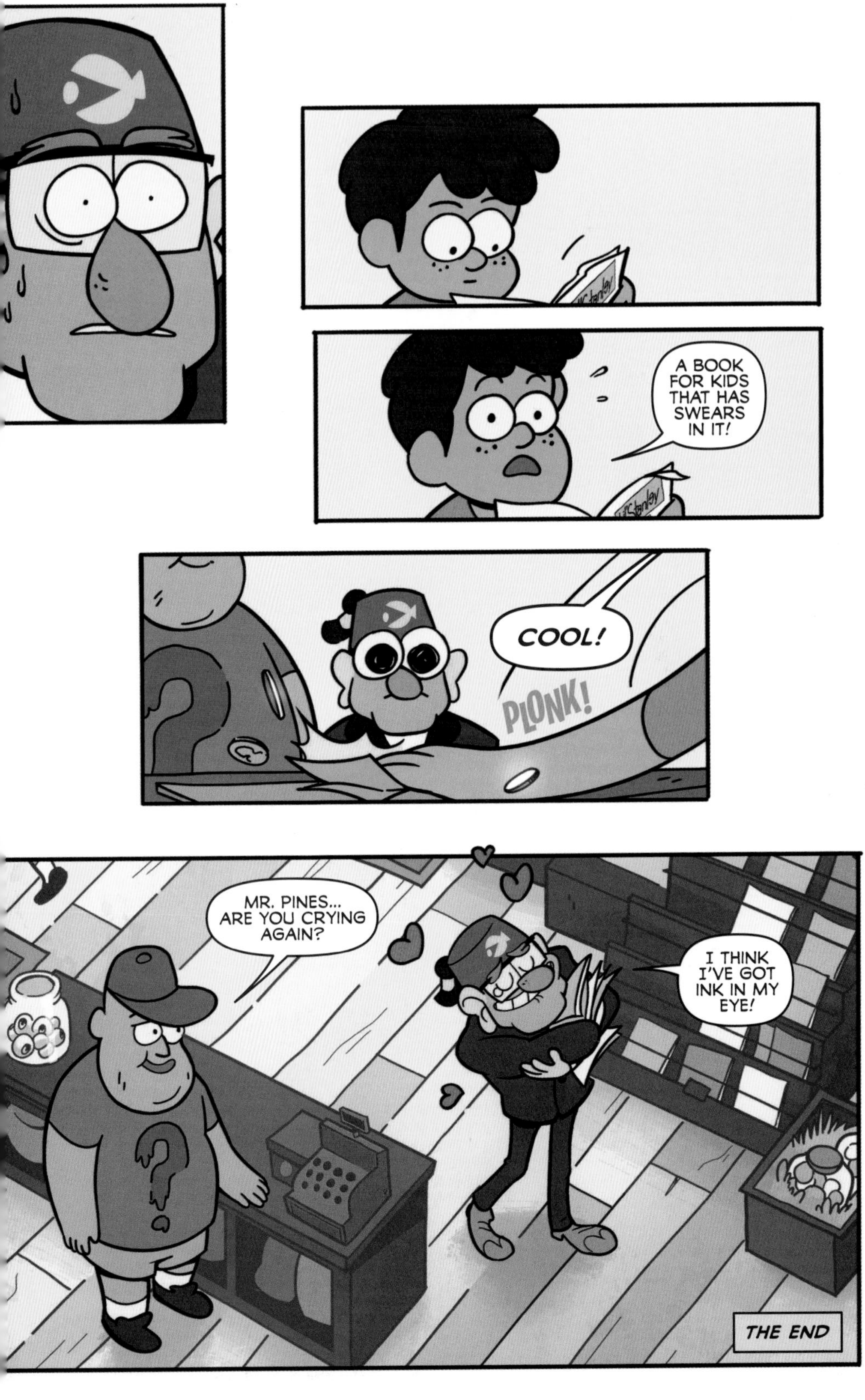
Lil'Stanley
A BOOK FOR KIDS THAT HAS SWEARS IN IT!
COOL!
PLONK!
MR. PINES... ARE YOU CRYING AGAIN?
I THINK I'VE GOT INK IN MY EYE!
THE END

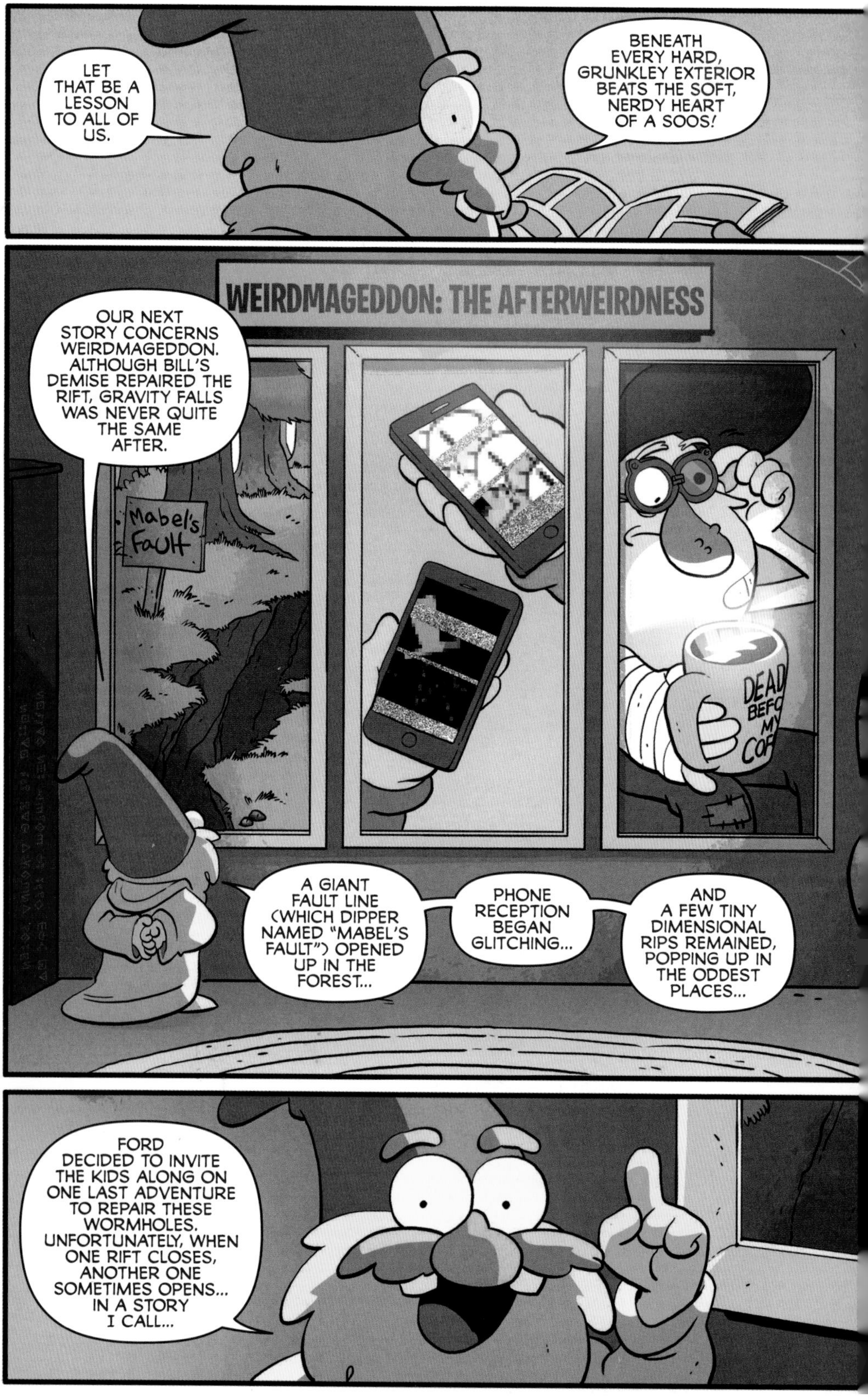
LET THAT BE A LESSON TO ALL OF US.
BENEATH EVERY HARD, GRUNKLEY EXTERIOR BEATS THE SOFT, NERDY HEART OF A SOOS!
WEIRDMAGEDDON: THE AFTERWEIRDNESS
OUR NEXT STORY CONCERNS WEIRDMAGEDDON. ALTHOUGH BILL'S DEMISE REPAIRED THE RIFT, GRAVITY FALLS WAS NEVER QUITE THE SAME AFTER.
Mabel's Fault
A GIANT FAULT LINE (WHICH DIPPER NAMED "MABEL'S FAULT") OPENED UP IN THE FOREST...
PHONE RECEPTION BEGAN GLITCHING...
AND A FEW TINY DIMENSIONAL RIPS REMAINED, POPPING UP IN THE ODDEST PLACES...
FORD DECIDED TO INVITE THE KIDS ALONG ON ONE LAST ADVENTURE TO REPAIR THESE WORMHOLES. UNFORTUNATELY, WHEN ONE RIFT CLOSES, ANOTHER ONE SOMETIMES OPENS... IN A STORY I CALL...

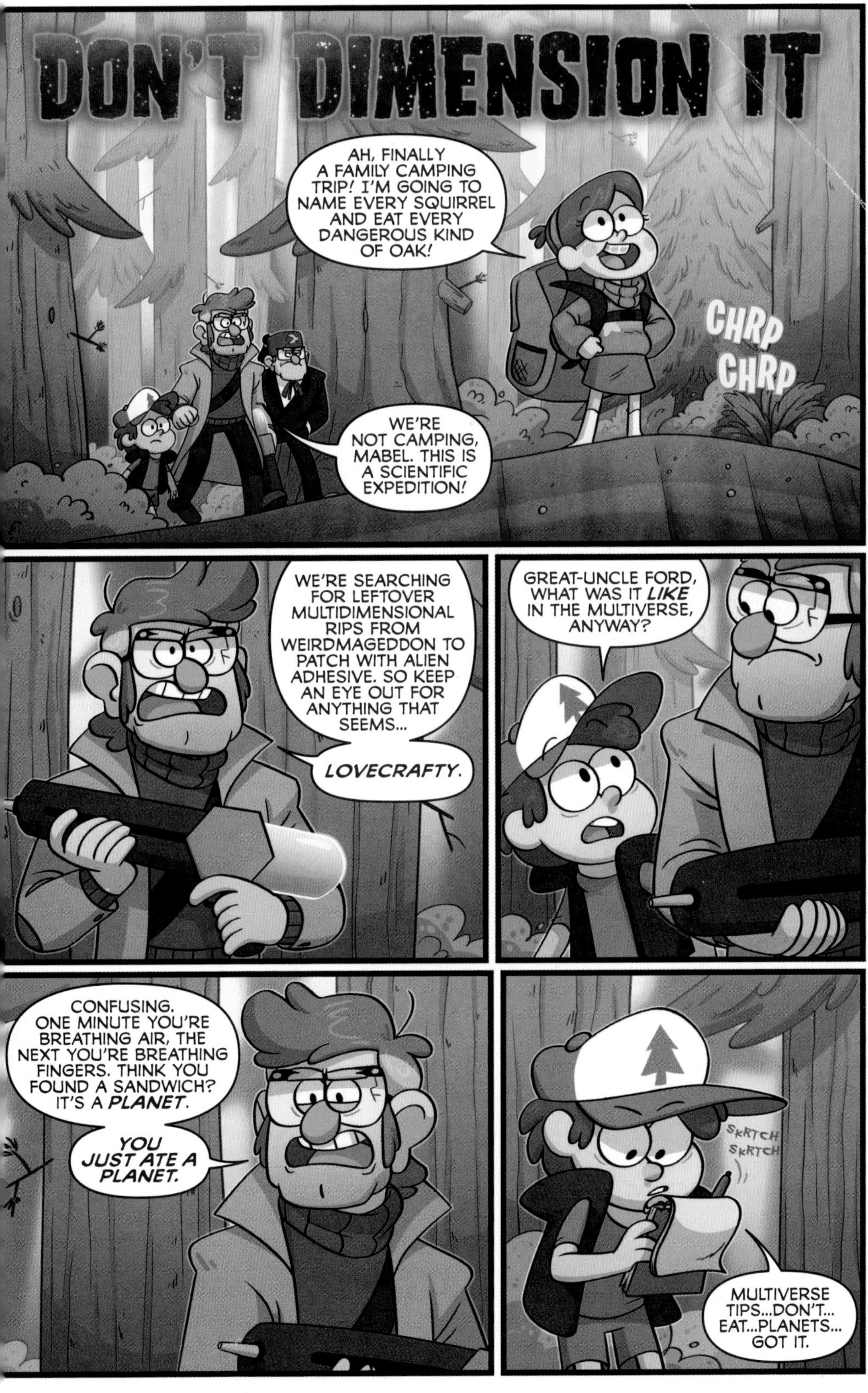
DON'T DIMENSION IT
AH, FINALLY A FAMILY CAMPING TRIP! I'M GOING TO NAME EVERY SQUIRREL AND EAT EVERY DANGEROUS KIND OF OAK!
CHRP CHRP
WE'RE NOT CAMPING, MABEL. THIS IS A SCIENTIFIC EXPEDITION!
WE'RE SEARCHING FOR LEFTOVER MULTIDIMENSIONAL RIPS FROM WEIRDMAGEDDON TO PATCH WITH ALIEN ADHESIVE. SO KEEP AN EYE OUT FOR ANYTHING THAT SEEMS...
LOVECRAFTY.
GREAT-UNCLE FORD, WHAT WAS IT LIKE IN THE MULTIVERSE, ANYWAY?
CONFUSING. ONE MINUTE YOU'RE BREATHING AIR, THE NEXT YOU'RE BREATHING FINGERS. THINK YOU FOUND A SANDWICH? IT'S A PLANET.
YOU JUST ATE A PLANET.
SKRTCH SKRTCH
MULTIVERSE TIPS...DON'T... EAT...PLANETS... GOT IT.

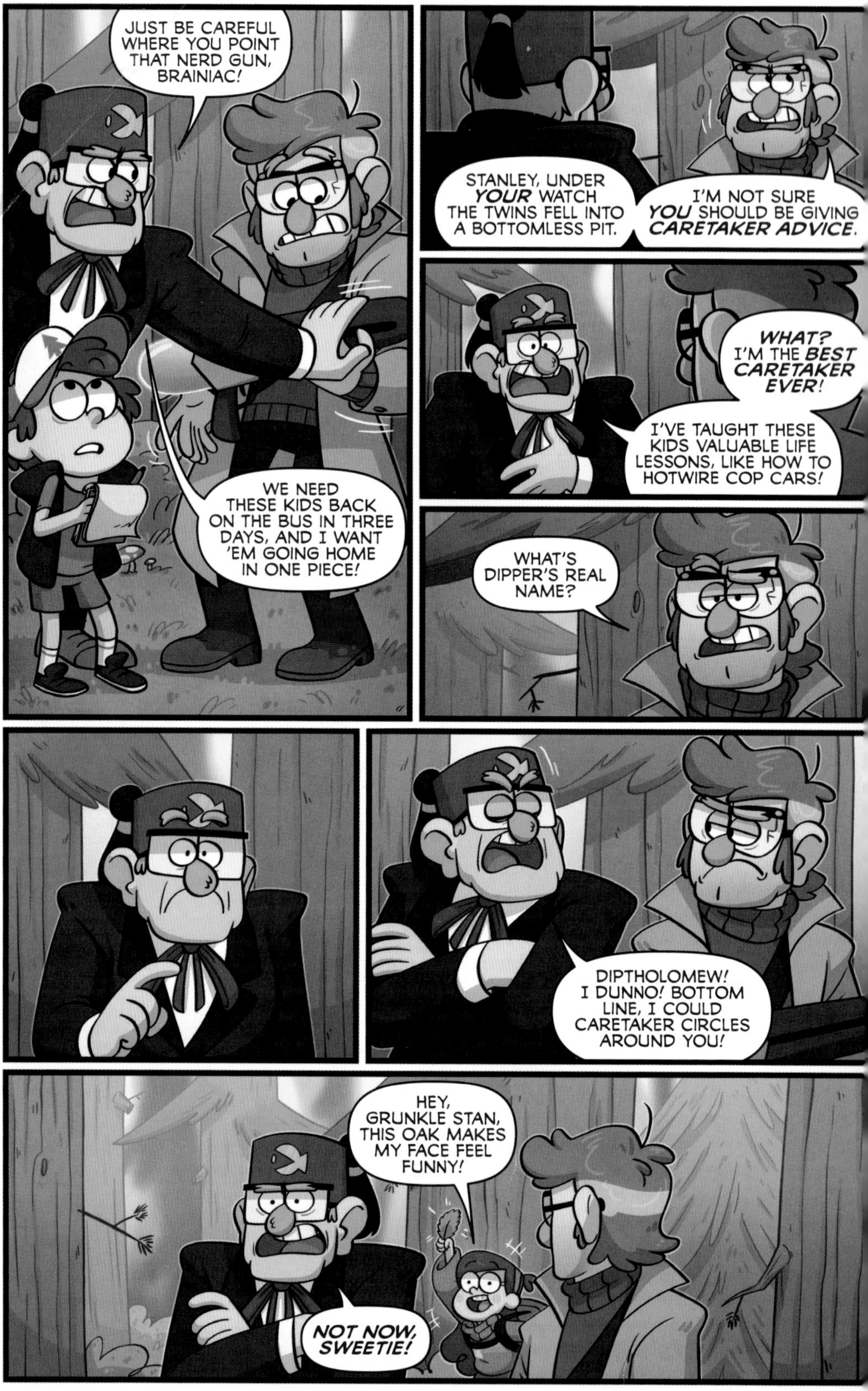
JUST BE CAREFUL WHERE YOU POINT THAT NERD GUN, BRAINIAC!
WE NEED THESE KIDS BACK ON THE BUS IN THREE DAYS, AND I WANT 'EM GOING HOME IN ONE PIECE!
STANLEY, UNDER YOUR WATCH THE TWINS FELL INTO A BOTTOMLESS PIT.
I'M NOT SURE YOU SHOULD BE GIVING CARETAKER ADVICE.
WHAT? I'M THE BEST CARETAKER EVER!
I'VE TAUGHT THESE KIDS VALUABLE LIFE LESSONS, LIKE HOW TO HOTWIRE COP CARS!
WHAT'S DIPPER'S REAL NAME?
DIPTHOLOMEW! I DUNNO! BOTTOM LINE, I COULD CARETAKER CIRCLES AROUND YOU!
HEY, GRUNKLE STAN, THIS OAK MAKES MY FACE FEEL FUNNY!
NOT NOW, SWEETIE!

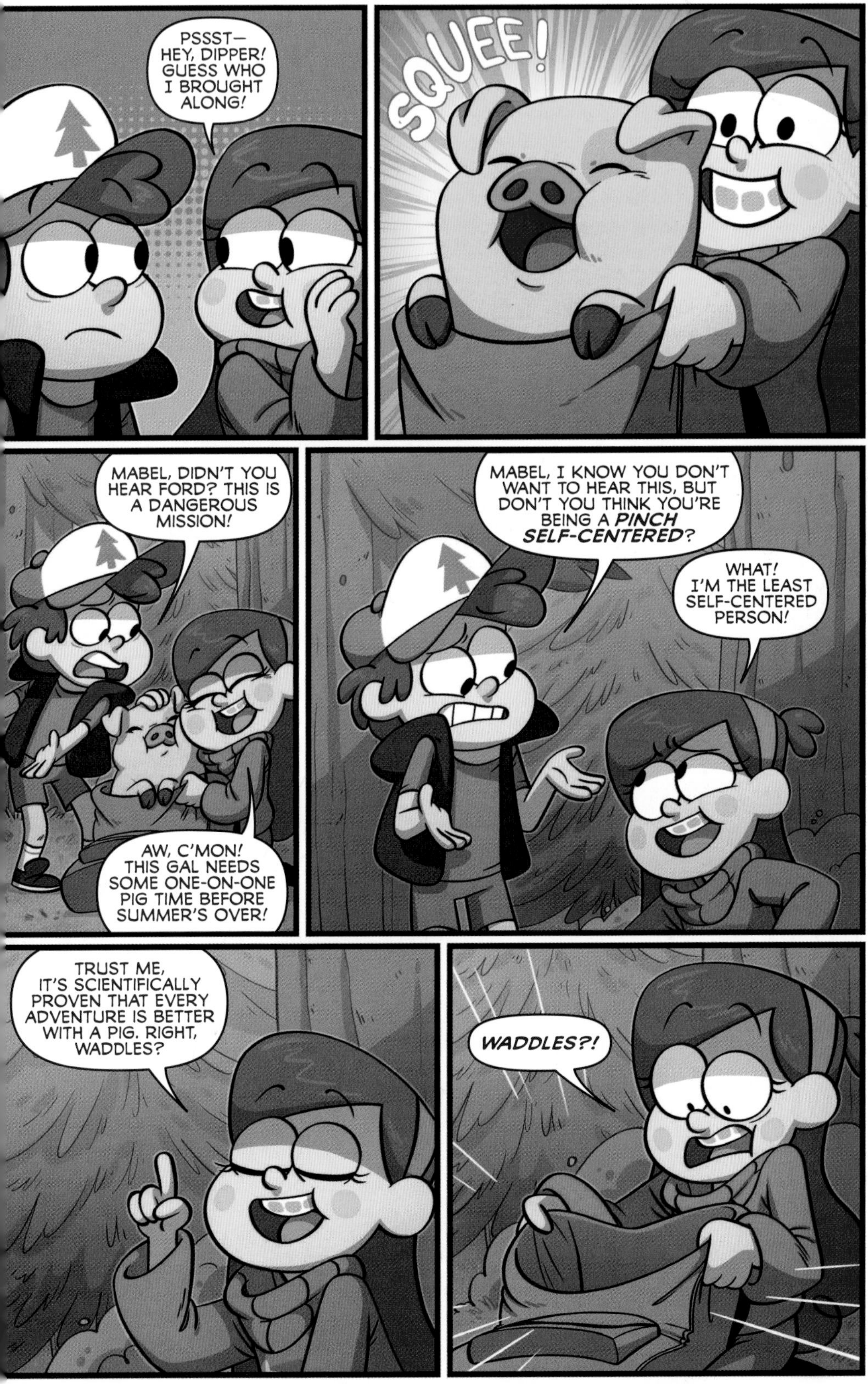
PSSST— HEY, DIPPER! GUESS WHO I BROUGHT ALONG!
SQUEE!
MABEL, DIDN'T YOU HEAR FORD? THIS IS A DANGEROUS MISSION!
AW, C'MON! THIS GAL NEEDS SOME ONE-ON-ONE PIG TIME BEFORE SUMMER'S OVER!
MABEL, I KNOW YOU DON'T WANT TO HEAR THIS, BUT DON'T YOU THINK YOU'RE BEING A *PINCH SELF-CENTERED*?
WHAT! I'M THE LEAST SELF-CENTERED PERSON!
TRUST ME, IT'S SCIENTIFICALLY PROVEN THAT EVERY ADVENTURE IS BETTER WITH A PIG. RIGHT, WADDLES?
WADDLES?!

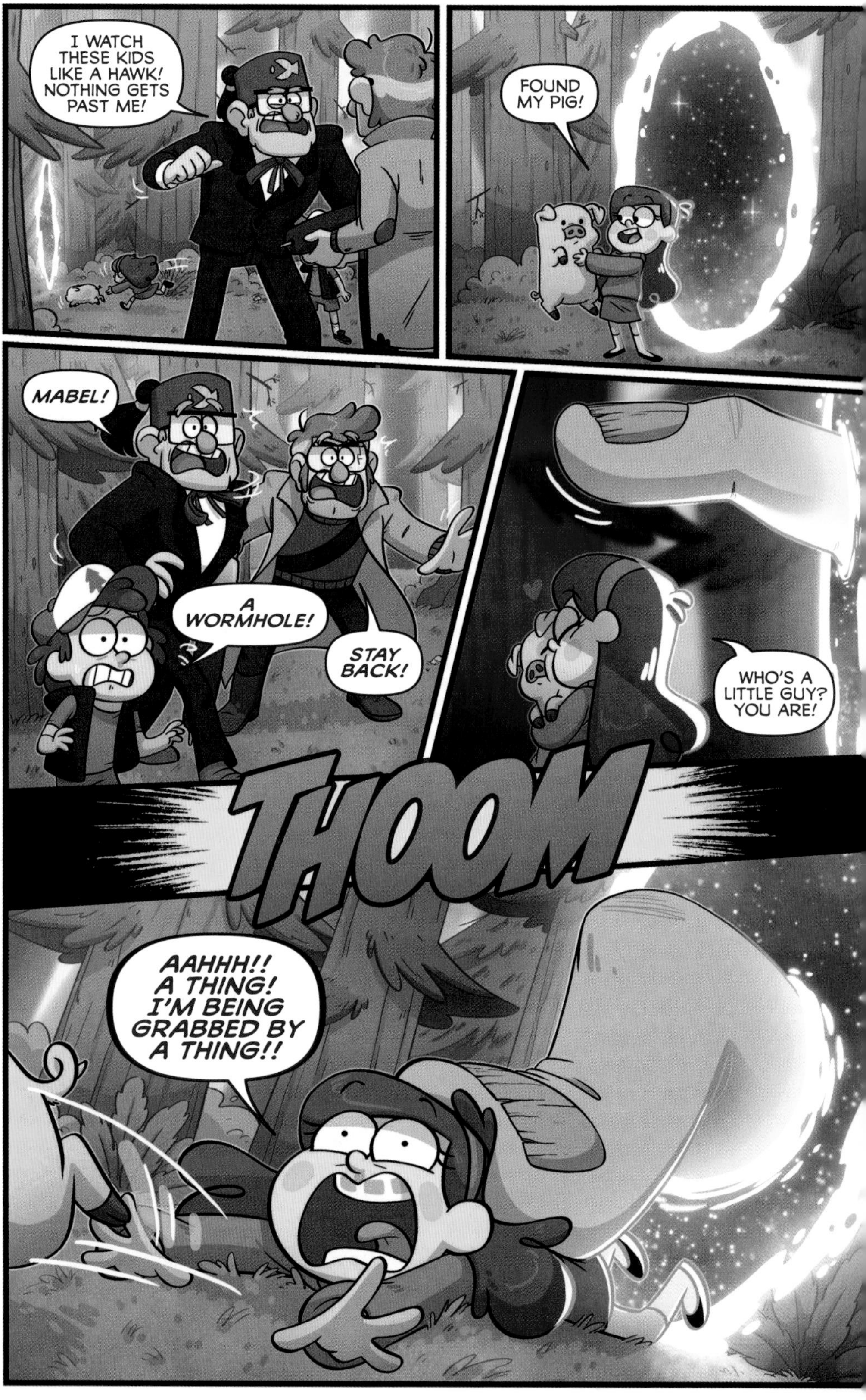
I WATCH THESE KIDS LIKE A HAWK! NOTHING GETS PAST ME!
FOUND MY PIG!
MABEL!
A WORMHOLE!
STAY BACK!
WHO'S A LITTLE GUY? YOU ARE!
THOOM
AAHHH!! A THING! I'M BEING GRABBED BY A THING!!

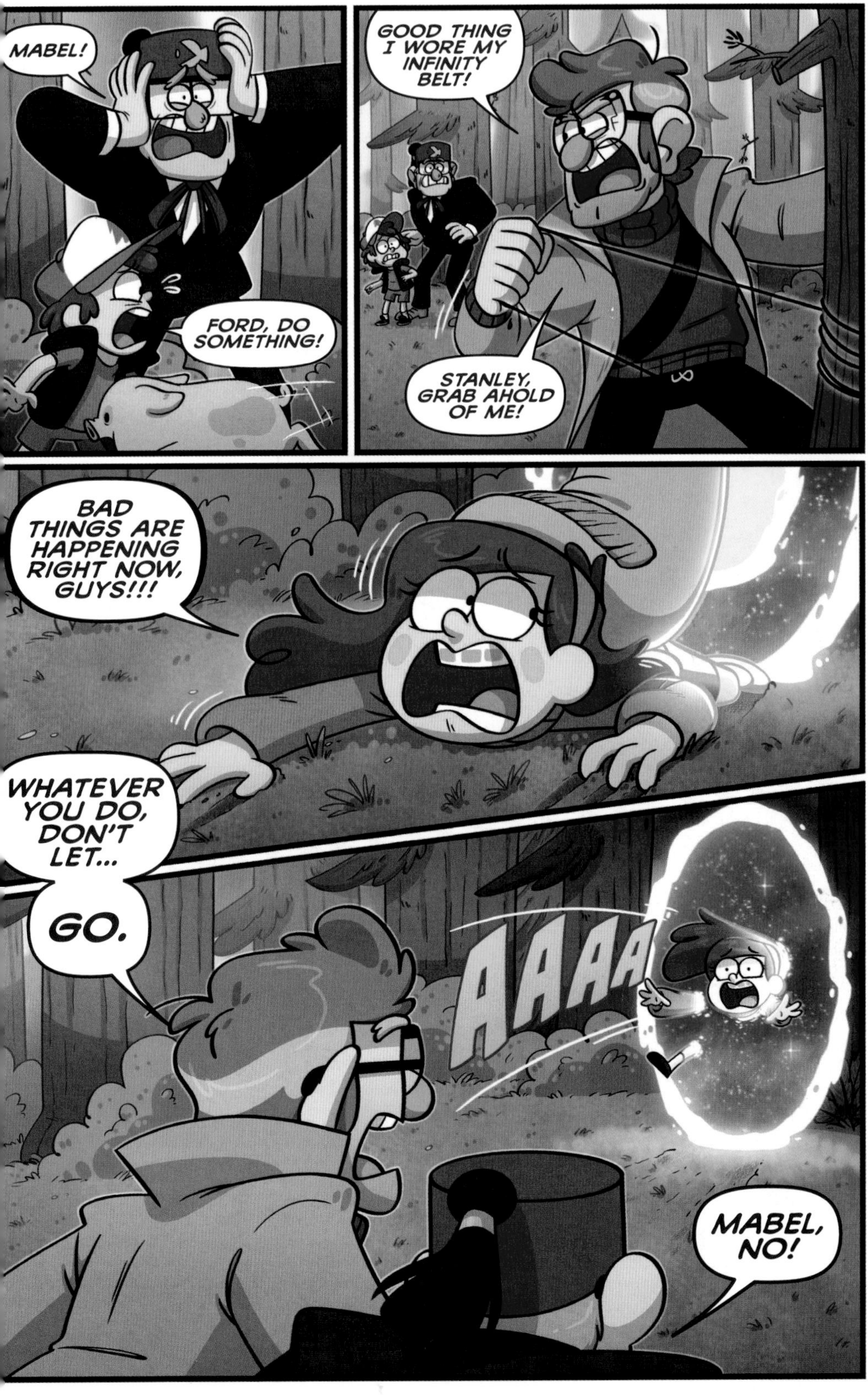
MABEL!
FORD, DO SOMETHING!
GOOD THING I WORE MY INFINITY BELT!
STANLEY, GRAB AHOLD OF ME!
BAD THINGS ARE HAPPENING RIGHT NOW, GUYS!!!
WHATEVER YOU DO, DON'T LET...
GO.
AAAA
MABEL, NO!

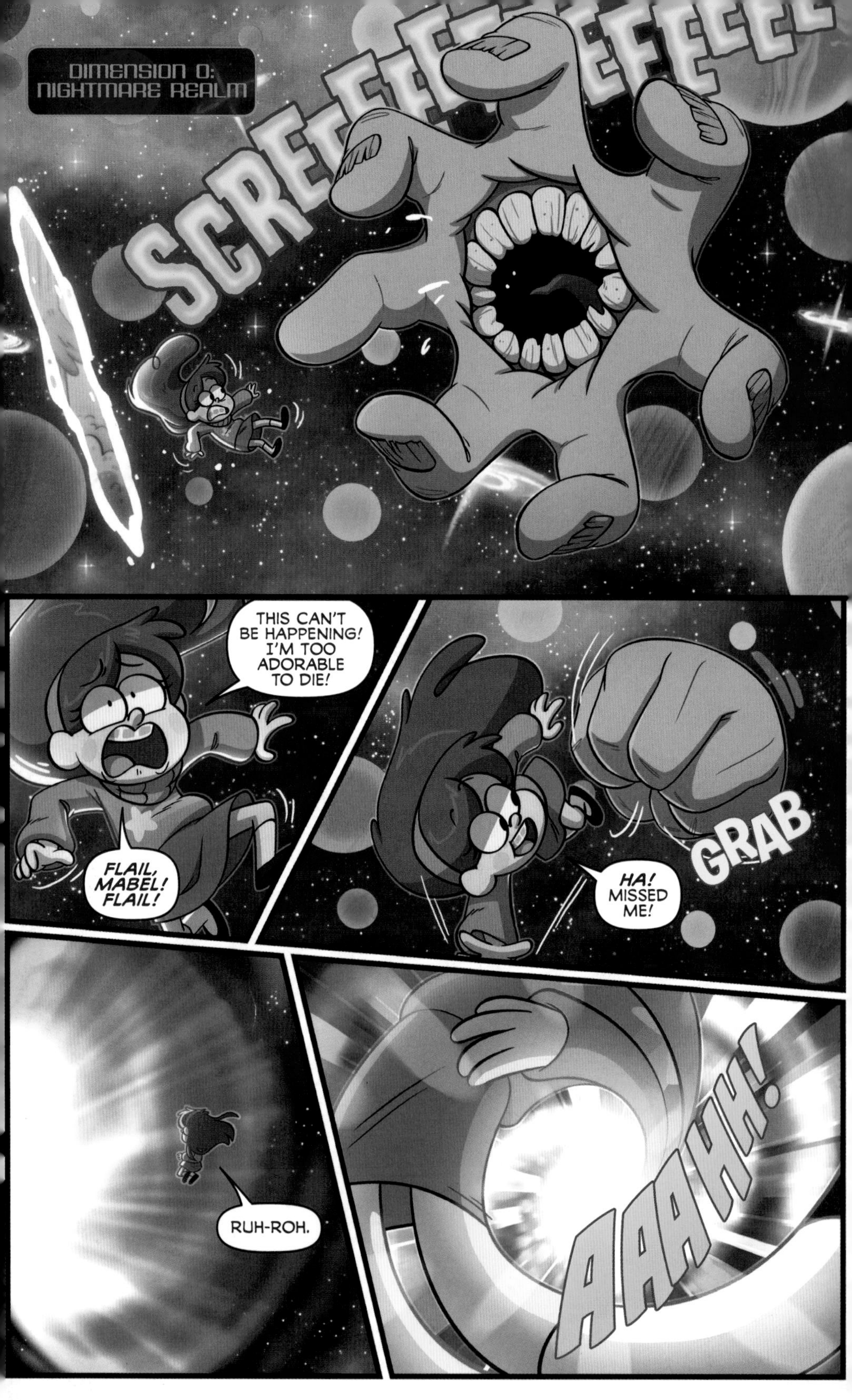
DIMENSION 0:
NIGHTMARE REALM
SCREEEEEEEEEEEEEL
THIS CAN'T BE HAPPENING! I'M TOO ADORABLE TO DIE!
FLAIL, MABEL! FLAIL!
GRAB
HA! MISSED ME!
RUH-ROH.
AAAHH!

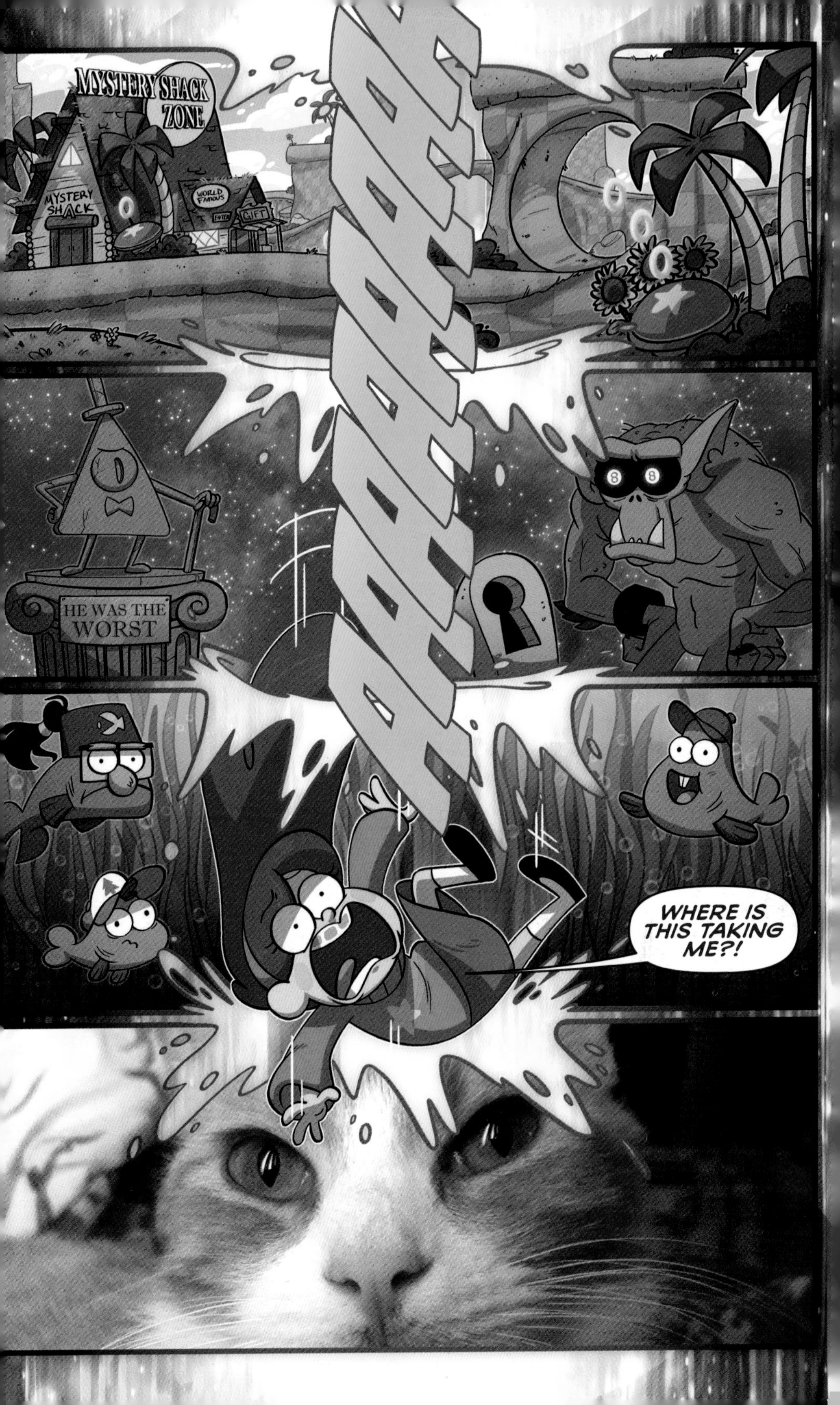
MYSTERY SHACK ZONE
MYSTERY SHACK
WORLD FAMOUS
GIFT
HE WAS THE WORST
WHERE IS THIS TAKING ME?!

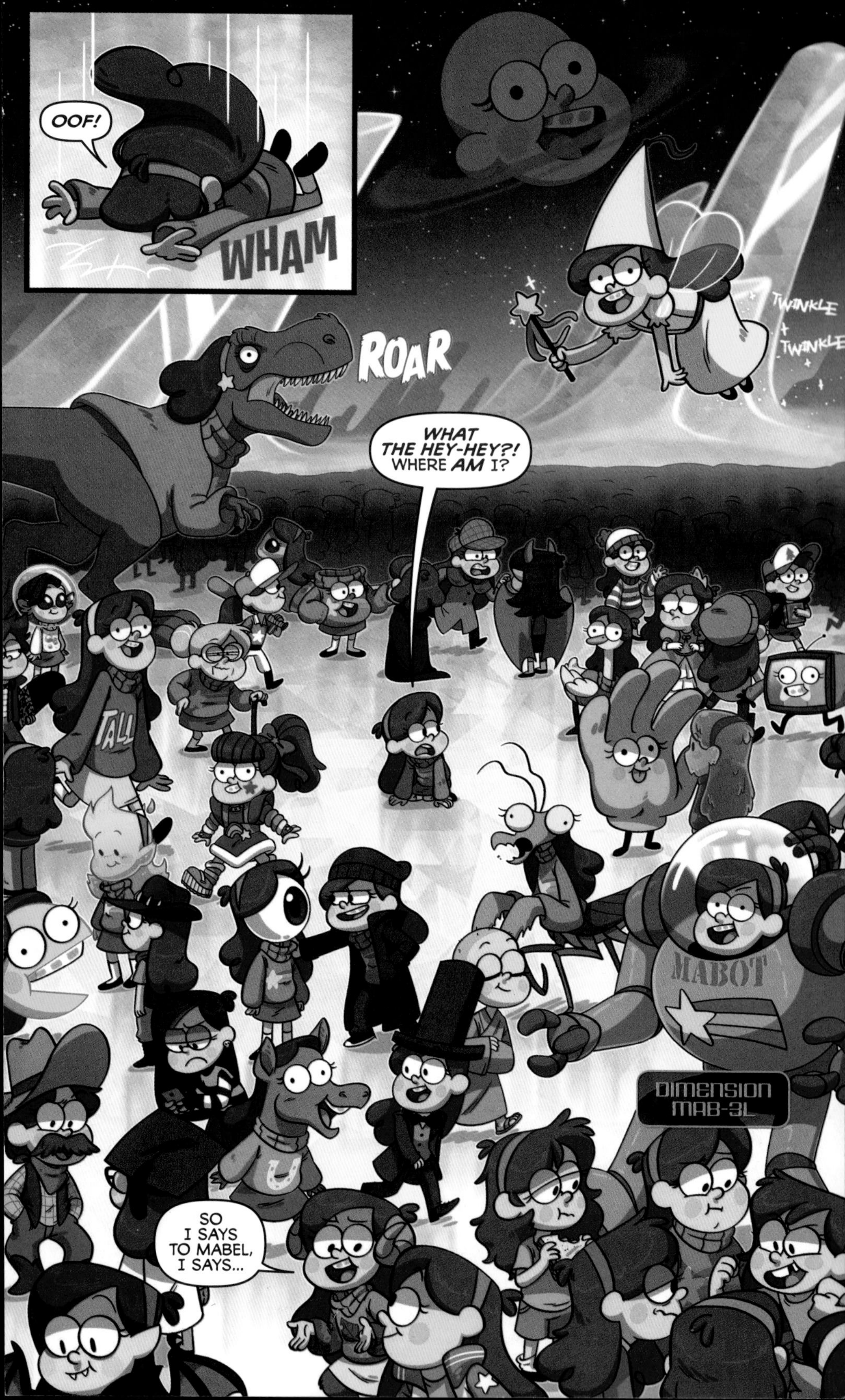
OOF!
WHAM
ROAR
TWINKLE TWINKLE
WHAT THE HEY-HEY?! WHERE AM I?
TALL
MABOT
DIMENSION MAB-3L
SO I SAYS TO MABEL, I SAYS...

RAZZLE MY DAZZLE, IT'S A *MABEL BONANZA!* THERE'S EVERY POSSIBLE VERSION OF ME...

TABLE MABEL...

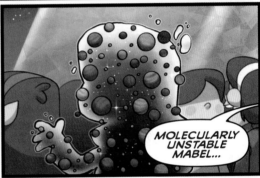

MOLECULARLY UNSTABLE MABEL...

AND HEY, YOU LOOK JUST LIKE ME!

WHOA, GIRL, YOU ARE FIERCE AND I *LOVE* IT.

REEE

HELLO THERE!

YOU MUST BE NEW HERE. WHICH MABEL ARE YOU?

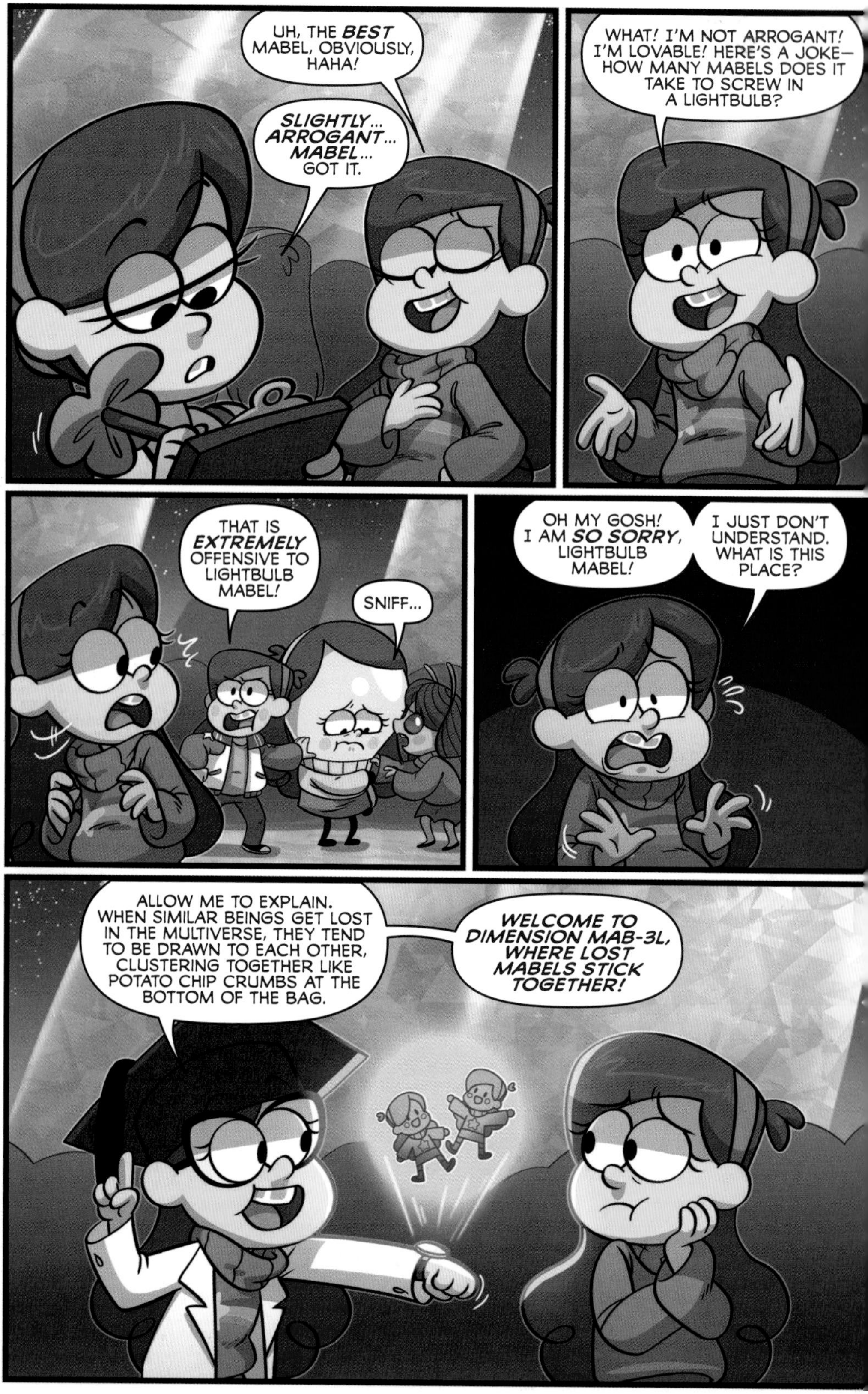
UH, THE BEST MABEL, OBVIOUSLY, HAHA!
SLIGHTLY... ARROGANT... MABEL... GOT IT.
WHAT! I'M NOT ARROGANT! I'M LOVABLE! HERE'S A JOKE— HOW MANY MABELS DOES IT TAKE TO SCREW IN A LIGHTBULB?
THAT IS EXTREMELY OFFENSIVE TO LIGHTBULB MABEL!
SNIFF...
OH MY GOSH! I AM SO SORRY, LIGHTBULB MABEL!
I JUST DON'T UNDERSTAND. WHAT IS THIS PLACE?
ALLOW ME TO EXPLAIN. WHEN SIMILAR BEINGS GET LOST IN THE MULTIVERSE, THEY TEND TO BE DRAWN TO EACH OTHER, CLUSTERING TOGETHER LIKE POTATO CHIP CRUMBS AT THE BOTTOM OF THE BAG.
WELCOME TO DIMENSION MAB-3L, WHERE LOST MABELS STICK TOGETHER!

THANKS, *EXPLAINBEL!* SUPER HELPFUL! BUT LIKE... HOW DO WE GET OUT OF HERE?

UNFORTUNATELY, WE'RE TRAPPED FOREVER.

THE SMARTEST MABEL HERE, *BRAINBEL,* TRIED TO INVENT A DIMENSIONAL ESCAPE POD, BUT SHE'S BEEN TOO BUSY WORKING ON HER STICKER COLLECTION TO FINISH IT.

WHAT?! I MEAN, I LOVE STICKERS AS MUCH AS THE NEXT MABEL, BUT WHAT ABOUT HOME?

I BET IF WE WORKED TOGETHER, WE COULD GET THAT PUPPY UP AND RUNNING!

SORRY, I TOTALLY LOST MY TRAIN OF THOUGHT WHEN YOU SAID *"PUPPY."*

WHO SAID *"PUPPY"*?!

PUPPY? WHERE?

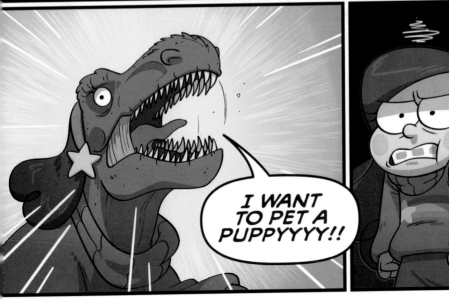

I WANT TO PET A PUPPYYYY!!

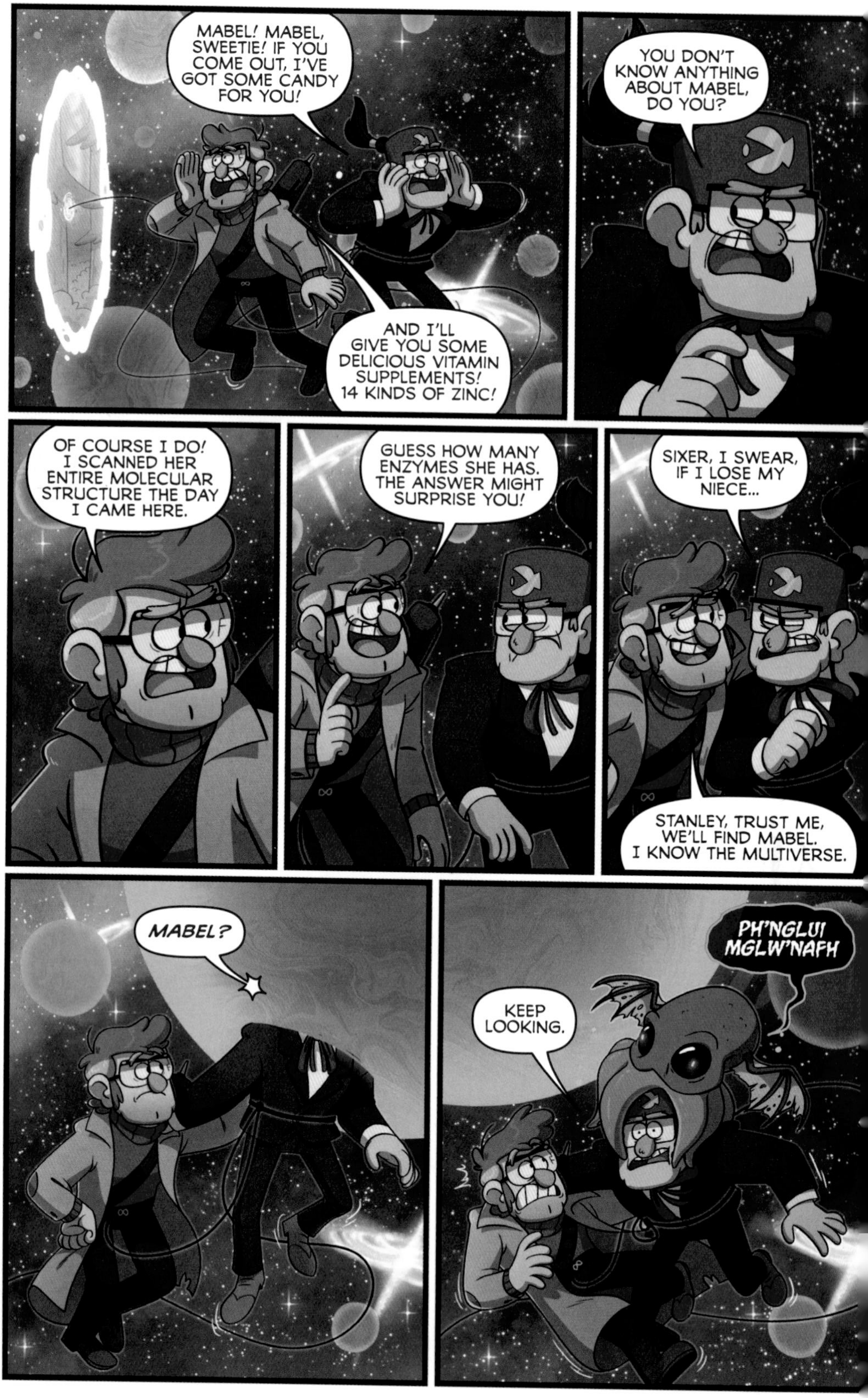

MABEL! MABEL, SWEETIE! IF YOU COME OUT, I'VE GOT SOME CANDY FOR YOU!
AND I'LL GIVE YOU SOME DELICIOUS VITAMIN SUPPLEMENTS! 14 KINDS OF ZINC!
YOU DON'T KNOW ANYTHING ABOUT MABEL, DO YOU?
OF COURSE I DO! I SCANNED HER ENTIRE MOLECULAR STRUCTURE THE DAY I CAME HERE.
GUESS HOW MANY ENZYMES SHE HAS. THE ANSWER MIGHT SURPRISE YOU!
SIXER, I SWEAR, IF I LOSE MY NIECE...
STANLEY, TRUST ME, WE'LL FIND MABEL. I KNOW THE MULTIVERSE.
MABEL?
KEEP LOOKING.
PH'NGLUI MGLW'NAFH

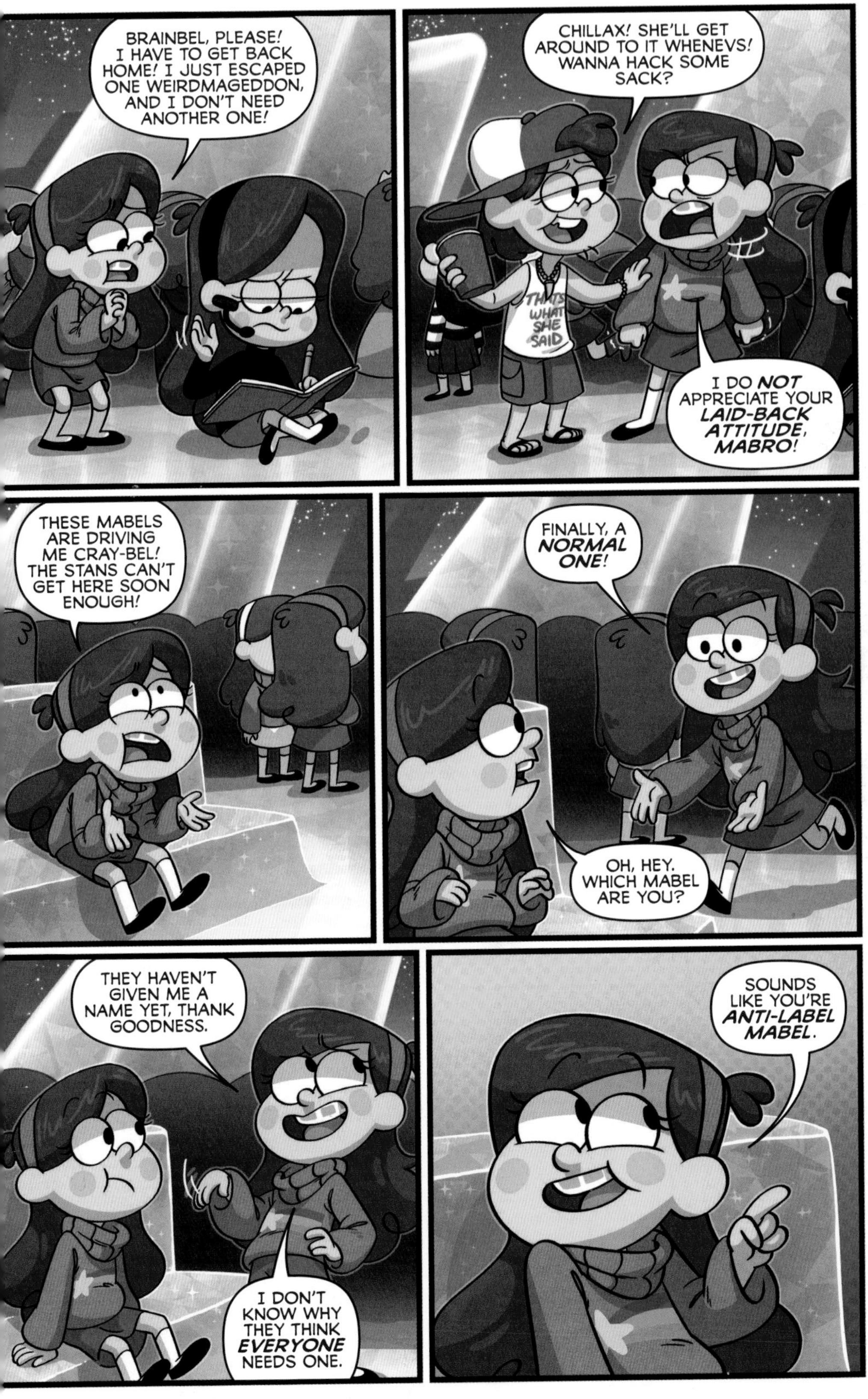
BRAINBEL, PLEASE! I HAVE TO GET BACK HOME! I JUST ESCAPED ONE WEIRDMAGEDDON, AND I DON'T NEED ANOTHER ONE!
CHILLAX! SHE'LL GET AROUND TO IT WHENEVS! WANNA HACK SOME SACK?
THAT'S WHAT SHE SAID
I DO NOT APPRECIATE YOUR LAID-BACK ATTITUDE, MABRO!
THESE MABELS ARE DRIVING ME CRAY-BEL! THE STANS CAN'T GET HERE SOON ENOUGH!
FINALLY, A NORMAL ONE!
OH, HEY. WHICH MABEL ARE YOU?
THEY HAVEN'T GIVEN ME A NAME YET, THANK GOODNESS.
I DON'T KNOW WHY THEY THINK EVERYONE NEEDS ONE.
SOUNDS LIKE YOU'RE ANTI-LABEL MABEL.

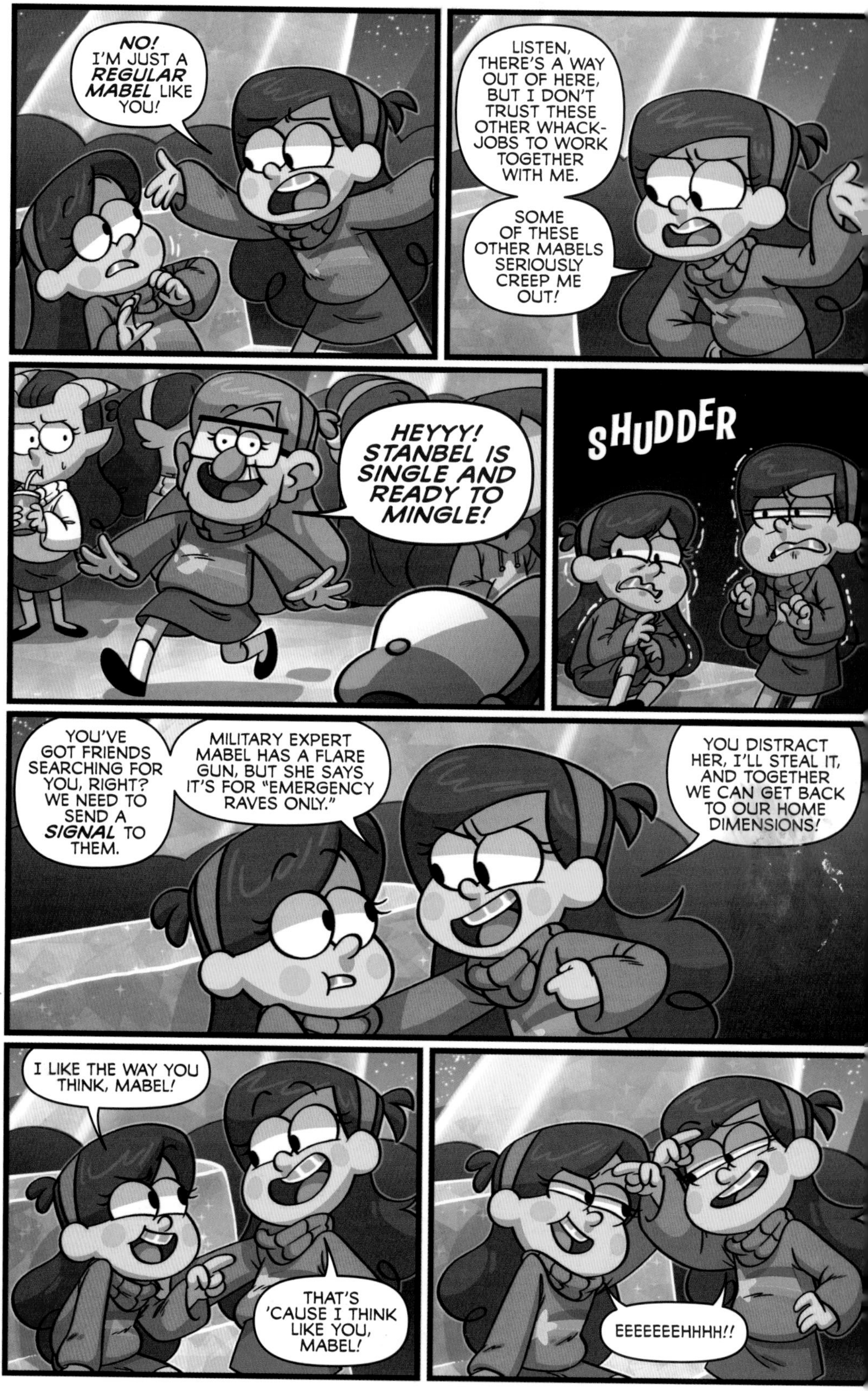
NO! I'M JUST A REGULAR MABEL LIKE YOU!
LISTEN, THERE'S A WAY OUT OF HERE, BUT I DON'T TRUST THESE OTHER WHACK-JOBS TO WORK TOGETHER WITH ME.
SOME OF THESE OTHER MABELS SERIOUSLY CREEP ME OUT!
HEYYY! STANBEL IS SINGLE AND READY TO MINGLE!
SHUDDER
YOU'VE GOT FRIENDS SEARCHING FOR YOU, RIGHT? WE NEED TO SEND A SIGNAL TO THEM.
MILITARY EXPERT MABEL HAS A FLARE GUN, BUT SHE SAYS IT'S FOR "EMERGENCY RAVES ONLY."
YOU DISTRACT HER, I'LL STEAL IT, AND TOGETHER WE CAN GET BACK TO OUR HOME DIMENSIONS!
I LIKE THE WAY YOU THINK, MABEL!
THAT'S 'CAUSE I THINK LIKE YOU, MABEL!
EEEEEEEHHHH!!

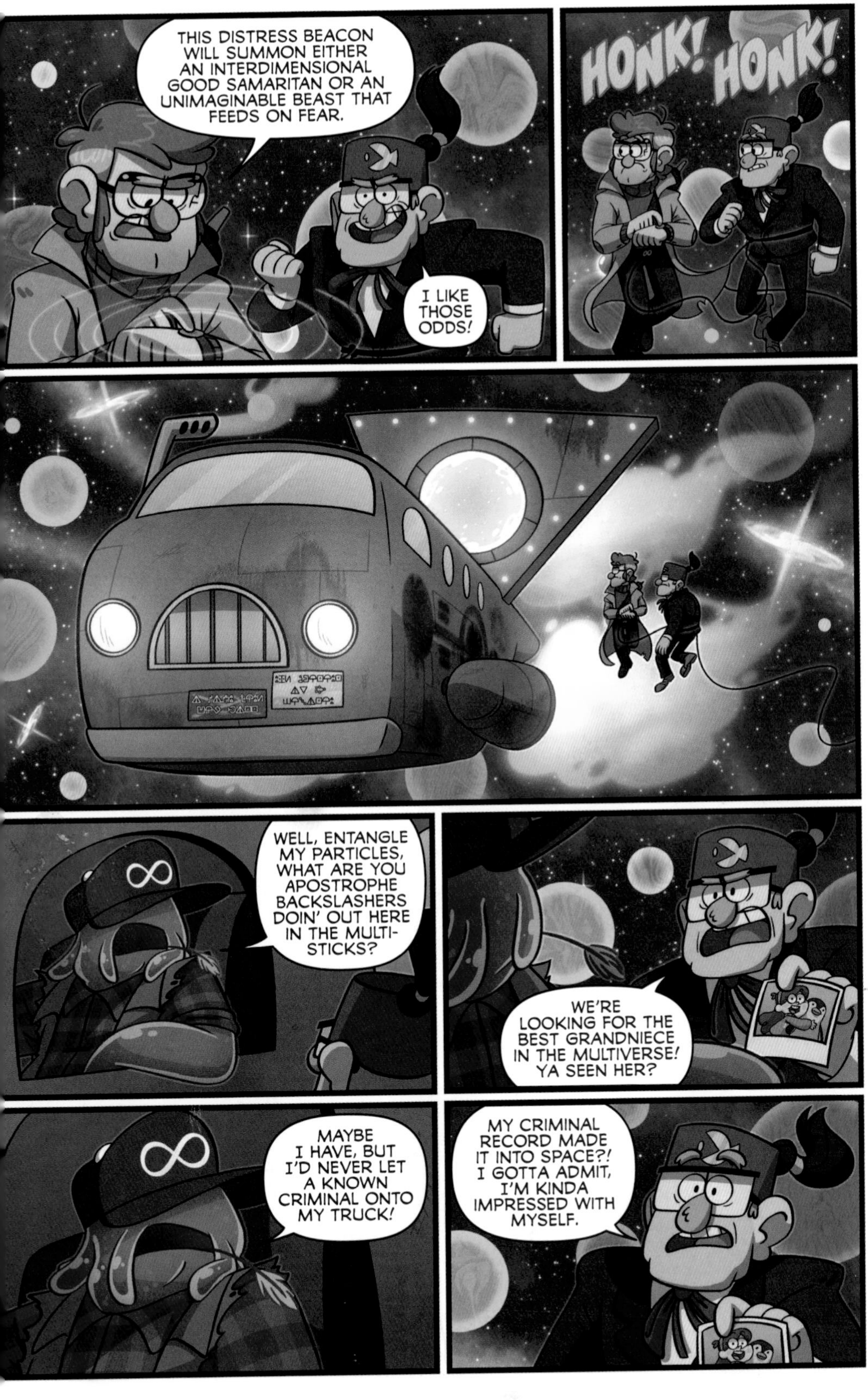
THIS DISTRESS BEACON WILL SUMMON EITHER AN INTERDIMENSIONAL GOOD SAMARITAN OR AN UNIMAGINABLE BEAST THAT FEEDS ON FEAR.
I LIKE THOSE ODDS!
HONK! HONK!
WELL, ENTANGLE MY PARTICLES, WHAT ARE YOU APOSTROPHE BACKSLASHERS DOIN' OUT HERE IN THE MULTI-STICKS?
WE'RE LOOKING FOR THE BEST GRANDNIECE IN THE MULTIVERSE! YA SEEN HER?
MAYBE I HAVE, BUT I'D NEVER LET A KNOWN CRIMINAL ONTO MY TRUCK!
MY CRIMINAL RECORD MADE IT INTO SPACE?! I GOTTA ADMIT, I'M KINDA IMPRESSED WITH MYSELF.

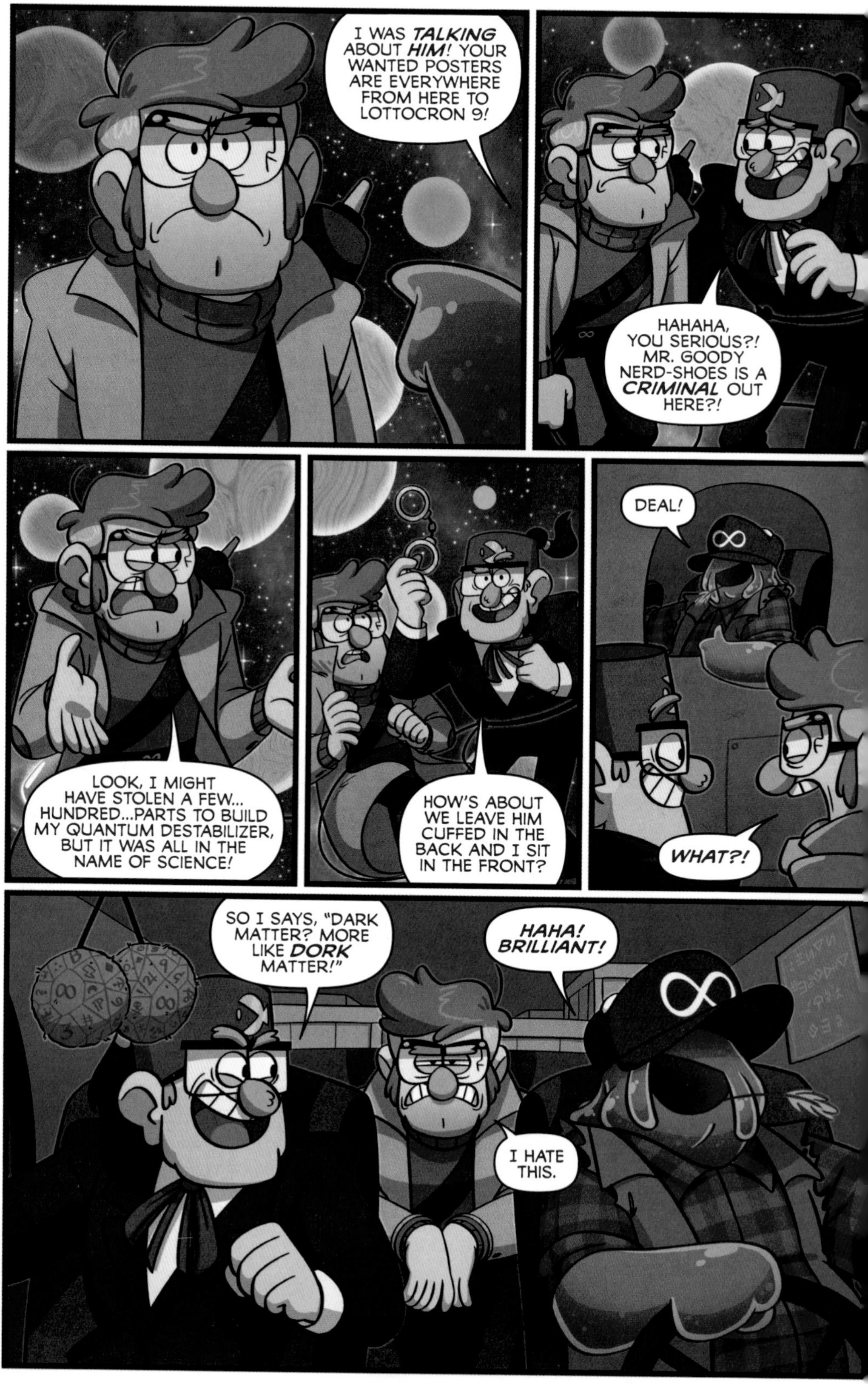

I WAS TALKING ABOUT HIM! YOUR WANTED POSTERS ARE EVERYWHERE FROM HERE TO LOTTOCRON 9!
HAHAHA, YOU SERIOUS?! MR. GOODY NERD-SHOES IS A CRIMINAL OUT HERE?!
LOOK, I MIGHT HAVE STOLEN A FEW... HUNDRED...PARTS TO BUILD MY QUANTUM DESTABILIZER, BUT IT WAS ALL IN THE NAME OF SCIENCE!
HOW'S ABOUT WE LEAVE HIM CUFFED IN THE BACK AND I SIT IN THE FRONT?
DEAL!
WHAT?!
SO I SAYS, "DARK MATTER? MORE LIKE DORK MATTER!"
HAHA! BRILLIANT!
I HATE THIS.

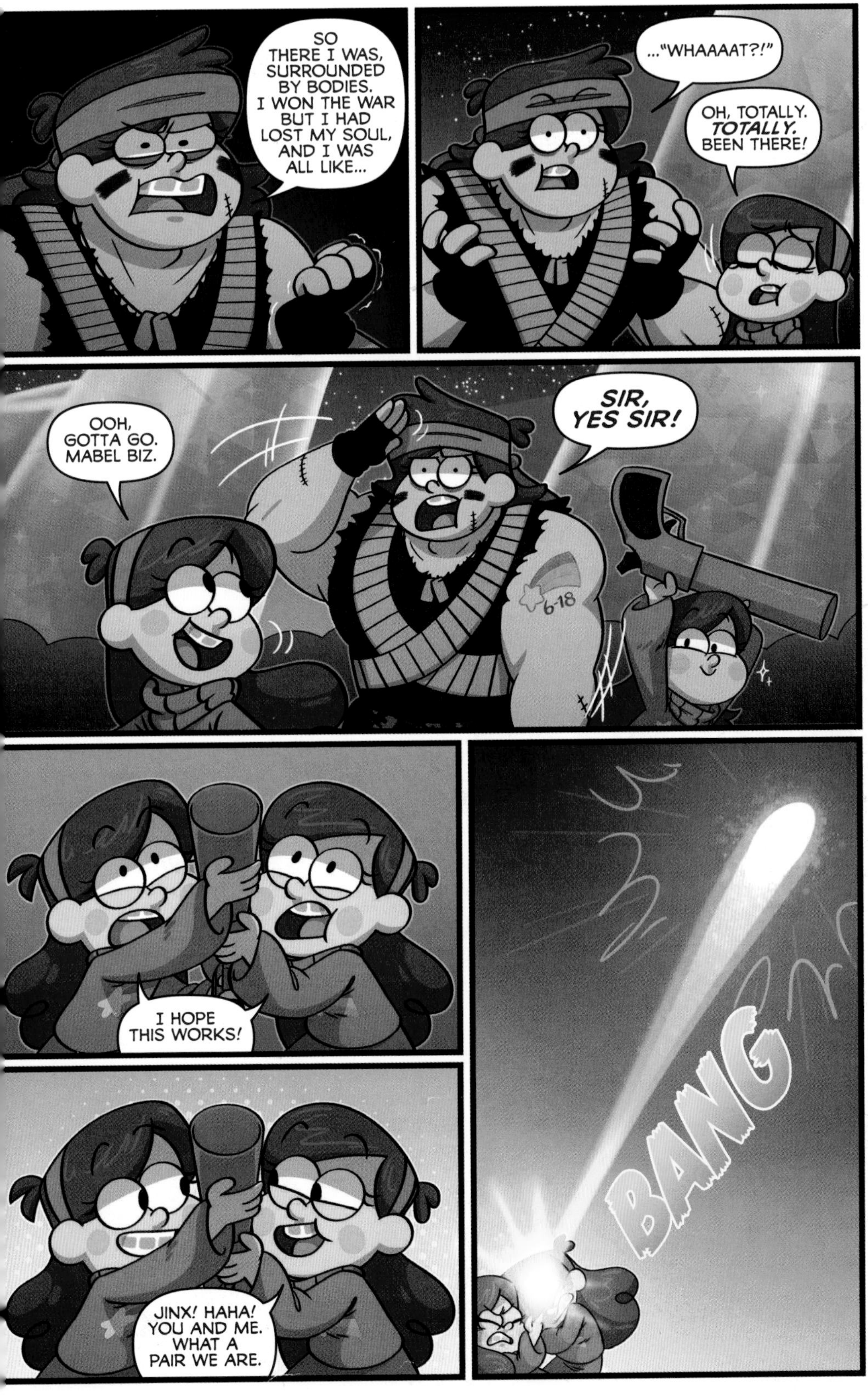
SO THERE I WAS, SURROUNDED BY BODIES. I WON THE WAR BUT I HAD LOST MY SOUL, AND I WAS ALL LIKE...
..."WHAAAAT?!"
OH, TOTALLY. *TOTALLY.* BEEN THERE!
OOH, GOTTA GO. MABEL BIZ.
SIR, YES SIR!
6-18
I HOPE THIS WORKS!
JINX! HAHA! YOU AND ME. WHAT A PAIR WE ARE.
BANG

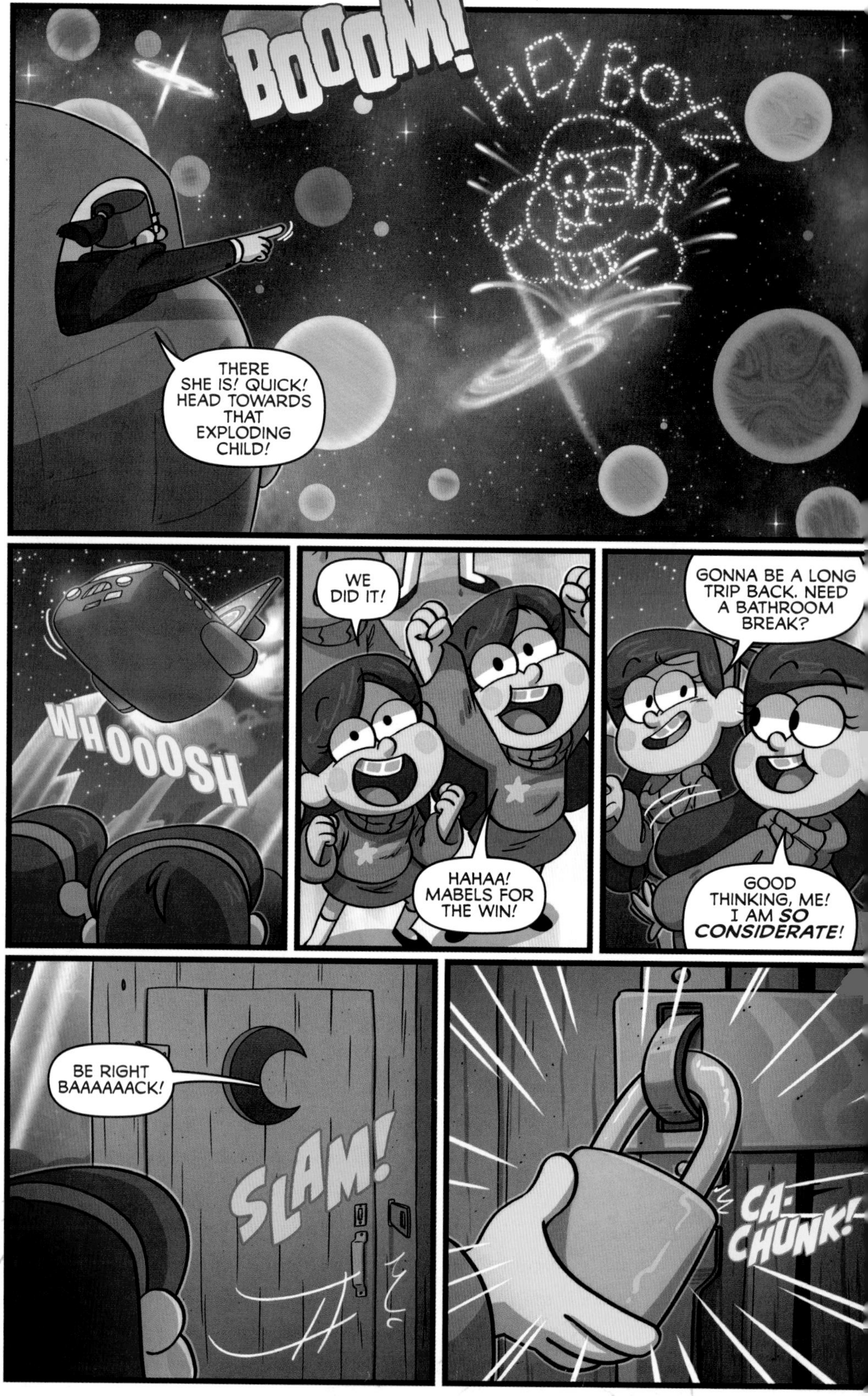
BOOOM!
HEY BOYZ
THERE SHE IS! QUICK! HEAD TOWARDS THAT EXPLODING CHILD!
WHOOOSH
WE DID IT!
HAHAA! MABELS FOR THE WIN!
GONNA BE A LONG TRIP BACK. NEED A BATHROOM BREAK?
GOOD THINKING, ME! I AM *SO CONSIDERATE!*
BE RIGHT BAAAAAACK!
SLAM!
CA-CHUNK!

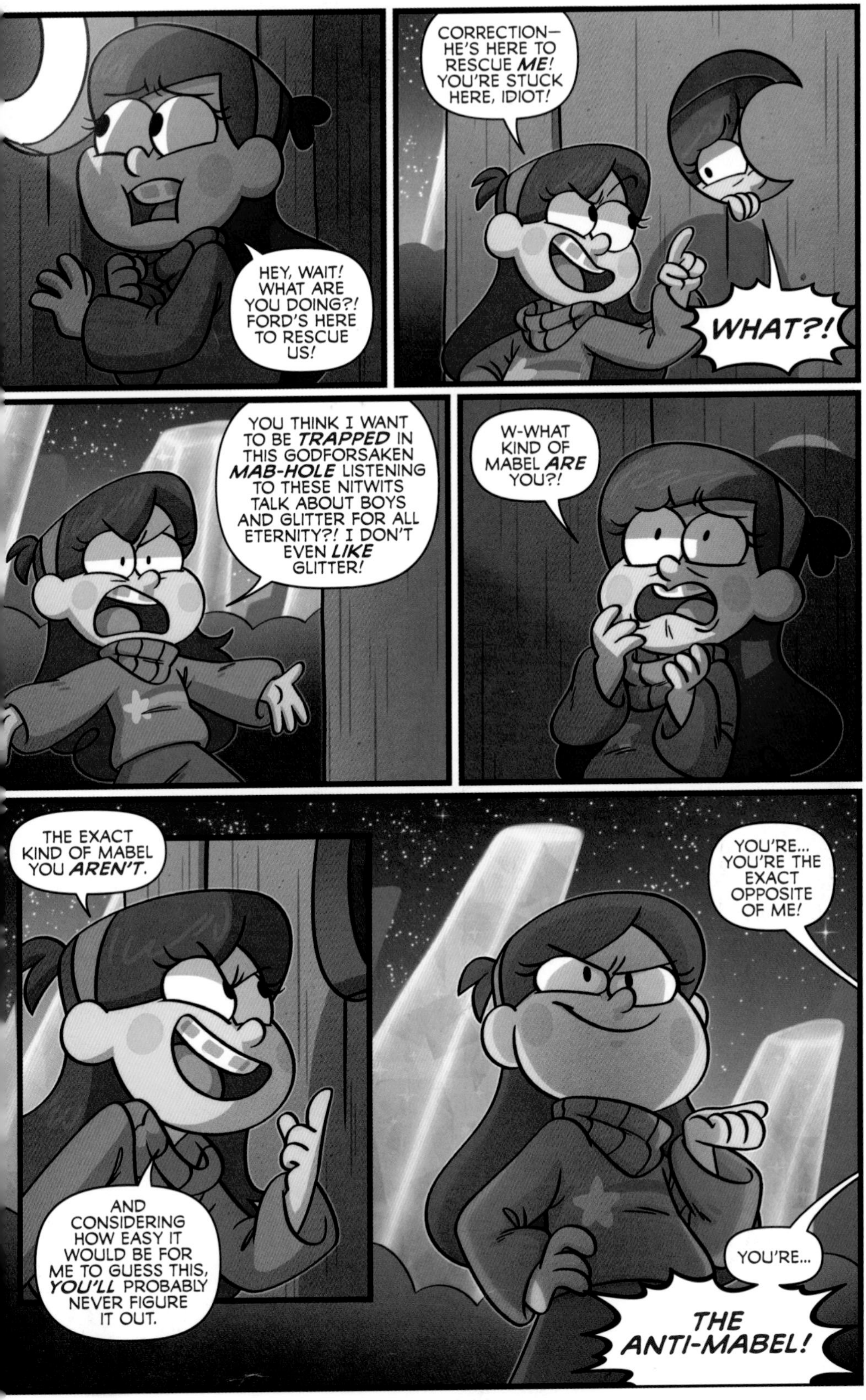
HEY, WAIT! WHAT ARE YOU DOING?! FORD'S HERE TO RESCUE US!
CORRECTION— HE'S HERE TO RESCUE ME! YOU'RE STUCK HERE, IDIOT!
WHAT?!
YOU THINK I WANT TO BE TRAPPED IN THIS GODFORSAKEN MAB-HOLE LISTENING TO THESE NITWITS TALK ABOUT BOYS AND GLITTER FOR ALL ETERNITY?! I DON'T EVEN LIKE GLITTER!
W-WHAT KIND OF MABEL ARE YOU?!
THE EXACT KIND OF MABEL YOU AREN'T.
AND CONSIDERING HOW EASY IT WOULD BE FOR ME TO GUESS THIS, YOU'LL PROBABLY NEVER FIGURE IT OUT.
YOU'RE... YOU'RE THE EXACT OPPOSITE OF ME!
YOU'RE...
THE ANTI-MABEL!

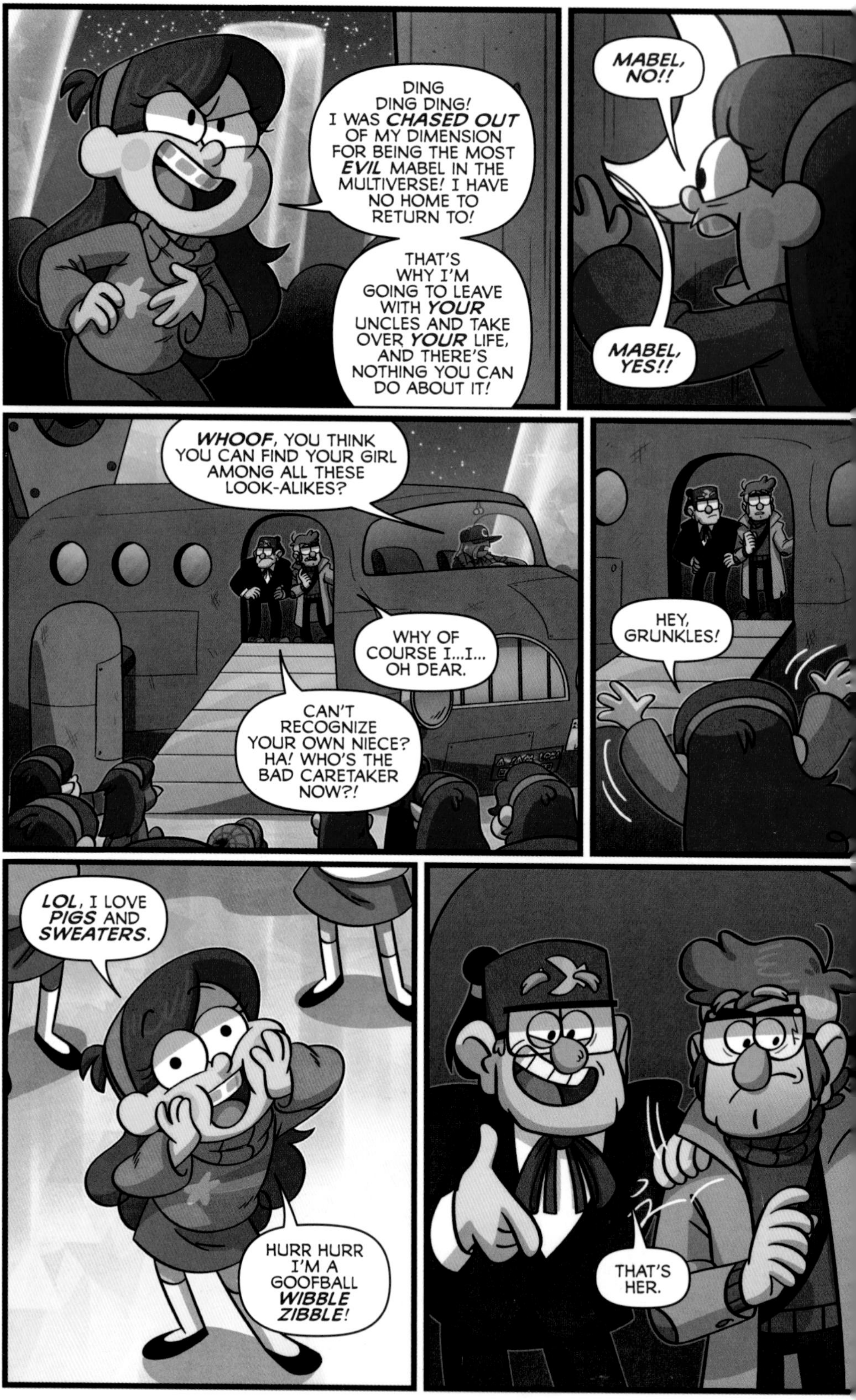

DING DING DING! I WAS ***CHASED OUT*** OF MY DIMENSION FOR BEING THE MOST ***EVIL*** MABEL IN THE MULTIVERSE! I HAVE NO HOME TO RETURN TO!
THAT'S WHY I'M GOING TO LEAVE WITH ***YOUR*** UNCLES AND TAKE OVER ***YOUR*** LIFE, AND THERE'S NOTHING YOU CAN DO ABOUT IT!
MABEL, NO!!
MABEL, YES!!
WHOOF, YOU THINK YOU CAN FIND YOUR GIRL AMONG ALL THESE LOOK-ALIKES?
WHY OF COURSE I...I... OH DEAR.
CAN'T RECOGNIZE YOUR OWN NIECE? HA! WHO'S THE BAD CARETAKER NOW?!
HEY, GRUNKLES!
LOL, I LOVE ***PIGS*** AND ***SWEATERS***.
HURR HURR I'M A GOOFBALL ***WIBBLE ZIBBLE***!
THAT'S HER.

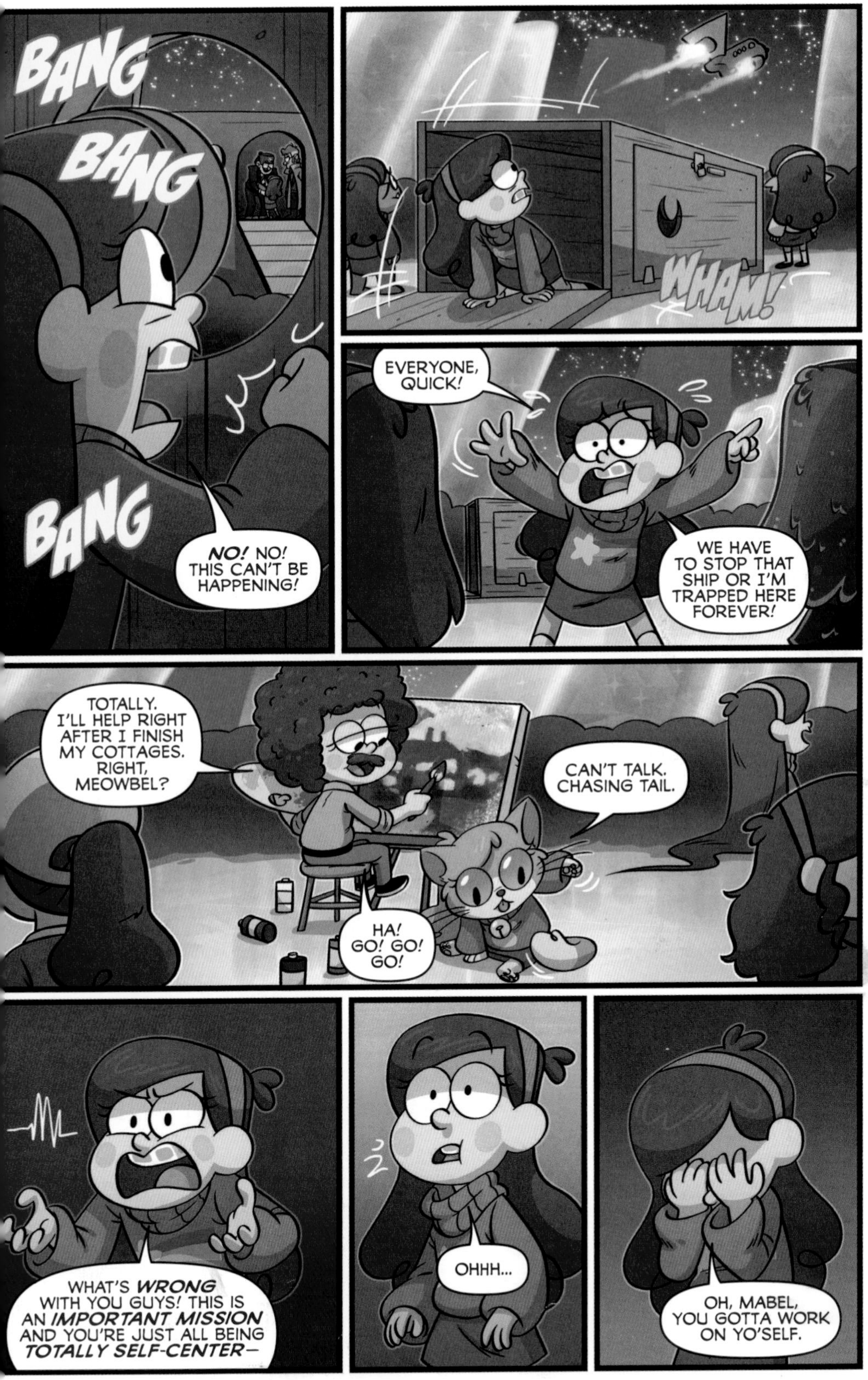
BANG
BANG
BANG
NO! NO! THIS CAN'T BE HAPPENING!
WHAM!
EVERYONE, QUICK!
WE HAVE TO STOP THAT SHIP OR I'M TRAPPED HERE FOREVER!
TOTALLY. I'LL HELP RIGHT AFTER I FINISH MY COTTAGES. RIGHT, MEOWBEL?
CAN'T TALK. CHASING TAIL.
HA! GO! GO! GO!
WHAT'S WRONG WITH YOU GUYS! THIS IS AN IMPORTANT MISSION AND YOU'RE JUST ALL BEING TOTALLY SELF-CENTER—
OHHH...
OH, MABEL, YOU GOTTA WORK ON YO'SELF.

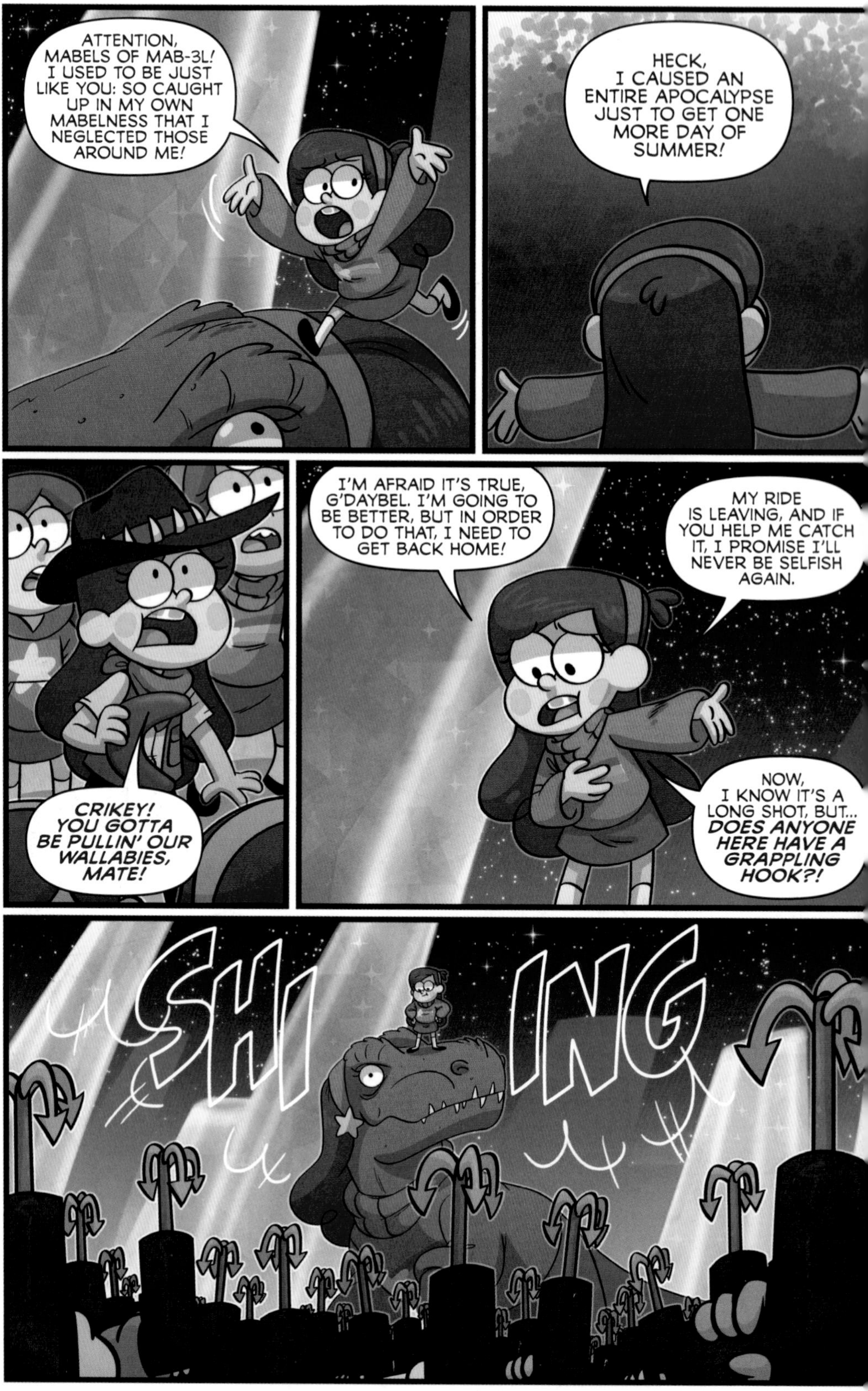
ATTENTION, MABELS OF MAB-3L! I USED TO BE JUST LIKE YOU: SO CAUGHT UP IN MY OWN MABELNESS THAT I NEGLECTED THOSE AROUND ME!
HECK, I CAUSED AN ENTIRE APOCALYPSE JUST TO GET ONE MORE DAY OF SUMMER!
CRIKEY! YOU GOTTA BE PULLIN' OUR WALLABIES, MATE!
I'M AFRAID IT'S TRUE, G'DAYBEL. I'M GOING TO BE BETTER, BUT IN ORDER TO DO THAT, I NEED TO GET BACK HOME!
MY RIDE IS LEAVING, AND IF YOU HELP ME CATCH IT, I PROMISE I'LL NEVER BE SELFISH AGAIN.
NOW, I KNOW IT'S A LONG SHOT, BUT... *DOES ANYONE HERE HAVE A GRAPPLING HOOK?!*
SHI ING

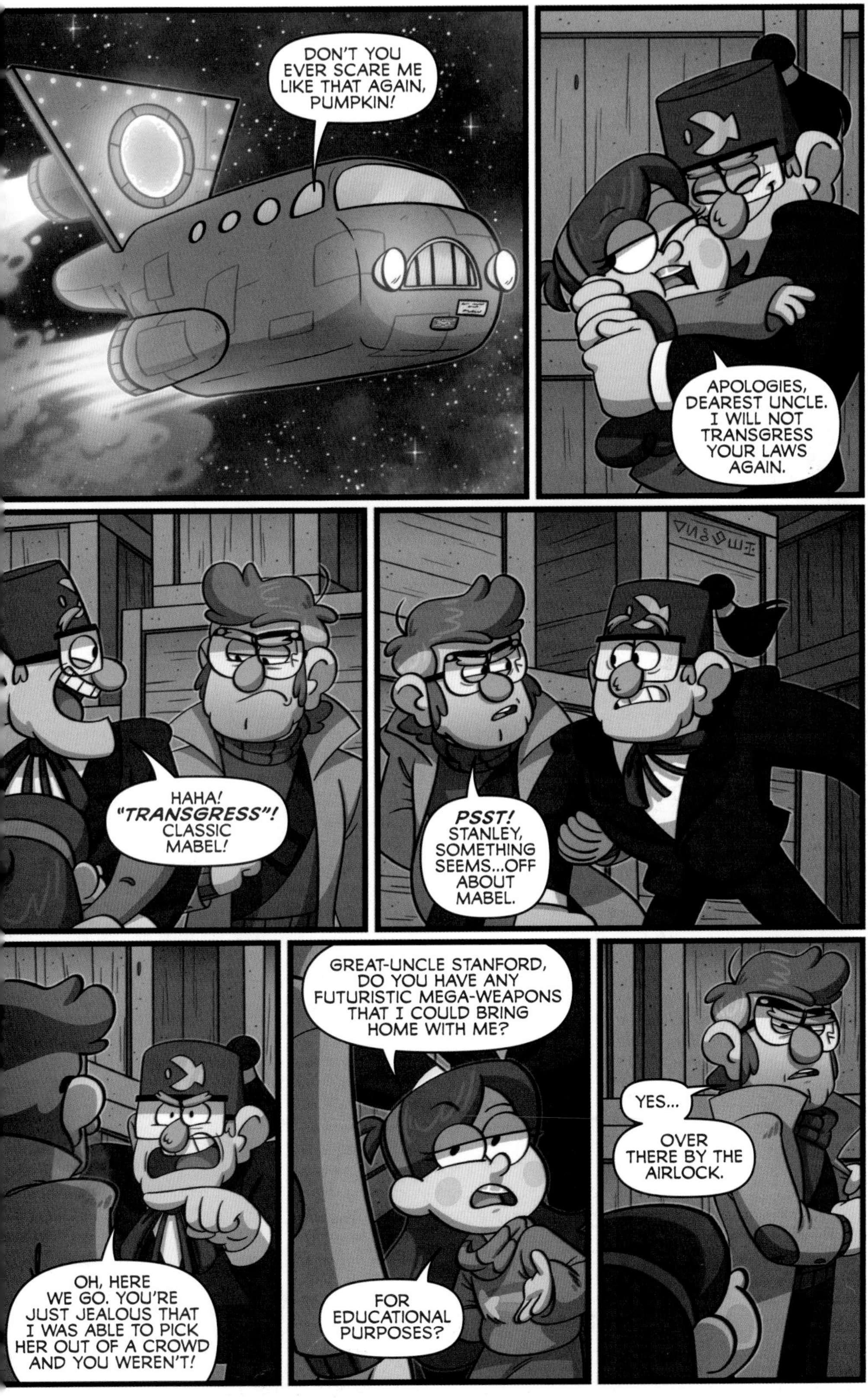
DON'T YOU EVER SCARE ME LIKE THAT AGAIN, PUMPKIN!
APOLOGIES, DEAREST UNCLE. I WILL NOT TRANSGRESS YOUR LAWS AGAIN.
HAHA! "TRANSGRESS"! CLASSIC MABEL!
PSST! STANLEY, SOMETHING SEEMS...OFF ABOUT MABEL.
OH, HERE WE GO. YOU'RE JUST JEALOUS THAT I WAS ABLE TO PICK HER OUT OF A CROWD AND YOU WEREN'T!
GREAT-UNCLE STANFORD, DO YOU HAVE ANY FUTURISTIC MEGA-WEAPONS THAT I COULD BRING HOME WITH ME?
FOR EDUCATIONAL PURPOSES?
YES...
OVER THERE BY THE AIRLOCK.

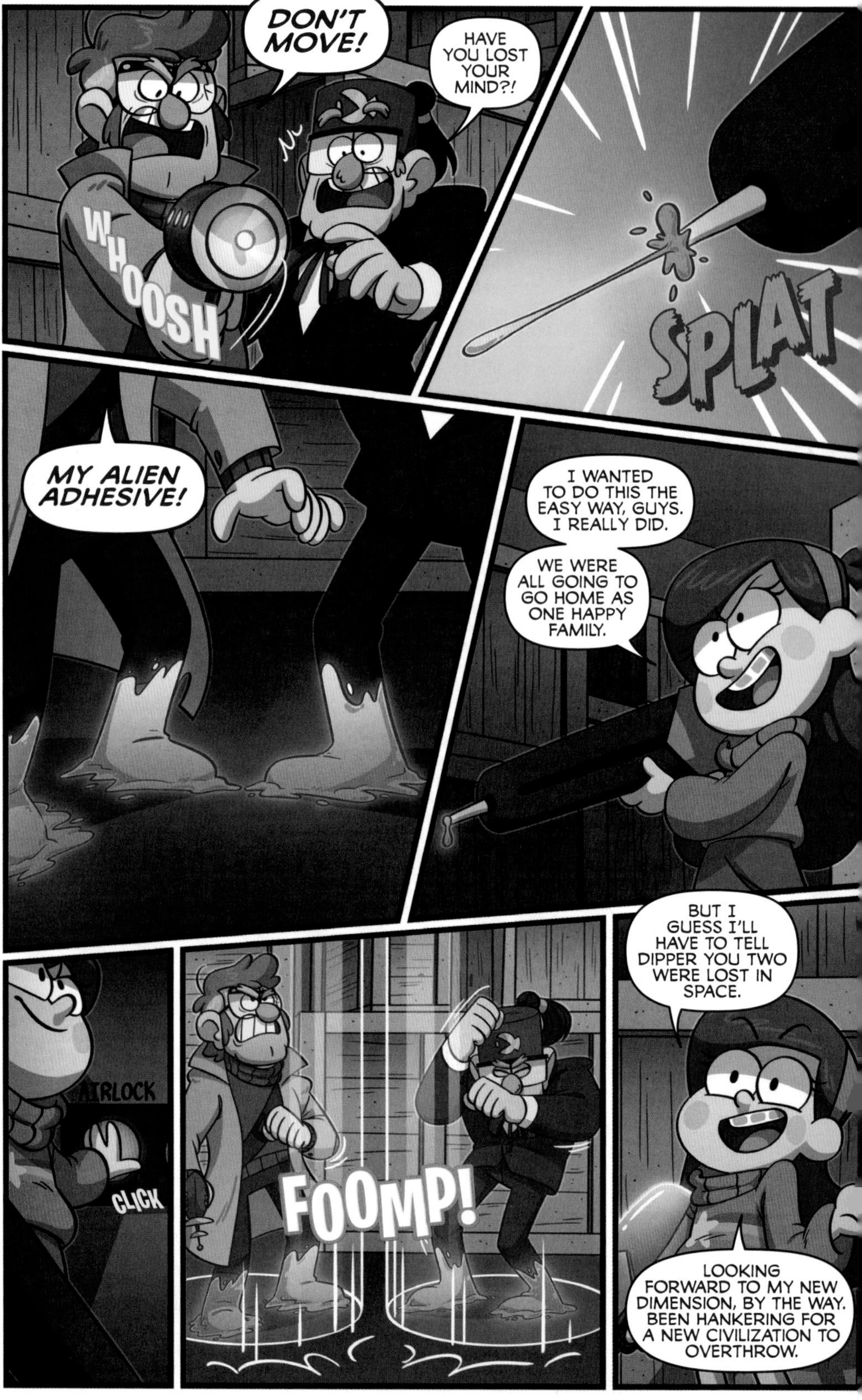

DON'T MOVE!
HAVE YOU LOST YOUR MIND?!
WHOOSH
SPLAT
MY ALIEN ADHESIVE!
I WANTED TO DO THIS THE EASY WAY, GUYS. I REALLY DID.
WE WERE ALL GOING TO GO HOME AS ONE HAPPY FAMILY.
AIRLOCK
CLICK
FOOMP!
BUT I GUESS I'LL HAVE TO TELL DIPPER YOU TWO WERE LOST IN SPACE.
LOOKING FORWARD TO MY NEW DIMENSION, BY THE WAY. BEEN HANKERING FOR A NEW CIVILIZATION TO OVERTHROW.

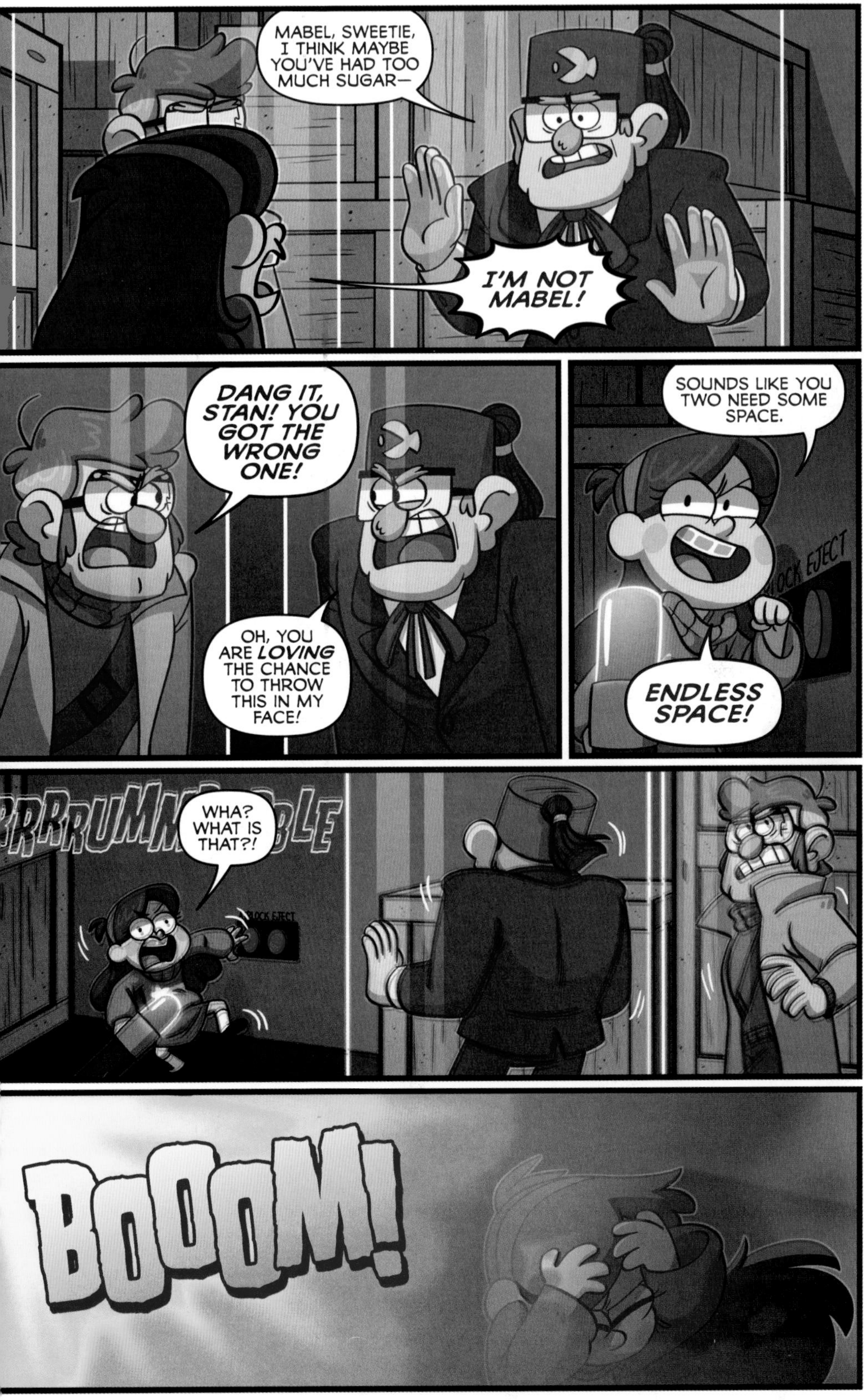

MABEL, SWEETIE, I THINK MAYBE YOU'VE HAD TOO MUCH SUGAR—
I'M NOT MABEL!
DANG IT, STAN! YOU GOT THE WRONG ONE!
OH, YOU ARE LOVING THE CHANCE TO THROW THIS IN MY FACE!
SOUNDS LIKE YOU TWO NEED SOME SPACE.
ENDLESS SPACE!
WHA? WHAT IS THAT?!
BOOOM!

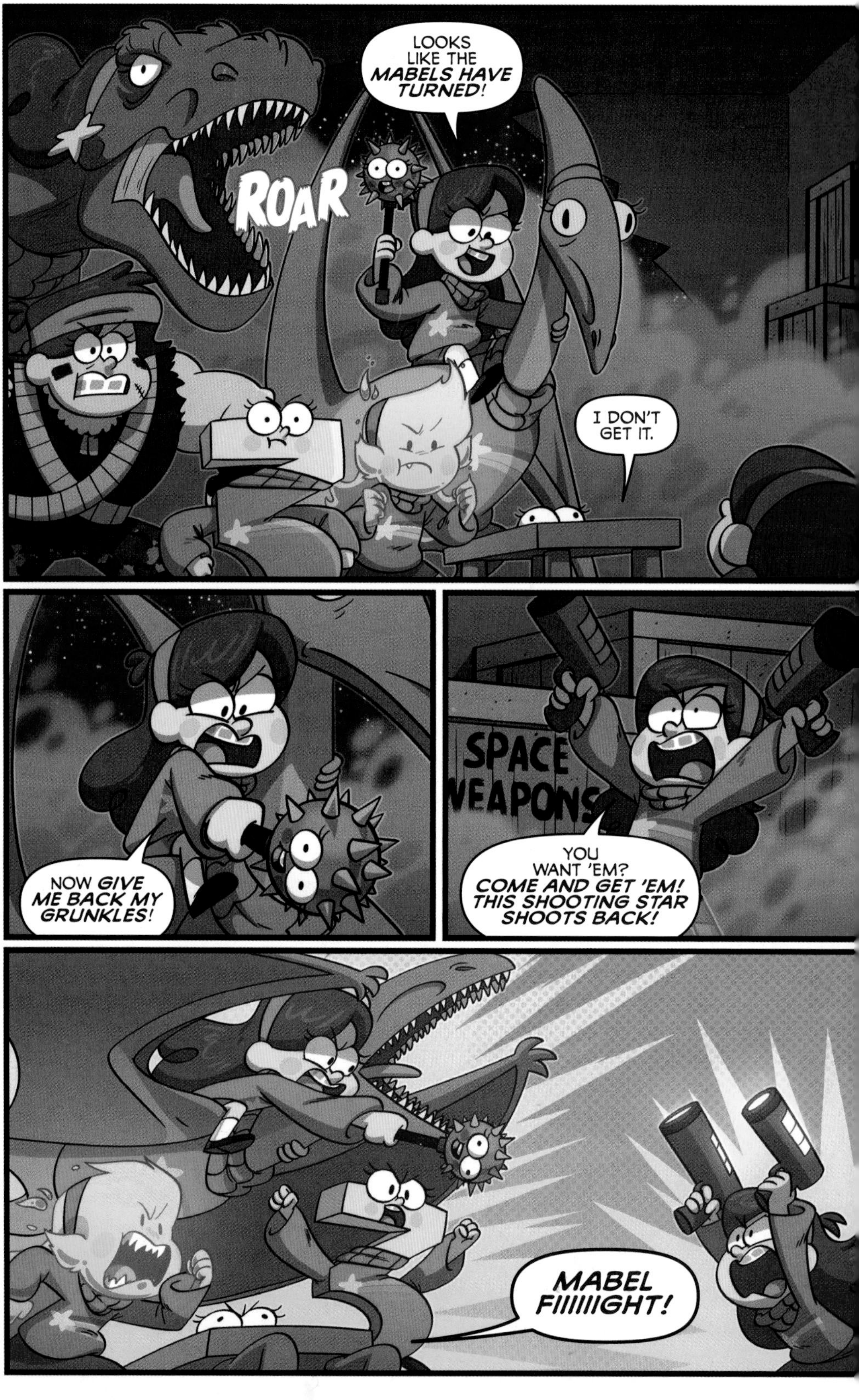
LOOKS LIKE THE MABELS HAVE TURNED!
ROAR
I DON'T GET IT.
NOW GIVE ME BACK MY GRUNKLES!
SPACE WEAPONS
YOU WANT 'EM? COME AND GET 'EM! THIS SHOOTING STAR SHOOTS BACK!
MABEL FIIIIIIGHT!

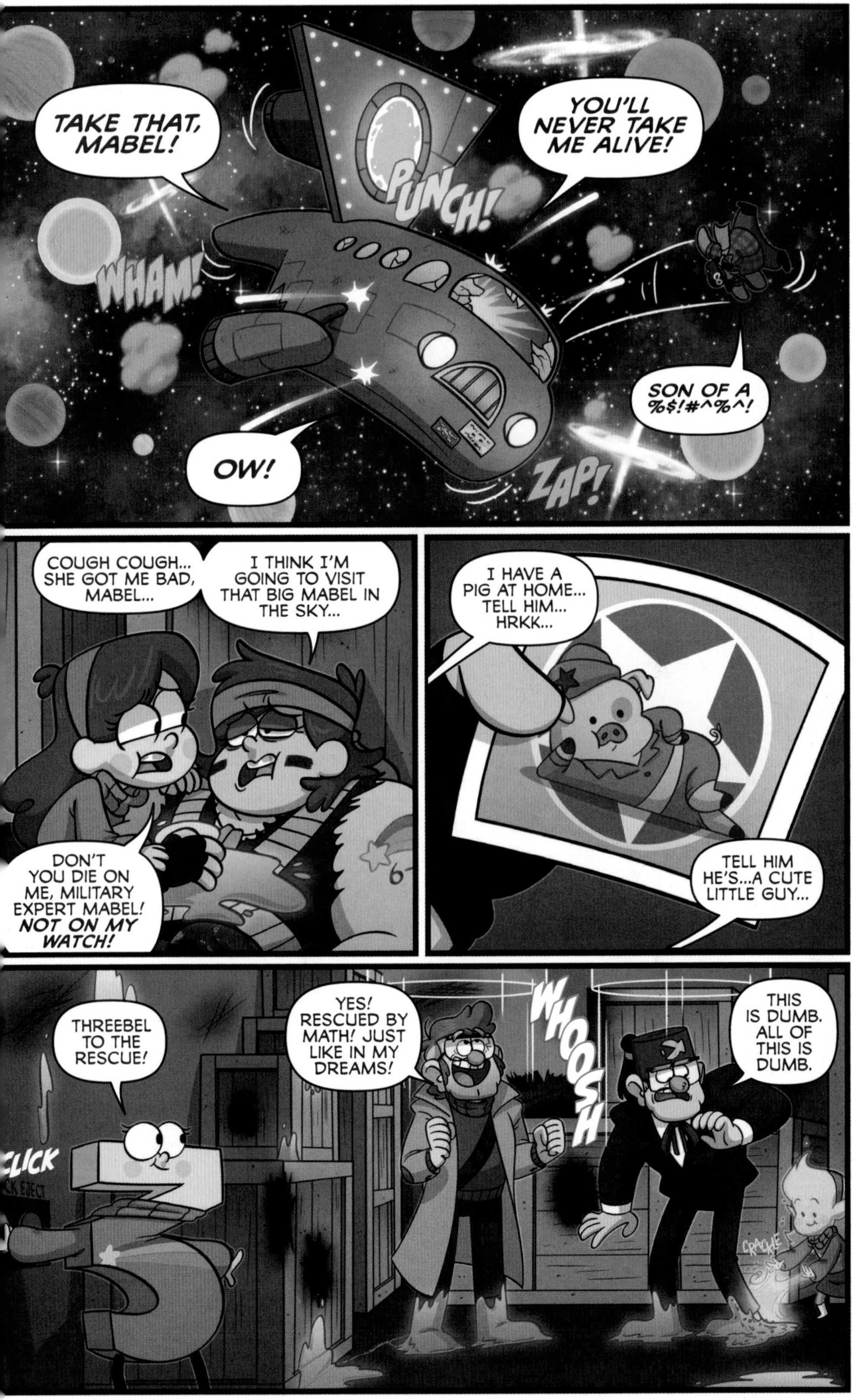
TAKE THAT, MABEL!
YOU'LL NEVER TAKE ME ALIVE!
PUNCH!
WHAM!
SON OF A %$!#^%^!
OW!
ZAP!
COUGH COUGH... SHE GOT ME BAD, MABEL...
I THINK I'M GOING TO VISIT THAT BIG MABEL IN THE SKY...
DON'T YOU DIE ON ME, MILITARY EXPERT MABEL! NOT ON MY WATCH!
I HAVE A PIG AT HOME... TELL HIM... HRKK...
TELL HIM HE'S...A CUTE LITTLE GUY...
THREEBEL TO THE RESCUE!
CLICK
YES! RESCUED BY MATH! JUST LIKE IN MY DREAMS!
WHOOSH
THIS IS DUMB. ALL OF THIS IS DUMB.
CRACKLE

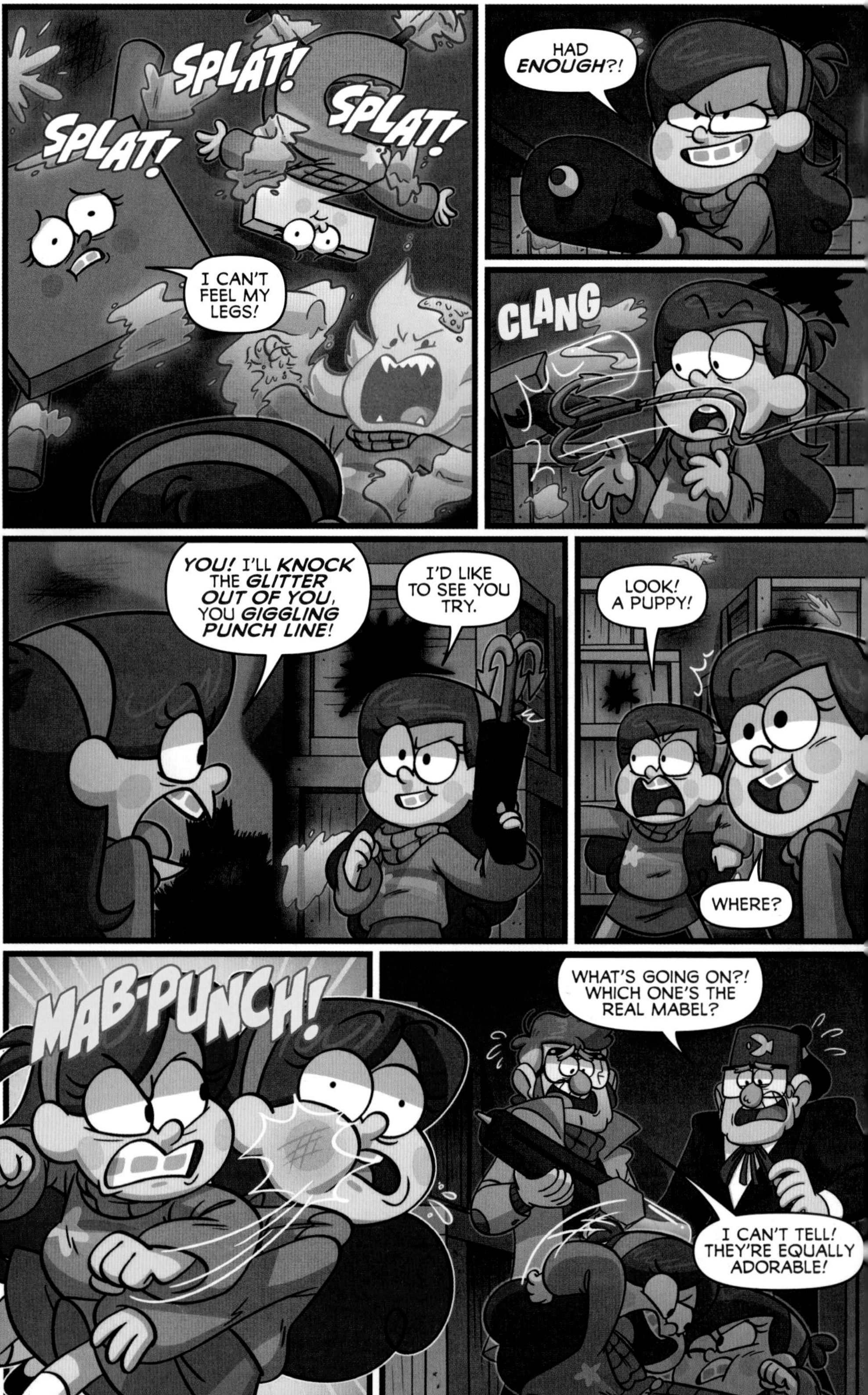
SPLAT!
SPLAT!
SPLAT!
I CAN'T FEEL MY LEGS!
HAD *ENOUGH*?!
CLANG
YOU! I'LL *KNOCK* THE *GLITTER OUT OF YOU*, YOU *GIGGLING PUNCH LINE*!
I'D LIKE TO SEE YOU TRY.
LOOK! A PUPPY!
WHERE?
MAB-PUNCH!
WHAT'S GOING ON?! WHICH ONE'S THE REAL MABEL?
I CAN'T TELL! THEY'RE EQUALLY ADORABLE!

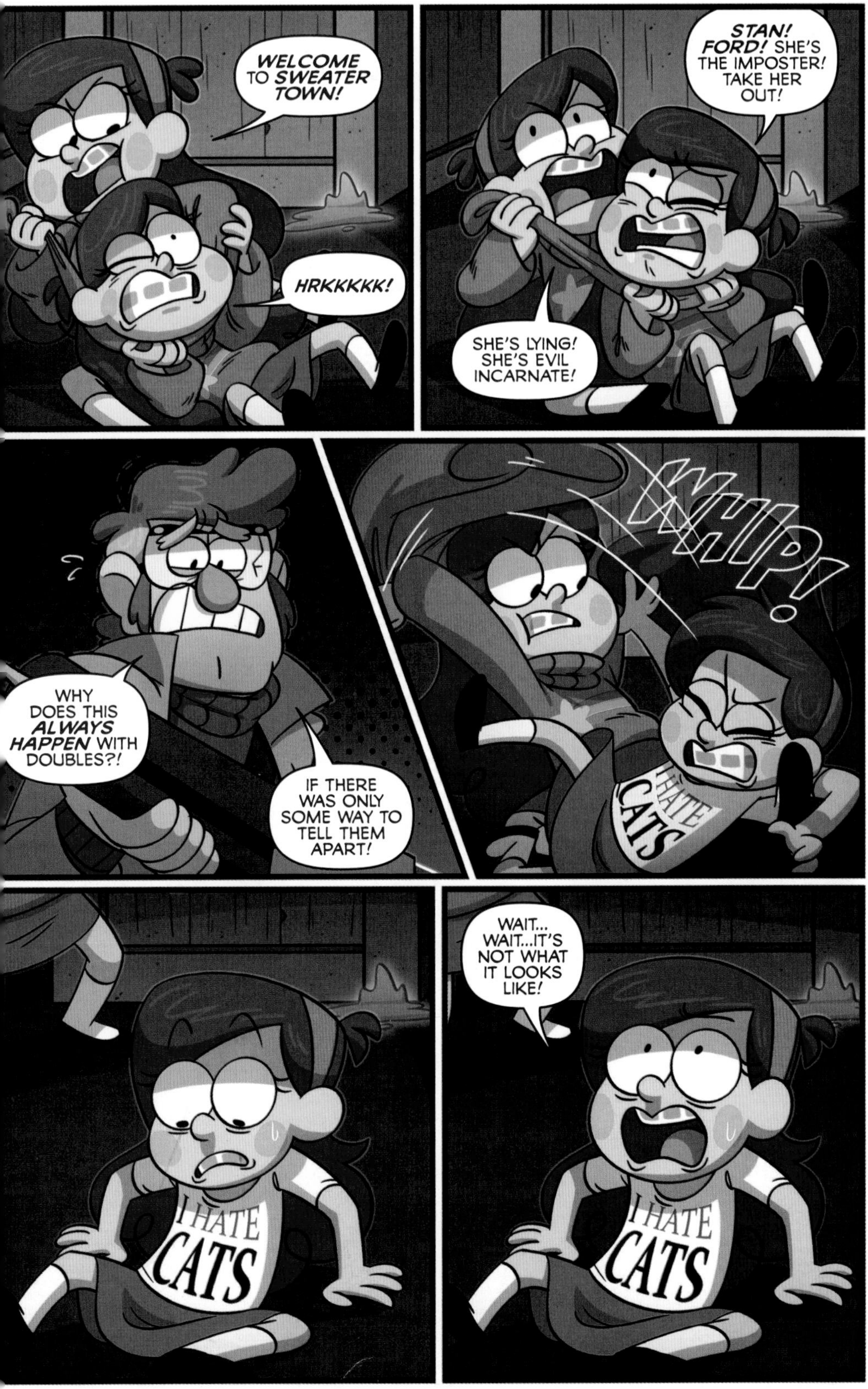
WELCOME TO SWEATER TOWN!
HRKKKKK!
STAN! FORD! SHE'S THE IMPOSTER! TAKE HER OUT!
SHE'S LYING! SHE'S EVIL INCARNATE!
WHY DOES THIS ALWAYS HAPPEN WITH DOUBLES?!
IF THERE WAS ONLY SOME WAY TO TELL THEM APART!
WHIP!
I HATE CATS
I HATE CATS
WAIT... WAIT...IT'S NOT WHAT IT LOOKS LIKE!
I HATE CATS

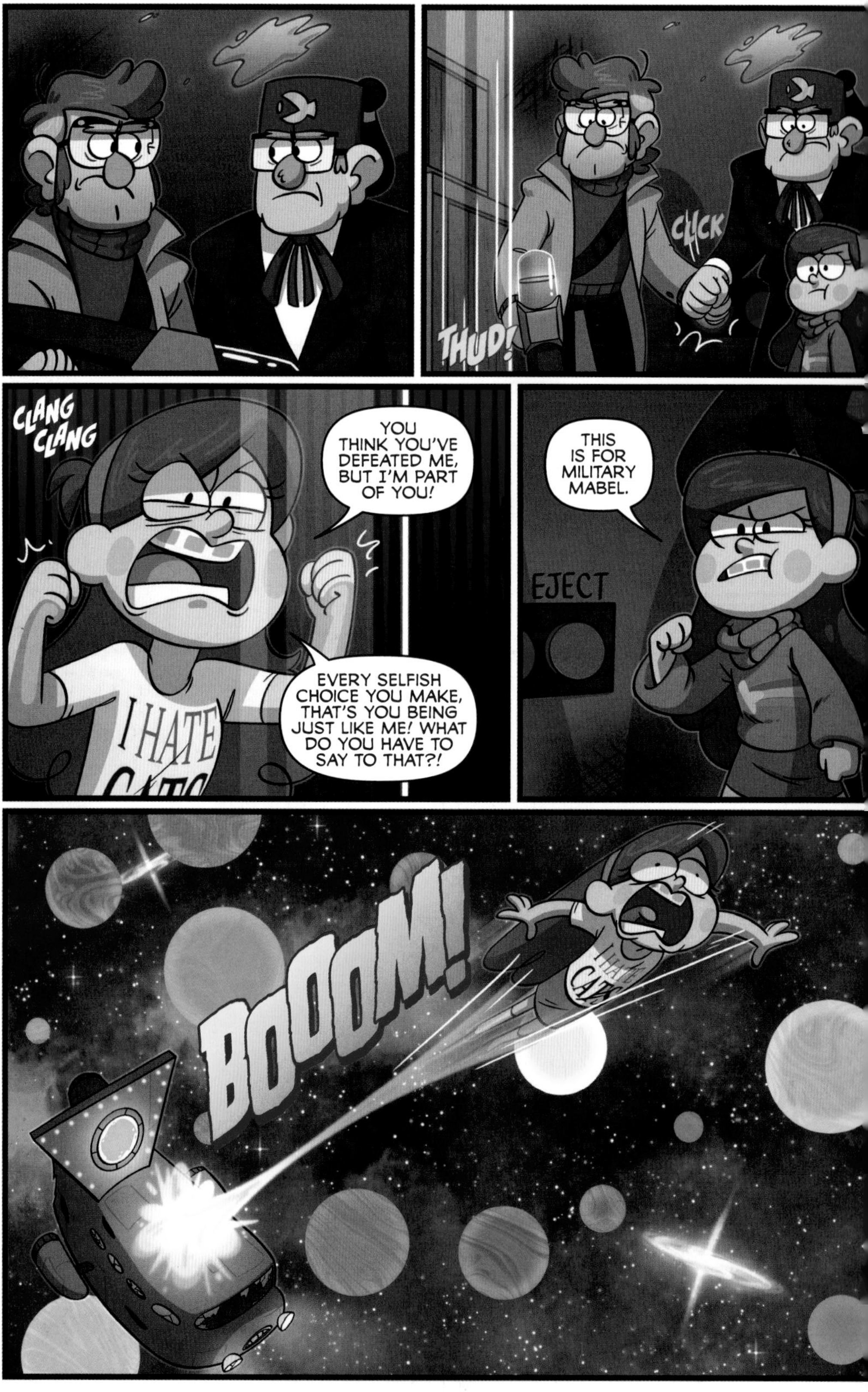
CLICK
THUD!
CLANG CLANG
YOU THINK YOU'VE DEFEATED ME, BUT I'M PART OF YOU!
EVERY SELFISH CHOICE YOU MAKE, THAT'S YOU BEING JUST LIKE ME! WHAT DO YOU HAVE TO SAY TO THAT?!
I HATE
THIS IS FOR MILITARY MABEL.
EJECT
BOOOM!

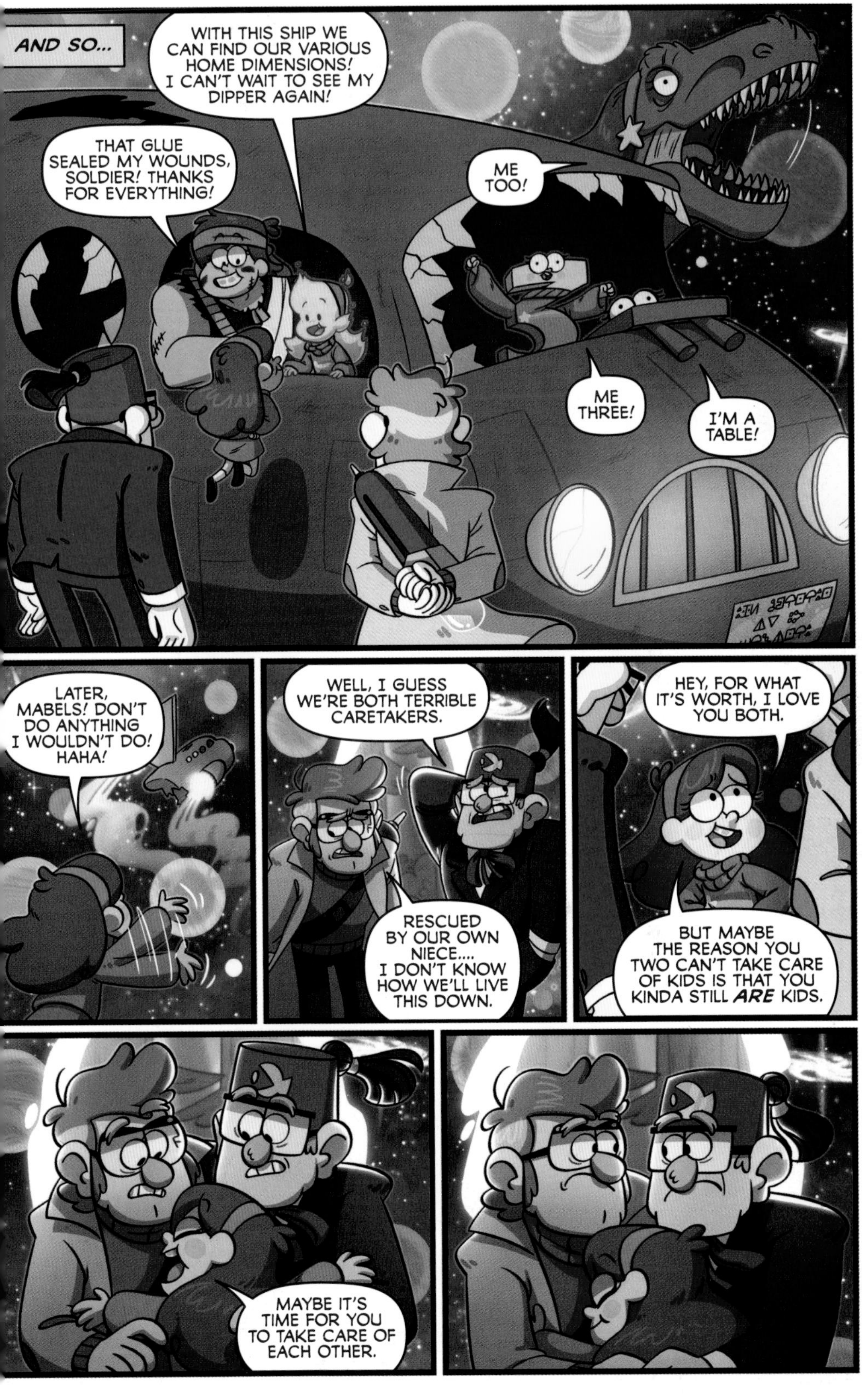
AND SO...
WITH THIS SHIP WE CAN FIND OUR VARIOUS HOME DIMENSIONS! I CAN'T WAIT TO SEE MY DIPPER AGAIN!
THAT GLUE SEALED MY WOUNDS, SOLDIER! THANKS FOR EVERYTHING!
ME TOO!
ME THREE!
I'M A TABLE!
LATER, MABELS! DON'T DO ANYTHING I WOULDN'T DO! HAHA!
WELL, I GUESS WE'RE BOTH TERRIBLE CARETAKERS.
RESCUED BY OUR OWN NIECE.... I DON'T KNOW HOW WE'LL LIVE THIS DOWN.
HEY, FOR WHAT IT'S WORTH, I LOVE YOU BOTH.
BUT MAYBE THE REASON YOU TWO CAN'T TAKE CARE OF KIDS IS THAT YOU KINDA STILL ARE KIDS.
MAYBE IT'S TIME FOR YOU TO TAKE CARE OF EACH OTHER.

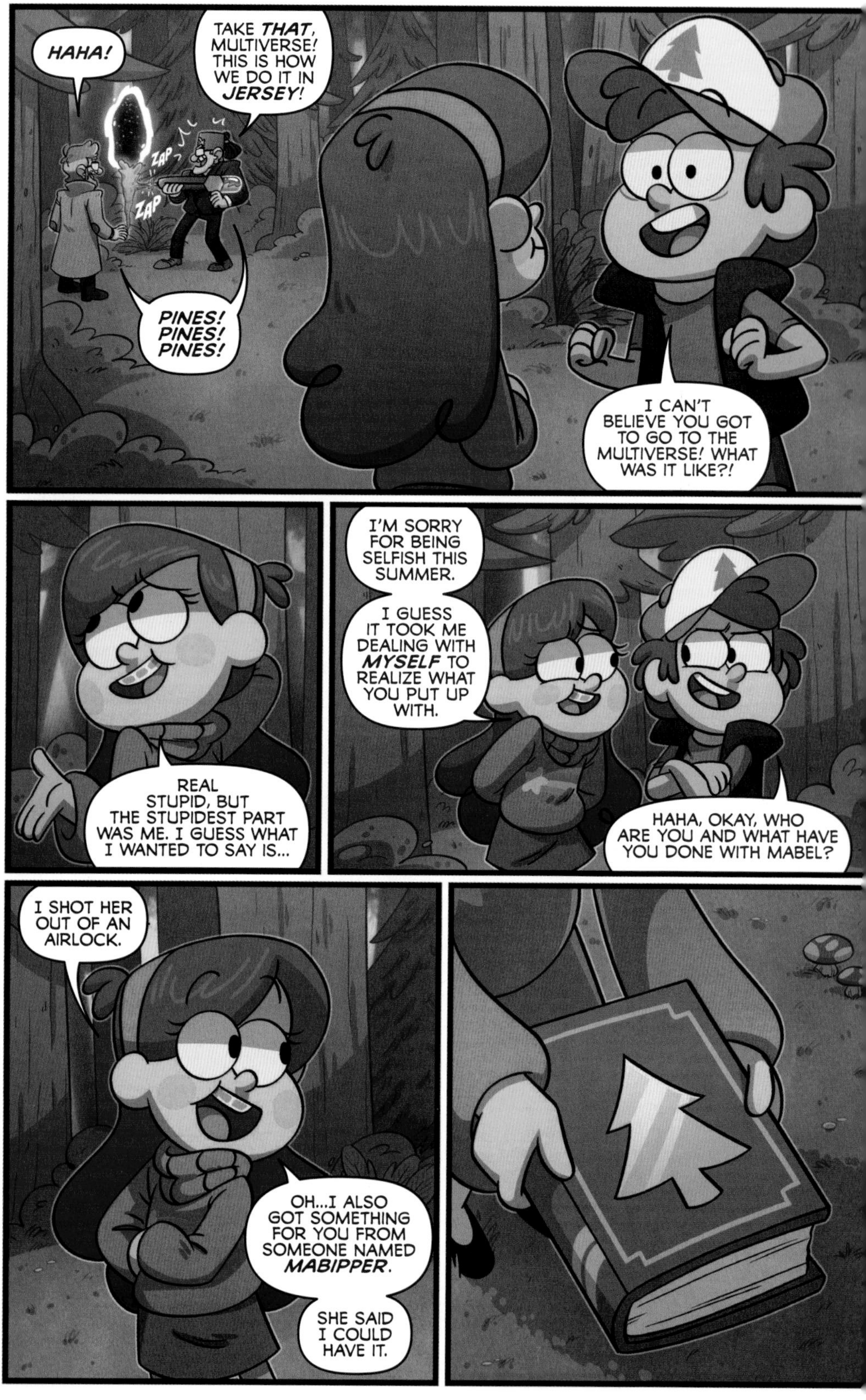
HAHA!
TAKE *THAT*, MULTIVERSE! THIS IS HOW WE DO IT IN *JERSEY*!
ZAP
ZAP
ZAP
PINES! PINES! PINES!
I CAN'T BELIEVE YOU GOT TO GO TO THE MULTIVERSE! WHAT WAS IT LIKE?!
REAL STUPID, BUT THE STUPIDEST PART WAS ME. I GUESS WHAT I WANTED TO SAY IS...
I'M SORRY FOR BEING SELFISH THIS SUMMER.
I GUESS IT TOOK ME DEALING WITH *MYSELF* TO REALIZE WHAT YOU PUT UP WITH.
HAHA, OKAY, WHO ARE YOU AND WHAT HAVE YOU DONE WITH MABEL?
I SHOT HER OUT OF AN AIRLOCK.
OH...I ALSO GOT SOMETHING FOR YOU FROM SOMEONE NAMED *MABIPPER*.
SHE SAID I COULD HAVE IT.

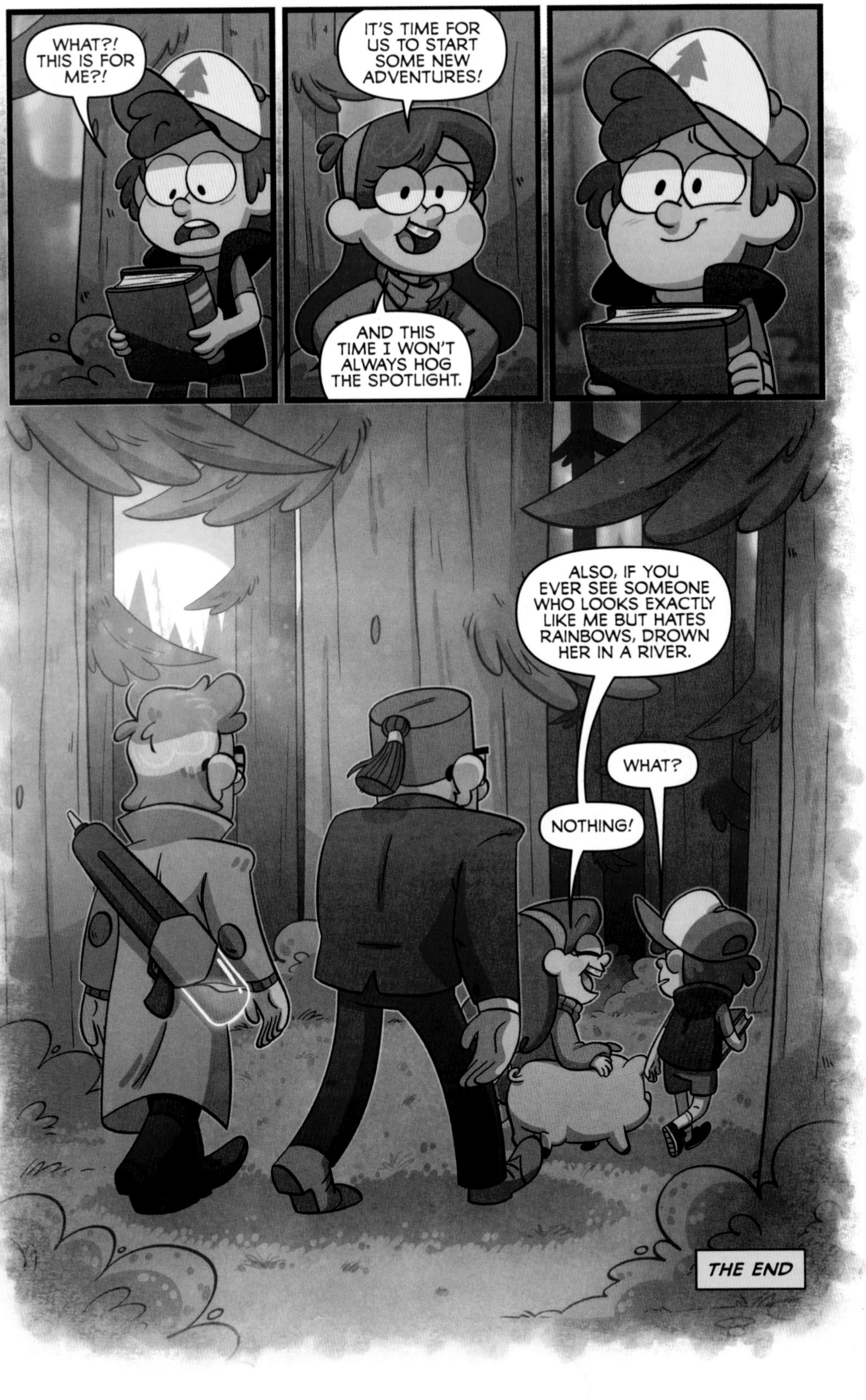
WHAT?! THIS IS FOR ME?!
IT'S TIME FOR US TO START SOME NEW ADVENTURES!
AND THIS TIME I WON'T ALWAYS HOG THE SPOTLIGHT.
ALSO, IF YOU EVER SEE SOMEONE WHO LOOKS EXACTLY LIKE ME BUT HATES RAINBOWS, DROWN HER IN A RIVER.
WHAT?
NOTHING!
THE END

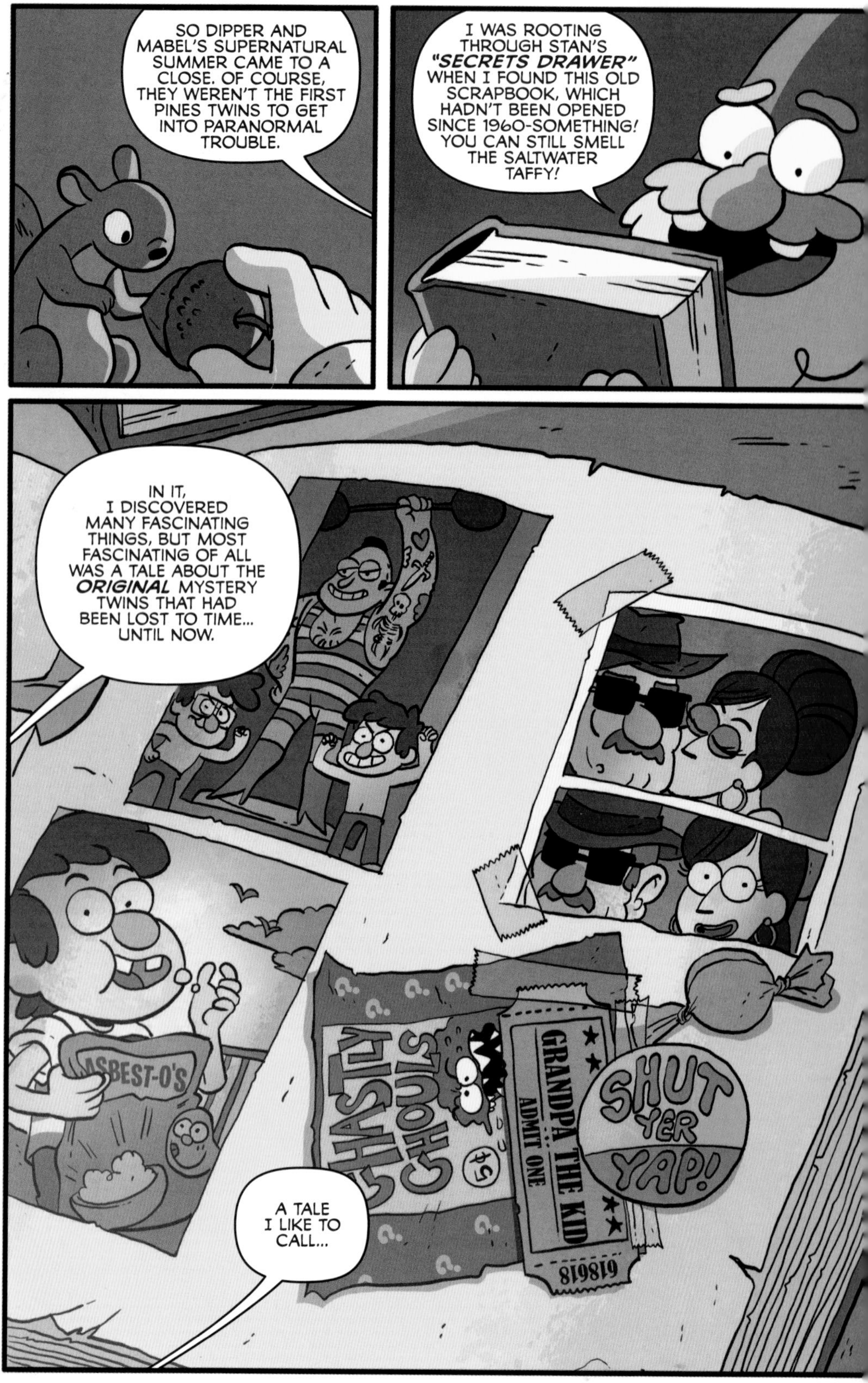
SO DIPPER AND MABEL'S SUPERNATURAL SUMMER CAME TO A CLOSE. OF COURSE, THEY WEREN'T THE FIRST PINES TWINS TO GET INTO PARANORMAL TROUBLE.
I WAS ROOTING THROUGH STAN'S *"SECRETS DRAWER"* WHEN I FOUND THIS OLD SCRAPBOOK, WHICH HADN'T BEEN OPENED SINCE 1960-SOMETHING! YOU CAN STILL SMELL THE SALTWATER TAFFY!
IN IT, I DISCOVERED MANY FASCINATING THINGS, BUT MOST FASCINATING OF ALL WAS A TALE ABOUT THE *ORIGINAL* MYSTERY TWINS THAT HAD BEEN LOST TO TIME... UNTIL NOW.
ASBEST-O'S
GRANDPA THE KID
ADMIT ONE
SHUT YER YAP!
A TALE I LIKE TO CALL...

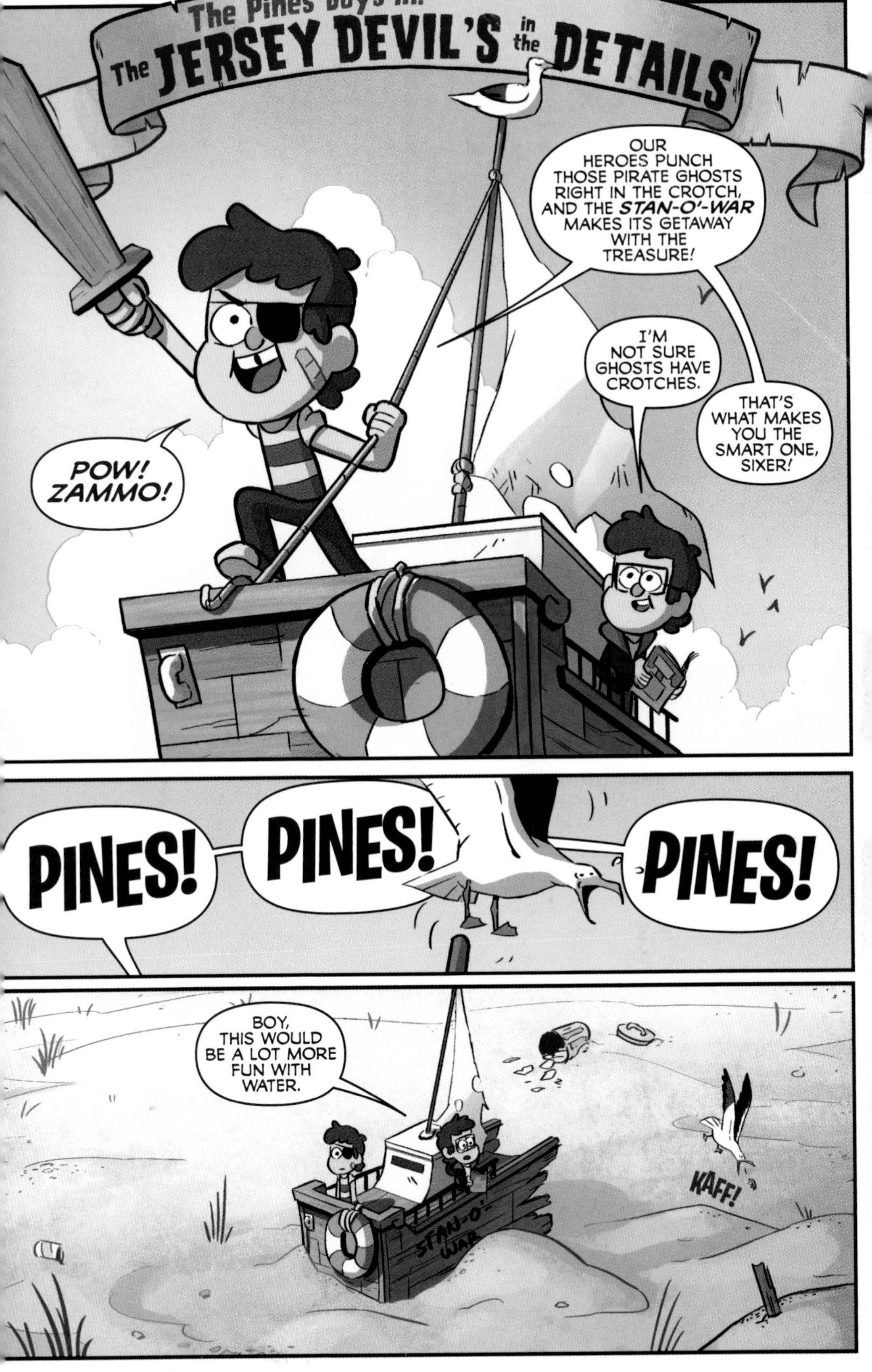
The Pines Boys in:
The JERSEY DEVIL'S in the DETAILS
OUR HEROES PUNCH THOSE PIRATE GHOSTS RIGHT IN THE CROTCH, AND THE STAN-O'-WAR MAKES ITS GETAWAY WITH THE TREASURE!
POW! ZAMMO!
I'M NOT SURE GHOSTS HAVE CROTCHES.
THAT'S WHAT MAKES YOU THE SMART ONE, SIXER!
PINES!
PINES!
PINES!
BOY, THIS WOULD BE A LOT MORE FUN WITH WATER.
STAN-O'-WAR
KAFF!

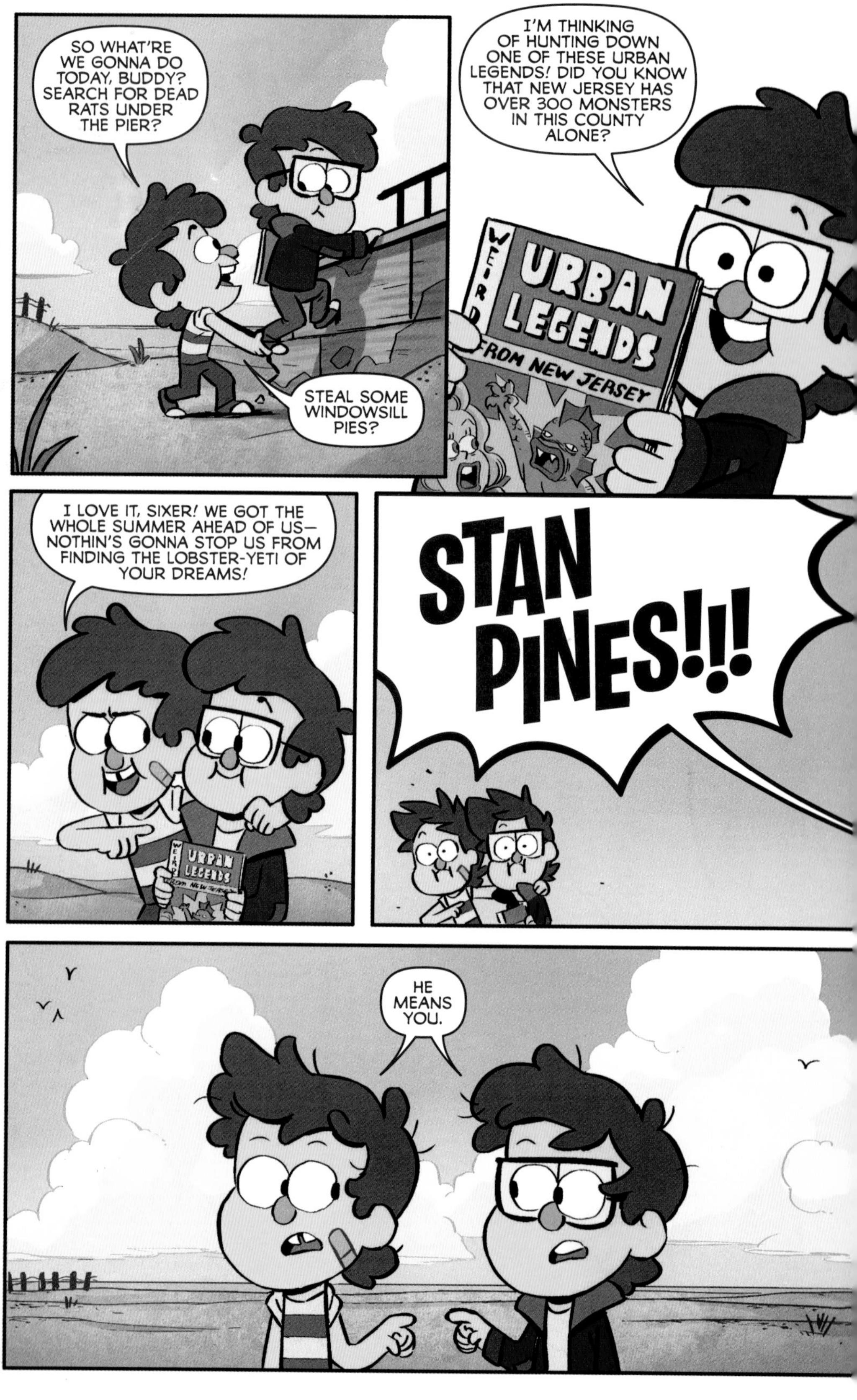
SO WHAT'RE WE GONNA DO TODAY, BUDDY? SEARCH FOR DEAD RATS UNDER THE PIER?
STEAL SOME WINDOWSILL PIES?
I'M THINKING OF HUNTING DOWN ONE OF THESE URBAN LEGENDS! DID YOU KNOW THAT NEW JERSEY HAS OVER 300 MONSTERS IN THIS COUNTY ALONE?
WEIRD
URBAN LEGENDS
FROM NEW JERSEY
I LOVE IT, SIXER! WE GOT THE WHOLE SUMMER AHEAD OF US—NOTHIN'S GONNA STOP US FROM FINDING THE LOBSTER-YETI OF YOUR DREAMS!
URBAN LEGENDS
STAN PINES!!!
HE MEANS YOU.

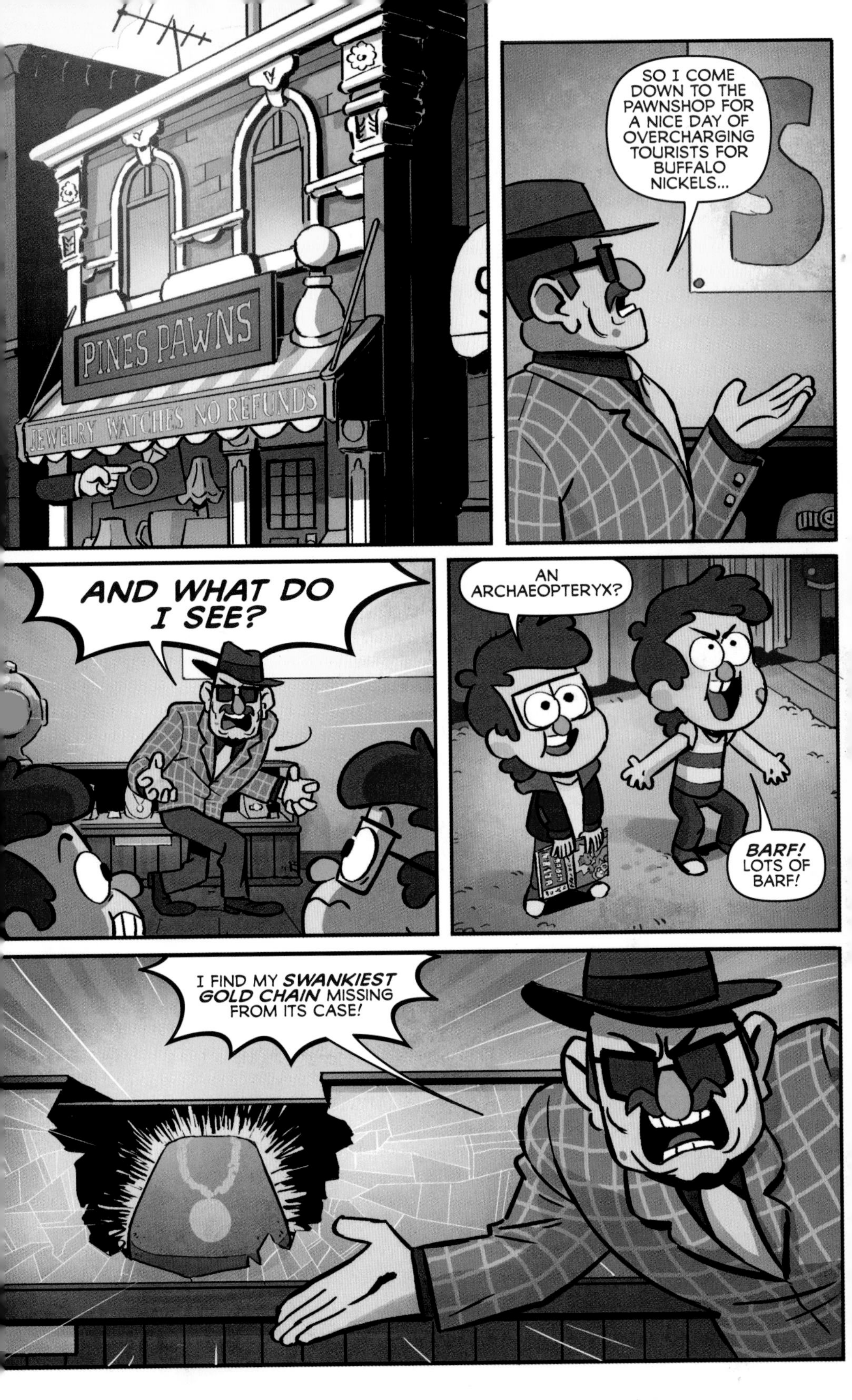
PINES PAWNS
JEWELRY WATCHES NO REFUNDS
SO I COME DOWN TO THE PAWNSHOP FOR A NICE DAY OF OVERCHARGING TOURISTS FOR BUFFALO NICKELS...
AND WHAT DO I SEE?
AN ARCHAEOPTERYX?
BARF! LOTS OF BARF!
I FIND MY SWANKIEST GOLD CHAIN MISSING FROM ITS CASE!

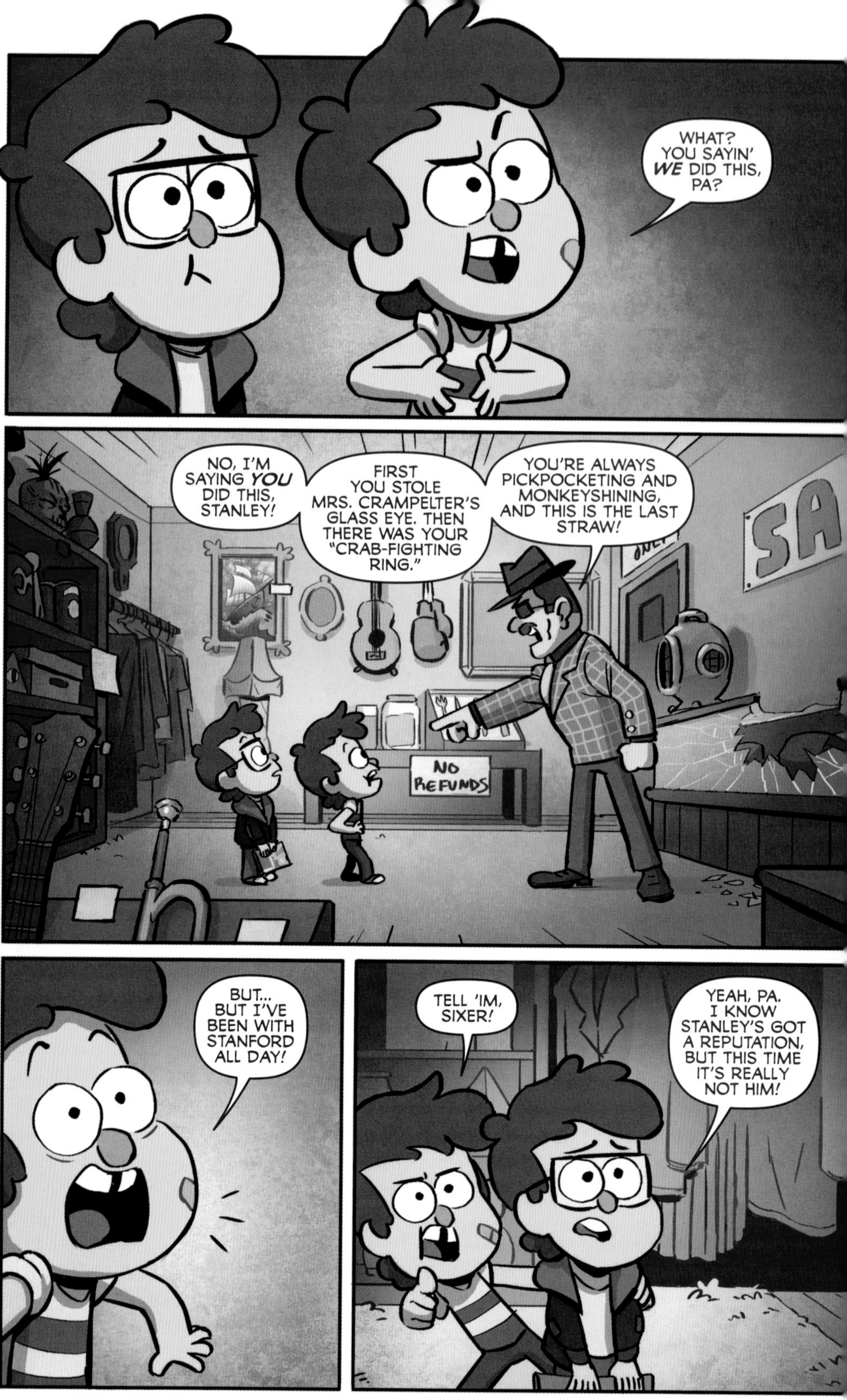
WHAT? YOU SAYIN' *WE* DID THIS, PA?
NO, I'M SAYING *YOU* DID THIS, STANLEY!
FIRST YOU STOLE MRS. CRAMPELTER'S GLASS EYE. THEN THERE WAS YOUR "CRAB-FIGHTING RING."
YOU'RE ALWAYS PICKPOCKETING AND MONKEYSHINING, AND THIS IS THE LAST STRAW!
NO REFUNDS
BUT... BUT I'VE BEEN WITH STANFORD ALL DAY!
TELL 'IM, SIXER!
YEAH, PA. I KNOW STANLEY'S GOT A REPUTATION, BUT THIS TIME IT'S REALLY NOT HIM!

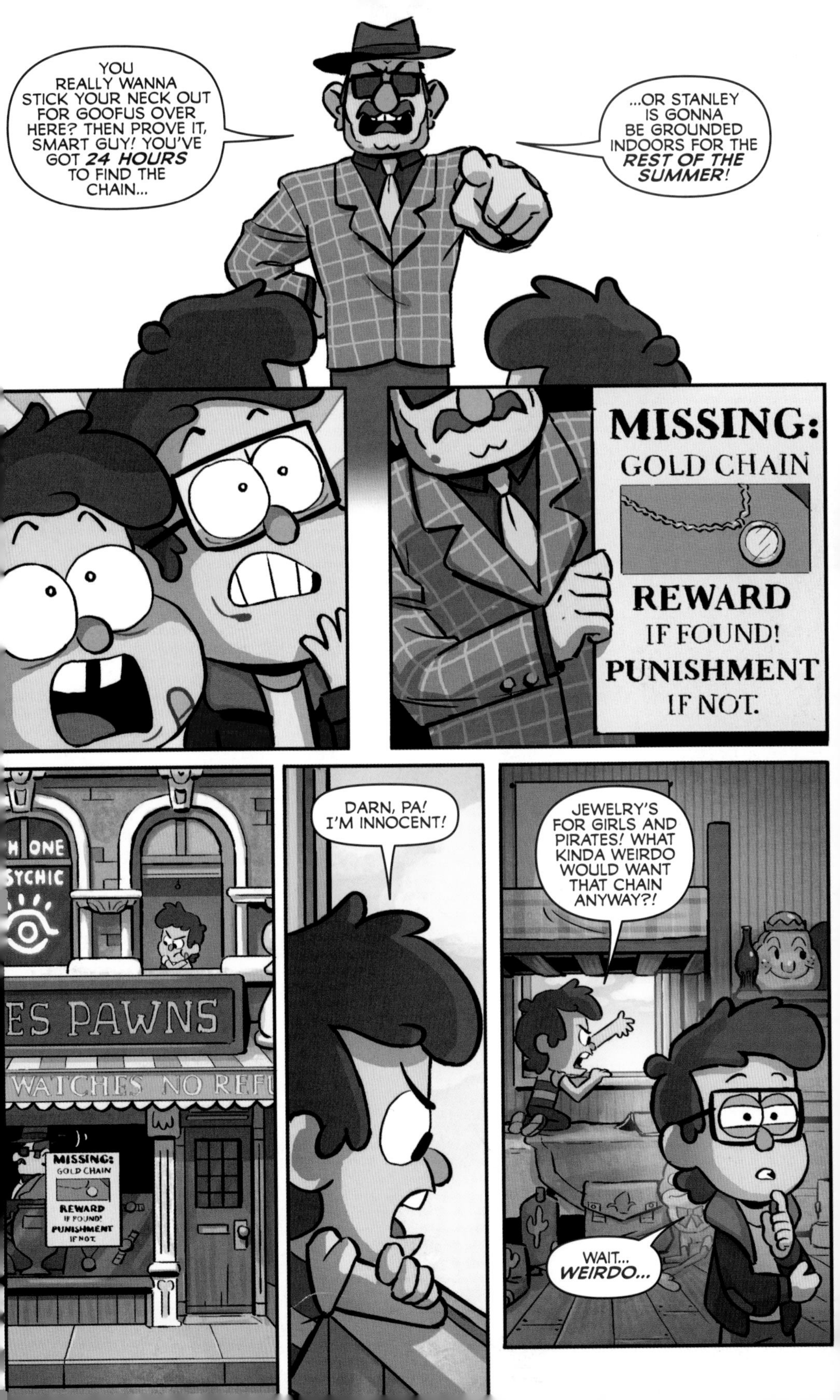
YOU REALLY WANNA STICK YOUR NECK OUT FOR GOOFUS OVER HERE? THEN PROVE IT, SMART GUY! YOU'VE GOT *24 HOURS* TO FIND THE CHAIN...
...OR STANLEY IS GONNA BE GROUNDED INDOORS FOR THE *REST OF THE SUMMER*!
MISSING: GOLD CHAIN
REWARD IF FOUND! PUNISHMENT IF NOT.
H ONE
SYCHIC
ES PAWNS
WATCHES NO REFU
MISSING: GOLD CHAIN REWARD IF FOUND! PUNISHMENT IF NOT.
DARN, PA! I'M INNOCENT!
JEWELRY'S FOR GIRLS AND PIRATES! WHAT KINDA WEIRDO WOULD WANT THAT CHAIN ANYWAY?!
WAIT... *WEIRDO...*

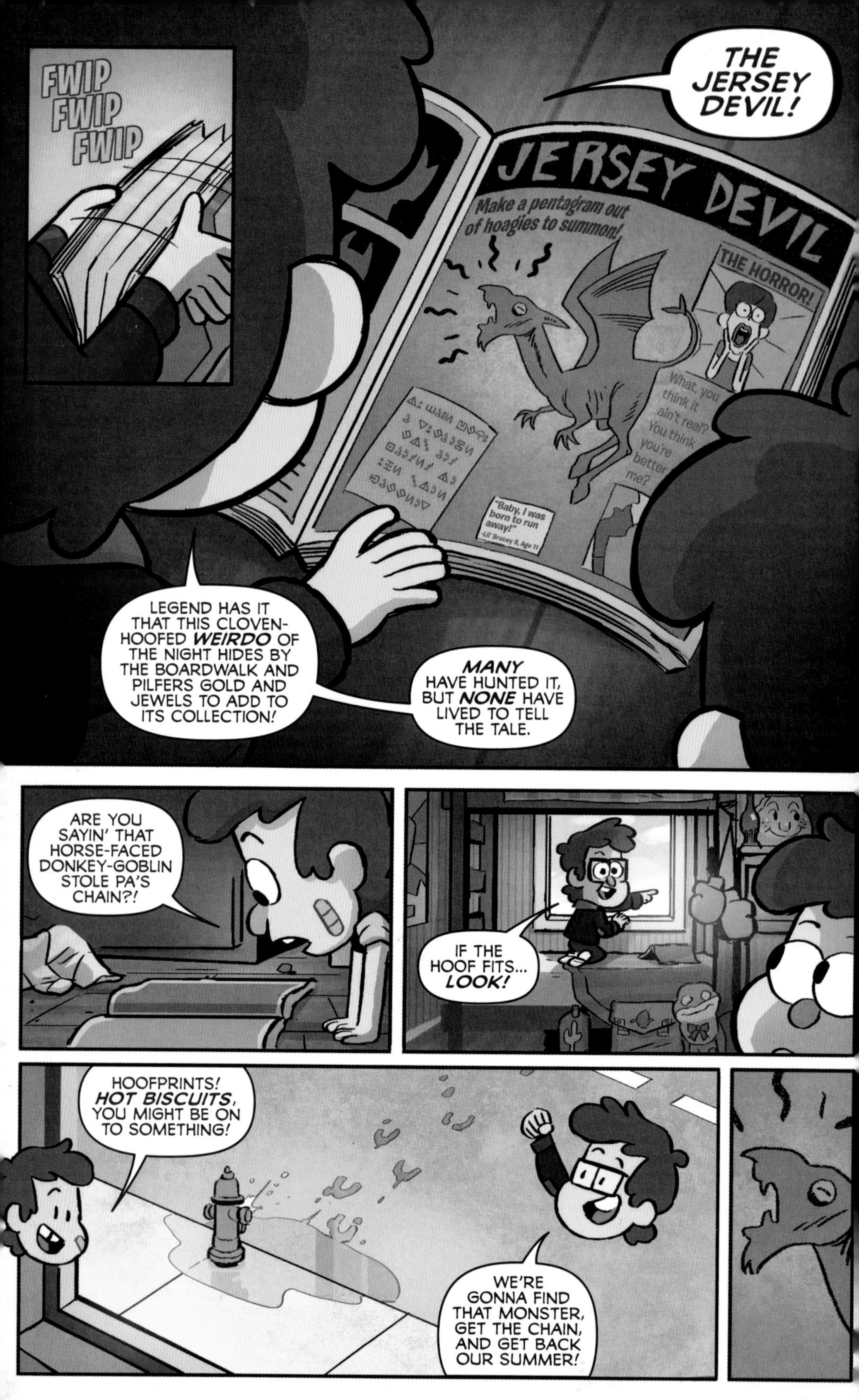
FWIP FWIP FWIP
THE JERSEY DEVIL!
JERSEY DEVIL
Make a pentagram out of hoagies to summon!
THE HORROR!
What, you think it ain't real? You think you're better me?
"Baby, I was born to run away!"
-Lil' Brucey S, Age 11
LEGEND HAS IT THAT THIS CLOVEN-HOOFED WEIRDO OF THE NIGHT HIDES BY THE BOARDWALK AND PILFERS GOLD AND JEWELS TO ADD TO ITS COLLECTION!
MANY HAVE HUNTED IT, BUT NONE HAVE LIVED TO TELL THE TALE.
ARE YOU SAYIN' THAT HORSE-FACED DONKEY-GOBLIN STOLE PA'S CHAIN?!
IF THE HOOF FITS... LOOK!
HOOFPRINTS! HOT BISCUITS, YOU MIGHT BE ON TO SOMETHING!
WE'RE GONNA FIND THAT MONSTER, GET THE CHAIN, AND GET BACK OUR SUMMER!

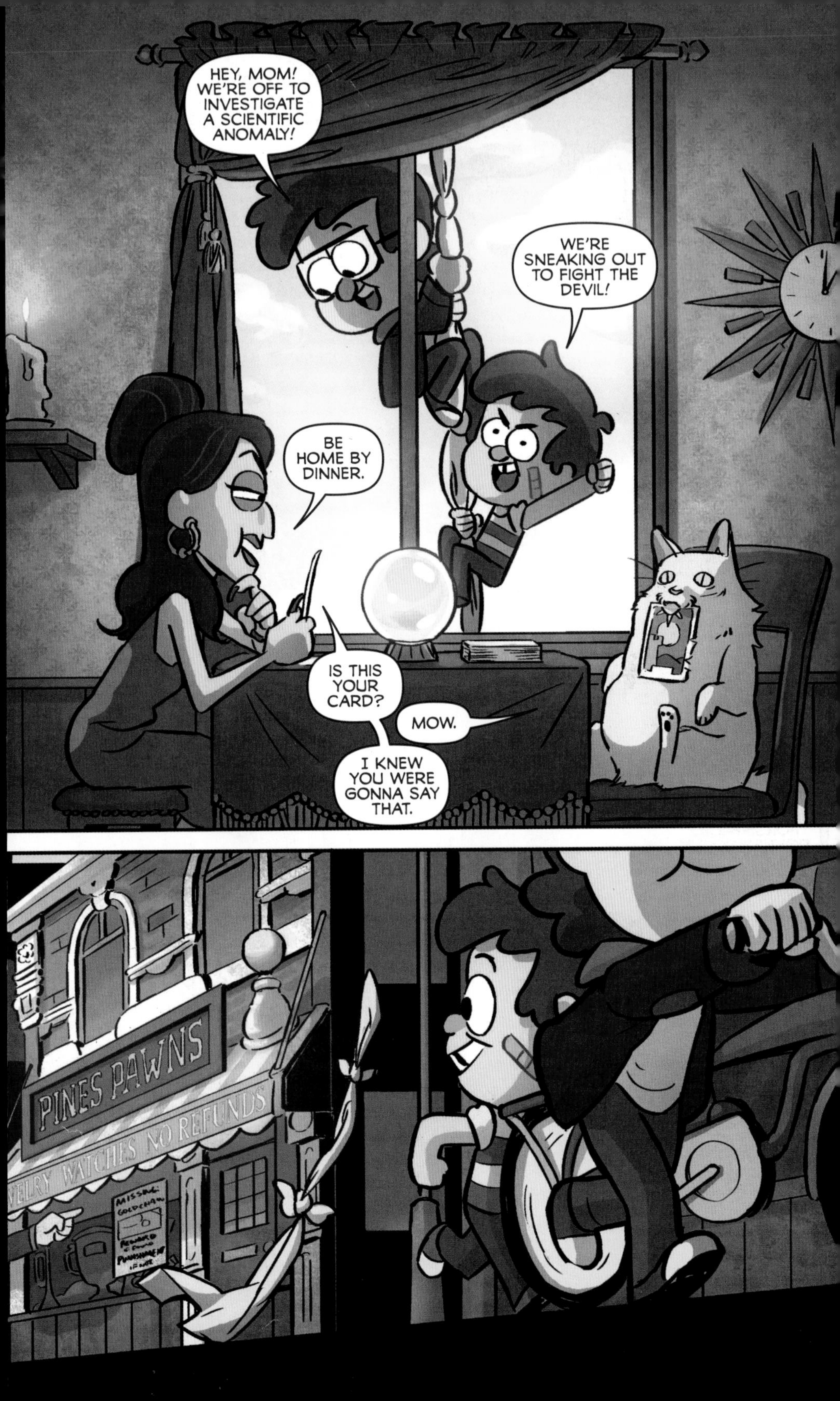
HEY, MOM! WE'RE OFF TO INVESTIGATE A SCIENTIFIC ANOMALY!
WE'RE SNEAKING OUT TO FIGHT THE DEVIL!
BE HOME BY DINNER.
IS THIS YOUR CARD?
MOW.
I KNEW YOU WERE GONNA SAY THAT.
PINES PAWNS
NO REFUNDS
WATCHES

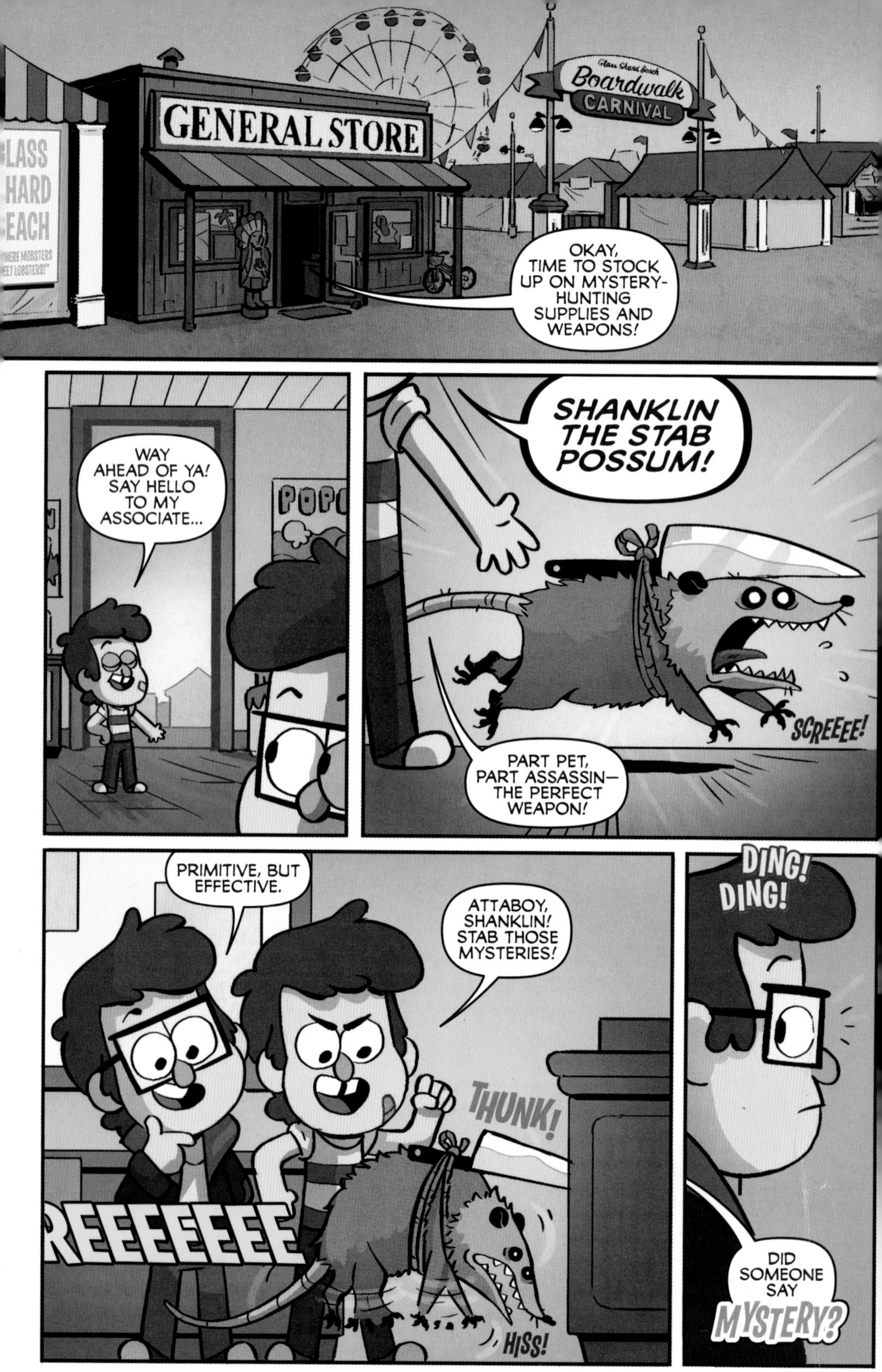
GENERAL STORE
Glass Shard Beach Boardwalk CARNIVAL
OKAY, TIME TO STOCK UP ON MYSTERY-HUNTING SUPPLIES AND WEAPONS!
WAY AHEAD OF YA! SAY HELLO TO MY ASSOCIATE...
SHANKLIN THE STAB POSSUM!
SCREEEE!
PART PET, PART ASSASSIN—THE PERFECT WEAPON!
PRIMITIVE, BUT EFFECTIVE.
ATTABOY, SHANKLIN! STAB THOSE MYSTERIES!
THUNK!
REEEEEEEE
HISS!
DING! DING!
DID SOMEONE SAY MYSTERY?

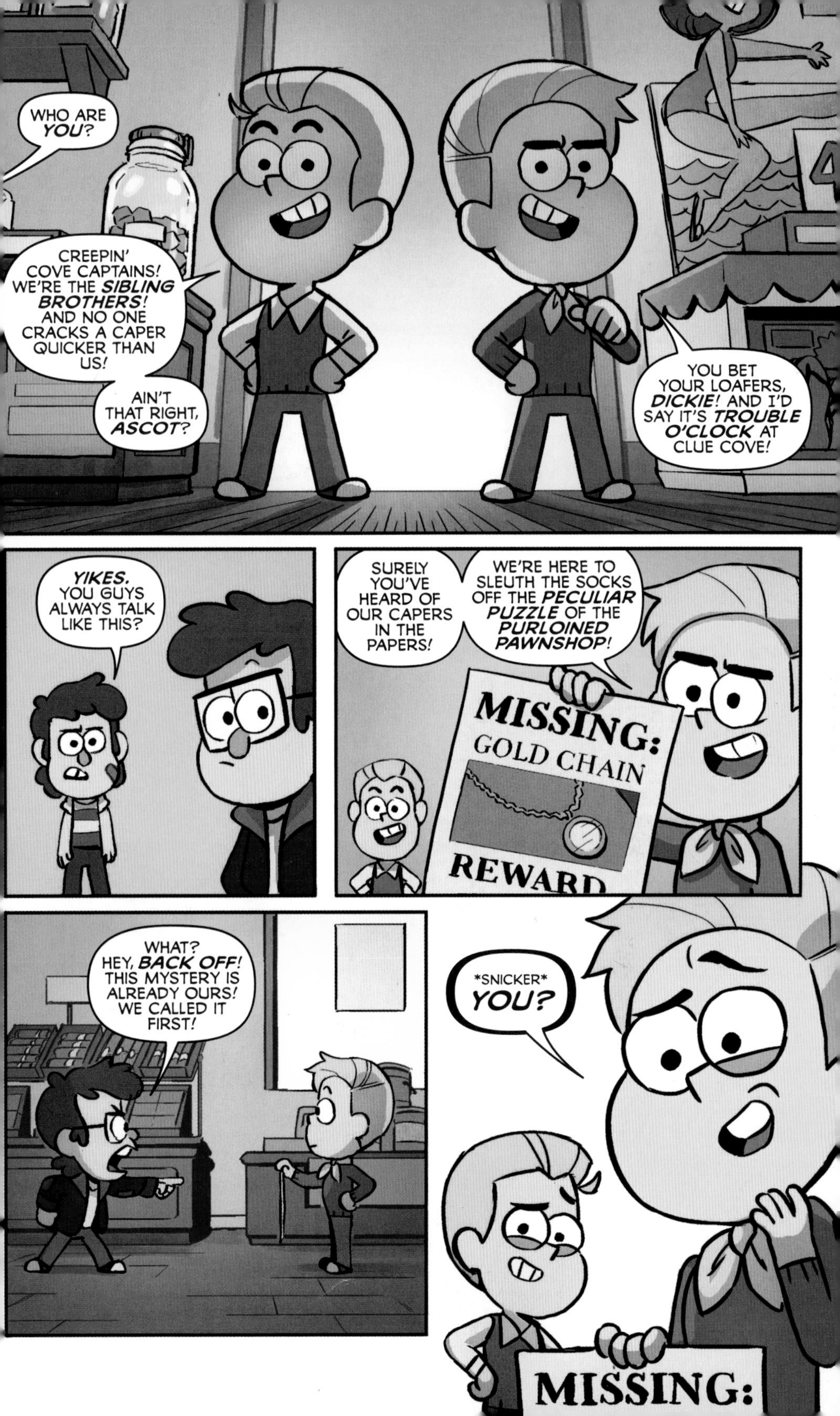
WHO ARE YOU?
CREEPIN' COVE CAPTAINS! WE'RE THE SIBLING BROTHERS! AND NO ONE CRACKS A CAPER QUICKER THAN US!
AIN'T THAT RIGHT, ASCOT?
YOU BET YOUR LOAFERS, DICKIE! AND I'D SAY IT'S TROUBLE O'CLOCK AT CLUE COVE!
YIKES. YOU GUYS ALWAYS TALK LIKE THIS?
SURELY YOU'VE HEARD OF OUR CAPERS IN THE PAPERS!
WE'RE HERE TO SLEUTH THE SOCKS OFF THE PECULIAR PUZZLE OF THE PURLOINED PAWNSHOP!
MISSING: GOLD CHAIN
REWARD
WHAT? HEY, BACK OFF! THIS MYSTERY IS ALREADY OURS! WE CALLED IT FIRST!
SNICKER YOU?
MISSING:

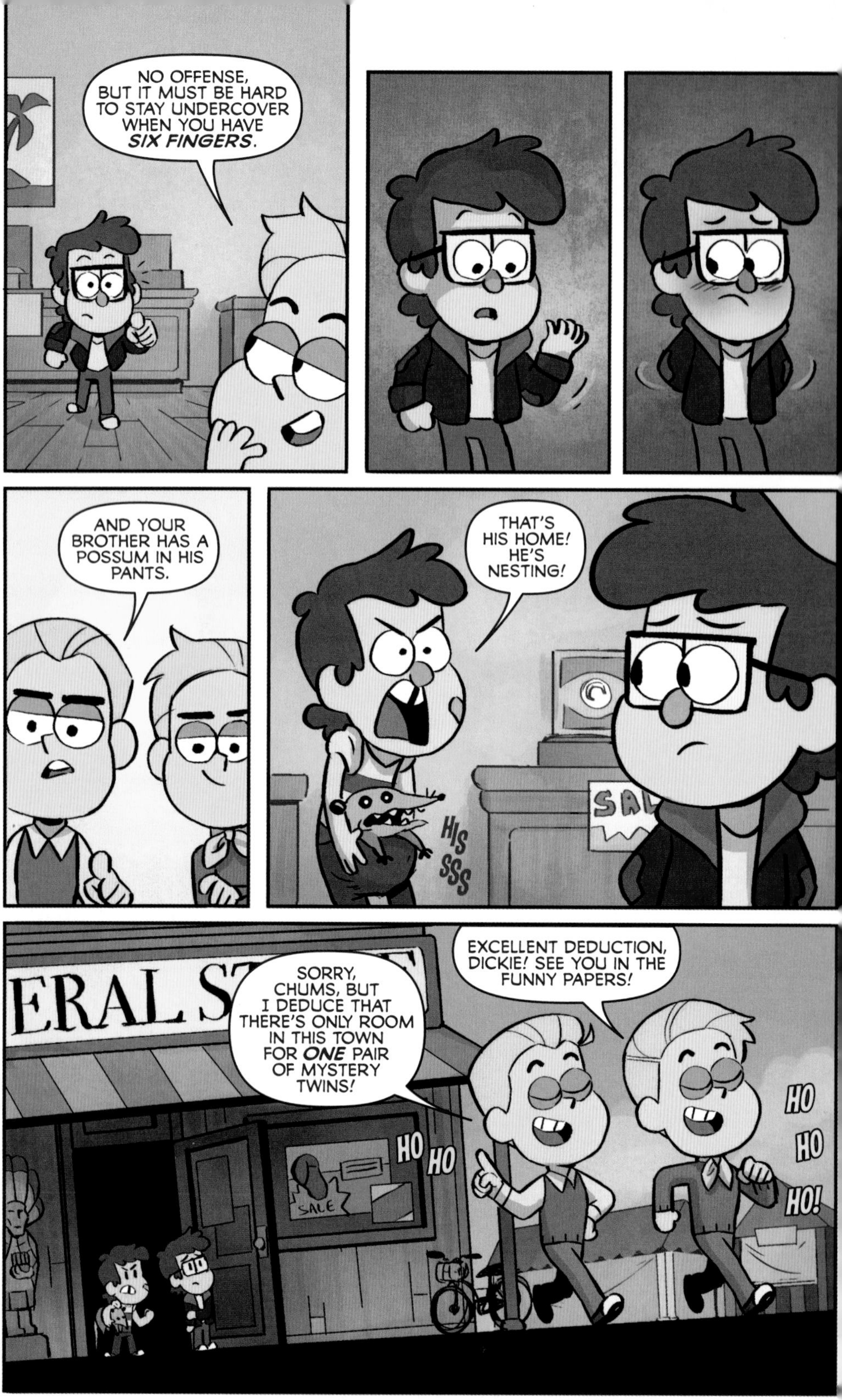
NO OFFENSE, BUT IT MUST BE HARD TO STAY UNDERCOVER WHEN YOU HAVE *SIX FINGERS*.
AND YOUR BROTHER HAS A POSSUM IN HIS PANTS.
THAT'S HIS HOME! HE'S NESTING!
HISSSS
SAL
ERAL ST
SORRY, CHUMS, BUT I DEDUCE THAT THERE'S ONLY ROOM IN THIS TOWN FOR *ONE* PAIR OF MYSTERY TWINS!
EXCELLENT DEDUCTION, DICKIE! SEE YOU IN THE FUNNY PAPERS!
HO HO
HO HO HO!
SALE

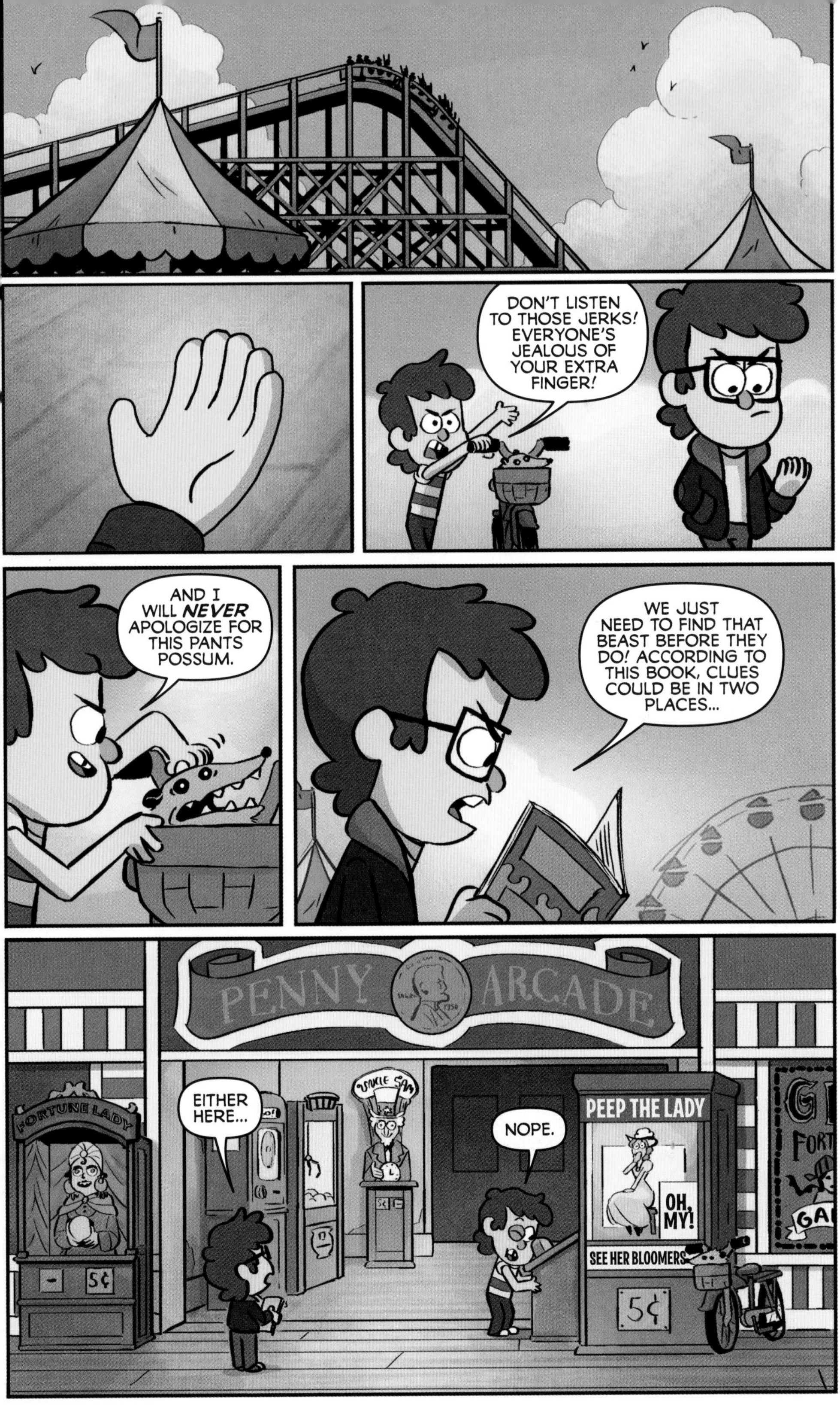
DON'T LISTEN TO THOSE JERKS! EVERYONE'S JEALOUS OF YOUR EXTRA FINGER!
AND I WILL ***NEVER*** APOLOGIZE FOR THIS PANTS POSSUM.
WE JUST NEED TO FIND THAT BEAST BEFORE THEY DO! ACCORDING TO THIS BOOK, CLUES COULD BE IN TWO PLACES...
PENNY ARCADE
FORTUNE LADY
5¢
UNCLE SAM
EITHER HERE...
NOPE.
PEEP THE LADY
OH, MY!
SEE HER BLOOMERS
5¢

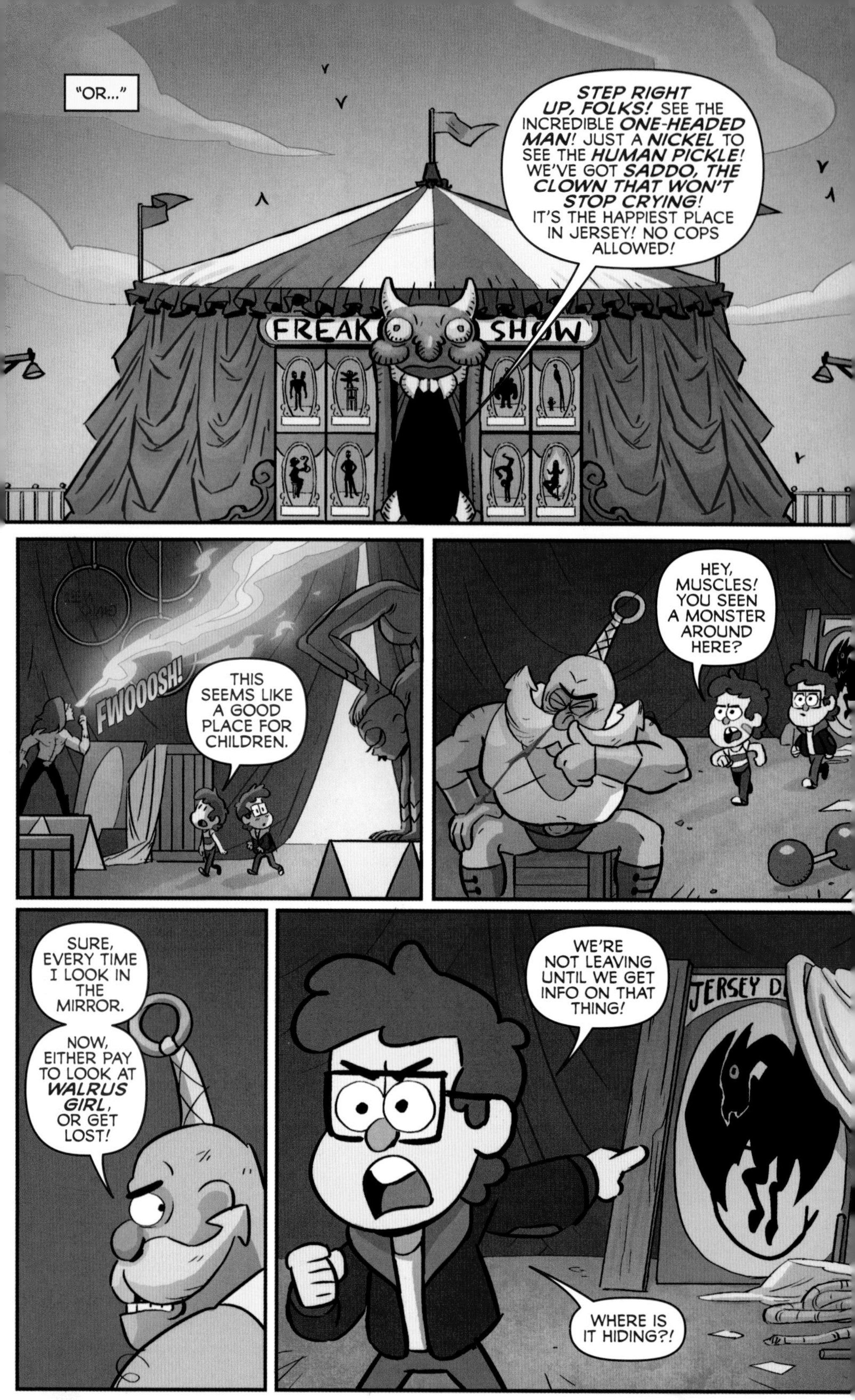
"OR..."
STEP RIGHT UP, FOLKS! SEE THE INCREDIBLE ONE-HEADED MAN! JUST A NICKEL TO SEE THE HUMAN PICKLE! WE'VE GOT SADDO, THE CLOWN THAT WON'T STOP CRYING! IT'S THE HAPPIEST PLACE IN JERSEY! NO COPS ALLOWED!
FREAK SHOW
FWOOOSH!
THIS SEEMS LIKE A GOOD PLACE FOR CHILDREN.
HEY, MUSCLES! YOU SEEN A MONSTER AROUND HERE?
SURE, EVERY TIME I LOOK IN THE MIRROR.
NOW, EITHER PAY TO LOOK AT WALRUS GIRL, OR GET LOST!
WE'RE NOT LEAVING UNTIL WE GET INFO ON THAT THING!
WHERE IS IT HIDING?!

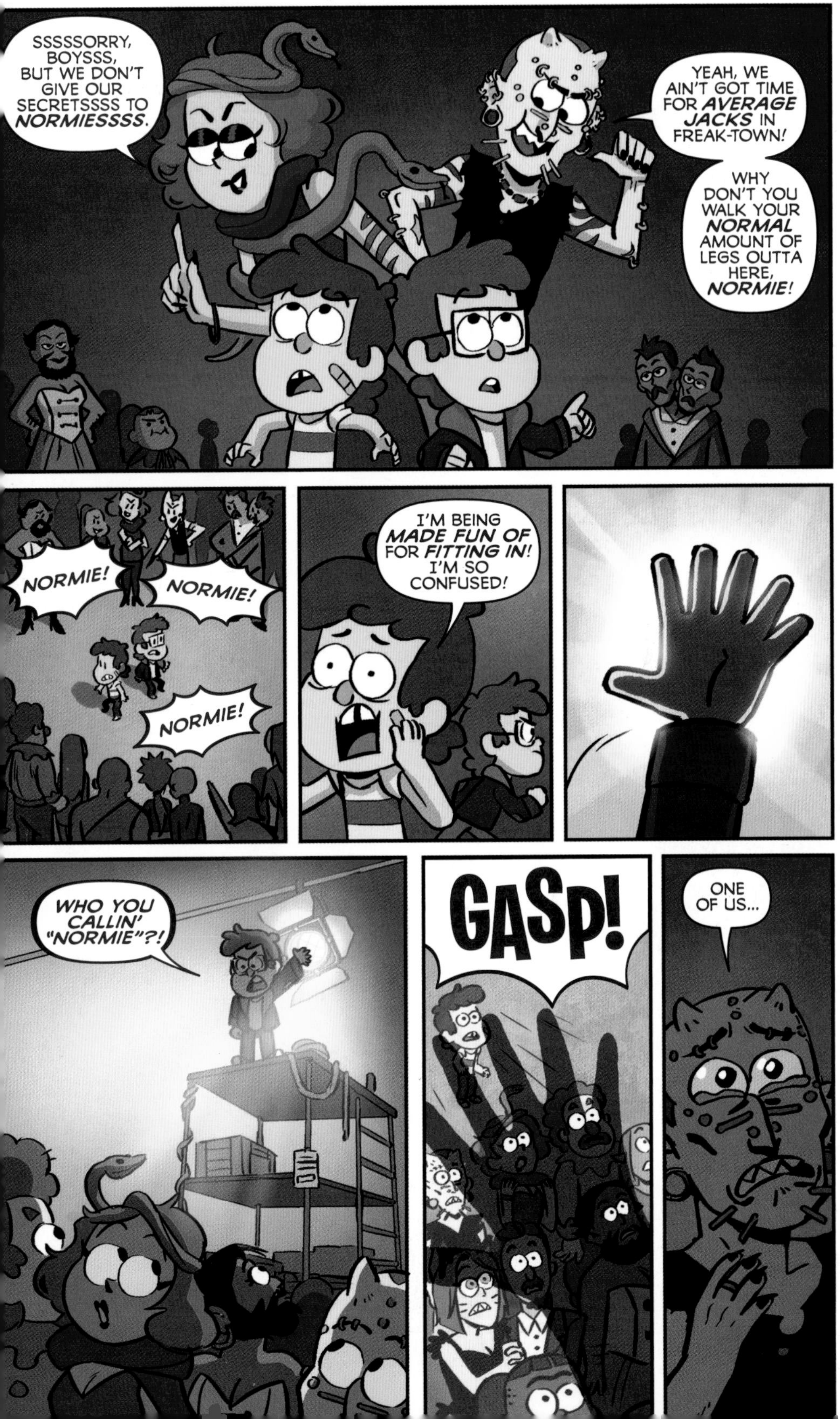
SSSSSORRY, BOYSSS, BUT WE DON'T GIVE OUR SECRETSSSS TO *NORMIESSSS*.
YEAH, WE AIN'T GOT TIME FOR *AVERAGE JACKS* IN FREAK-TOWN!
WHY DON'T YOU WALK YOUR *NORMAL* AMOUNT OF LEGS OUTTA HERE, *NORMIE*!
NORMIE!
NORMIE!
NORMIE!
I'M BEING *MADE FUN OF* FOR *FITTING IN*! I'M SO CONFUSED!
WHO YOU CALLIN' "NORMIE"?!
GASP!
ONE OF US...

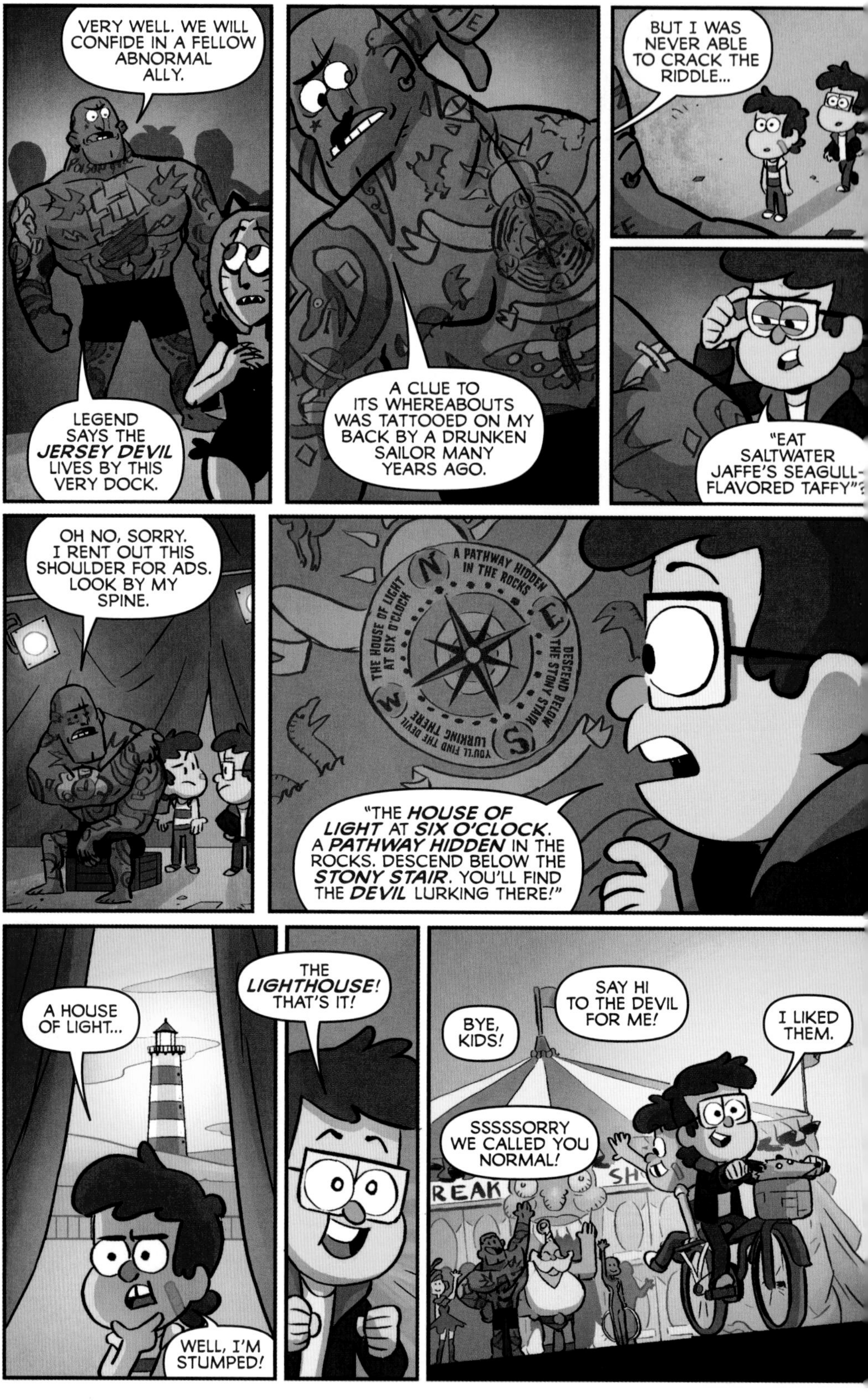
VERY WELL. WE WILL CONFIDE IN A FELLOW ABNORMAL ALLY.
LEGEND SAYS THE *JERSEY DEVIL* LIVES BY THIS VERY DOCK.
A CLUE TO ITS WHEREABOUTS WAS TATTOOED ON MY BACK BY A DRUNKEN SAILOR MANY YEARS AGO.
BUT I WAS NEVER ABLE TO CRACK THE RIDDLE...
"EAT SALTWATER JAFFE'S SEAGULL-FLAVORED TAFFY"?
OH NO, SORRY. I RENT OUT THIS SHOULDER FOR ADS. LOOK BY MY SPINE.
N
E
S
W
A PATHWAY HIDDEN IN THE ROCKS
DESCEND BELOW THE STONY STAIR
YOU'LL FIND THE DEVIL LURKING THERE
THE HOUSE OF LIGHT AT SIX O'CLOCK
"THE *HOUSE OF LIGHT* AT *SIX O'CLOCK*. A *PATHWAY HIDDEN* IN THE ROCKS. DESCEND BELOW THE *STONY STAIR*. YOU'LL FIND THE *DEVIL* LURKING THERE!"
A HOUSE OF LIGHT...
WELL, I'M STUMPED!
THE *LIGHTHOUSE!* THAT'S IT!
BYE, KIDS!
SAY HI TO THE DEVIL FOR ME!
I LIKED THEM.
SSSSSORRY WE CALLED YOU NORMAL!

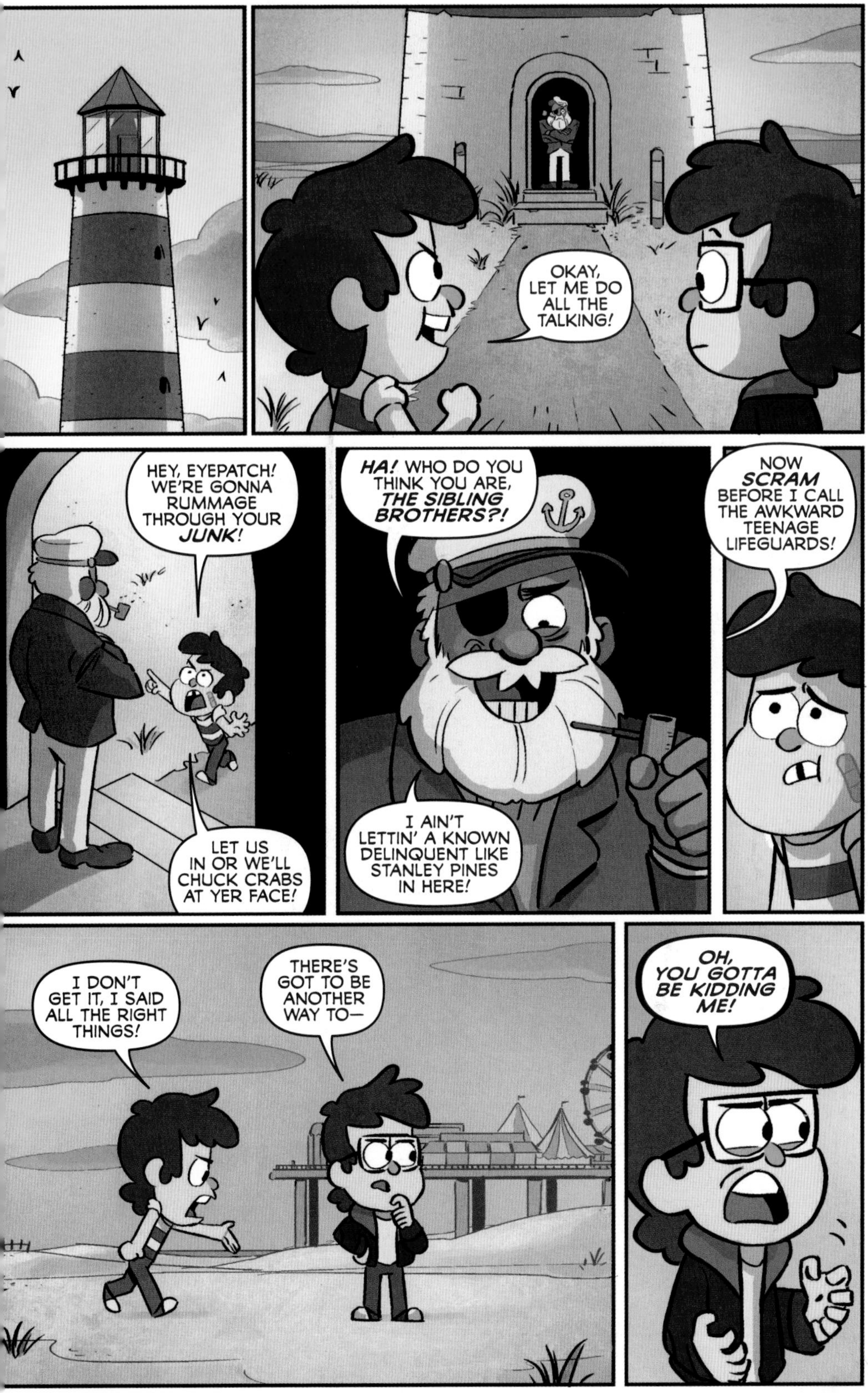
OKAY, LET ME DO ALL THE TALKING!
HEY, EYEPATCH! WE'RE GONNA RUMMAGE THROUGH YOUR *JUNK*!
LET US IN OR WE'LL CHUCK CRABS AT YER FACE!
HA! WHO DO YOU THINK YOU ARE, ***THE SIBLING BROTHERS?!***
I AIN'T LETTIN' A KNOWN DELINQUENT LIKE STANLEY PINES IN HERE!
NOW ***SCRAM*** BEFORE I CALL THE AWKWARD TEENAGE LIFEGUARDS!
I DON'T GET IT, I SAID ALL THE RIGHT THINGS!
THERE'S GOT TO BE ANOTHER WAY TO—
OH, YOU GOTTA BE KIDDING ME!

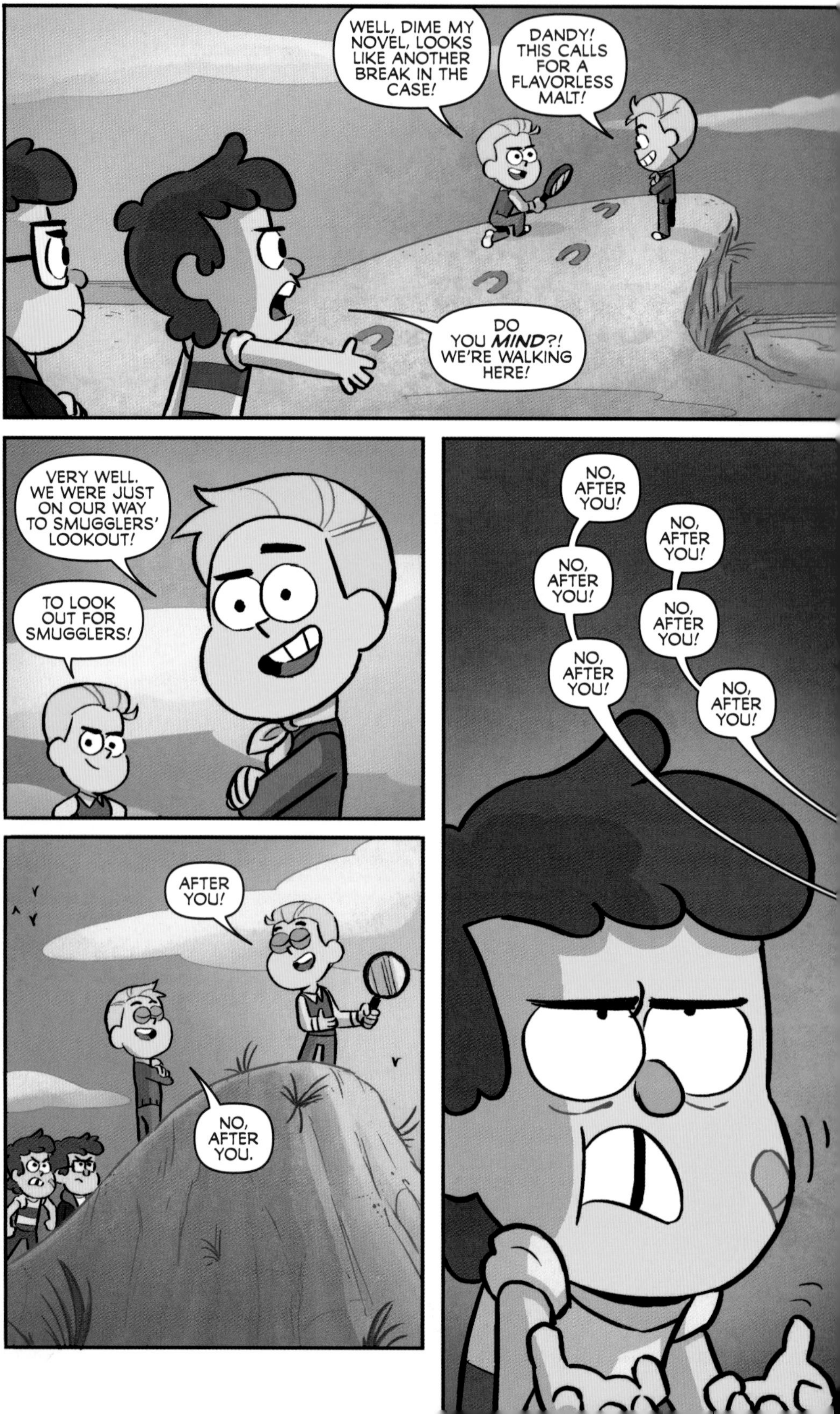
WELL, DIME MY NOVEL, LOOKS LIKE ANOTHER BREAK IN THE CASE!
DANDY! THIS CALLS FOR A FLAVORLESS MALT!
DO YOU *MIND*?! WE'RE WALKING HERE!
VERY WELL. WE WERE JUST ON OUR WAY TO SMUGGLERS' LOOKOUT!
TO LOOK OUT FOR SMUGGLERS!
AFTER YOU!
NO, AFTER YOU.
NO, AFTER YOU!
NO, AFTER YOU!
NO, AFTER YOU!
NO, AFTER YOU!
NO, AFTER YOU!
NO, AFTER YOU!

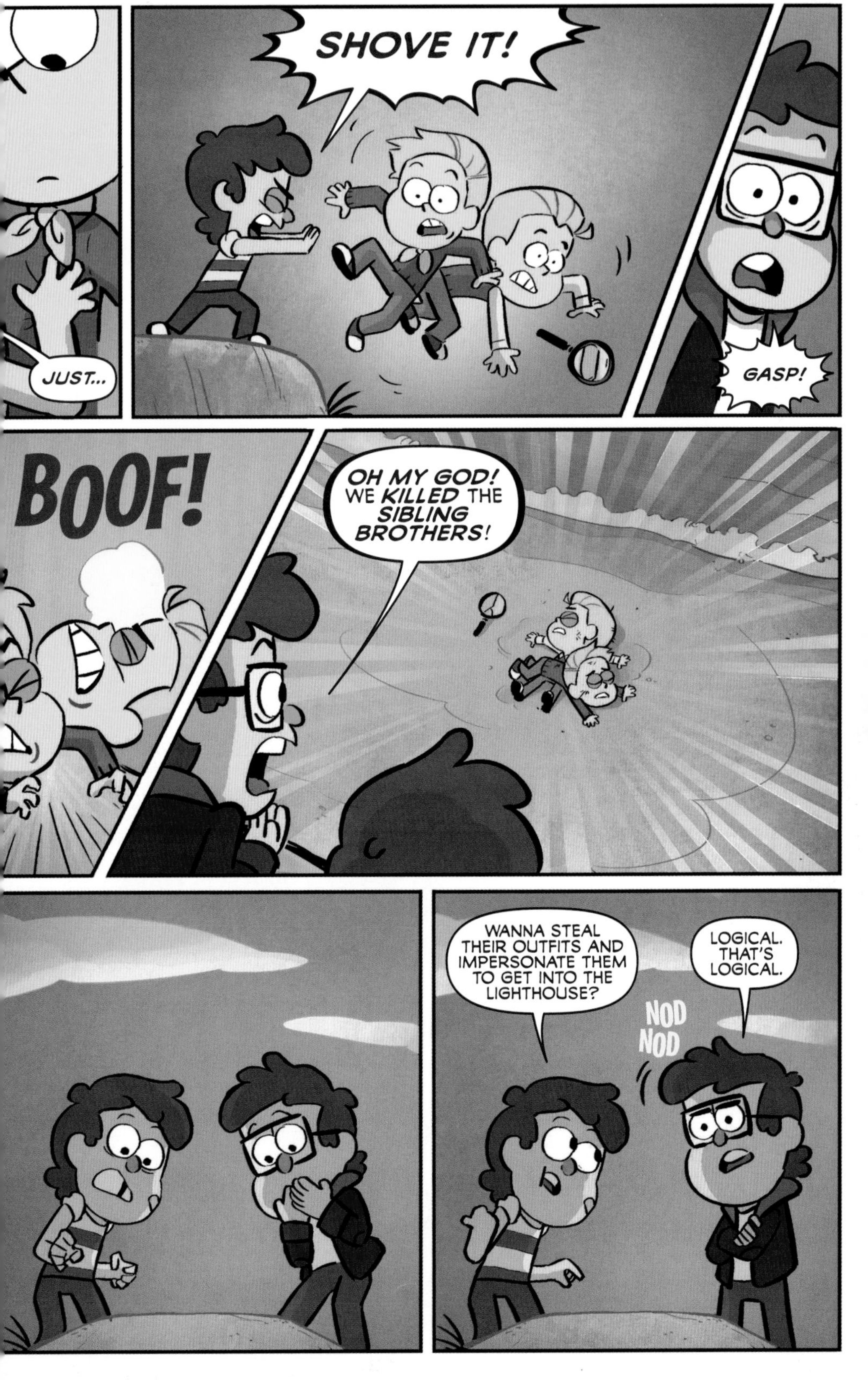
JUST...
SHOVE IT!
GASP!
BOOF!
OH MY GOD! WE KILLED THE SIBLING BROTHERS!
WANNA STEAL THEIR OUTFITS AND IMPERSONATE THEM TO GET INTO THE LIGHTHOUSE?
NOD NOD
LOGICAL. THAT'S LOGICAL.

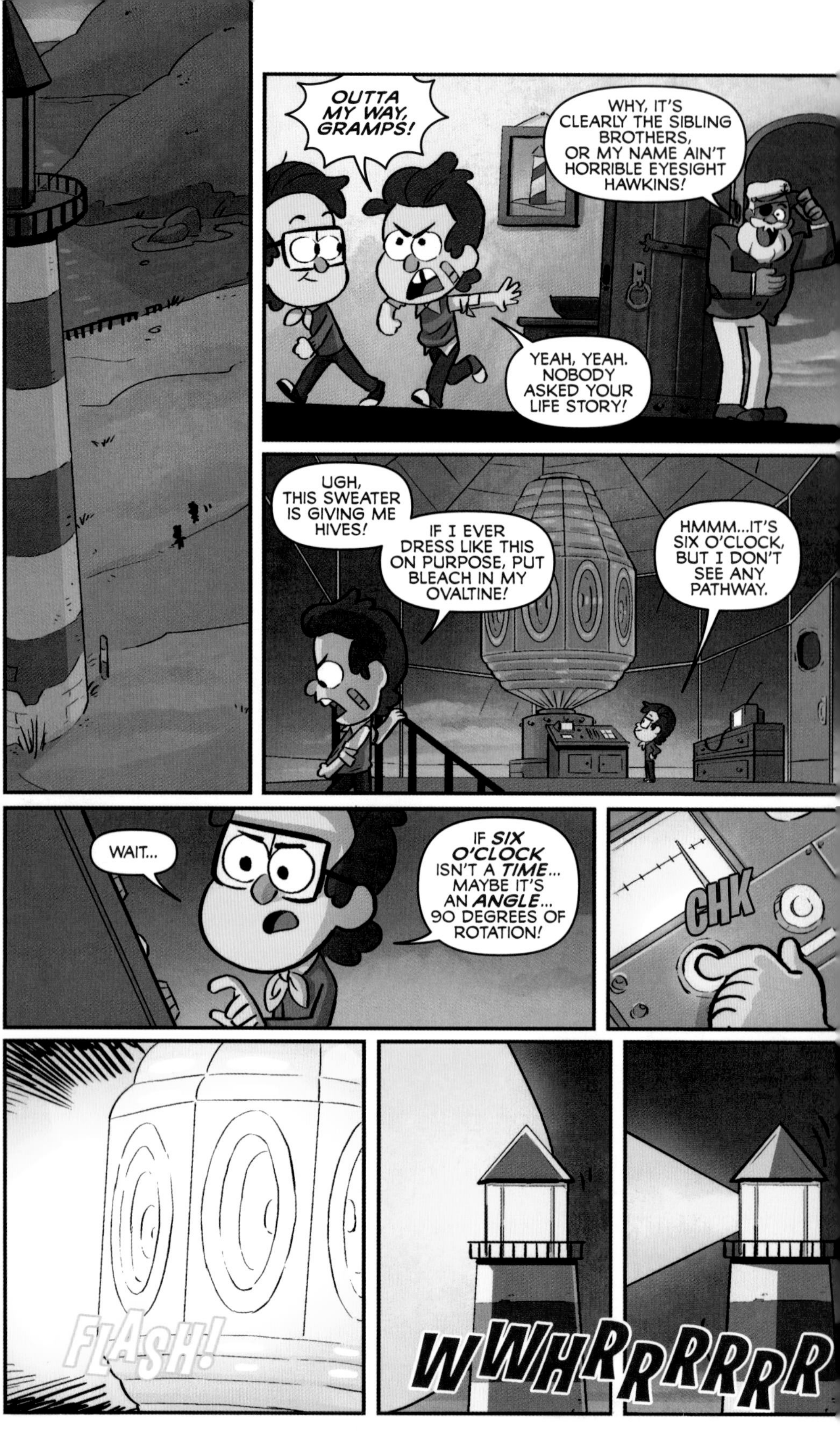
OUTTA MY WAY, GRAMPS!
WHY, IT'S CLEARLY THE SIBLING BROTHERS, OR MY NAME AIN'T HORRIBLE EYESIGHT HAWKINS!
YEAH, YEAH. NOBODY ASKED YOUR LIFE STORY!
UGH, THIS SWEATER IS GIVING ME HIVES!
IF I EVER DRESS LIKE THIS ON PURPOSE, PUT BLEACH IN MY OVALTINE!
HMMM...IT'S SIX O'CLOCK, BUT I DON'T SEE ANY PATHWAY.
WAIT...
IF SIX O'CLOCK ISN'T A TIME... MAYBE IT'S AN ANGLE... 90 DEGREES OF ROTATION!
CHK
FLASH!
WWHRRRRRR

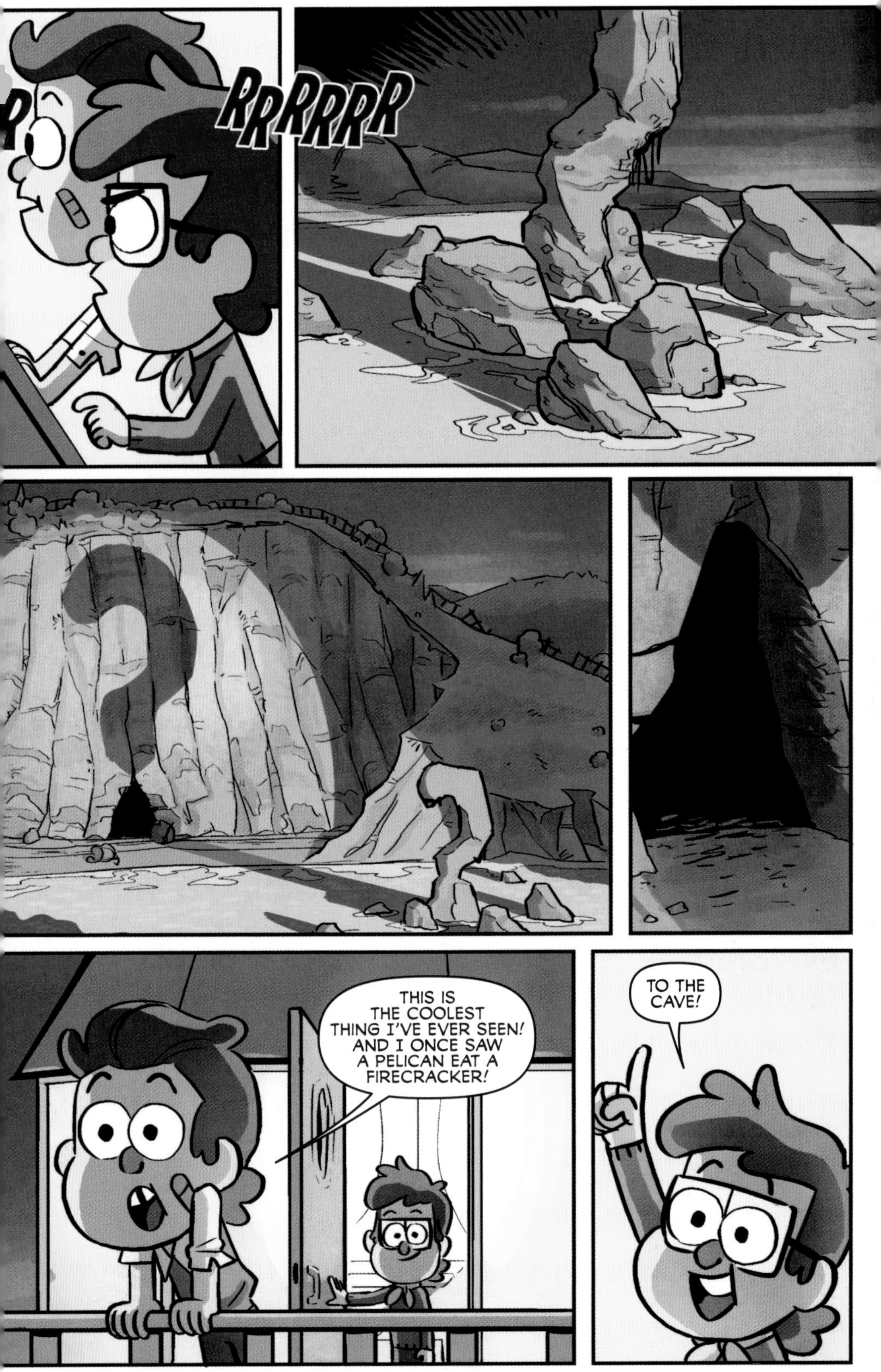
RRRRRRR
THIS IS THE COOLEST THING I'VE EVER SEEN! AND I ONCE SAW A PELICAN EAT A FIRECRACKER!
TO THE CAVE!

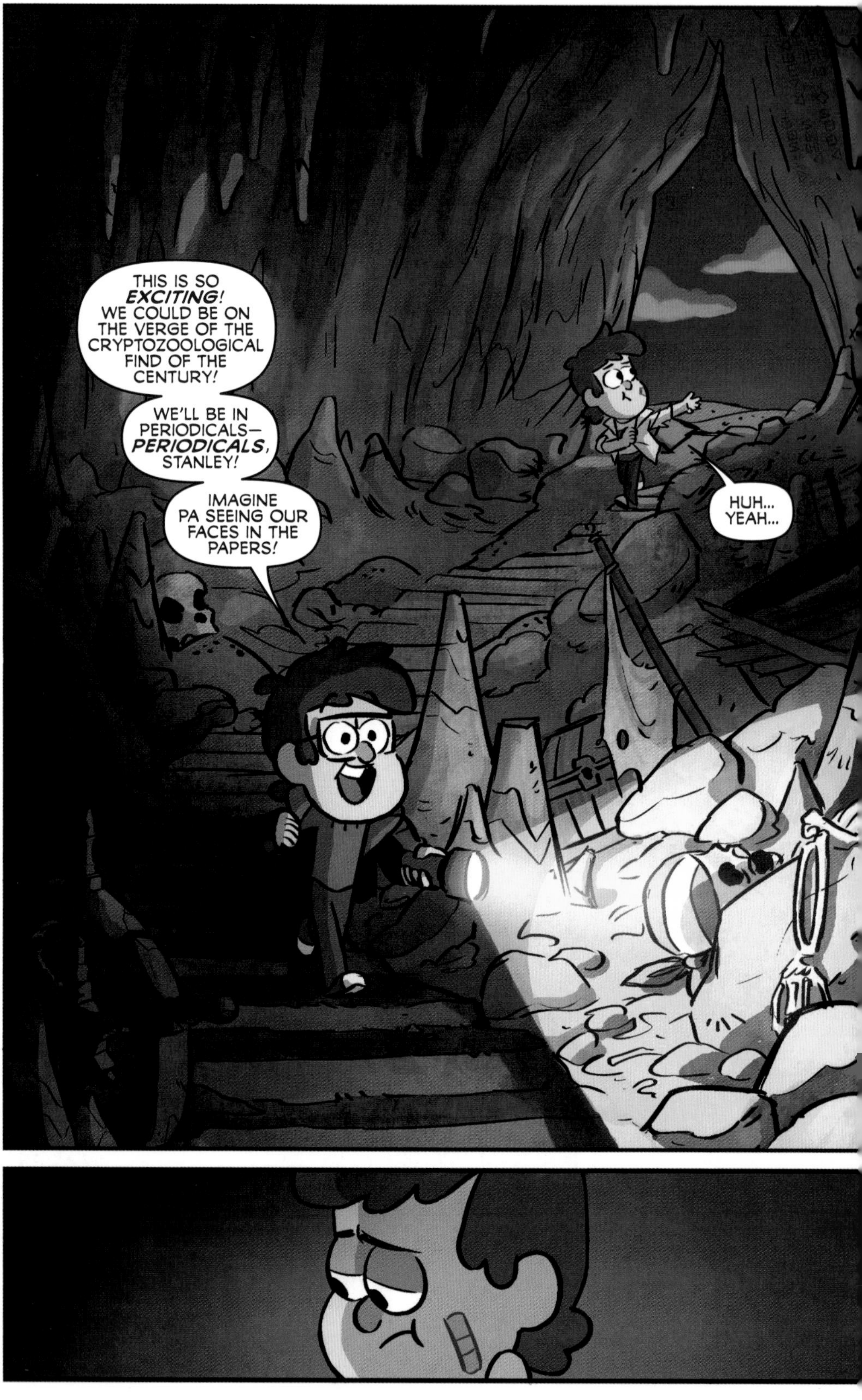
THIS IS SO *EXCITING*! WE COULD BE ON THE VERGE OF THE CRYPTOZOOLOGICAL FIND OF THE CENTURY!
WE'LL BE IN PERIODICALS— *PERIODICALS*, STANLEY!
IMAGINE PA SEEING OUR FACES IN THE PAPERS!
HUH... YEAH...

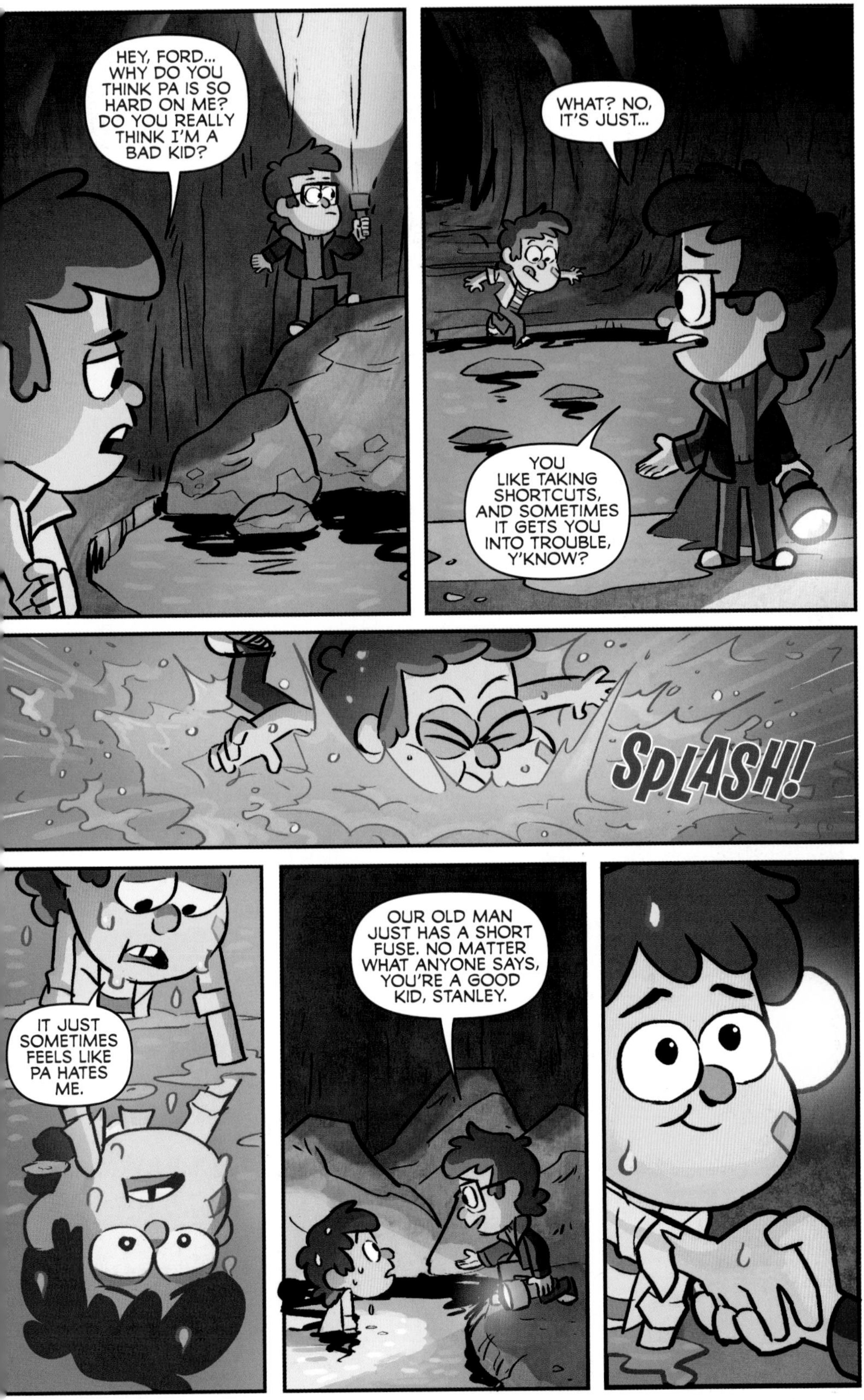
HEY, FORD... WHY DO YOU THINK PA IS SO HARD ON ME? DO YOU REALLY THINK I'M A BAD KID?
WHAT? NO, IT'S JUST...
YOU LIKE TAKING SHORTCUTS, AND SOMETIMES IT GETS YOU INTO TROUBLE, Y'KNOW?
SPLASH!
IT JUST SOMETIMES FEELS LIKE PA HATES ME.
OUR OLD MAN JUST HAS A SHORT FUSE. NO MATTER WHAT ANYONE SAYS, YOU'RE A GOOD KID, STANLEY.

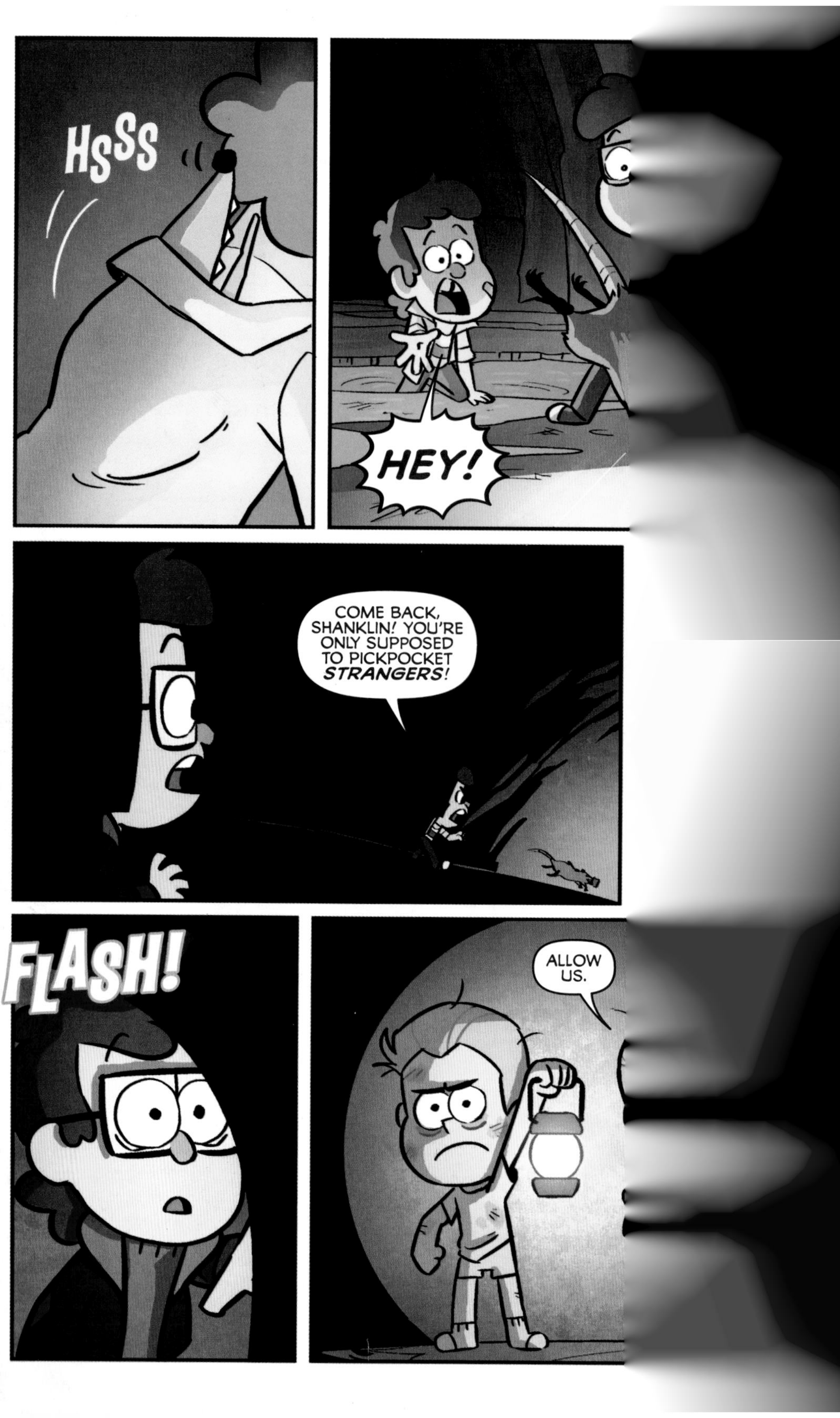
HSSS
HEY!
COME BACK, SHANKLIN! YOU'RE ONLY SUPPOSED TO PICKPOCKET STRANGERS!
FLASH!
ALLOW US.

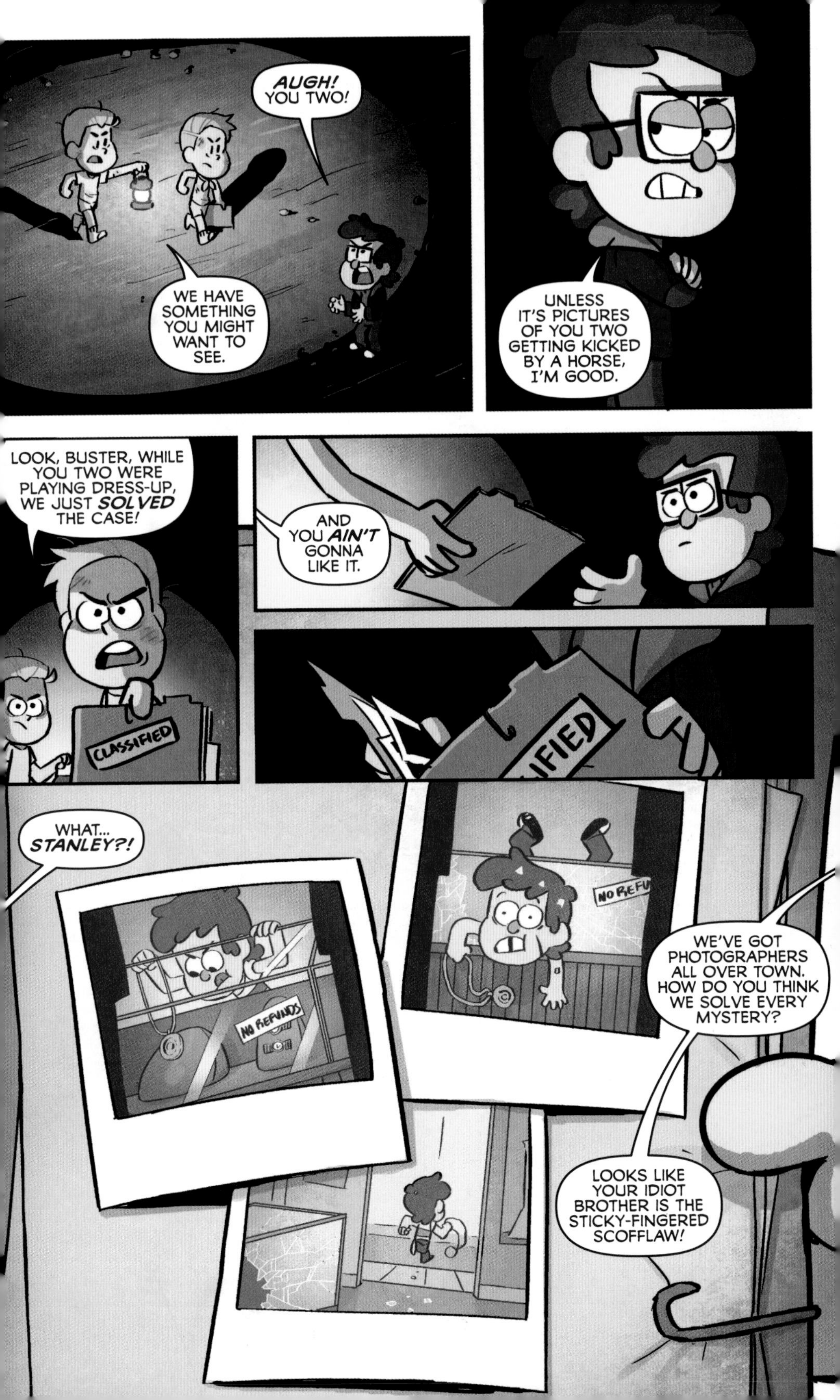

AUGH! YOU TWO!
WE HAVE SOMETHING YOU MIGHT WANT TO SEE.
UNLESS IT'S PICTURES OF YOU TWO GETTING KICKED BY A HORSE, I'M GOOD.
LOOK, BUSTER, WHILE YOU TWO WERE PLAYING DRESS-UP, WE JUST SOLVED THE CASE!
CLASSIFIED
AND YOU AIN'T GONNA LIKE IT.
WHAT... STANLEY?!
NO REFUNDS
WE'VE GOT PHOTOGRAPHERS ALL OVER TOWN. HOW DO YOU THINK WE SOLVE EVERY MYSTERY?
LOOKS LIKE YOUR IDIOT BROTHER IS THE STICKY-FINGERED SCOFFLAW!

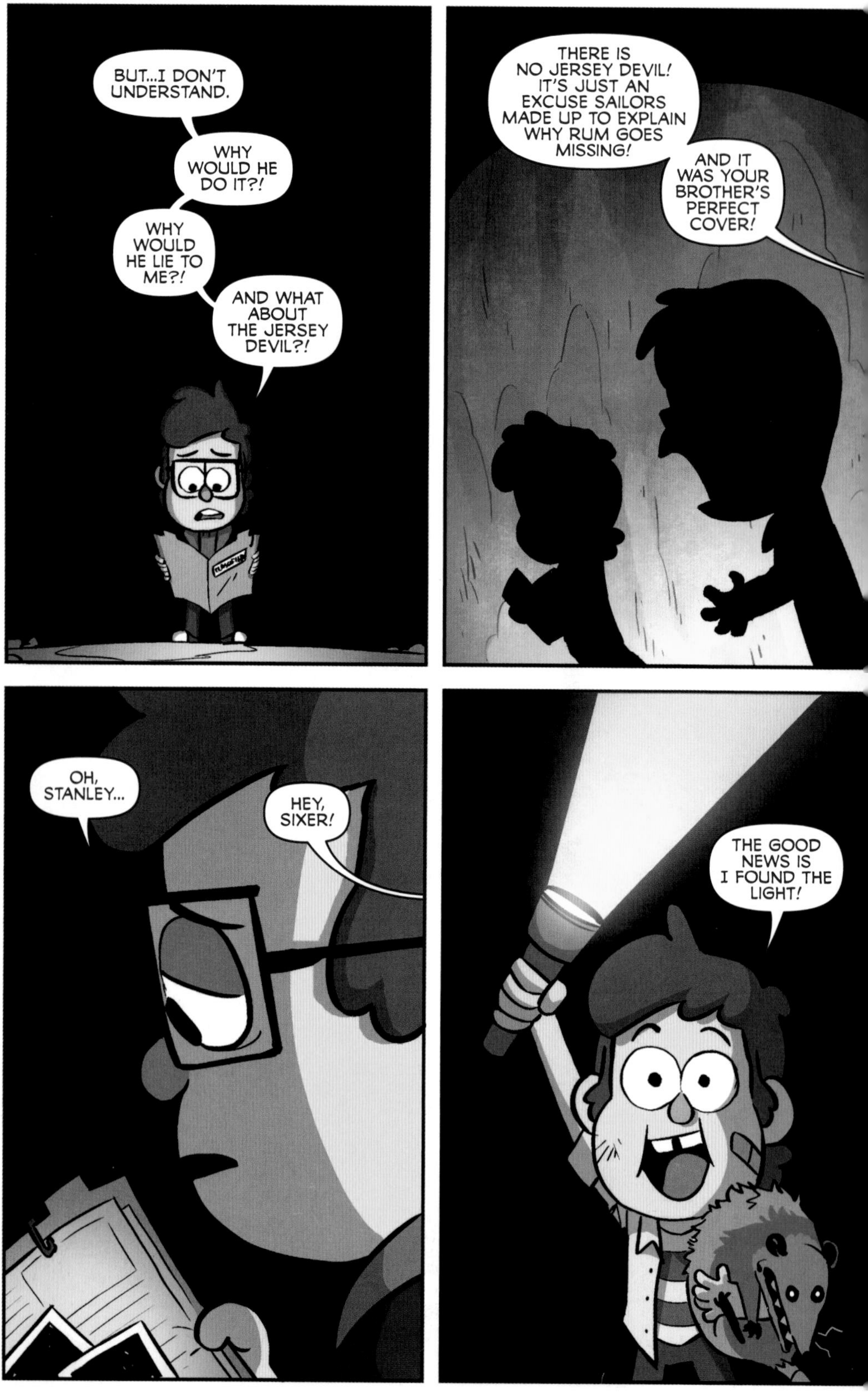
BUT...I DON'T UNDERSTAND.
WHY WOULD HE DO IT?!
WHY WOULD HE LIE TO ME?!
AND WHAT ABOUT THE JERSEY DEVIL?!
THERE IS NO JERSEY DEVIL! IT'S JUST AN EXCUSE SAILORS MADE UP TO EXPLAIN WHY RUM GOES MISSING!
AND IT WAS YOUR BROTHER'S PERFECT COVER!
OH, STANLEY...
HEY, SIXER!
THE GOOD NEWS IS I FOUND THE LIGHT!

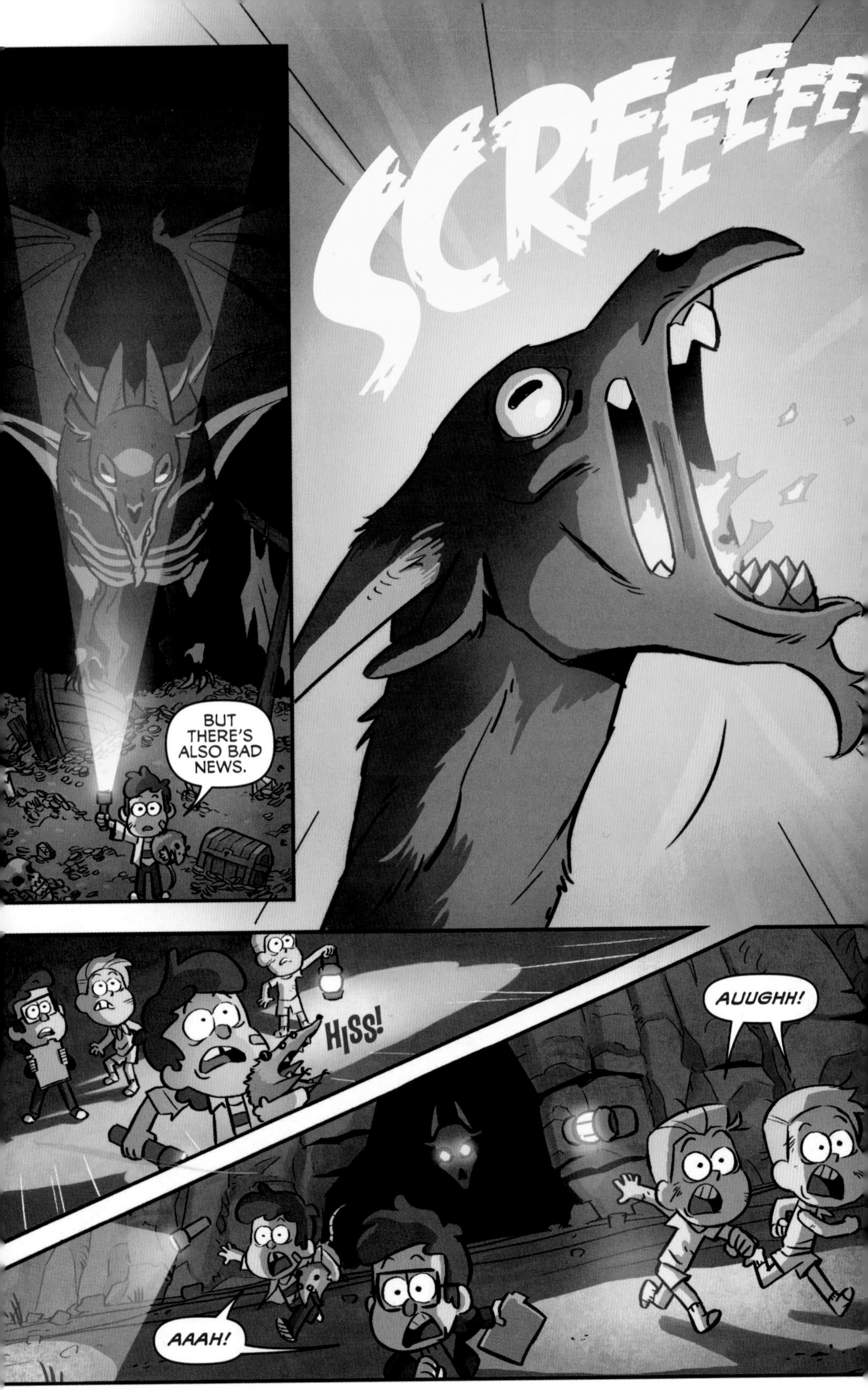
BUT THERE'S ALSO BAD NEWS.
SCREEEEEE
HISS!
AUUGHH!
AAAH!

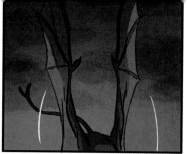

WHOOSH

SCREEECH!

GALLOPING GUMSHOES, WHAT IS THAT?!

IT'S THE JERSEY DEVIL! IT'S REAL! I'D BE EXCITED IF I WASN'T SO TERRIFIED!

#@$!

HEY, HEY! LOOK WHO FINALLY LEARNED TO SWEAR!

Glass Shard Beach
Boardwalk
CARNIVAL

AAUGHH!!

THUD!

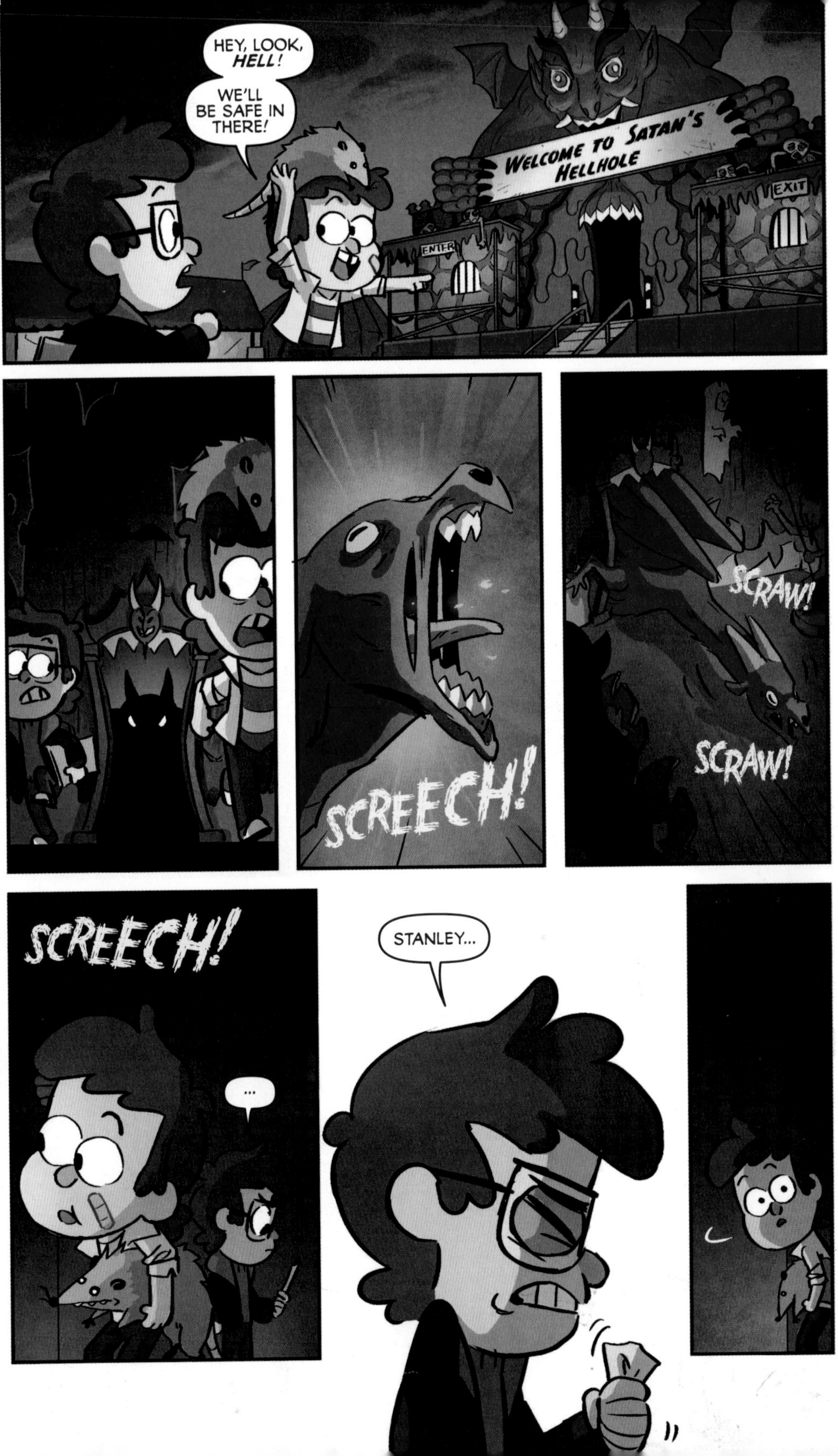
HEY, LOOK, *HELL!*
WE'LL BE SAFE IN THERE!
WELCOME TO SATAN'S HELLHOLE
ENTER
EXIT
SCREECH!
SCRAW!
SCRAW!
SCREECH!
...
STANLEY...

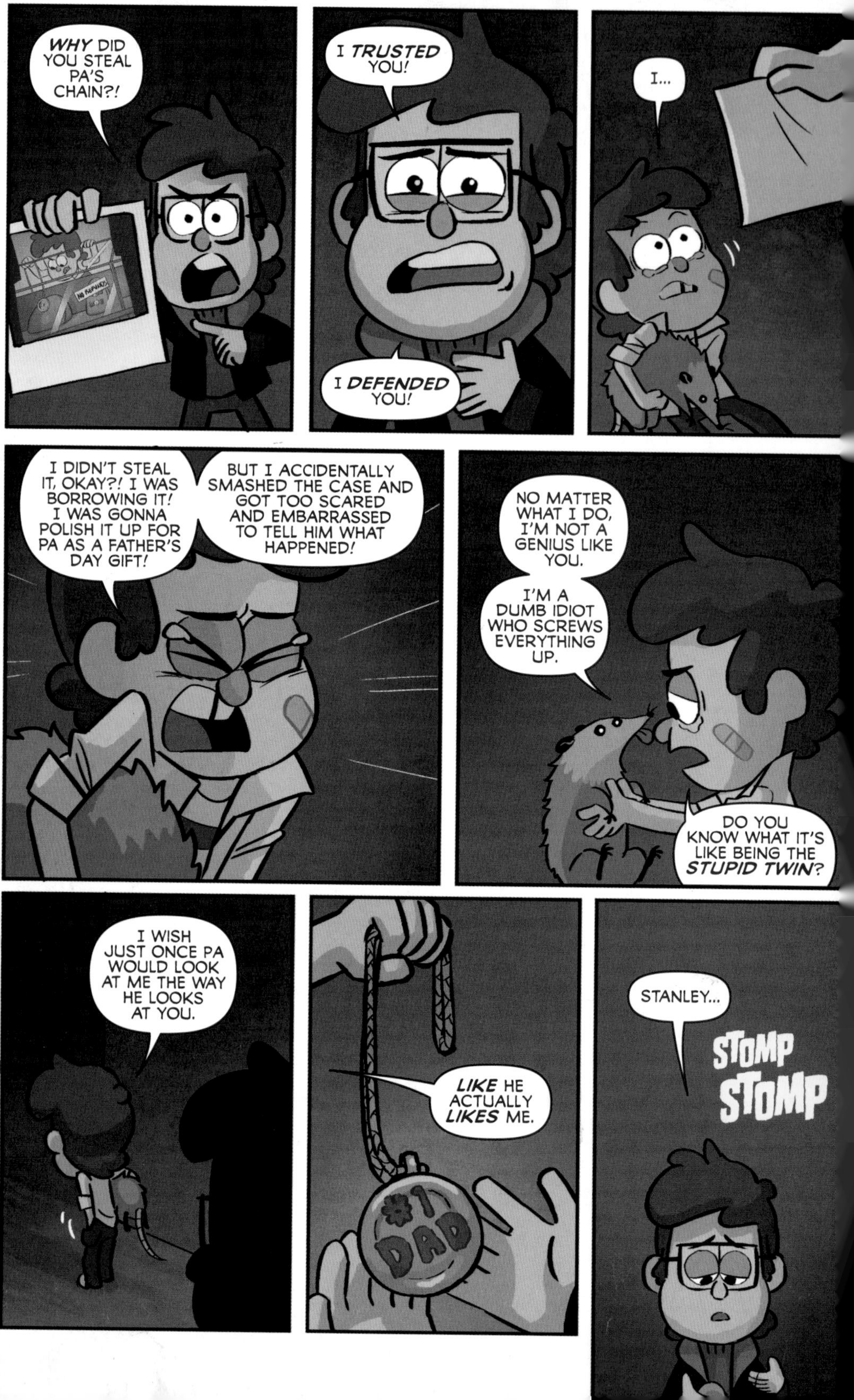
WHY DID YOU STEAL PA'S CHAIN?!
I TRUSTED YOU!
I DEFENDED YOU!
I...
I DIDN'T STEAL IT, OKAY?! I WAS BORROWING IT! I WAS GONNA POLISH IT UP FOR PA AS A FATHER'S DAY GIFT!
BUT I ACCIDENTALLY SMASHED THE CASE AND GOT TOO SCARED AND EMBARRASSED TO TELL HIM WHAT HAPPENED!
NO MATTER WHAT I DO, I'M NOT A GENIUS LIKE YOU.
I'M A DUMB IDIOT WHO SCREWS EVERYTHING UP.
DO YOU KNOW WHAT IT'S LIKE BEING THE STUPID TWIN?
I WISH JUST ONCE PA WOULD LOOK AT ME THE WAY HE LOOKS AT YOU.
LIKE HE ACTUALLY LIKES ME.
#1 DAD
STANLEY...
STOMP
STOMP

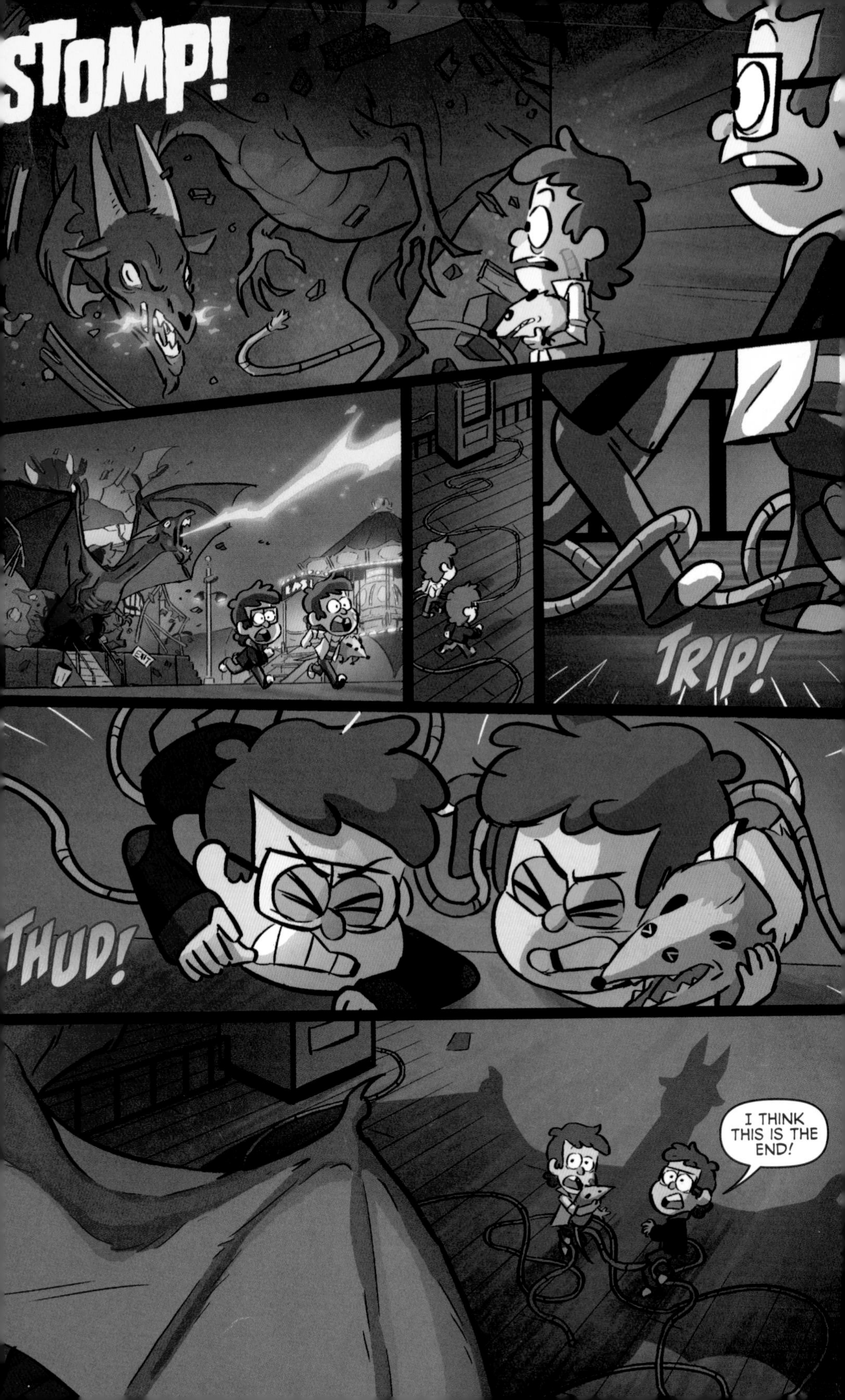
STOMP!
TRIP!
THUD!
I THINK THIS IS THE END!

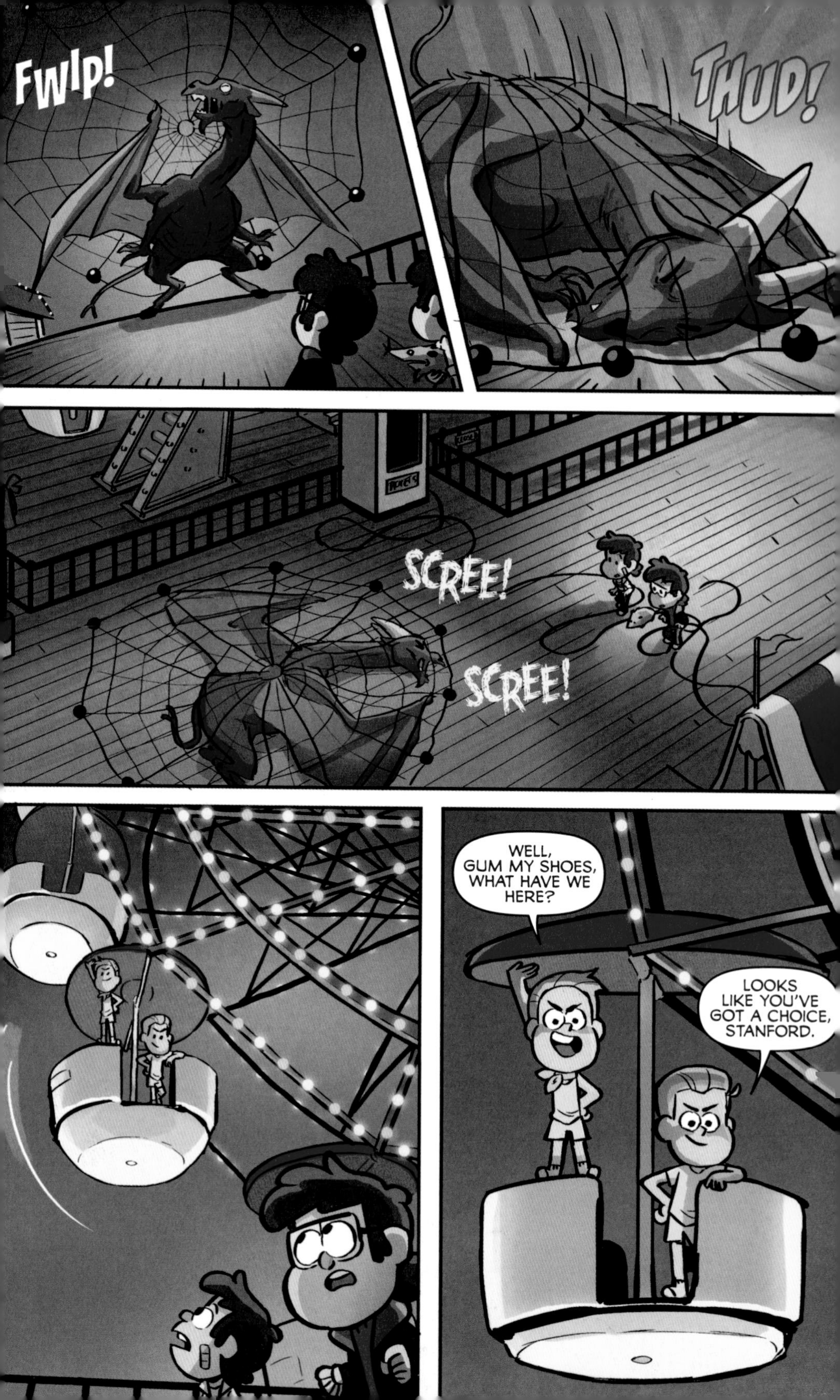
FWIP!
THUD!
SCREE!
SCREE!
WELL, GUM MY SHOES, WHAT HAVE WE HERE?
LOOKS LIKE YOU'VE GOT A CHOICE, STANFORD.

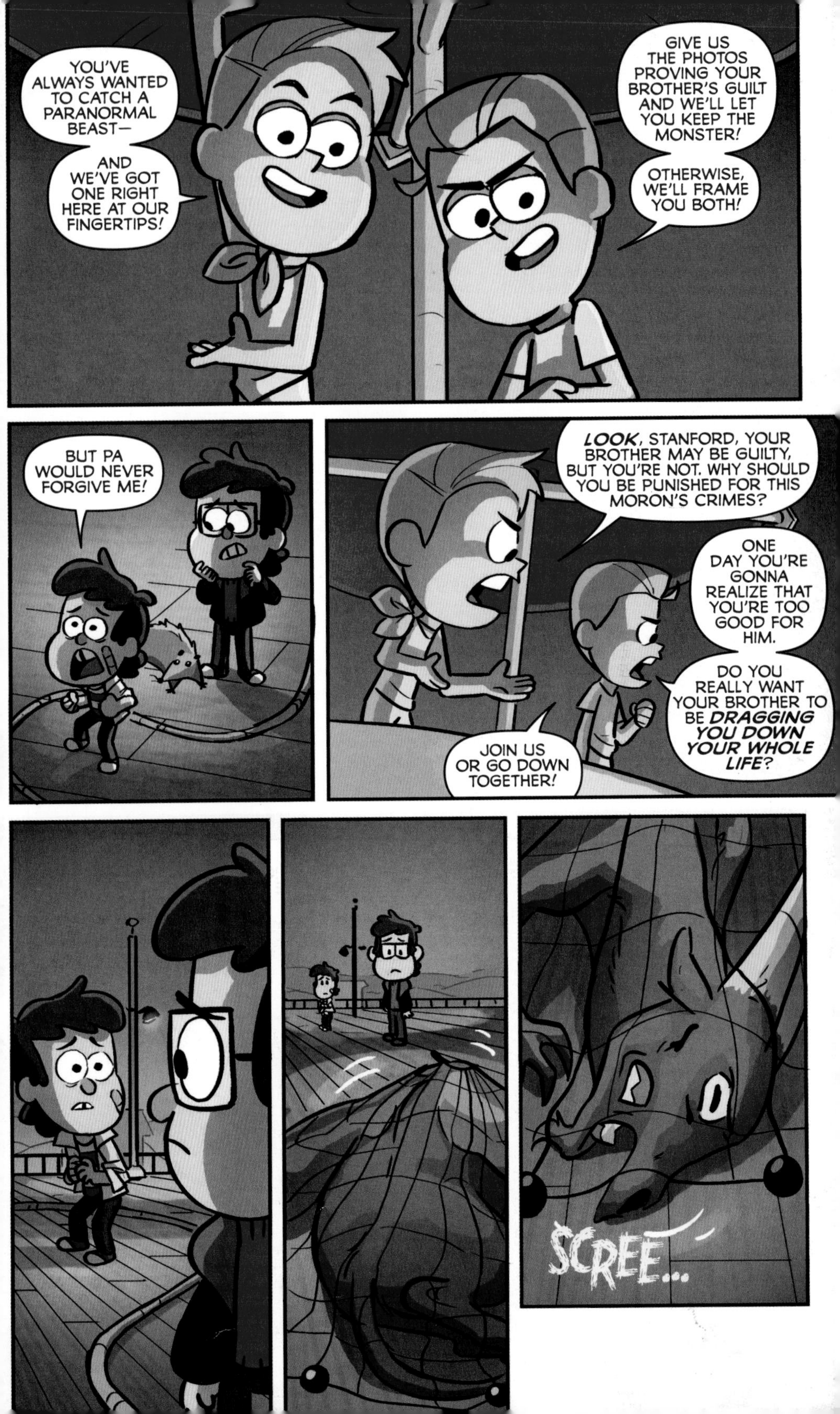
YOU'VE ALWAYS WANTED TO CATCH A PARANORMAL BEAST—
AND WE'VE GOT ONE RIGHT HERE AT OUR FINGERTIPS!
GIVE US THE PHOTOS PROVING YOUR BROTHER'S GUILT AND WE'LL LET YOU KEEP THE MONSTER!
OTHERWISE, WE'LL FRAME YOU BOTH!
BUT PA WOULD NEVER FORGIVE ME!
LOOK, STANFORD, YOUR BROTHER MAY BE GUILTY, BUT YOU'RE NOT. WHY SHOULD YOU BE PUNISHED FOR THIS MORON'S CRIMES?
ONE DAY YOU'RE GONNA REALIZE THAT YOU'RE TOO GOOD FOR HIM.
DO YOU REALLY WANT YOUR BROTHER TO BE ***DRAGGING YOU DOWN YOUR WHOLE LIFE***?
JOIN US OR GO DOWN TOGETHER!
SCREE...

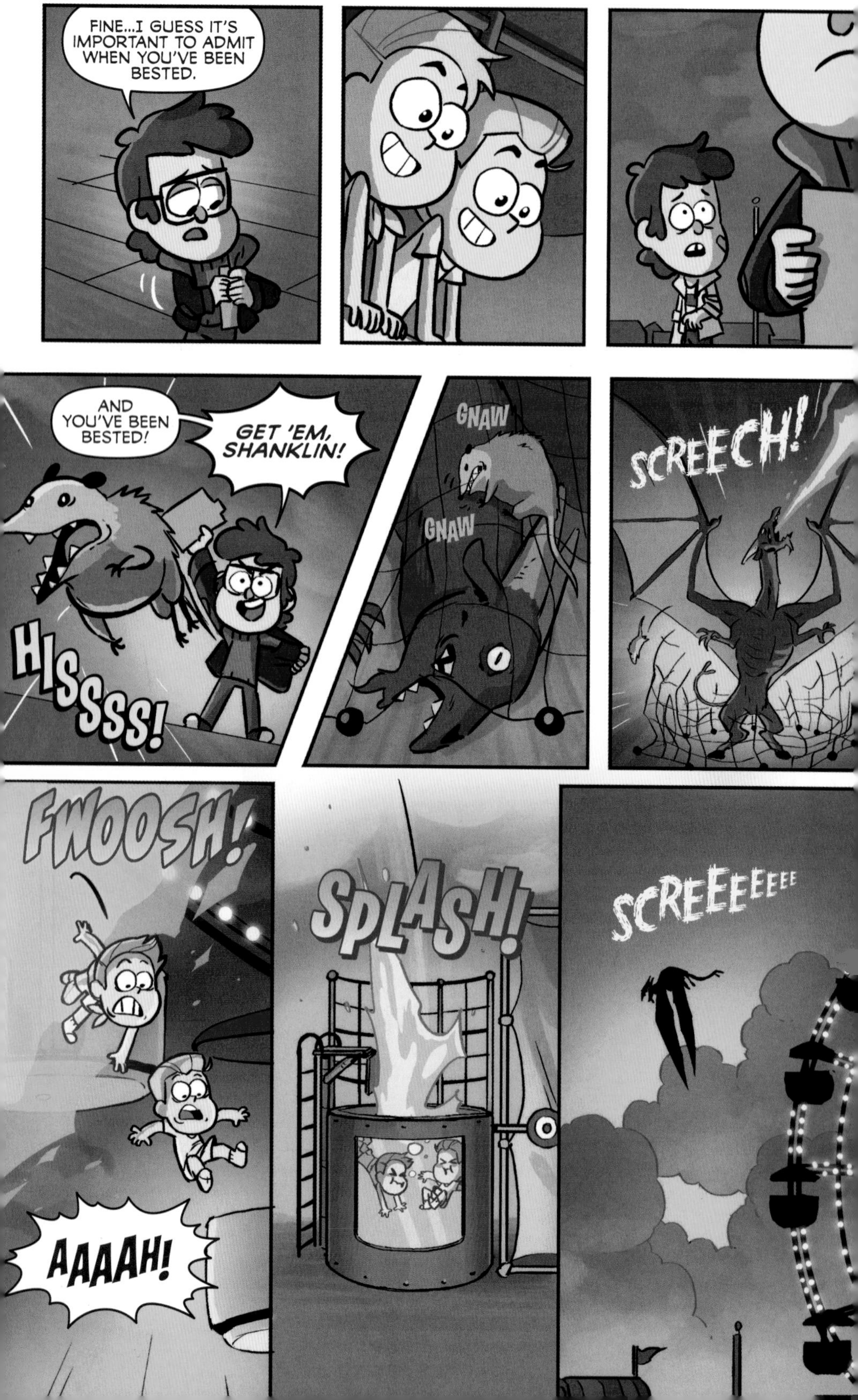
FINE...I GUESS IT'S IMPORTANT TO ADMIT WHEN YOU'VE BEEN BESTED.
AND YOU'VE BEEN BESTED!
GET 'EM, SHANKLIN!
HISSSSS!
GNAW
GNAW
SCREECH!
FWOOSH!
AAAAH!
SPLASH!
SCREEEEEEE

HUFF...HUFF... YOU IDIOT! NOW NO ONE WILL KNOW YOU FOUND THE BEAST!

JUST WHO DO YOU TWO THINK YOU ARE?!

I'LL TELL YOU WHO WE ARE! WE'RE THE PINES TWINS, *KINGS OF NEW JERSEY!*

WE'RE WEIRDOS AND HOOLIGANS, AND WE LOOK OUT FOR EACH OTHER AND MISFITS LIKE US!

NOW GET OFF MY DOCK!

JUST YOU WAIT, WE'LL GET OUR REVENGE!

THERE'S NO ROOM IN THIS TOWN FOR FREAKS LIKE YOU!

OH YEAH?

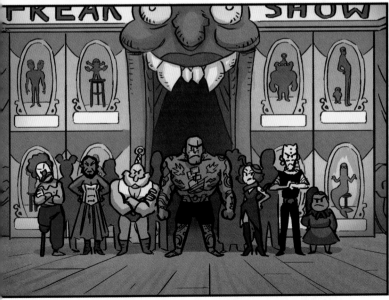

WHO YOU CALLIN' FREAKS?!

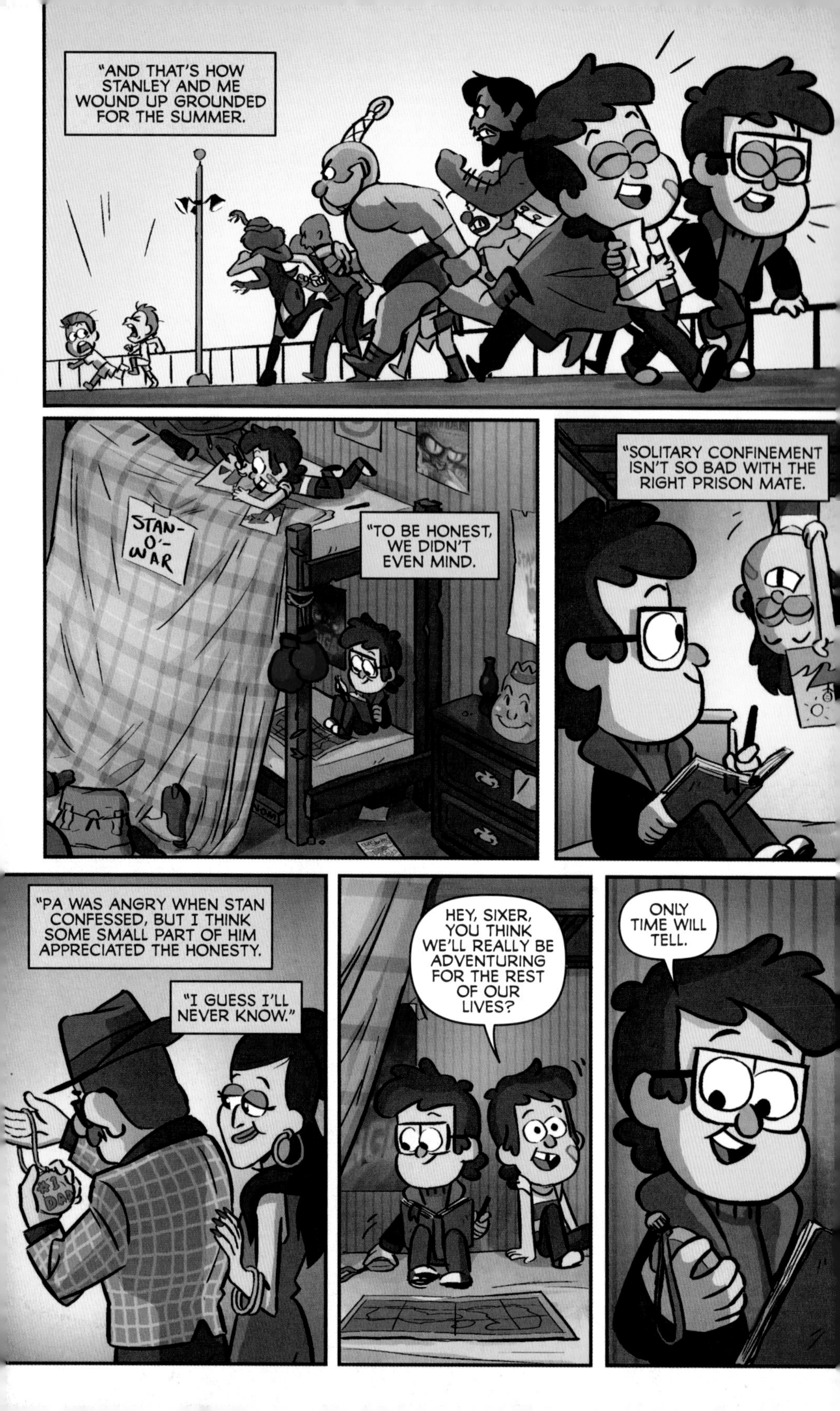

"AND THAT'S HOW STANLEY AND ME WOUND UP GROUNDED FOR THE SUMMER.
STAN-O'-WAR
"TO BE HONEST, WE DIDN'T EVEN MIND.
"SOLITARY CONFINEMENT ISN'T SO BAD WITH THE RIGHT PRISON MATE.
"PA WAS ANGRY WHEN STAN CONFESSED, BUT I THINK SOME SMALL PART OF HIM APPRECIATED THE HONESTY.
"I GUESS I'LL NEVER KNOW."
#1 DAD
HEY, SIXER, YOU THINK WE'LL REALLY BE ADVENTURING FOR THE REST OF OUR LIVES?
ONLY TIME WILL TELL.

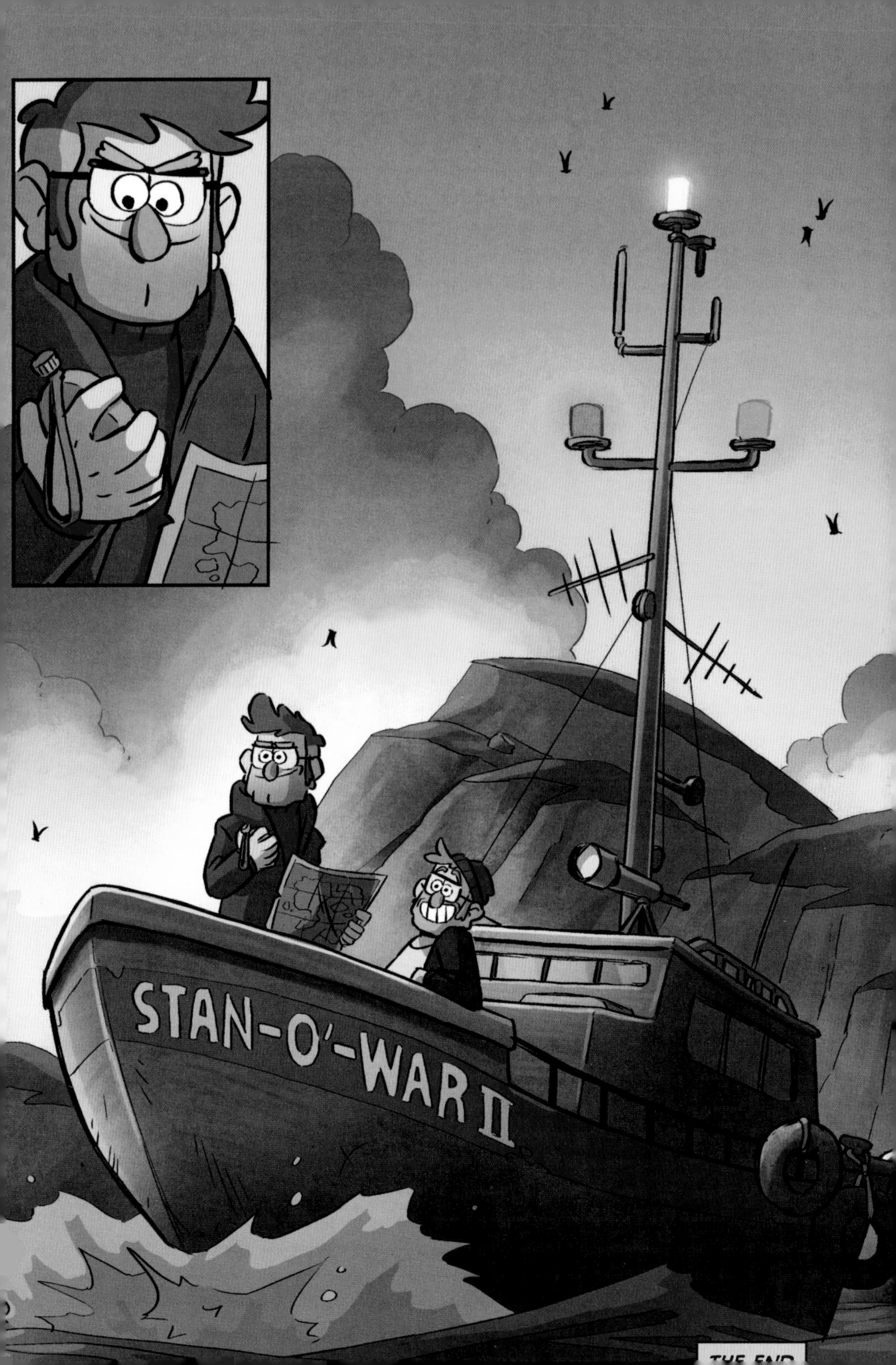
STAN-O'-WAR II

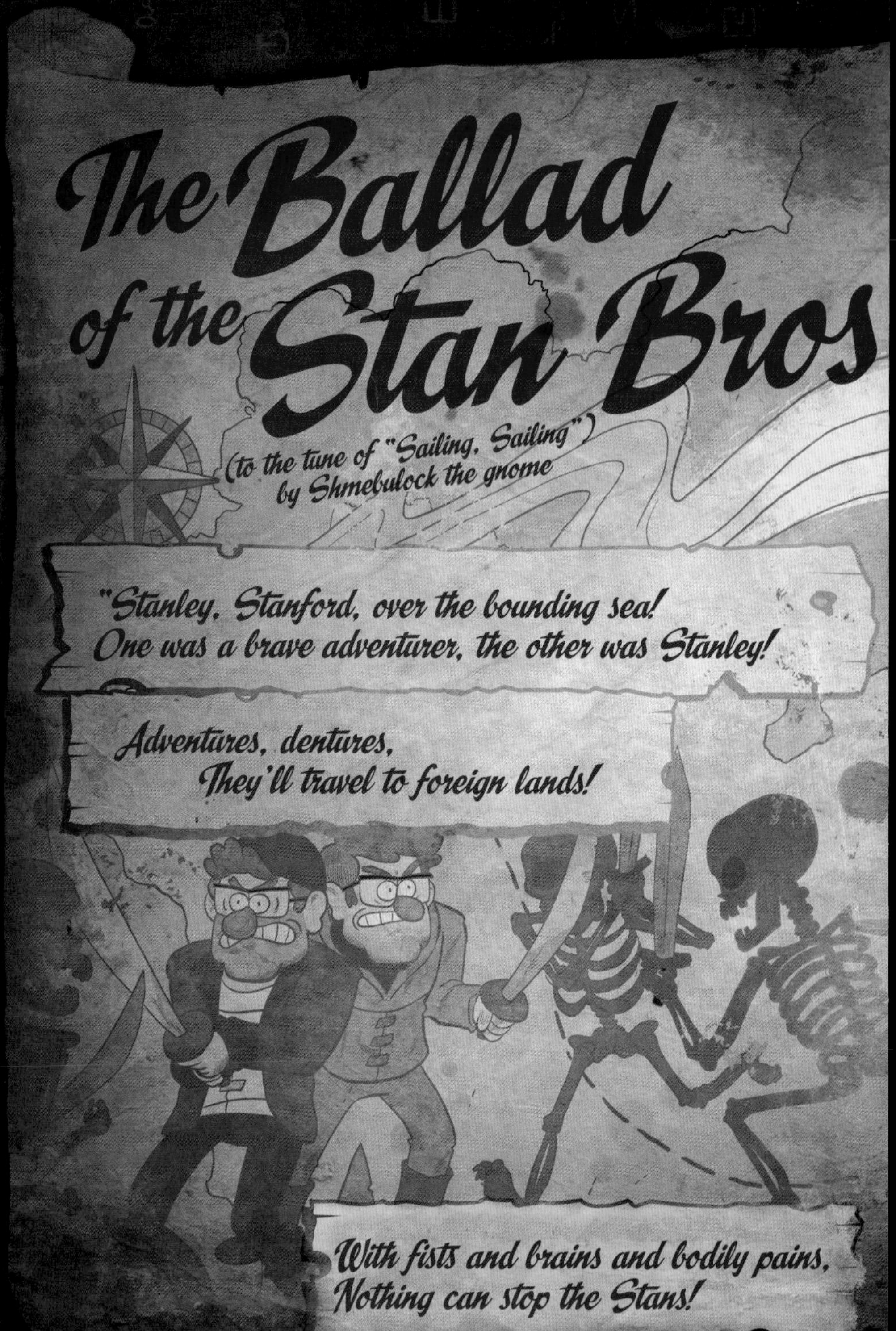
The Ballad of the Stan Bros
(to the tune of "Sailing, Sailing")
by Shmebulock the gnome
"Stanley, Stanford, over the bounding sea!
One was a brave adventurer, the other was Stanley!
Adventures, dentures,
They'll travel to foreign lands!
With fists and brains and bodily pains,
Nothing can stop the Stans!

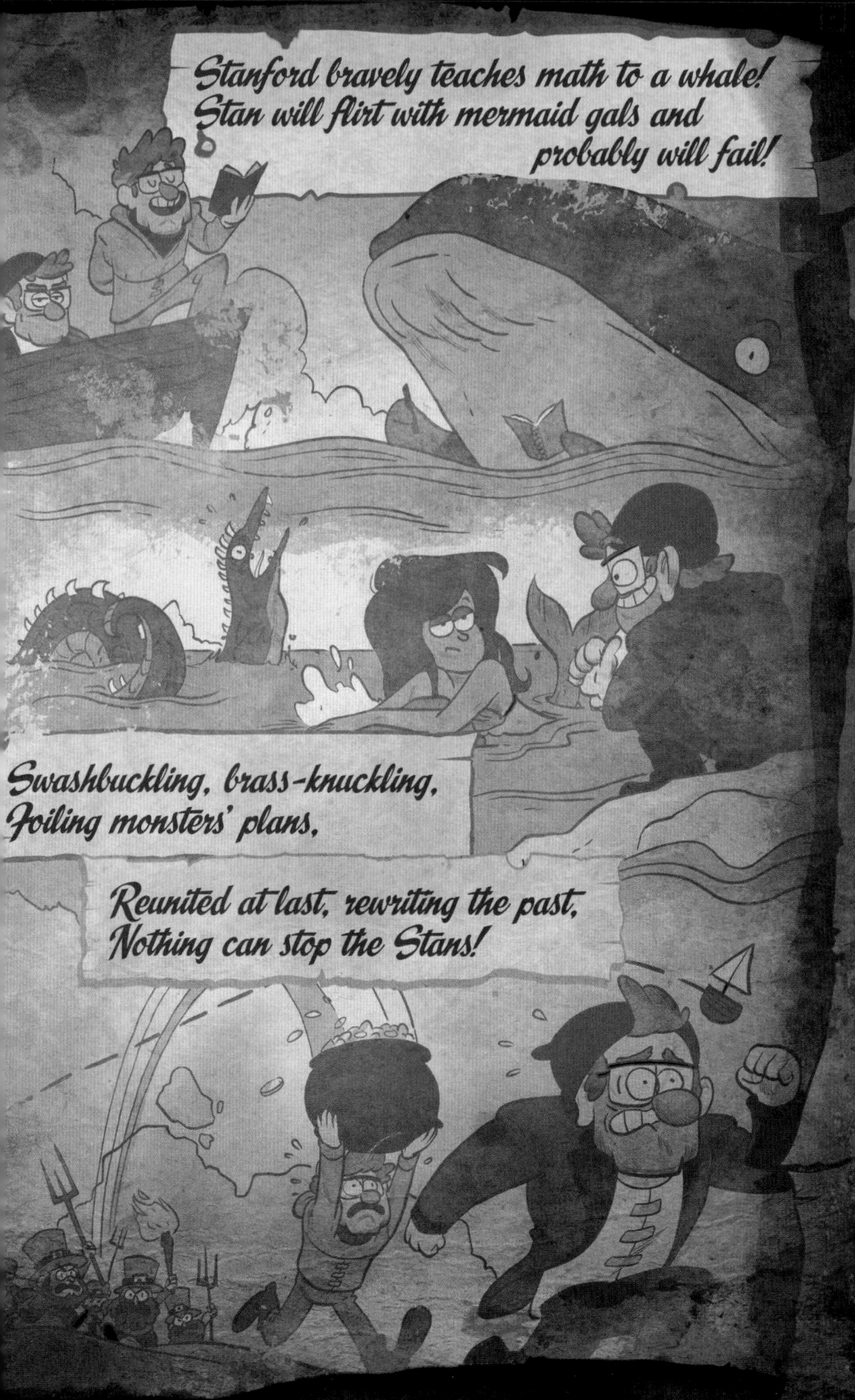
Stanford bravely teaches math to a whale!
Stan will flirt with mermaid gals and probably will fail!
Swashbuckling, brass-knuckling,
Foiling monsters' plans,
Reunited at last, rewriting the past,
Nothing can stop the Stans!

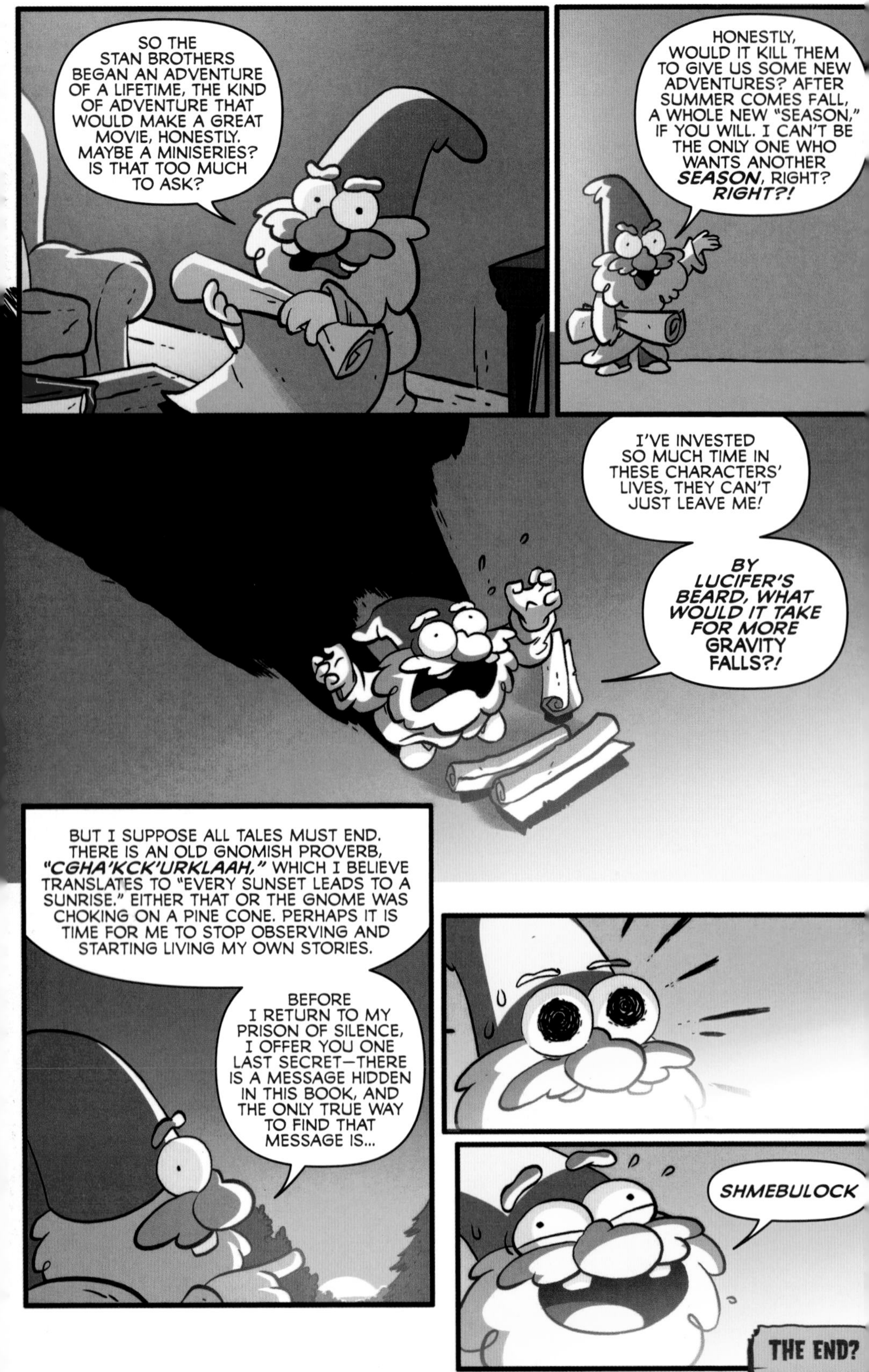
SO THE STAN BROTHERS BEGAN AN ADVENTURE OF A LIFETIME, THE KIND OF ADVENTURE THAT WOULD MAKE A GREAT MOVIE, HONESTLY. MAYBE A MINISERIES? IS THAT TOO MUCH TO ASK?
HONESTLY, WOULD IT KILL THEM TO GIVE US SOME NEW ADVENTURES? AFTER SUMMER COMES FALL, A WHOLE NEW "SEASON," IF YOU WILL. I CAN'T BE THE ONLY ONE WHO WANTS ANOTHER SEASON, RIGHT? RIGHT?!
I'VE INVESTED SO MUCH TIME IN THESE CHARACTERS' LIVES, THEY CAN'T JUST LEAVE ME!
BY LUCIFER'S BEARD, WHAT WOULD IT TAKE FOR MORE GRAVITY FALLS?!
BUT I SUPPOSE ALL TALES MUST END. THERE IS AN OLD GNOMISH PROVERB, "CGHA'KCK'URKLAAH," WHICH I BELIEVE TRANSLATES TO "EVERY SUNSET LEADS TO A SUNRISE." EITHER THAT OR THE GNOME WAS CHOKING ON A PINE CONE. PERHAPS IT IS TIME FOR ME TO STOP OBSERVING AND STARTING LIVING MY OWN STORIES.
BEFORE I RETURN TO MY PRISON OF SILENCE, I OFFER YOU ONE LAST SECRET—THERE IS A MESSAGE HIDDEN IN THIS BOOK, AND THE ONLY TRUE WAY TO FIND THAT MESSAGE IS...
SHMEBULOCK
THE END?

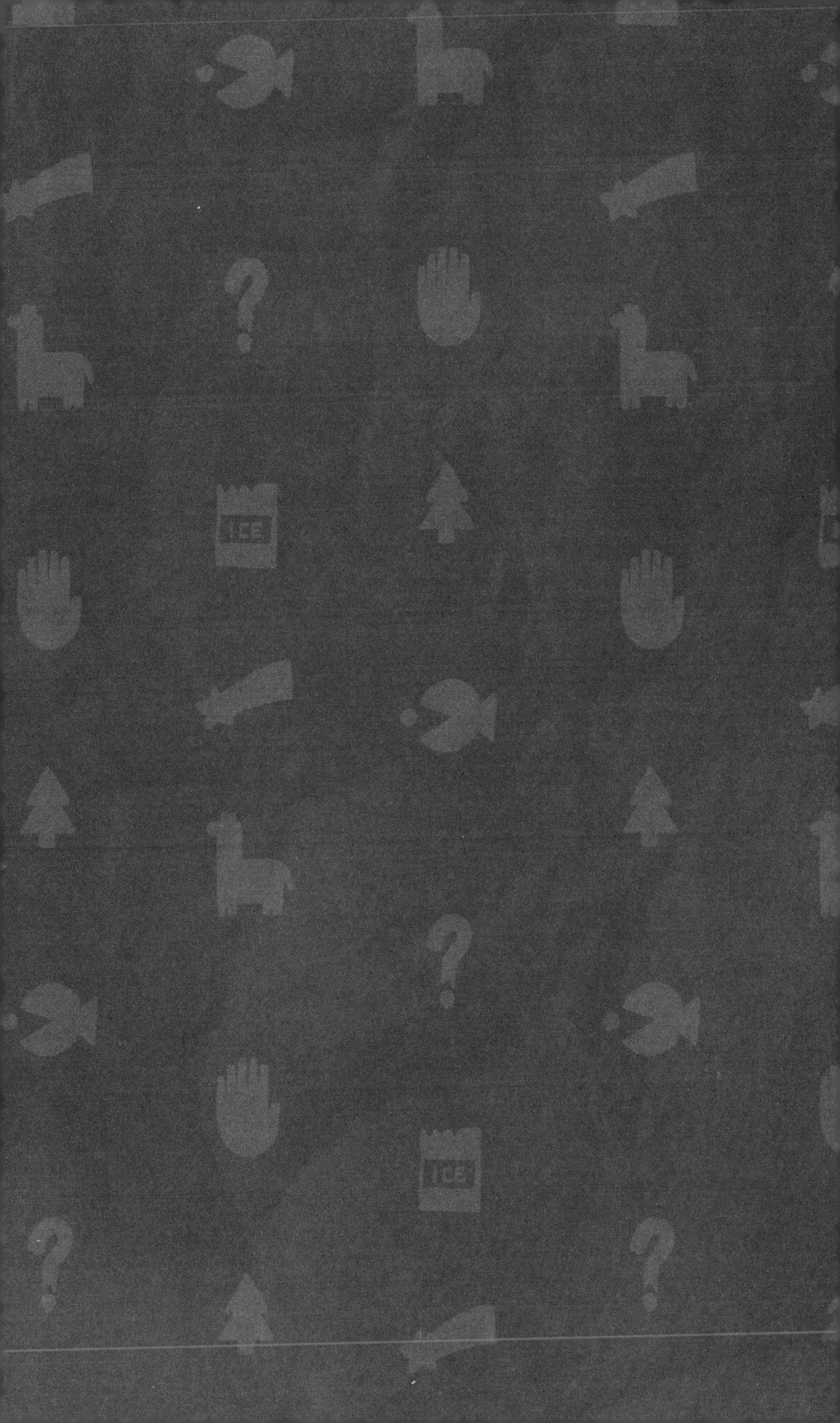
ICE
ICE